NONE
STOOD
TALLER
The Final Year

didn't admit it openly, but Dotty had taken up the role of the wire cage holding down the champagne cork. I'm not sure that any of us realised how much we were suppressing. Rolo's announcement released something even greater than our unbridled joy about Dotty and Rob. Three years of concentrated effort, stress, and anxiety had been compressed into the events of a single day. And there it remained, a highly unstable mix of suppressed emotion, just waiting to explode.

Rolo's announcement lit the fuse, and a second later it exploded. I leapt up from my chair and found myself jumping up and down with my arms in the air. Fiona hugged me, and we jumped up and down together, looking completely ridiculous. Patrick picked me up and swung me around, before kissing me fully on the lips. Then everyone hugged and kissed everyone else. We were all the same; the spontaneous release of all that tension and suppressed emotion resulted in a euphoria which transcended any concept of appropriate behaviour. In truth, we completely lost it!

The only person trying to maintain his aristocratic reserve was, of course, Edward, but he too was swept along in the outburst of emotion. When Fiona confronted him she just put her arms around him and kissed him. Feeling my hand on his shoulder, he turned and smiled. For once in our tortured relationship, he didn't hesitate, he took me in his arms and kissed me! In the ensuing euphoria, it was several seconds before I realised I was standing in a close embrace, locked in a kiss *with Edward!* The realisation made my heart race even faster, in that moment we were alone together, nothing else existed. It might have started spontaneously but that was not how it ended. In an instant it became a passionate kiss.

The commotion was so loud that Corporal Harris and Private Thomson came rushing into the Manor armed with their rifles. They were followed into the office by most of the household staff. Suddenly it wasn't just Edward and me standing in the room, everyone else miraculously appeared as if conjured out of the air. Jennings was the last of the household staff to appear. Looking bewildered, he approached Edward, providing a much-needed distraction.

"Is there something I should be aware of, My Lord?"

"Yes, Jennings, we are in receipt of wonderful news. Our colleagues Dorothy and Rob are both in safe hands in Normandy."

Florence's startled expression filled the room.

"Do you mean Dotty's *not* dead? Dotty's *alive*?" she shouted.

She ran across the office and put her arms around me.

"She's really alive?" she asked.

"She is, she must have escaped, she's okay!"

"Oh, Lily, I'm so pleased."

As far as I was aware it was only Jennings and Florence who knew about Dotty. Jennings, as always, maintained his impeccable air of authority and was not best pleased with Florence. He quietly took her to one side.

"What on earth do you think you are doing, Florence?" he said discreetly. "You can't put your arms around Mrs Heywood, what were you thinking? And you will certainly not refer to her by her Christian name. Be off with you now, I'll deal with you later."

Florence could not suppress her glee, even as she scurried off. I took Jennings by the arm.

"Don't be too hard on her, Mr Jennings. I've become very attached to her."

"I am aware of that, Mrs Heywood. This is why I unofficially appointed her to the position of your lady's maid."

"I'm not sure I ever thanked you for that, Mr Jennings."

"Quite unnecessary, I assure you."

"Please don't be hard on her."

"Do not concern yourself, Mrs Heywood, my bark is far worse than my bite."

He walked away towards Edward. "Will there be anything else, My Lord?"

Edward had regained some of his composure. In fact, we were all trying to do the same.

"Yes, Jennings. Do you remember when Wing Commander Albright was forced to bail out over France, and we heard the good news?"

"Indeed I do, My Lord. Champagne and glasses for everyone."

Jennings gestured to the rest of the staff and they left in an orderly fashion. The guard stood down and returned to their post. We each tried to replace our feet on the ground, but there was no suppressing the elation in the room. The joyful conversation was all about Dotty and Rob. We had no information except that they were alive, but it didn't stop us from speculating about their escape. Gradually the conversation broadened to encompass the invasion. All our doubts and fears were finally being expressed, together with some well-earned self-congratulation.

Jennings returned with bottles of champagne, and the girls carried trays of glasses. When everyone was standing, glass in hand, we naturally looked towards Edward to say something and propose a toast. He looked very thoughtful, his expression making me aware of the gravity of the situation. A moment ago we had shared together a moment of huge significance for us, but now he felt obliged to address the whole room.

"Ladies and gentlemen," he said. "That was quite a moment!" There was a buzz of agreement before Edward could continue. "Three years ago, we came together as a group of people with a common purpose, but I feel we have become much more. We created an organisation which is greater than the sum of its parts. When one part of that organisation became missing, we were no longer complete, such is the bond we have created. Dorothy and Rob are safe and thus we are united as a group once again. I propose a toast to their safe return: *To Dorothy and Rob!*"

We all raised our glasses to a chorus of '*Dorothy and Rob*'.

Edward obviously had more to say, so we drank the toast and waited for him to continue.

"It is now reasonably safe for us to assume that D-Day has been a success. That success is due in no small part to the contribution of each and every person in this room. Perhaps we can allow ourselves a moment to consider the magnitude of our achievement. Operation Overlord will take its place in history, not only as one of our country's finest moments, but also as one of the free world's greatest achievements. I am reminded of Winston Churchill's words when he addressed us here at Middlebourne. The great day of celebration which he described draws closer. He said when that day comes, no-one will stand taller than the people gathered in this room. He was absolutely right, and it is with great pride that I stand among you. Well done, everyone! I propose a toast: *To D-Day!*"

I found his words deeply moving, and the toast was drunk in silence. No-one suggested we stand in silence, it just happened spontaneously. We stood silently to honour those who fell during D-Day. It is that tradition which we repeat each year at our reunion. We just waited until Edward addressed us again.

"I can't imagine we could ever repeat an occasion like this," he said, "so I would just like to say one more thing. It seems almost invidious to thank any one person, everyone's contribution has been invaluable. However, I cannot allow this moment to pass without thanking my Chief of Staff. Lily has been with me right from the start. As we are all aware, she is an unbreakable spirit, and it is her spirit which has helped to shape us, and to hold us together. This is as much your success as anyone's, Lily. I would like to propose a toast to my invaluable Chief of Staff, *To Lily.*"

I was struck silent, not knowing what to do or say as everyone raised their glass to me. They were all so kind and generous, but they were expecting me to say something. I held my handkerchief to my eyes, but could hardly keep pace with my tears. I didn't want to say anything, I just wanted to hold Edward in my arms. Not knowing what to say, I just said the first thing that came to mind.

"The only person who knows how I feel at this moment is Patrick's Mammy." There was a moment of laughter which eased my tension. "That was such a kind thing to say, Edward, thank you. If only it were true! We all know who really created Station M. Your knowledge and connection with the intelligence community is without parallel. This is *your* creation, Edward, and yours alone. I came here as a Land Girl and nothing more. I'm a part of your creation, you made me, Edward. Whatever contribution I've been able to make has been because of you. Everyone here owes you a vote of thanks, the nation owes you a vote of thanks, but above all I want to thank you. It has been such an honour, thank you for believing in me. I would like to propose a toast to my mentor, to our leader, *Edward, Lord Middlebourne!*"

Woody raised the occasion to an even higher level by proposing three cheers for Edward. For once in his life, he actually appeared humbled! He did his best to dismiss it all, but I could see he was deeply moved. The afternoon continued with more bottles of champagne being opened, and our spirits reaching new heights. We all drank far too much, and the afternoon quickly developed into a party atmosphere. Our normal British reserve probably disappeared with the pop of the second champagne cork. Even Rolo, who rarely drinks much, showed another side of his personality. He normally existed on an intellectual level somewhere up in the stratosphere, yet here he was, putting his arm around Susan, and laughing and joking with everyone.

Johnny had been flying over Normandy that morning, and when he returned with his film, he found the photo reconnaissance room locked and empty. He then went to the communications hut looking for Susan, and then onto Hut 3, but no-one was to be found. When he finally appeared at the office door, our party was complete. Fiona shouted '*Johnny*', at the top of her voice, and ran across the room to him. Edward came and stood next to me, we smiled at each other as Fiona and Johnny seemed to meld into one person. And then Edward put his arm around my waist!

Even after several glasses of champagne, he still took me completely by surprise. I put my arm around him without thinking, and we looked at each other.

"They make a lovely couple, don't they?" I said, referring to Fiona and Johnny.

"They certainly do, and they are not afraid for the world to see, are they?"

"Well, why should they? I don't think the rest of the world exists for them."

"I suppose you're right. I'm just not used to seeing such a public display of affection."

"You're not offended, are you, Edward?"

"I think a year or two ago I might have been."

"What has changed you then?"

"You, Lily! You have changed me."

"Me - how have I changed your opinion?"

"You've changed everything! I might say that you have completely changed the time-honoured order of things."

"I'm intrigued, Edward, but I'm not sure changing the time-honoured order is something I am aware of having done!"

Even in their cups, the boys were desperate to hear what Johnny had witnessed flying over Normandy. It was certainly not with Fiona's blessing, but the boys surrounded Johnny, asking him questions. They all seemed to possess a photographic memory, and Corky especially could literally visualise just about every hedgerow in Normandy. They quizzed Johnny about the finest detail, the exact positions of the troops on the ground, providing them with a mental picture which Montgomery would have given his right arm for.

"Your speech, Lily, I was deeply moved," Edward said, "it

was … well, it was not what I was expecting. It was exceedingly generous of you."

"No more generous than you were to me, Edward, but you know I'm right. I am what you made me."

"Far be it for me to introduce a note of discord," he said jokingly, "but I cannot entirely agree with you, Lily. You are a wonderful, and may I say an extraordinary, woman! I couldn't possibly create those attributes, you brought those attributes to me, and in doing so I have learned far more from you than you might imagine."

"Edward, this isn't like you to be so open, that's a lovely thing to say! I suspect you must have had too much to drink."

"I suspect you may be right. Perhaps we should form a self-appreciation society."

"Good idea, first thing I would do is to exclude anyone else from joining."

"That would be the whole point, Lily. Perhaps we should make it a lifelong membership!"

Suddenly I was stone-cold sober. What was Edward saying? At that point we became embroiled in the conversation between Johnny and the boys. I listened, but I didn't hear them. We had both drunk an awful lot of champagne, Edward was not even steady on his feet, but that didn't change what had just been said. My head was spinning, and it wasn't just the champagne.

Chapter Three
Things Left Unsaid

Our celebration continued into the evening. It had been a heady concoction of champagne and emotion. It was not sustainable and inevitably our euphoria seeped away, deflating like a gradually leaking balloon. Those wonderful feelings of joy and pride remained, but slowly we had to surrender to our growing fatigue. As the party broke up, Edward asked if I was having dinner with him. Having arranged to be with Greg, I should have declined, but instead I just accepted Edward's offer without thinking. Realising what I'd done, I felt my heart jump in my chest, not knowing what to do. I didn't want to impose upon Fiona, but I found myself looking at her with a quizzical expression.

"Would you mind calling in on Greg as you go home, Fi?" I asked.

"I know what you want me to say, that's all right. I'll tell him it's Station M business."

"Thanks Fi, I'm sorry to ask."

"You know you can't go on like this, don't you?"

"I know, believe me, I know."

Edward came so close to telling me something that afternoon, I felt sure he was reaching out to me. I was compelled to accept his dinner invitation, as I had to offer him the opportunity to continue that conversation. As powerless as I was to refuse, I remained tormented, still thinking about Greg. Fiona's words came back to haunt me, no-one knew better than me that I was playing with fire. I loathed and despised myself, and much as I tried to justify my situation, I knew it could not continue. Walking away from the office with Edward, I managed to smile at Fiona, but guilt was my constant companion.

"Shall we dress for dinner, Lily?" he asked.

"That would be lovely, Edward, but would you mind if we didn't? It's getting awfully late."

"Quite right, shall we say twenty minutes in the Drawing Room?"

I agreed and hurried upstairs to my bedroom. Every step up the central staircase seemed to invite a fresh thought into my mind. One moment, I could see Dotty's smiling face, then it was Greg's inviting eyes. The solid oak handrail beneath my hand was a stark reminder of the here and now. There was nothing as permanent or dependable as that solid oak in my life. I had no idea where my future lay, it terrified me. Florence was waiting for me as I approached, and it was lovely to see a friendly, non-judgmental face.

"It's lovely to see you looking so happy, Florence. Do I assume Mr Jennings has forgiven you for your indiscretion?"

"He gave me a good telling-off, but I know he doesn't really mean it. Isn't it wonderful news about Dotty? I'm so happy for you, I hated seeing you that upset."

"I can't tell you how relieved I am, I'm not sure how I would cope without Dotty. There's nobody else like her, is there?"

I explained that I was short of time, just needing a quick freshen up and a change of clothes before dinner with His Lordship. When I returned from the bathroom she had selected my outfit for me, and laid everything out on the bed, including my pearl and ruby necklace and earrings.

"It's only a casual dinner, Florence, I wasn't thinking of my best cocktail dress."

"You and His Lordship were standing with your arms around each other this afternoon. I think this is definitely what you should wear this evening."

"You don't miss a thing, do you! How am I going to manage without you? I mean that, Florence. We have grown really close, haven't we?"

"I know, I do enjoy being your lady's maid, I can't imagine not doing it."

"Don't worry, I won't desert you."

"I know you won't, Mrs Heywood, I think of you as my friend."

"Good, I'm pleased. Now, I'm going to take your advice about the cocktail dress."

Florence also insisted I wear my hair up, which made me late for Edward. As I left my bedroom, I felt terribly over-dressed for a casual evening, but had to admit I felt wonderful as I entered the Drawing Room. It was a knee-length black dress, closely fitting, finished with a beautiful sleeveless lace top, and a little bow at the neck. A sleeveless dress was considered racy at the time; the slightly low-cut neckline certainly was, but the lace top gave it a wonderful elegance. I wore it with a thin black belt, and black high heels with a white trim. Going by the look on Edward's face, I think I made quite an impression. He sprang to his feet with a lovely smile.

"I didn't expect you to go to so much trouble, Lily. You look … breath-taking!"

"You're definitely getting better at this, Edward, that was exactly the right thing to say!"

"Yes, I am trying, the trick I find is to take a moment and breathe deeply. In that way, when you take my breath away, I have time to regain my composure."

"I'm not sure that you realise, Edward, but there are occasions when you can be utterly adorable."

He wasn't used to flattery, and I wasn't used to giving him any. That day was the first time I really appreciated that beneath his aristocratic veneer, Lord Middlebourne had passions like any other man. He stood with the same beguiling expression on his face as Lady Caroline came into the Drawing Room. She was dressed as she always was for dinner, and it reminded me that however elegant I felt, I was dressed casually.

"Good evening, Caroline, may I say you look lovely this evening."

"Thank you, my dear, but I believe it is I who is standing in your shadow this evening. I can't think when I have seen you looking more lovely. Are we celebrating an occasion?"

"That's very kind, Caroline, thank you. Actually, we are celebrating. My dear friend Dorothy, and another of our agents, have both been found alive and well in Normandy. We have been celebrating all afternoon."

"Oh, what wonderful news, I am so pleased. Isn't that wonderful, Edward?"

"Yes, it is the best possible news," Edward replied, "and good evening, Mother. If I might interrupt you ladies, perhaps you might care to join me."

"Yes, of course, Edward. Now, Lily, you must tell me all about your friend in Normandy."

Mr Jennings asked us if we would like drinks and I recoiled at the prospect of further alcohol. I asked for a glass of tonic water, while Caroline decided upon a glass of sherry. Edward agreed with me, tonic water sounded ideal. I noticed how he sat back in his Chesterfield armchair with an arm resting on each wing, watching Caroline and I discussing things together.

His idea of casual was to change his three-piece suit for a double-breasted blazer, bow tie, and light cavalry twill trousers. Edward had a way of always looking elegant. It didn't matter if he was sitting or standing, he just had that knack of looking perfect, not just his clothes, but his natural elegance in both posture and movement. He possessed another alluring charm that evening, I could see it in his eyes.

I told Caroline all about Dotty and Rob, she was genuinely

interested and delighted at the outcome. We talked until Jennings invited us in for dinner, and we took our places at the table. Poor Edward hardly got a word in.

"I wanted to discuss Mary with you, Lily," Caroline said. "You were so right about her. She is such a bright girl. I have concluded that we are wasting her talents by employing her as a maid."

"This was my feeling, Caroline. I feared we would only lose her if we retained her as a maid."

"I was very doubtful when you raised the matter with me, I have to admit, Lily. When you suggested I might enjoy taking her under my wing and teaching her how to do the accounts, well, I can tell you I was a little surprised at the suggestion."

"Yes, I remember that occasion, you put me in my place if I remember correctly! I based that belief upon my own experience. A skill or experience shared with someone else is something special, it makes you appreciate your own ability. It's a wonderful thing to be able to do. When I saw how capable you were, Caroline, I wondered if it was a gift which you took for granted. I was sure teaching Mary would be valuable for both of you. But I agree, it was not my decision to make, I shouldn't have suggested it."

"Well, I am pleased you did. I have surprised myself; it has been a really worthwhile experience. You were right, Lily, I have enjoyed it enormously."

"Oh, I'm delighted. And while I'm confessing, there's something else. What would you think about Mary extending her talents towards the estate office? If Jennings agrees, Norton needs an assistant. Now, I do know such a position is normally a male preserve, but I think Mary has the ability to grow into a position like that."

"Assistant estate manager! Can you really envisage Mary in that position?"

"I can, I think she's more than capable."

"In that case, I trust your opinion, Lily. What do you

think, Edward, does Lily have your blessing to promote Mary to such a position, do you trust her opinion?"

"Oh, I'm sorry, are you asking my opinion?" he joked.

"If you disapprove, Edward, I'll drop the matter immediately," I said.

"Disapprove! I can't make my presence known this evening, let alone disapprove! I would trust you with my life, Lily. If this is your considered opinion, then I know it to be correct."

Edward still had the same lovely expression on his face, and so did Caroline. I looked from one to the other as we made our way into the Dining Room. We had barely sat down when Jennings came back into the room and stood next to Edward. He casually leaned forward and whispered.

"There is a telephone call for you, My Lord."

"Oh no, can't it wait, Jennings?"

"It's the Prime Minister, My Lord."

Edward looked disappointed. "I think I know what this is about, will you please excuse me?"

He walked out of the Dining Room, leaving me smiling at Caroline.

"I often wonder if Winston abuses our friendship on occasions like this. It's very inconsiderate to telephone at such a time!"

"Well, we are at war, Caroline, and we have just invaded Europe. I'm not sure the Prime Minister has the time to differentiate between day and night."

"Yes, of course, how silly you must think I am."

"Not at all, you're remembering how things should be, and how they will be again."

"I cannot believe things will ever be the same again. The country will struggle to rebuild itself."

"You're right, it will, but Britain will be great again."

"When you say so, Lily, you make it sound possible. I suspect that you and Edward together could achieve anything."

I smiled, not quite knowing the meaning of what she had

just said. When Edward returned his delightful expression was absent. Jennings replaced his chair beneath him, and he sat down, obviously deep in thought.

"That must have been important, Edward, what did the PM want?" I asked.

"Nothing urgent at all. The PM has not seen daylight since D-Day, he had no idea what the time was. I knew there was going to be a general assessment of SOE operations post D-Day, it seems that General Gubbins has brought that forward. I have to go to SOE headquarters tomorrow."

"Do you think our future will be discussed?"

"Well, in terms of personnel, we are insignificant. But yes, I fear we may have served our purpose. Our field agents will likely be reassigned."

We discussed it throughout dinner. It was inconsiderate in front of Caroline, but at that moment, the future of Station M inevitably took precedence in our minds.

"It's late," Caroline said. "I think I shall retire and leave you two to discuss these matters."

Edward walked around the table to remove her chair, and Caroline wished us both goodnight. She gave me a lovely hug, and Edward kissed her cheek. She left us in the same graceful manner with which she had entered. The Countess was the most impressive woman I have ever known. Her charm, grace and poise were legendary which, combined with her intellect, ensured she had the full attention of any room full of people, simply by entering. In her heyday, she was also blessed with incomparable beauty. I could easily imagine her presence at one of the many Middlebourne functions - regardless of the guest list, she would have been the only woman in the room.

It was late, Edward and I sat down again at the table rather than retiring to the Drawing Room. I felt there were important things to be said between us, but the prospect of closing down Station M obviously filled our minds.

"With all that has been happening, we've never discussed what's going to happen to Station M," I said.

"Well, we both knew our assignment had an end date, but after all we have been through, it doesn't seem possible that it can all come to an end."

"Perhaps we will be assigned something else," I said hopefully.

"That's perfectly possible. I shall find out soon enough, but it is likely to mean considerable change."

"What kind of changes do you mean?"

"Well, you see, it goes back to when the Prime Minister asked me to take over the location planning for the D-Day landings. We had to break away from SIS because it was too large to control. The only organisation which is outside of the establishment is SOE. Our SOE designation has really been a convenience, we are effectively nothing more than an affiliate of that organisation."

"Our agents are all SOE-trained."

"They are, and that reinforces our SOE designation. If we were given another assignment, the problem I can see coming is that the War Ministry will want to regularise us by putting as many of us as possible in uniform."

"That would be a disaster, Edward! It would mean us becoming salaried members of the armed forces. I claim all of our costs as expenses, we would no longer be able to do that."

"You're right, Lily, if I can avoid that outcome I certainly shall."

"Forgive me if I'm wrong, Edward, but I had the impression earlier this evening that there was something else you wanted to tell me."

"There was something, Lily, but in view of this development, perhaps it will be best if we have that discussion when I return."

"Edward, you're frightening me! If Station M is to be closed, and I am to go, please Edward, I need to know."

"Go! Oh Lily, you're not going anywhere! What on earth gave you that absurd idea?"

"Well, what will I do when Station M is no more?"

"That is precisely what I would like to talk about. We have a lot to discuss, but first I think it best if I go to Baker Street to find out what lies ahead."

My heart was almost bursting out of my chest. I had no home of my own outside of Middlebourne; all my anxieties and insecurities coalesced around that one unforeseeable place - the future. Perhaps I had a future with Greg, perhaps I had a future with Edward in Middlebourne. In that moment, I finally came face-to-face with my greatest fear of all, that my future might contain neither of those things!

"Edward, please, do you not realise how important this is to me? When you say I'm not going anywhere, please tell me, do I have a future here at Middlebourne?"

"Oh, my darling Lily, I thought we both understood that this is your future. My fear was that you might not want that future. Forgive me for being so inept, I wanted us to have this conversation in totally different circumstances. I have so many things to consider, but losing you is not one of them."

I didn't know if he was offering me a future as his wife, or as his Chief of Staff. But I knew him well enough to know he had his reasons for being evasive. Edward did nothing without due consideration, he never made a rash decision. Beneath it all he was a warm, and as I recently found out, a passionate man. I also realised being the Ninth Earl presented him with obligations that I could barely comprehend. He was as conflicted as I was, that was obvious to see. Everything about Edward told me he wanted me as passionately as I wanted him. I suppose it was very much to his credit as a gentleman that he was determined not to cross that line. In order to do so, his sense of gallantry dictated that he must first ask for my hand.

I confess at the time I found it all slightly ridiculous, but then again I was judging him by my East End standards. The forces that combined to compel Edward to marry Beatrice were stronger than any commitment I could imagine. I felt powerless to stand up against those insurmountable forces, it seemed I had no option but to watch Edward's self-torment while concealing my own. We left the Dining Room together.

He then escorted me to my room, which was something he had only done once before. I knew he was not about to come in with me, but for the first time, I felt sure he wanted to! He kissed my cheek, but it was not how he would kiss his mother. We smiled at each other, and it was definitely not how he would have smiled at his mother. He was telling me something with his eyes, I just couldn't be sure what it was. When he left me, I looked around, but Florence was nowhere to be seen. She was skilled in the art of discretion, but I knew she'd soon appear. The moment I entered my room, she knocked on my door.

"Have you had a lovely evening, Mrs Heywood?"

"I have, Florence, it has been unusual, but it's an evening I will never forget."

"That sounds wonderful."

She was hesitant, I knew how well she understood me.

"No, he didn't propose to me, if that's what you're thinking!"

"Well, I did wonder, you have that sparkle back in your eyes."

"Can I not have *any* private thoughts without you knowing them!"

"Oh, I didn't mean to pry, I'm sorry."

"That was intended to be a compliment, Florence."

She put my clothes away and tidied up for me, and all the while she retained a knowing expression. Florence has such an expressive face. I knew what she was thinking, she didn't have to ask. I didn't have an answer for her, so we maintained our unspoken conversation until she left.

"See you in the morning, Mrs Heywood, sweet dreams."

Chapter Four
Our Proudest Moment

The days immediately following D-Day were an awful time for Fiona and for me. Dotty was always in our minds, we just wanted her back home. For the wider nation, D-Day marked the defining point of the Second World War. Hopefully it was the beginning of the end, and it couldn't come soon enough. It had been two and a half years since the Blitz, and for Londoners the scars were deep. In January 1944, the Germans began what they called Operation Steinbock. There were fourteen air raids on London, and more on Bristol, Hull, and Cardiff. Over fifteen hundred people were killed and three thousand were injured.

For Londoners especially, D-Day was greeted with relief as well as celebration, but it was tinged with apprehension. We all knew what the consequences of failure would be; the collective spirit of the British people stood shoulder to shoulder with the Allied troops. News from the battle front became the nation's life blood. Newspaper reports were eagerly devoured, while the evening ritual of the family sitting around their wireless sets became the norm.

On June 13th, there was some good news from Normandy. Following a prolonged and bloody battle, Carentan fell to the Allies. The French Resistance, together with the SAS and SOE units of F-Section disrupted the German lines of supply. Combined with air power, the disruption severely limited German reinforcements to the front. Field Marshal Rommel finally had to report back to Germany that the Allies had complete control of Carentan. The strategically important port city of Caen was still in enemy hands, but the consolidation of the landings gave Londoners the hope that the air raids were finally over.

June 13th 1944 was a significant day for two reasons. The hope of Londoners that the air raids had ended was soon to be cruelly dashed, but paradoxically for us at Station M, it was our proudest day. Edward was in his office preparing for his journey to London, Fiona and I were occupied with some household issues. My green phone rang, it was Elizabeth Layton, the PM's secretary.

"Good morning, Lily, how are you?"

"Fine, thank you, Elizabeth, how are you?"

"Rushed off my feet as always. He wants to talk to you, Lily, to all of you - he's been writing a little speech. It must be important; he's spent quite a bit of time on it."

"Crikey, I'll get Lord Middlebourne, give me a moment."

I went through to Edward's office, where he was sorting files in his briefcase.

"Edward, the Prime Minister wants to talk to us, all of us."

The three of us gathered around the telephone; just as Edward was sitting down, the PM's familiar voice came through the green handset.

"To whom am I speaking?"

"It's Lily, sir."

"Ah, Lily, how are you, my dear?"

"I'm well, sir, thank you."

"Is Edward there with you?"

"Yes, we're all close to the telephone."

"Good, because I want to address you all. I am pleased to confirm that the greatest invasion force that the world has ever seen has gained an unyielding foothold in Normandy. The Allied forces will now advance with unshakable resolve. This magnificent achievement has turned the tide against the Nazi tyranny. The darkness which fell upon the people of Europe and beyond may now give way to the light of a new dawn. One day soon that light will shine upon a free and grateful nation. I cannot exaggerate the debt which our people, and those of Europe, owe to you and to your colleagues. The work that you have undertaken at Middlebourne has helped to change the course of history. It saddens me to think you will never receive the recognition which you all so justly deserve. So I speak for the nation when I say to you all, thank you. On this occasion, Lily, it is you who should ask me if this conversation is an honour or a pleasure, and I would tell you, it is a *very great* honour. God bless you all."

"God bless you, Prime Minister."

With that he was gone, and we sat there in silence! We just looked at each other, until eventually Fiona spoke.

"That was wonderful."

"You must be so proud, Edward," I said. "What a tribute!"

"Yes I am," he replied, "I'm proud of everyone."

"We must write it down word for word, before we forget anything," I said.

Just as soon as we had produced a transcript, it was obvious what we had to do. The three of us immediately went over to Hut 3, gathering Susan and Mac on the way. There were white cotton wool clouds blowing gently across the sky, but for that moment we walked beneath a large patch of blue, and the sunshine raised our spirits even higher. Edward immediately gathered everyone together in Hut 3, where we all stood in eager anticipation.

"Ladies and gentlemen, the following words were spoken to me just ten minutes ago. This message was directed to us all at Station M by the Prime Minister, Sir Winston Churchill."

Edward then read the Prime Minister's words. They greeted

the message with silence, just as we had done, they just stood looking at each other. Patrick was finally the one who knocked the cork out of the bottle.

"Well, me Mammy rarely had cause to be proud of me, but by heaven, she does today."

The subsequent outpouring was almost like when the news of Dotty arrived. The Prime Minister's wonderful words not only raised our spirits; he finally provided the cathartic moment we needed to end our direct involvement in D-Day. We had done it, and our place in history was secure, though only we would know. Celebrations continued over lunch in the canteen. Our spirits were high and our pride knew no bounds. I'm sure Brenda wondered what had come over us. The time just seemed to disappear. Edward planned to catch the three o'clock train from Tunbridge Wells, so reluctantly we had to leave them to their celebrations.

We set off to walk back to the Manor, still in a celebratory mood. Our high spirits were abruptly interrupted when we heard a strange sound approaching from the southeast. The noise was sufficiently loud that it grabbed our attention, we stopped immediately to look up. Fi spotted it first, initially we assumed it was a small aircraft. The wings were short and square-ended, and as best as we could estimate, it appeared to be smaller than a Spitfire. What we found alarming was that it was heading straight for us! I'm sure we all had the same reaction, was this a new enemy fighter plane? As it grew closer, we realised how fast it was going, and the ever-increasing noise was like no aeroplane we had ever heard.

"There doesn't appear to be a propeller!" Edward said.

"There must be," I replied.

We were relieved as it flew over us, each spinning around to watch it speed away. It sounded like a motorcycle with no exhaust pipe, a strange pulsing, rasping sound. From behind, it was obvious to Edward what it was.

"That is some kind of pulse jet."

"What's that?" I asked.

"It's a propulsion system based upon the expulsion of burning gases. Each of those pulses is an injection of fuel."

"How do you know this, Edward?"

"It's an interesting subject, jet propulsion. It's just basic physics really."

Corky came rushing over to us. "Was that what I think it was? I didn't see it, but it sounded like a pulse jet."

"That's exactly what it was, and it's heading straight for London."

"Was it what we were expecting?" he asked.

"I'm afraid so!"

"So the reports are correct?" Corky replied.

"Yes, when I get to Baker Street, I'll try to find out more. This might represent a serious turn of events."

I had no idea what they were talking about, but Edward's reaction alarmed me. Both he and Corky looked worried. Edward didn't say much more about it as we hastened on our way to the Manor. Now, of course, we know precisely what it was. That was June 13th, and it was the first V1 flying bomb launched against London!

Arriving back at the Manor, we saw that William was already waiting, standing by the Rolls-Royce. He looked mightily pleased with himself in his pale blue chauffeur's uniform, not a button out of place. The colour matched the lighter section of the car's gleaming two-tone paintwork. Edward went on ahead, needing to get his things together. I stayed with William, having already decided I would go to the station with him. It was some little time later when he appeared, looking slightly harassed.

"Where were you, Lily? I've been looking for you."

"Oh, I'm sorry, I've been waiting for you here with William. I'm going with you to the station."

"It's not necessary for you to do that."

"It may not be necessary, Edward, but I want to."

"Well, that's awfully thoughtful. I am not used to a send-off."

William opened the door for me and loaded Edward's overnight case, while I sat with him in the back of the car. This was a first, I hadn't ridden in the Rolls-Royce with him before. We had worked so closely for so long that I confess I was used to thinking of him as Edward. In that moment, sitting next to him outside the Manor, he was very much Lord Middlebourne. It served to remind me how close we had become. William set off at a sedate pace, and the wonderful smell of leather retained the opulence of the Manor within the car. I was enjoying every second of the journey, but Edward brought me back to reality.

"Find every camera we possess and make sure everyone knows where one is at all times. If the opportunity arises, take a photograph of one of those 'things', it may be useful."

"You sound like you expect more of them."

"Yes, I am afraid that would be the logical conclusion. That might have been a test flight or a prototype, but it will not be the only one."

"You're worried about it, aren't you, Edward? Do you consider this to be serious?"

"I do! It could be extremely serious. If this is what I assume it is, we may not have a defence against it. There may be no way of stopping them."

"I'll make everyone aware of what to do, don't worry. I'll ask the guard to be extra vigilant, they're outside all the time. They'll be ready with a camera."

As we drove into the station car park, there was the familiar crunching of gravel beneath the tyres as the car sedately drew to a halt. William opened the doors for us. As I stepped out, the sight of the clock tower brought my childhood memories flooding back. Tunbridge Wells West Station made a big impression on me as a little girl. In the early years, Mum would travel with my brother Ian and me to Gran's. Then, when I was a little older, I had to take care of Ian after Mum put us on the train in London. We were alone until Gran was there to meet us. Worst of all was when it was just me, and I felt rejected and frightened. It reminded me of my relief when I saw Gran standing on the platform. The sight of the clock tower getting ever closer as the train approached the station was my abiding memory. For me, the tower was synonymous with Gran's smiling face.

"I travelled to this station so often as a child, Edward, this place is full of memories for me."

"Happy memories, I hope," he said.

"Well, no, actually it was a sad time for me."

"When I return, perhaps you might consider sharing those memories with me."

"I would like that."

I always associated those memories with my fear of the train. Either I was looking forward to getting off, or I was frightened of getting on. This was to be an altogether different experience, I was the person who would wave from the platform, while the train took someone away from me. The train pulled into the station on time, bringing with it those familiar sounds and smells that used to frighten me as a child. First the variable pitch of the steam whistle, as it neared the station. Clouds of steam mingled with the smoke from the stack, billowing and swirling under the station platform canopy. Finally, it drew to a halt with a screech of brakes and a last hiss of steam.

For a little girl, the mighty engine was like a fire-breathing dragon that towered over me, I could even smell its breath. I was sad that day, I didn't want to see Edward go. It was only intended to be for a couple of days, but I didn't want him to leave me. The carriage doors opened and passengers disembarked. Then there was that other familiar sound as they slammed the doors shut, reminding me that when my carriage door slammed shut, my time with Gran and Middlebourne was over. I was heading back to London, and I hated it.

He lifted his case into the first-class carriage and turned towards me to say goodbye. Edward's words during our conversation the evening before still rang in my ears. It all slightly overwhelmed me. I wasn't thinking, it wasn't planned, I put my arms around him and kissed him on the lips. It was only a brief kiss, but then we stood for a moment with our arms around each other. It was much more than just the kiss, that was the very first occasion when Edward and I crossed that unseen barrier into each other's space. For me, it was a wonderfully special moment, it sent a tingle down my spine. It was a new experience for us both, neither of us knew how to react. Edward hesitated as he stepped into the carriage, looking back at me as if to say, what just happened?

The last of the doors slammed shut, and the guard blew his whistle. The dragon sprang into life, engulfing me in its fiery breath as it took Edward away from me. I waved goodbye with all the enthusiasm with which, as a little girl, I used to wave to Gran. I walked back to the car park with mixed emotions, but mostly I was re-living that kiss. I was happy. I recognised one of the passengers who had disembarked; it was the same arrogant woman I met on the train a couple of years ago, and who interviewed me for the WLA. She also recognised me and said hello.

"I remember you, my dear, you made quite an impression on me during your WLA interview. Are you defeating Hitler single-handedly?"

"Not single-handedly, no, I have some help now," I quipped.

We walked into the car park together. I so well remembered the first occasion I met her, how dismissive of me she was, and my humiliation when she saw Jim arrive there to pick me up in a trailer! This time, William opened the door of the Rolls-Royce for me. As I stepped into the car, I allowed myself a genteel smile. I confess my encounter was a good end to my day. While William drove me back to Middlebourne, my genteel smile grew larger by the mile. As we gently slowed to a halt outside the Grand Entrance, Corporal Harris stood to attention. It wasn't his place to open my door, but he did it anyway!

"Thank you, Corporal, but you do realise you've just deserted your post?"

"I wouldn't be the first soldier to desert his post for the sake of a pretty woman."

"Make a note of that, William. Corporal Harris has just admitted to deserting his post and has made an inappropriate comment to the Chief of Staff."

"That sounds like a serious charge," William said.

"Will you put in a friendly word for me, Mrs Heywood?"

"Do you mean I should testify as to your excellent character?"

"Well, yes, I can see the problem."

"Rely on me, Corporal, I'll make up a redeeming feature for you."

We laughed as we always did and I went on my way, feeling better for the encounter. Still smiling about Harris, I went into the office to find Fiona concentrating on some figures. The look on her face clearly indicated that she would welcome a break from it. I had no idea how quickly my mood was about to change.

"Did Edward catch his train okay?"

"Oh yes, plenty of time."

"Has something happened between you two - these last couple of days he's been extremely attentive, hasn't he?"

"Something has happened, Fi. I've just kissed him goodbye, I mean, I really kissed him goodbye!"

"Wow, that *is* progress."

"It's more than that, Fi. Last night he told me my future is here at Middlebourne! He didn't elaborate, that's typical isn't it, but you know what I want it to mean, don't you?"

"Oh, Lily, I would be so happy for you, I know how you

feel about Edward. You've made a decision, haven't you? So you must do what you always do - you must act upon it and break it off with Greg. He's such a lovely man, you can't let him believe he has a future with you. I'm not making any more excuses for you, that was the second time last night."

"It's just so difficult, Fi, hurting him is the same as hurting myself, that's how close we are."

"You love him, don't you? You love both of them!"

"Heaven help me, Fi, you're right, I do."

"Is that even possible?"

"It is, I can't explain it, but it's true."

"I can't understand, Lily, but if it's true, it can only end in heartache. You don't need me to tell you what to do."

"I know, why do you think I can't face up to it?"

"It's always been Edward, hasn't it? I told you, you were gooey-eyed right from the start."

"You did, Fi. You also told me if I had a chance of happiness with Greg I should take it."

"I did, didn't I? But don't forget you were convinced Edward would marry Lady Beatrice."

"I'm still not sure that isn't the case, but I can't live without him. I know what I have to do."

"I don't envy you, Lily, when will you tell Greg?"

"He's probably expecting me tonight."

"Why don't you see him now and then come home to Gran's tonight?"

"That's a good idea, Fi. I know what will happen otherwise. He'll put his arms around me, and well, I'll be powerless to leave."

"That would be a terrible mistake, Lily. I'll tell Gran you're coming, so make sure you do!"

Fiona had become such a wonderful friend, the only person who knew my most intimate secrets, and whose opinion I trusted completely. I left the office feeling awful but knowing she was right. Having created that heart-breaking situation for myself, I was damned if I did and damned if I didn't. The prospect terrified me. It would have been extremely convenient if Florence had appeared. I wanted to tell her I would go to my grandmother's that evening, and perhaps she could also inform Lady Caroline. In reality, I was just looking for any reason to delay. Unfortunately, Florence didn't appear so nothing stood between me and the inevitable.

My memory of walking over to the estate office is almost entirely erased. I probably spoke to William, and I must have spoken to the guard at the door, but I cannot recall. The only memory I have is of forcing myself to knock on the estate office door. Raising my arm felt like an impossible ordeal, I knew this one simple action was about to change my life. I knocked with my heart in my mouth, and my hand shaking. When Greg appeared, I stood unable to react. He looked at me and instantly realised I was in distress. He put his arms around me and we kissed. When two people are as close as we were, you hardly need words to express your deepest thoughts.

"What's wrong, Lily, what's happened, it's not bad news about Dotty, is it?"

As I drew a deep breath, I could feel every beat of my heart. My hands were trembling and my eyes welled up with tears.

"No, it's nothing like that."

Greg stepped back half a pace, holding my hands. As he looked at me, his expression changed.

"This is the end, isn't it? I've been expecting this day to come."

I didn't have to tell him how broken-hearted I was, my tears were saying that for me.

"I'm so sorry, Greg. I always thought relationships broke up when couples fell out of love, not when they were falling in love. Please don't hate me, the days we've shared together have been wonderful."

"Why then, Lily? Why does it have to end? Is it Lord Middlebourne?"

"I don't have a relationship with him, nothing like that has ever happened."

"But this is still all about him, isn't it?"

"It is, I work with him every day, we know each other's minds, it's as if we are one person. I'm tortured by it every day, we don't have a relationship, but he's a part of me. I have to accept that I can't live without him."

"You can't live without him, but how can you live with him? The Earl of Middlebourne is not going to marry a woman from the East End of London, Lily. What kind of future do you see for yourself?"

"I don't know!"

He held me close again, then guided me towards a chair. We sat looking at each other. Nothing was said for a while, he just held my hand with such a sad look in his eyes.

"I know you, Lily Heywood, this is final isn't it, you have decided?"

"I'm sorry, Greg, I have to. I'm consumed with guilt, it's as though I'm being unfaithful to both of you. That's not who I am, I can't do that."

"I always thought I was on borrowed time, but that doesn't make it any easier, does it?"

"I can't ask you to understand, Greg, walking away from this is the hardest thing I've ever had to do."

"Then why do it?"

"Because the more I fall in love with you, the more tortured I'm becoming."

It was an unfortunate choice of words; I was falling ever more in love with him, but it was hardly an appropriate time to admit it. He forced a smile and squeezed my hand.

"It has been amazing, hasn't it?"

"Oh, believe me, it has. It's the most wonderful relationship I've ever experienced."

"I've always admired your strength of character, Lily. I might have guessed it would eventually come between us."

"Can you forgive me, Greg, can we still work together?"

"That's going to be difficult, you'll always know I want you."

"You'll always know I want you."

"All we can do is try. I promised I would remain with you until the end of the war. I'll continue to do that."

"Thank you. Can I kiss you before I go?"

"You mean our farewell kiss?"

"I suppose so."

"Try leaving without!"

I've never forgotten our last kiss; we were both reaching for a part of each other that we could keep forever. We held each other tightly. I was aware of every part of his body pressed against me, the feel of his skin against mine, the touch of his hand. When we finally broke apart, our physical relationship was over, but everything else remained. As I walked through the door, I knew I was leaving a part of myself behind. After a dozen paces, as I stopped and turned to see Greg standing in the doorway looking forlorn, I made no effort to disguise my tears. I wanted to run back into his arms and I'm sure he felt the same, but somehow I continued on my way.

It was one of those heart-wrenching moments when the pain is so exquisite, it burns an indelible memory in your mind. I was convinced it was the right decision, but as I walked towards the sanctity of my bedroom, self-doubt tormented me. Private Thomson was on duty at the door and I was embarrassed when he asked if I was all right. Then William saw me, he was also concerned by my appearance. Mrs Morgan, who was equally worried, met me in the hall. My embarrassment was finally compounded when I confronted Jennings.

"Are you all right, Mrs Heywood, you look terribly upset, is there anything I can do?"

"Bless you, Mr Jennings, that's very kind, but I'll be fine."

"As you wish, Mrs Heywood."

When finally I leaned back against my bedroom door, I

breathed an enormous sigh of relief. It was only moments later when Florence came to the door. She knocked and came straight in.

"Mr Jennings sent me, what's wrong, Mrs Heywood?"

"It's nothing, I'm upset, that's all."

"It's not nothing, though, is it? Why don't you cry on my shoulder?"

It took me an age to compose myself and when I did, Florence's shoulder was wet with tears. The lovely thing was that I wasn't embarrassed, I sobbed my heart out without a care.

"You needed that," she said with a smile.

"You'll never know how much, Florence, thank you."

"Are you going to tell me?"

Florence knew where I was those nights when I was not in my bedroom, so there was no point trying to deny it.

"I've broken it off with Greg Norton."

"I'm sorry to see you so upset, but I think I know why you've done that. It's not for me to say really, but I think it's for the best."

"It is for the best, but it's been a horrible thing to do."

"Are you dining with Her Ladyship tonight?"

"No, I'm going to my grandmother's tonight. Will you tell Her Ladyship for me?"

"Of course I will. Why don't you freshen up in the bathroom? I'll get your clothes ready for you, and then I can make you look presentable again."

Florence had become indispensable to me. I said nothing, but more than ever that evening I wondered how I would manage without her. She did so much to help me through that dreadful experience. When I finally left to go to Gran's, I looked like my old self, even if I didn't feel like it. It had been more than two weeks since I last saw Gran. Fiona had been clever asking me to come that night, knowing that going home would lift my spirits when I needed it the most. Even though it had been a while, Spencer Tracy recognised my footsteps as I walked along the footpath. I could hear Fi shouting at him, but to no avail. He remained determined to greet me as I opened the door.

"Get down, Spencer, that's a good boy. Yes, I'm pleased to see you too."

The silly dog was quite beside himself, and his tail couldn't possibly have wagged any faster. He seemed to be pushing me towards the kitchen where Gran and Fiona had dinner waiting for me. Gran struggled up onto her feet and hugged me for ages.

"What's all this, Gran? It's not been that long!"

"I'm just so pleased to see you, Lily. Fiona won't tell me, but I know you girls had something to do with D-Day and that's why you haven't been home. I'm so proud of you both."

"We had quite a bit to do with it, Gran, but you must tell no-one."

"I know, I won't say a word, not even to Mavis. Just think, my girls had a lot to do with D-Day, it's wonderful."

Fiona smiled from ear to ear! Fi was such a part of the family that Gran called her 'one of her girls'.

"Now, will you tell me where Dotty is? Fiona just tells me she's away somewhere."

"That's right, she is. If I tell you something, Gran, will you really promise me never to repeat it?"

"Of course, love, not even to Mavis."

"Well, you know Dotty's sort of in the army now, well, she's in Normandy. I can't tell you what she did, but when D-Day started, she did something really vital towards the landings. Our Dotty is a real heroine, Gran. She's alive and well, and she should be home soon."

I hadn't realised how worried she'd been, the joy in her eyes was obvious to see. Her pride in 'her girls' was contagious; Fiona and I couldn't help but bask in a little of Dotty's reflected glory. I wanted so much to tell her more, but that was how it was, we just didn't talk about it. Fiona said nothing about

Greg, but she would occasionally look at me as if seeking reassurance. Gran was in good form, knowing Dotty would be home soon had raised her spirits.

We didn't mention the flying bomb incident, concentrating more on the prospect that an end to the war might finally be in sight. We had a lovely time together, albeit slightly surreal for me, with Greg always in my mind. I did my best not to let my mood affect the evening but must admit it was a relief when it came time to go to bed. Fi was the first to go upstairs, and as soon as I had finished putting away the last of the dishes I followed her. I held Gran tightly when I kissed her goodnight. More than ever, she was the unchanging centre of my universe.

"I love you, Gran, I'll see you in the morning." She then took me totally by surprise.

"Whoever has broken your heart, Lily, life will go on, you know."

"How did you know?"

"I'm a part of you, Lily, you can't hide anything from me."

We smiled at each other. She had the same sparkle in her eye that I remember from when I was a little girl. Walking up the stairs, I stopped and looked back at her.

"You're right, Gran, life does go on, but why does it have to be so painful?"

"I don't know, luv, but it often is," she said, walking away.

The moment I stepped into the bedroom, Fiona was sitting up, waiting to ask me about Greg.

"Did you tell him?"

"I did."

"Was it awful?"

"It was, I don't know how I managed to do it."

"How did Greg take it?"

"He said he was expecting it, so I don't think it was a surprise. He dealt with it a lot better than I did, but knowing him, he just didn't show it until I was gone. It feels dreadful to have done that to him."

"Can you still work together, what's going to happen?"

"I think we can, but it could be difficult."

"You've done the right thing, Lily, you had to distance yourself from one of them, and you've made your decision."

"I just hope I've made the right decision, but I'm not sure I had any other option."

It was the end of an emotional day, a day that I have never forgotten.

Chapter Five
The Calm Before The Storm

The boys in Hut 3 were all strangely quiet. Rather than moving symbols around on a map of the Normandy beaches they were looking at a map of South East England and London.

"Morning, Lily," said Corky, "that thing we saw yesterday was exactly what we thought it was. It's effectively a flying bomb, propelled by a pulse jet, I'm afraid this is serious."

"How serious, Corky?"

"We don't know, but my guess is *very* serious. Rolo has picked up on an interim report from Bletchley Park. We think they launched several, there's a report that two fell into the Channel, but four have struck home."

"Have they hit London?"

"They were obviously aimed at London, but all except one fell short. They hit Cuckfield in West Sussex, and Swanscombe in Kent."

"Swanscombe, that's a bit close to home."

"One was even closer, Lily. Sevenoaks has been hit!"

"*Sevenoaks*! Oh my goodness."

"As far as we know the only casualties are in Bethnal Green in London, at Grove Road. We hear at least six are dead."

The boys had read some of the early reports about Hitler's

new reprisal weapon, or 'Vergeltungswaffen', and hence the term V1. It was obviously serious. At that stage, only two days after the first sighting, we didn't understand just how serious the new threat would turn out to be. The other concern which had been preoccupying them was Omaha Beach. Johnny had been asked to make an aerial survey of the whole area, the analysis was ongoing.

"Have you formed any opinions yet about Omaha?" I asked.

"It's not possible to be sure yet," replied Woody. "We need a lot more access to the decision-making on the day, but we're getting a clearer picture."

"Did we make a mistake?" I asked apprehensively.

"Sometimes events have a way of conspiring against you," said Patrick. "Not even me Mammy can control everything."

"That sounds like we *did* make a mistake," I replied.

"Why did we select Omaha in the first place, Lily?" asked Corky.

"Well, it was 7000 yards of gently shelving crescent-shaped beach, and in 1943 it was virtually undefended. It was also in reasonably close proximity to the other four beaches."

"Yes, it was the perfect choice," said Woody. "However, after the decision was made, they started to fortify it."

"But we were aware of every permanent defence," I replied.

"Everyone agreed it wasn't practical to consider an alternative; we couldn't leave a defensible gap between the landing beaches," Woody replied. "The strategy was to destroy the defences. What we didn't see was that a German infantry division had moved in to reinforce their defensive position."

"I didn't know that; didn't anyone spot this?"

"We've looked again at the reconnaissance photographs from the days before, we can't see any troop movements."

"Even so, Woody, the plan was to destroy all the coastal defences with aerial bombing and naval bombardment."

"We missed!"

"We couldn't have missed, we dropped thousands of tons of bombs!"

"It's clear what happened from Johnny's latest reconnaissance. The bombers had to go in just ahead of the invasion force at daybreak - they were afraid of hitting our own forces so they erred on the side of caution. What was an error was that they flew over the beaches; they didn't fly parallel to them. Apart from destroying the defences, they were supposed to provide craters on the beach to act as shelter for the advancing troops. The fact is that most of the bombs fell inland."

"And the naval bombardment, what happened to that?"

"Same thing, couldn't open fire until daybreak when the invasion force was closing in, most of the fire missed."

"That was bad enough," said Corky, "but the plan was to land the amphibious tanks first in order to provide cover fire for the troops."

"Don't tell me that went wrong as well."

"They launched twenty-nine DD-tanks in the first wave, twenty-seven of them sank in the high seas!"

"Oh my God!"

"The weather was against us, Lily," said Patrick. "It wasn't just the tanks - ten landing craft sank. Men were scattered along the beach, the weather that day cost us dearly."

"The engineers were supposed to clear a path through the beach obstacles," said Woody. "It seems that wasn't a success either."

"It sounds like it was a miracle the Americans succeeded at all."

"Not a miracle, Lily, just guts, determination, and men's lives."

It was a sobering discussion, one that we continue to this day. There was still so much that we didn't know, perhaps there are things we'll never know. At one point, General Bradley considered evacuating Omaha. If that had happened, who knows what the outcome of D-Day might have been. In the end, the slaughter resulted in a triumph, but we must never forget the cost; 2000 U.S. troops were killed or wounded on Omaha. The British on Gold and Sword beaches lost another 2000 troops killed or wounded, while on Juno beach the Canadians had over 900 killed or wounded. Our foothold into Europe came at a price.

Rolo had been absent from our discussion; he was trying to find out more about the flying bombs from his connections at Bletchley. When he finally came back to Hut 3, we all assumed he had additional news to tell us.

"Is it more bad news, Rolo?" I asked.

"No, if I can believe it, it's amazing news."

"Well, tell us, what's happened?"

"This has come from Bletchley. It says there has been an armed conflict involving the French Resistance in Caen."

"But there's heavy fighting around Caen," said Woody. "The place is a German stronghold, it's hardly the place for an uprising."

"This wasn't really an uprising. It seems a prisoner was being held by the Gestapo in the municipal building. The French Resistance attacked and destroyed much of the building, freeing the prisoner. What followed was a running battle in the streets that lasted more than an hour. The fighting was so intense the German army thought it was the Allied invasion forces and they sent in reinforcements, including tanks. Somehow two SOE agents are reported to have escaped in a stolen German military vehicle."

"It's Dotty, isn't it, it must be!" I exclaimed.

"I agree," replied Rolo. "The Americans said they apprehended them abandoning a German vehicle, and they found discarded German uniforms. That's why they thought they were fifth column. It has to be them."

"They're both bloody heroes, what they've done is incredible," said Woody.

"She told me she would drag herself back by her fingertips if she had to, and now she has."

"Do we know who this came from?" asked Patrick.

"It obviously originated from someone who knew they were SOE, someone within FR with knowledge of who to contact."

"It's going to be a proud moment when we welcome them back," said Mac.

"We all feel the same, Mac, when do you expect them?"

"I expect them any time, they'll come back on a supply ship."

"We must lay on a welcome for them," I said, "bunting, the whole works."

"Great idea," Mac replied.

"I'll see to it," I said. "I bet Jennings or Mrs Morgan will know where to lay their hands on some bunting."

Rolo confirmed that there were no more reports of the flying bombs. We all breathed a sigh of relief. I wanted to believe that was the end of it, but Corky in particular seemed quite sure there would be more to follow. I walked back to the Manor hoping he was wrong, but fearing he was right. On the way, I glanced over towards the estate office, and could see Greg standing by his van. My heart jumped, my common sense told me to ignore him, but I turned right instead of left, and found myself walking towards him.

"Morning, Greg, how are you?"

"When someone like you, asks someone like me, 'how are you', what you're really asking is how are you without me?"

"That's exactly what I'm asking, Greg."

"I can manage nearly ten minutes without thinking about you."

"As long as that, I can't manage that long."

"You will, Lily, you have Lord Middlebourne to fill your mind."

"I can't keep on telling you how sorry I am every time we meet, Greg, but please know that I am. You're the last person on earth I wanted to hurt."

"I know, so don't go on apologising."

"Thank you. I'm going to organise a big welcome home for Dotty and Rob. It should be any day now."

"Can I be there?"

"I don't see why not."

I was pleased I turned right and hadn't gone straight on to the Manor. Greg and I had to coexist, and more than that, I wanted him in my life. As luck would have it, the first person I met when I returned to the Manor was Mrs Morgan. Sure enough, she knew where to lay her hands on some bunting. When I told her what it was for, she was as excited about the idea as I was.

"Leave it to me, Mrs Heywood, we can put it up for you, with a big 'Welcome Home Dotty and Rob' banner."

"That would be perfect, Mrs Morgan. They mustn't be seen from outside, so let's have them all around the Great Hall. I'll have a word with Her Ladyship, but I'm sure it will be fine."

Mr Jennings came over to us and he also approved of the arrangements for Dotty and Rob.

"While you're here, Mr Jennings - have you thought about allowing Mary time off to work with the estate manager?"

"I have, Mrs Heywood. I think it is an absurd idea! However, you wouldn't have asked me if you didn't think the idea had merit. Therefore, I have discussed it with Mrs Morgan, and I will allow Mary two afternoons a week. If this is to continue, we shall have to consider engaging another maid, it will be more than Florence can cope with."

"I agree, Mr Jennings, I'm very grateful for your decision. I think Mary will make you proud. Do you mind if I tell her today?"

"Not at all, I shall send her to your office."

"If I might venture an opinion, Mr Jennings, I think it would be wise to start interviewing girls right away."

Jennings surprised me because for a notoriously stubborn man, he was being extraordinarily cooperative. I thanked him and Mrs Morgan before going on my way. As I walked to the office, I felt I was finally beginning to take back control. The moment I entered the office, I couldn't wait to tell Fiona about the report we received from Bletchley about the uprising in Caen. We agreed it had to be Dotty and Rob. We barely had time to discuss it when there was a knock on the door, it was Mary.

"Mr Jennings said you wanted to see me about something, Mrs Heywood."

"That's right, Mary, would you sit down for a moment?"

"Nothing wrong, is there?"

"No, nothing. I wanted to ask you how you feel your career is developing."

"My career! I'm not sure being a maid is really a career."

"Well, it can be, if you choose it to be. But I was thinking more of the extra work you've been doing for Mrs Morgan, and for Her Ladyship."

"I much prefer doing that, I really like working with Her Ladyship."

"How do you get on with her?"

"I was scared stiff to start with. The first few times, I felt she didn't really want to teach me, and I wondered why she had asked me. I tried so hard, just like you told me to, Mrs Heywood. I looked things up in those books you gave me. As soon as I understood things, Her Ladyship seemed to warm towards me. I look forward to it now."

"I'm so pleased. It was a big step for Her Ladyship taking you under her wing. The Countess wouldn't normally do such a thing."

"I realise that, and I can't help but think you had a lot to do with it, Mrs Heywood."

"I might have mentioned it, but you have to take your own chances in life, Mary, and you took yours."

"Well, I'm doing my best."

"There's another opportunity I would like you to consider.

This would be an enormous step up for you, Mary, it wouldn't be like helping Her Ladyship. What I am going to suggest could define the rest of your life."

"You make it sound really serious, Mrs Heywood, I'm not sure I understand."

"As we go through life, Mary, we all have to make decisions along the way. Mostly they'll be occasions where, if we get it wrong we learn from the experience and try not to do it again. But then there are those decisions that you might call life changing. Those are the occasions when you will not get a second chance. Your entire life can depend upon just two or three decisions."

"Are you telling me I have a really important decision to make?"

"I am, Mary. I'm going to offer you something that you will think is beyond you. A step you may be frightened to take."

"What is it?"

"I'm offering you the position of trainee assistant estate manager, which in the fullness of time, could result in you becoming an estate manager. You would start a couple of afternoons a week as a trainee, and then it's up to you, but you will be burning your bridges, there'll be no going back."

"I can't be an estate manager, I'm a housemaid!"

"I told you before, Mary, that's *what* you are, not *who* you are. Forget your title as a housemaid. You're a very intelligent young woman who is more than capable of doing whatever you set your mind to. Believe in yourself, Mary, this is your moment, please take it."

"I remember when you told me about your uncle, and how he offered you your chance in life. You said that you didn't hesitate, Mrs Heywood, you accepted the job. I've never forgotten our conversation that day, you really inspired me."

"Does that mean you'll accept the position?"

"If you think I can do it, Mrs Heywood, then so do I!"

Fiona walked over to Mary and put her hand on her shoulder. "You've just made the best decision of your life, Mary, well done!"

Chapter Six

The Phone Call

Mary was still standing in the office with us when my green phone rang, I had to answer it.

"Excuse me, Mary. Hello," I said.

"Lily, it's Elizabeth Layton."

I put my hand over the mouthpiece. Something about Elizabeth's tone alarmed me.

"I'm sorry, Mary, we'll have to finish this conversation another time."

Mary understood and politely left the office immediately.

"Sorry, Elizabeth, I was with someone."

"There have been several incidents in London, Lily, it's those flying bombs. He's asked me to tell you. Now don't be alarmed, because we have no details, but it sounds like Lord Middlebourne has been involved."

"What do you mean, involved?"

"As far as we know, he was travelling in a car with some other very senior people, and we believe they were involved in one of the explosions. I'm sorry, Lily, it sounds serious. We believe the casualties have been taken to hospital."

"Edward is in hospital, which hospital?"

"I don't know, this has literally only just come in. The PM was informed by the Home Secretary because the police say some very senior officials are involved. It would be extremely bad for morale if it became public knowledge."

"I'm trying not to panic, Elizabeth, please tell me if you know anything else."

"I'm afraid there are fatalities, Lily, but the PM doesn't know who."

"Oh my God, no!"

I dropped the phone and slumped back into my chair. I felt as if I was spiralling down into a bottomless well. Fiona stepped forward and grabbed the phone.

"Elizabeth, it's Fiona Robinson. Lily is in shock, she can't respond, what did you tell her, I need to know everything."

Fi was simply brilliant, she acted calmly and efficiently, doing everything I was incapable of doing. When I was told about Dotty's apparent death, I didn't think there was any greater pain that death could inflict on me. I was wrong, now I fell headlong into something even more exquisitely painful. Fiona organised more tea, and all the while she was making telephone enquiries. She didn't stop to comfort me, she did exactly what she had to do. It felt like an eternity, and all the while I sat shaking, trying desperately to exclude reality. I overheard Fi say 'are you sure'. I looked up at her expecting a knife to be plunged into my heart.

"He's alive, Lily, he's in St Thomas' Hospital. He's badly injured, but he's alive."

It didn't sink in for a moment. It was Fi's reassuring smile which brought me back from the hell I had descended into.

"He's alive, you're sure?"

"Yes, he's listed as Edward Sinclair. Right, get yourself tidied up. I'll ask Florence to pack you a case. I'll inform Lady Caroline, and I'll have William waiting with the car by the door. If you hurry, you can catch the 11.30 train."

"Fi, you've been amazing."

"I had a wonderful teacher, now off you go."

I ran to my room, my mind racing in all directions. Edward

was seriously injured, that prospect filled me with terror, but he was alive and that gave me hope, even some joy. I realised I was panicking, not thinking clearly. Amongst my maelstrom of thoughts, one crystal clear imperative rose into prominence: Edward needed me. That was the only clear thought I needed in order to motivate myself. Florence appeared as I was going into the bathroom.

"Florence, pack me a case for a week, I have no idea what I will need, so try to think of everything."

When I returned, she was busy folding clothes into my largest case.

"Miss Robinson told me His Lordship has been injured, he will be all right, Mrs Heywood, I just know he will."

"How can you be so sure?"

"Nothing will happen to His Lordship if you're there."

"I hope you're right, Florence."

Albert appeared at my door to carry my case to the car, and Jennings spoke to me briefly as I was leaving.

"He will be in excellent hands, Mrs Heywood. Will you pass on the best wishes of every member of the household, and will you keep us informed?"

"I will, Mr Jennings, and could you and Mrs Evans take care of Her Ladyship, she will be very distressed."

"Of course, and you take care of yourself, Lily."

"Don't worry, Charles, I'm not about to fail His Lordship in his hour of need."

He raised his chin, pressing his lips together in a proud gesture. I smiled an acknowledgement and continued quickly outside to the waiting car. William was there with the door of the Rolls-Royce open. Elsie Morgan and Joyce Evans appeared at the door with the kitchen staff, the girls quickly following with Albert. Fiona had motivated the entire household. They all waved as William pulled away, I raised my hand. In retrospect, I must have looked like the Queen, but that was hardly my intention.

We were in good time arriving at the station, and William escorted me onto the platform. When I saw the train approaching and heard the whistle it failed to rouse those childhood memories of fear. The dragon's breath and squealing brakes were there to take me to Edward. William placed my case in the carriage, and the slamming doors marked the beginning of my journey, not the end. I thanked William and waved goodbye as the engine roared into life. The carriage couplings clunked together as the dragon sped me on my way.

It was an uneventful journey. I was so far away in my thoughts that I hardly remember it. When the train pulled into Charing Cross, it seemed as if only minutes had elapsed. The platforms were thronging with people. There were far more men in uniform than civilians, making the station feel like an army transit camp. Miraculously I managed to get a porter to carry my case to the taxi rank, where a friendly cabby asked, "Where to, luv?" to which I replied, "St Thomas' Hospital."

The journey from the station was fairly straightforward. Compared with the last time I was in London, it was noticeable that the roads were passable. The bomb sites were everywhere, but the roads were clear. There were many damaged houses, one after another, each one the broken fragments of people's lives, the debris cleared into piles. Many more were simply spaces where someone's home once stood, all memory of the people erased. Builders were working everywhere as part of a national programme to repair damaged property. I could see a lot of progress had been made since 1941, but not all the destruction we drove past was dated back to that time. The more recent raids had also taken their toll. I was anxious to get to the hospital and asked the cabby if he could drive any faster.

"You got someone there, luv?"

"Yes, he's been injured."

"Don't worry, luv, I'll get you there."

When I arrived, it was not what I was expecting. St Thomas' suffered terrible bomb damage in September 1940.

I later found out that it had been hit several times during the Blitz, with many people killed. A barrage balloon was tethered within the grounds, one of many floating over London. The building stood in defiance, bearing its wounds like a proud soldier, but the damage was extensive. Big Ben towered in the distance, on the other side of the river, reminding us all that Britain would never be cowed. I thanked my cabby and rushed into the building, struggling with my case. I asked a lady where I would find Edward Sinclair. She was slow and ponderous, searching through her records.

"Can you hurry, please."

"Is he a new admission?"

"Yes, he's a bomb casualty, they admitted several at the same time."

"Oh yes, I know, terrible business. They won't let you see him. Nobody is allowed to go into that ward."

"Please, just tell me which ward he is in."

"It's no good taking that attitude, dear, you had better come back another day."

"Of course, I understand, perhaps in a couple of days' time."

"That would probably be best."

"That's fine, which ward should I ask for when I come back?"

"Ask for Ward Five, that's one of the underground wards, all the casualties have been put down there."

"And where will I find Ward Five?"

The exasperating woman explained where to go, I thanked her kindly and set off immediately towards the ward. Her protests receded as I distanced myself from her. I rushed off down the stairs and entered a strange subterranean world. The basement had been converted into wards and operating theatres, but all the trappings of the basement remained. It was an incongruous world of white linen sheets amongst pipes and girders. Curtain rails were suspended from the ceiling along with leaking pipes and cables.

Ward Five was relatively narrow with beds along each side. I could see a frenzy of activity around several of the patients. It was like a battlefield, with blood everywhere, and nurses were running around wearing what looked like butcher's aprons. There must have been twenty injured people. One bed had a blood-stained sheet draped over a body; they must have been too rushed to draw the curtain. The scene confronting me completely took my breath away, was that Edward lying there beneath the blood-stained sheet?

None of the patients appeared to be Edward, and so I walked through, checking each bed. I didn't find him, not unless he was the patient with his head in bandages. I went to that bed and picked up the notes, it was Edward! I gasped at the sight which confronted me. His chest was bound, and his head was almost covered in a blood-stained bandage. I rushed to his side and grabbed his hand, but he didn't respond. My heart was already exploding in my chest, but his lack of response filled me with a terror that seemed to inhabit every inch of my body.

"Can you hear me, Edward? It's Lily."

He was completely motionless, I desperately needed to speak to someone, but was paralysed with fear. In amongst all the activity, no-one appeared to have noticed me entering the ward, the nurses all huddling around patients. Not thinking beyond what lay before me, I tried to shout for one of the nurses.

"I need the doctor who is tending this patient, can someone help me?"

"That's not possible. Who are you? You shouldn't be here," one of the nurses responded.

"I'm not going anywhere."

The young nurse left me and quickly returned with a matron who marched up to me with as much menace as she could muster. Middle-aged and rotund, she was quite intimidating, demanding I leave immediately.

"I'm staying with this man," I said tearfully.

"I do not know how you got in here, but I will have you removed, if necessary."

"The Luftwaffe couldn't do that, so you certainly won't, I'm staying here. You can beat me to the ground and drag me out screaming, and I'll come straight back. I'll never leave this man's side."

She took a step back, looking quite aghast. I could see she was considering her options.

"Who are you, who is this man to you?"

"I love him, that's all you need to know."

"That explains a lot. In that case you had best have a chair, my dear, it may be a long wait." She beckoned a nurse. "Nurse, fetch this lady a chair."

"Thank you, Matron, I will cooperate with you. I'll not be in the way, but I am not leaving. Can you explain to me what this man's condition is?"

"He has broken ribs, and multiple minor injuries which will heal, but he has a serious head injury, he's in a coma."

"When will he come out of the coma?"

"I'm sorry, my dear, but he might not come out of it."

She might as well have drawn a knife from her belt and plunged it into me. My legs buckled beneath me, I had to lean against the bed. Closing my eyes for a moment and taking a deep breath, I tried to compose myself, but the room appeared to be spinning around me.

"Thank you for being honest with me, Matron, but I can assure you he will come out of the coma and make a full recovery. I need to speak to whoever is in charge of his treatment."

"That's Dr Wisniewski, he's with another patient. Would you like a nurse to fetch you a cup of tea? You look like you need it."

"That would be greatly appreciated, thank you. What's your name, Matron?"

"Mrs Horworthy."

"And your first name?"

"I'm known as Matron, my dear, but my first name is Marion."

"Thank you again, Marion, I'm Mrs Heywood, Lily Heywood."

She was totally bemused because in an institution like a hospital, they strictly adhered to the social protocols, nobody would ever call her Marion. In this way, I made sure she was not about to forget me. Content that I wouldn't be removed, I tried to calm down and gather my senses. I was not sure if the staff knew who the casualties were; it was possible they were just names, perhaps I was the only person who knew who they were. I looked at the man in the next bed, he was conscious, but appeared to be in a very bad way. Glancing around at the others, I recognised two of them. One was General Ashton. I met him, albeit briefly, when I was in Baker Street meeting General Gubbins. The other was Sir John Cornwallis. I went straight over to General Ashton. He was not in the best shape, but he was conscious.

"General Ashton, how are you?"

"I'm sorry, do I know you?" his voice was weak.

"We met once in Baker Street."

"Who are you?"

"I'm Mrs Heywood, Lord Middlebourne's Chief of Staff."

"Oh thank heavens, I wasn't sure if anyone knew we were here."

"The PM's office informed me, they know something happened, but they have no details."

"All I know is there was a damned almighty explosion, and the building we were driving past blew out across the road. We took the full brunt of it."

"They think it was one of these flying bombs."

"Oh good Lord, we were half expecting that. Now look here, Heywood, none of us are in a fit state to do anything. You must take charge."

"Don't worry, sir, I have it in hand. How many of you are involved?"

"Four of us, plus the driver. Damn tight squeeze in the car. Ponsonby was by the window, I'm afraid he bought it. Middlebourne was in the front on that side, he didn't look too good either. Cornwallis and I fared better."

"What about the driver?"

"Private Hawkins, reliable man, he's here somewhere."

I looked around for my friendly matron, but she was nowhere to be seen.

"Nurse, will you find Matron for me, please."

She looked at me quizzically but did as I asked. I realised I had to confide in someone, I had no authority in the hospital. When Matron appeared, she looked slightly annoyed at being summoned.

"Well, what is it now?"

I led her to a quiet corner and turned my back to the rest of the occupants.

"When these men came in, Marion, did you not notice from their uniforms that two of them are top-ranking officers?"

"Well, yes, now that you mention it, but we see uniforms all the time."

"How have you identified them?"

"Mr Sinclair was conscious when he came in, but if people can't tell us who they are, we look at whatever documents they have on them."

"That's what I thought. Now look, Marion, I have to confide in someone here, and I don't know anyone else. Do you understand the meaning of keeping a State secret?"

"Of course I do."

"You must not repeat what I am going to tell you. Three of the survivors involved in that bomb blast are very important people, they're vital to the war effort. There are several things I need to do, and I need some authority so I need your help, Marion. Above all, we must not draw attention to ourselves. Do you recognise that man over there?"

"The face looks familiar."

"He's a member of the War Cabinet, you might have seen his picture in the paper. The thing is, Marion, if it was generally known that one of Hitler's new flying bombs had injured public figures - well, it would be bad for public morale wouldn't it?"

"What do you mean, flying bombs?"

"Do you not read the papers?"

"I don't have time."

"Let's just say it's a new and very dangerous weapon. I imagine you'll be seeing more of its consequences."

"Who are you, Mrs Heywood?"

"I can't tell you who I am, but I'm asking you to help me."

"Do you work for the government?"

"Yes, I suppose I do."

"So you don't love that patient, you deceived me, you were very convincing."

"I was convincing, Marion, because it's true. I can't live without him. That's why I know he will recover."

"I certainly think if you have anything to do with it, he will. What can I do to help?"

"I need to see the doctor in charge, you need to pave the way for me. First and foremost, I must know everything about Edward's condition. Then I need to have a full medical report on each of the men involved. I need access to an equipped office with a telephone, and I need two messengers standing by."

"You can use the hospital secretary's office; I'll talk to her. Dr Wisniewski is going to be a different matter, he will not like what you are suggesting."

"Talk to him, Marion, pave the way for me, and do it quickly, will you?"

She left me then, looking quite motivated, making me hopeful I had found an ally. I sat a short time with Edward again; it was desperately difficult to tear myself away from him, but I knew I had to go back to General Ashton.

"I've just had another thought, General, you must have had documents, briefcases and the like. Where are they?"

"Good point, Heywood, I was in no state to notice. Oh good grief, they could be anywhere."

"Hopefully the police have picked them up. I'll inform Baker Street. They'll know what to do. I'm also going to send them a medical report on each of you. They can have their own medical experts assess you. I expect they will try to have you moved somewhere less public."

"We need to keep this hush-hush, Heywood, not good for the public to know about this."

"Yes, I'm dealing with that."

I broke away from the General when I saw who I presumed was Dr Wisniewski approaching me. I led him to Edward's side.

"Now look here, Mrs Heywood, or whatever your name is. Matron has spoken to me, tells me you're from some sort of government department. I'm not releasing hospital records to you or anyone else. I deeply resent timewasters like you walking into an emergency like this and expecting cooperation. Who the hell do you people think you are? Why don't you leave it to the people who actually get things done!"

His English was perfect, but his slight Polish accent made it perfectly clear what his background was.

"Your ignorance of this situation is perfectly understandable, but that's no excuse for such arrogance. Let me explain something to you, Dr Wisniewski. There are people in this ward who have contributed enormously to the invasion of Europe, and I'm proud to count myself among them. Allied soldiers are fighting for our freedom in Normandy right now. The people of Poland know better than anyone what Nazi occupation means, and yet they continue to fight through their magnificent resistance movement. I'm asking you to do something for this county. If you don't value what we are fighting for, then shame on you, you're a disgrace to your own brave countrymen!"

"Are you threatening me, Mrs Heywood?"

"I am!"

His eyes widened and he stepped back from me. I wasn't sure if he was defiant or deflated as he took a moment before answering.

"Perhaps I do need to know more about this situation. I too have been fighting today, I've been fighting to save lives, but I apologise if I've appeared arrogant."

"I've also had a traumatic day, Doctor, I would normally be far more courteous. Some of the men in this ward serve this country at the very highest level. I mean no disrespect to you or your staff, but I *will* forward their medical notes to higher authority. The wellbeing of these people is not for you to decide. I'm particularly concerned about this man, kindly explain to me what his condition is."

"He has a serious traumatic brain injury, there is bleeding within his brain which is increasing internal pressure. If that pressure is not released, he will die."

I couldn't answer, I just stood there frozen.

"Your reaction tells me you care deeply for this man."

"I do. So tell me, what are you going to do to prevent that build-up of pressure?"

"He will have surgery as soon as possible."

"And what are the chances of success?"

"Very low, I am afraid, we simply don't have this kind of expertise here."

"Who does?"

"This is not my field, but there is a surgeon, I believe his name is Cairns."

"Is he the best?"

"I believe so."

"What time-scale are we looking at?"

"It is very urgent, no more than twelve hours."

"Where will I find Cairns?"

"I think he is associated with Oxford University."

"Thank you, Doctor. I want you to bring me the medical records for four of the patients in this ward. I will point out the ones I am concerned with. Please ensure they include every medical detail, and your opinion. Right now, I need the use of the secretary's office, so I will detain you no longer, Matron will show me where to go."

I left him standing there looking bewildered. I went straight to the matron, who was standing close by.

"Have you told the secretary to vacate her office, Marion?"

"I have, follow me, Mrs Heywood."

I didn't say a word as we walked along the corridor. Every fibre of my body wanted to be with Edward so I had to cling desperately to my determination to do what I knew had to be done. She showed me to the office, which amounted to a small space in a store room. There were filing cabinets and cardboard boxes everywhere. It was obviously an emergency measure following the bomb damage. At least there was a telephone, and a typewriter. As I went inside, I asked Marion to wait outside with the secretary. I grabbed the telephone and dialled the office. My finger trembled as I reached for the dial. When Fiona answered, I could have burst into tears. I told her everything I knew as quickly as I could.

"Slow down, Lily," she said.

"I can't, Fi, there isn't time. Edward needs an urgent operation."

"Oh that's terrible. Oh Lily, this is awful. Will they do it?"

"This is the problem, Fi, there are very few experts in brain surgery. They will attempt it, but I need something much better than that. I've been told about one expert whose name is Cairns. I don't know which hospital he works in, but I believe he has a connection with Oxford University. I need you to find out for me, Fi. I need you to phone everyone you can think of, use all our contacts, including Elizabeth if necessary."

"Don't worry, Lily, I'll find the best surgeon there is."

"Last thing, Fi, give me the telephone number for General Gubbins' office."

"I've got it right here, Lily."

"Thank you, phone me back here, I'll have the secretary waiting to come and call me."

At last, some of the weight was lifted from my shoulders. Fi would move heaven and earth for me, there was no need to concern myself on that score. I telephoned Gubbins' office and spoke to his assistant Margaret Jackson, giving her the full story. When I mentioned the briefcases, there was consternation. General Gubbins himself came to the phone and I could tell from his tone of voice that things were going to happen rapidly. The telephone was not secure, but I had no option.

The moment I had finished conveying the salient details, Gubbins hung up, I understood why. No doubt questions were about to be asked - how did Fiona find out where the men had been taken quicker than the intelligence services? A breakdown of communications with the civil authorities seemed like a likely explanation to me. I replaced the receiver gently, relieved that I had relinquished another responsibility. I asked Matron and the secretary to come in.

"You must be used to arranging ambulances, Marion?"

"Well yes, sometimes we have to transfer patients to other hospitals."

"Good, I want you to have an ambulance equipped and ready to take Edward to wherever I send him. Do you advise that a nurse should travel with him?"

"Yes, I do, but I'm not sure we can spare one."

"Find someone, Marion, you must have women you can call upon."

"Well, I'll do my best."

"In situations like this, Marion, don't think in terms of doing your best. Only think how you will succeed."

"I'm sorry, I don't know your name," I said to the secretary.

"Mrs Riley."

"And your first name?"

"Evelyn."

"Ok, Evelyn. If you have an urgent phone call to make, do it immediately. After that, I need this line available at all times. If someone telephones you, be as brief as you can, get rid of them. A woman called Fiona Robinson will call, when she does, run and find me."

"Yes, Mrs Heywood."

"As soon as Matron gives you the medical notes, I want you to copy them for me. I want two copies of each."

"Yes, I can do that."

"Good. Now, Marion, I need you to help me with the patient records."

"How can I help?"

"I'll tell you in a minute."

We left the office and proceeded back towards the ward.

"When the doctor has completed the medical notes, I want you to remove the names from your records. We will call them by their Christian names and the first letter of their surname."

"This is very irregular."

"It is, indeed, Marion, I'm not sure I've ever had such an irregular day."

She went on her way, and all I wanted to do was to be with Edward but realised I should report to the General first. I found him looking slightly better, he seemed pleased to me.

"What progress?" he asked.

"I am erasing all records of your being here. I've spoken to Baker Street; they will track down your briefcases immediately. I shall send your medical notes with a report to both Baker Street and the Prime Minister's office within the hour. I'm proposing to have Lord Middlebourne moved to another hospital for an urgent operation as soon as possible."

"Damn fine job, Heywood, good to have you on board."

"You relax and get yourself better, General."

At last I had time to sit with Edward and almost ran to his side. I longed to see his face, but only his mouth and nose were visible. It felt as if my beautiful Edward had been removed, placed somewhere for safekeeping, leaving behind the broken shell that lay before me. I held his hand and spoke to him continually hoping maybe he could hear me.

"I'm here, Edward. I'm with you, can you hear me, Edward?"

The sight of his helpless body lying there filled me with dread. The waiting was by far the worst part. Feeling so helpless and being reliant upon other people didn't come easily for me. As long as I felt in charge of things I could cope, but the moment I stayed there with Edward, the fear surged through my body again. When the doctor walked towards me holding the medical notes, I welcomed his appearance as a distraction from my torment.

"Would you be kind enough to give these to Matron, Doctor? She knows what to do with them."

He cooperated with me, or at least he didn't question my request. As he was leaving, I called him back to thank him. He nodded a gesture, I wasn't sure if it was whole-hearted cooperation, or a begrudged willingness. Either way, he did as I asked. It must have been some time later when Marion placed her hand on my shoulder.

"I'm sure he can't hear you, Lily, you're only upsetting yourself."

"I know, I just have to."

"I overheard what you said earlier to the Doctor, about these men here, and yourself. I don't know what you do, but I have the feeling we should all be grateful to you."

"That's kind of you, Marion. I can't tell you what we do, but I'm proud to be a part of it. And I am so proud of this man, he's the most amazing, and wonderful person I have ever met."

"And you love him, I can see that."

"I do, and I'm fighting for him. That's why I have to stay focused on what I need to do."

"Evelyn has finished copying the records, and I changed the names as you asked. The ambulance is waiting for you."

"What about messenger boys?"

"Yes, Evelyn has someone standing by."

"We make a good team, Marion, thank you."

We continued talking until Evelyn appeared, waving frantically at the end of the ward. It was my phone call. I rushed with her to the office, thanking her on the way for all her efforts. I grabbed the phone as if it were the last straw floating on the water, and I was drowning, which in many ways I was.

"Hello, Fi."

"I've found him, Lily, quite easy really. He's your man, no doubt about it. His name is Hugh Cairns, he's at St Hugh's Military Hospital, it's in Oxford. This is where all the ground-breaking research into brain injury is being done. Edward couldn't possibly go to a better place, Lily. I've spoken with them, they know who Edward is, and they'll be ready."

"Oh Fi, what a relief! I'll have him in an ambulance as soon as possible. Make sure Caroline knows what's happening, and would you make a point of telling Jennings. And tell Elizabeth I'll send a report with the medical notes via messenger before I leave here. I'm sending another to Baker Street. Between them they can contact the next of kin, they will be so worried."

"What else can I do, Lily?"

"Pray for Edward."

"I will. Keep in touch, Lily. I'll stay by the phone until late tonight in case you need me. I'll stay all night if necessary."

"I'll telephone you from St Hugh's, and thanks, Fi."

Handing Marion the details of St Hugh's Military Hospital, I asked her to get Edward ready to leave in the ambulance. My typed reports for Baker Street and the PM were brief, but concise. Combining the single sheet with the medical notes, I addressed the envelopes. When Evelyn saw the address, she looked up at me with wide eyes. Now she understood the importance of what she had been doing.

"Give these to your two messenger boys immediately, Evelyn, and thank you for all you have done."

"It's a pleasure, Mrs Heywood. Will you let us know how Mr Sinclair is?"

"Of course I will."

As I walked back towards the ward, I saw Marion and a nurse walking briskly alongside a trolly being pushed by a porter. The nurse was holding a drip feed steady, I walked along with them towards the waiting ambulance. I realised I had left my suitcase somewhere, and so I asked the same woman that I annoyed earlier if she knew where it was.

"Are you still here?" she said, "I told you to leave, there's your case, you really must go."

"Thank you, I will."

Chapter Seven
St Hugh's Military Hospital

As we left the hospital entrance, another ambulance came rushing in with casualties. They laid the victims out on stretchers. There were at least four of them, and all in a bad way. I had been in their position in 1941 and knew precisely what they were feeling. The horrible disorientation, the awful grey choking dust in their eyes and lungs. Their only connection with their former lives was the pain coursing through their bodies. A fire engine sped by with its bell ringing as people were running down the road. It was all horribly reminiscent of the Blitz. Marion asked the ambulance driver what had happened; his answer was chilling. More V1's were falling on London, one had exploded close by.

"I must go and take care of these people, Lily, there are more on the way."

"I can't thank you enough, Marion, I am so grateful."

"Edward is going to be fine, Lily, I share your confidence. Just make sure you let me know."

"I will, you can be sure of that."

Marion's attention turned towards the casualties, while mine turned towards getting Edward to Oxford. Our ambulance driver was a cheerful East Ender who said he'd been given his orders by Matron and assured me he would get Edward to

Oxford in next to no time. Marion was obviously a force to be reckoned with.

"Matron will have my guts for garters if I'm not quick about it," he joked. There were casualties lying on the ground on stretchers, with more on the way. His gentle humour might seem to have been out of place, but the reality was that the driver felt exactly the same anguish for the casualties as I did. Standing with his smiling face against the backdrop of Big Ben, just across the river, he personified the defiance of the British people, the spirit of the Blitz.

The nurse assigned to Edward seemed to be very young, but she too was equally defiant. She instructed the porters to lift Edward into the ambulance with great care. Self-possessed, her calm confidence was reassuring. The moment the driver closed the ambulance doors against the commotion outside, it was as if he had turned off my power supply. I slumped onto the bench next to Edward, and had it not been for embarrassing myself in front of the nurse, I would have burst into tears. Staying in control of the situation had completely drained me. With that need removed, the seriousness of Edward's condition filled me with fear; my heart raced, and I became cold and clammy.

"I want you to lie down, Mrs Heywood, before you fall down," the nurse said. "You look really pasty; I think you're about to faint."

The time for being strong had gone, I couldn't pretend otherwise. Lying there with the motion of the ambulance moving me from side to side, it all felt as if it was happening to someone else. The nurse was lovely, holding my hand and sharing her time between her 'two patients'. When I recovered a little, she offered me some water.

"You look a bit better now, how do you feel?"

"I'm so sorry, I don't know what came over me."

"Matron told me something about what you did back at the hospital, and she told me what this man means to you.

Don't apologise, Mrs Heywood, there's only so much a body can take."

"You're very kind, nurse, what's your name?"

"Joan."

"I'm Lily, and this is Edward."

"It's shocking to see someone in a coma, especially someone you love. I see this a lot, Lily, but nearly always the patient wakes up complaining about a sore head."

"He has to wake up, Joan, he just has to."

On one occasion Edward's head moved to one side, I looked up at Joan, but she assured me it was only the movement of the ambulance. She placed an extra pillow next to his head to prevent him moving. For much of the remaining journey, I clung tightly to Edward's hand, while Joan's attention never wavered. When the ambulance came to a halt, I thought we were stopping at a crossroad or perhaps a hold-up somewhere, it seemed too soon to be in Oxford.

When the driver opened the doors, and I realised where we were, I was expecting to see a recognisable hospital. Instead it was a beautiful building with a line of dormer windows and chimney pots. An army ambulance was leaving and some army personnel walking about. Three nurses and a doctor came rushing towards us, it was quickly apparent that they were used to receiving casualties. I remembered Fiona telling me it was a military hospital. Joan presented the doctor with the medical notes, and with no more ado, they wheeled Edward away. I rushed after them before I realised Joan was going back to the ambulance. Not intending to stop, I turned and shouted back to her.

"Thank you, Joan, thank you for everything."

"What about your suitcase?" she shouted back.

She waved with a cheery smile. I suppose for her it was all in a day's work. I rushed back to grab my case, thanking her and the driver again before following Edward into the building. This was quite different to St Thomas' - very much a military hospital. As I pushed my way past an orderly to be by Edward's side; I became aware we were standing in an enormous room. It was reminiscent of the Great Hall at Middlebourne, with long flowing curtains at the tall windows and beautiful crystal glass lights hanging from the high ceiling. It appeared to be a reception area for the assessment of incoming casualties. Many were in uniform, so my assumption was that they were probably all soldiers, casualties from Normandy.

A doctor quickly came over to me and read the notes. There was an air of military efficiency about the place, I didn't feel the need to do or say anything. The doctor looked around the hall and raised his hand, looking over to the far side. Another doctor walked towards us. He was middle-aged, thin grey hair combed back from his face, his white coat partially covering his high-ranking military uniform. The other doctor handed him the medical notes and stood back subserviently. I wanted to say something, but like the other doctor, I stood waiting.

"I know who this man is, who are you, madam?" he asked.

"I'm Lord Middlebourne's Chief of Staff, Mrs Heywood."

"Hugh Cairns, Mrs Heywood. I've been briefed from on high, you and Lord Middlebourne have some extremely high connections."

"Is it possible to make an assessment from what you have seen?"

"No, far too early, I'm afraid. We're ready for surgery and time is of the essence, so I suggest you go and have a cup of tea, Mrs Heywood, the orderly will show you where to go. I shall come and find you the moment his surgery is over."

I lifted Edward's hand and kissed it. The prospect of leaving him to go into surgery sent shivers down my spine. Cairns put his hand on my shoulder, he had a kind face and a lovely smile, and an immensely reassuring air of confidence. An orderly walked me away towards a delightfully furnished room, where I crumpled into an armchair. A pretty young nurse eventually followed on behind me and asked if I would like a cup of tea.

My eager acceptance must have sounded desperate because she asked when I had last eaten. When I said I couldn't remember, she kindly offered to get me something.

After ten or fifteen minutes, she came back with a cup of tea and a sandwich, I was so grateful. She was a particularly well-educated young woman, obviously from a fine family. Thankfully, she was both talkative and knowledgeable because I had a lot of questions. I learned that St Hugh's was in fact St Hugh's College, part of Oxford University. The government requisitioned it to be deployed as a military hospital specialising in head injury. Cairns, along with others, was instrumental in its creation. They had 430 beds; she said the grounds were full of brick-built huts, acting as wards. It was the centre of excellence for head injury in the United Kingdom, I was so relieved to be there.

Revived with tea and sustenance, I could only sit there listening to my heart beating. Every time that I glanced at my watch, the hands appeared to be stationary. I found myself continually praying for God's help. "Please bring him back to me," was my continual plea. Every part of my body ached with tension and the palms of my hands were sore where I was pressing my fingers into them. It had been almost three hours; the evening was transitioning into the night. My heart was beating like a drum when Cairns eventually appeared at the door. I jumped to my feet, but was totally unable to speak, or even draw breath. He must have seen the state I was in, because the first thing he said was that I should sit down.

"You can relax, Mrs Heywood. Dr Wisniewski's diagnosis of an intracerebral haematoma was overly pessimistic. Lord Middlebourne has suffered a straightforward epidural haematoma."

"Will he be all right?"

"Oh yes, he should be as right as rain!"

I can't explain what then happened to me. I didn't know what to do, my hands moved involuntarily towards my face, and I burst into floods of tears. When I tried to speak, I couldn't string two words together. Struggling back onto my feet, I poured myself into his arms, as much to support my trembling legs as it was to show gratitude.

"I was expecting you to be happy, Mrs Heywood!"

Something Florence once told me sprang into my mind. "I *am* happy," I replied, "this is me being the happiest I have ever been!"

"It's gratifying to be so appreciated, Mrs Heywood. I can see Lord Middlebourne means a lot to you."

"He means absolutely everything to me. I can never thank you enough for saving his life."

I asked when I could see him, and it was clear that for the moment I would be unnecessarily in the way. Edward would remain unconscious, probably throughout the night; the expectation was that he might regain consciousness the next day. We talked for some time; Dr Cairns was an immense comfort. When a nurse came into the room and spoke to him, it became obvious that Edward was only one of many such patients. Despite the ever-encroaching night, he had another surgery to perform. He left with a smile, seemingly a reservoir of energy. I can't imagine how many people's lives he must have saved. The Brigadier, later Sir Hugh Cairns, was instrumental in developing brain surgery and his legacy continues to this day.

It was now almost dark, and the kind young nurse asked me where I was staying. It was only then that I realised I had nowhere to go. She must have taken pity on me because she said there was a vacant room in the nurses' quarters, and provided no one else knew about it, she thought it would be fine. Not only that, but she also invited me to join her with the other nurses in their canteen.

"You won't get into trouble, will you?" I asked.

"I'm not a career nurse, Lily, I'm a volunteer, they need me."

She was probably right. Young women like Patricia from a private school background often had scant regard for regulation, but that did nothing to decrease her value as a nurse. She made me feel as if I was taking part in a schoolgirl prank, but secretly I was immensely grateful. She even led me to a telephone that I could use. I could hardly wait to tell Fi.

"They say he should be fine, Fi, … I haven't lost him." I broke down for a moment before regaining my composure.

"Oh thank goodness, I've been so worried, Lily, everyone has."

"I know, it's been one of the worst days I've ever been through, but thanks to you, we've been treated like royalty here."

"Oh good, I told Elizabeth we had to move heaven and earth, she said she would make sure it was done."

"It really was done, Fi, everyone has been brilliant, I'm even staying the night here. Would you ring the servant bell, Fi? I'd like to tell Jennings myself. And will you assure Lady Caroline that Edward will be fine. He is still unconscious, but that's normal, we're hoping he will regain consciousness tomorrow."

We talked some more until I could hear Jennings entering the office, and he came to the telephone.

"Is there news, Mrs Heywood?"

"There is, Mr Jennings, he's had an operation to relieve the pressure on his brain, and they assure me he's going to be fine."

There was a long pause. "That is the most wonderful news, Mrs Heywood. I have been concerned for both of you."

"We'll both be fine, Charles, I promise you."

"Welcome news, indeed, will that be all, Mrs Heywood?"

Fiona came back onto the phone. "What did you say to Jennings? He's just left with a tear in his eye!"

"We didn't need to say much, we've become surprisingly close."

"I've noticed, it seems like you've won him over."

"Or perhaps he's won me over."

"When you say the medics assure you Edward will be fine, what did they really say, Lily?"

"I can't hide anything from you, can I, Fi! They said they cannot be sure until he is conscious and talking, but they are genuinely hopeful."

"I prefer your version, Lily, will you let me know as soon as you find out?"

"Of course I will."

"Well, I've got good news for you. Dotty and Rob are back! It was not exactly the celebration we planned, but they're here."

"Oh, that's wonderful, tell her I can't wait to see her. Is she all right?"

"She says she's never felt better, but she isn't. They did horrible things to her fingers; the MO said she'll fully recover, but she must be in pain. They've both been to hell and back, Lily, but you know Dotty - she'll never admit it."

"Oh, I can't wait to see her, and how is Lady Caroline, she must be so worried?"

"She seems to be coping well, but you're right, she must be worried. She asked me to send a telegram to Edward's sister, Lady Elizabeth. I gathered that she might come back from America."

"I'm not sure Edward would want that. Oh, someone else wants to use this telephone, I must go. Thank you for everything you've done, I'll phone back when I know more. Bye, Fi."

"Bye, Lily."

What was left of the day went by very quickly. I played my role as the naughty schoolgirl, much to Patricia's obvious delight. She smuggled me into the canteen, which at that late hour was almost empty. The journey from the canteen into the nurses' quarters was much more Patricia's idea of fun. She cleared the path ahead of me, waving me on when the coast was clear. She blatantly enjoyed every second of her prank. Had I been in charge, I'm afraid I would have given her a lecture about growing up and accepting her responsibilities. In the circumstances, I was being equally irresponsible and scurried into my room feeling just as triumphant as she did.

"Keep your head down, Lily, put a nightdress on when you go to the bathroom, no one will notice. I'll fetch you in the morning."

Chapter Eight
The Concert

Patricia insisted I had breakfast with her, even introducing me to some other nurses. What it was not to have a care in the world! I felt so envious of her. There was only one thing on my mind, at least she had the sense to realise that. I left my suitcase in the room and once again, with no authorisation, she marched me off directly towards the recovery ward where Edward had been sent. My gratitude knew no bounds, I was about to thank her when I saw Edward lying in one of the beds. Only the top of his head was bandaged, I could at last see his face. For the first time, Patricia showed maturity beyond her years.

"Just go, Lily," she said, and walked away. I rushed to Edward's side.

"Edward, can you hear me? Squeeze my hand if you can hear me."

There was no response, but I'd been told to expect that. I kissed his hand, I stroked his face, I kissed his cheek, I didn't stop talking. Oblivious to the world around me, I didn't notice a nurse walk up behind me, not until she tapped me on the shoulder. My first thought was, 'here we go again, I shouldn't be here,' but she took me completely by surprise.

"Would you like a chair, Mrs Heywood?"

"Well, yes, if it's not too much trouble."

The ward was in one of the many outbuildings, not dissimilar to our huts at Middlebourne. A simple, uncluttered room with a row of beds on either side, with the nurses' station by the entrance. A patient occupied each bed, some with obvious multiple injuries. What they shared in common was a bandaged head. I felt very conspicuous being the only visitor, but the staff knew who I was, and didn't object. When the nurse came back with a chair, I asked if I was doing the right thing, continually talking to Edward.

"Oh yes, they can often hear, but are unable to respond. It's usually a significant voice or even a song which brings them back."

"Do you think he knows it's me?"

"Quite possibly, keep at it, Mrs Heywood. It's a wonderful moment when they come out of a coma, it's the most rewarding part of my job."

I didn't need encouragement, I talked all morning, only stopping briefly for a cup of tea. The man in the next bed was fully conscious, he must have been sick of my endless chatter, but couldn't have been kinder.

"I was like your Edward, luv, if I'd had you talking to me I reckon I would have come out of it much sooner."

"I'm sorry if I'm disturbing you."

"Not a bit of it, luv, I like the sound of your voice."

He made me think of that memorable night we shared in the 'Forge' when I sang 'Over The Rainbow'. That was such a wonderful memory. I started to quietly sing the song, holding Edward's hand all the while. I sang it in 'half voice' or mezza voce, as my voice coach used to say. It was how I often practiced, rather than disturbing people.

"Sing up, luv, I can't hear you," the man next door said.

"Oh no, I can't, it will disturb everyone."

"Sing up, luv, we need disturbing," shouted a man from the far end of the ward.

"Yes, come on, Mrs Heywood," said the nurse. "We all like a good song."

"Well, if you're sure," I replied.

I closed my eyes for a moment and imagined that night at the 'Forge', with the boys gathered around me, Cole encouraging me. I didn't need the piano or the harmonica to accompany me, I could still hear them playing in my mind. I sang the song as if Edward's life depended upon it. When I reached the crescendo, I had to look away for a moment, when my eyes returned to Edward, he was looking at me!

"Edward, can you hear me?"

"Lily," he replied.

The nurse ran over, there were cheers from the other patients. Unable to help myself, I put my arms out and almost fell onto him. I hugged and kissed him, oblivious to his groans.

"Careful, Mrs Heywood, don't forget he has broken ribs," the nurse said.

I pulled away in horror; poor Edward, what was I thinking! Gently cupping his face in my hands, I looked into his eyes.

"Welcome back, Edward, how do you feel?"

"Terrible! What do you mean, welcome back, where have I been?"

"You've been unconscious for a day and a half. I've never been so frightened in my entire life but thank God you've come back to me."

"Where am I, what's happened to me?"

"You're in hospital, and you're going to be just fine. I've been with you every step of the way."

"I know you have."

"You knew? You were unconscious."

"I just knew you were with me, Lily."

The nurse put her hand on my shoulder. "That's enough for the moment, Mrs Heywood. I need to assess Lord Middlebourne properly. You can stay if you like, provided you don't sit on his ribs again. And by the way, you're a beautiful singer, I've not heard that song sung like that before."

In her own way, she was reassuring me that assessing Edward was normal procedure. I let his fingers slip out of my hand and stepped aside for the nurse. As I walked over to the nurses' station, I could almost feel the tension draining out of my feet. The other nurse invited me to sit down, which I readily accepted.

"It's wonderful when they regain consciousness, isn't it?" she said.

"Oh, it's more than wonderful! It's like being reborn, it's as if we've been given another life together, I'm so happy."

"My husband came here as a casualty. His coma lasted for over a week, I felt sure I'd lost him. It changed my life when he came back to me, we never stop counting our blessings now. That's why I applied to work here."

"So you know how grateful I am, don't you?"

"That's why we do it, Mrs Heywood, we really make a difference. What do you and Lord Middlebourne do? Going by the priority they've given to him I'm guessing it must be something important."

"I wish I could tell you, let's just say we also make a difference."

"That's good enough for me. So tell me about your singing, you're a proper singer, aren't you?"

"I could have been, it's only a passion now, I just love singing."

"It shows, I thought you were quite amazing. Do you think you could sing some more for us? The patients would love it."

"If you're sure it would be allowed?"

"There's an upright piano in the reception hall, I could ask the orderlies to bring it over. Ruth, one of our nurses, is a great pianist."

"It seems like a lot of trouble."

"The men would love it, Mrs Heywood, but I'm thinking beyond that. There are patients who have been in a coma for days, some of them for weeks. You saw the effect your singing had on Lord Middlebourne."

"When you put it like that, it would be an honour to sing for them."

The week which followed was one of the most memorable of my life, as well as being one of the most rewarding. Edward made tremendous progress. We soon found that he'd lost none of his mental ability. He was initially weak and in pain, but he grew stronger every day. There were few opportunities for us to be alone together, but we had never been closer. Every day, when I spoke to Fiona, she would tell me the latest news about the war in Normandy, and about the V1's. Edward wanted to know every detail. When caught in the explosion, they were on their way to a meeting to discuss our response to the V1. He thought Station M could contribute towards the intelligence work. We quietly discussed what we were capable of doing.

I also talked to the other patients, listening to their accounts of the D-Day landings. Each and every one gave me a graphic account of what they encountered. Perhaps the most moving was a young American soldier who sustained his head injury on Omaha beach when he landed as part of the second wave. Both he and his comrades had seen the amphibious tanks sink during the initial assault of the beach. As they approached the beach in their landing craft, they thought they knew the nature of the hell they were entering, but nothing could have prepared this young man for what he was about to encounter.

"The sea was so rough, every one of us felt sick, we were either seasick or sick with fear. I didn't know what to expect when the ramp was released, that was our first view of Omaha beach. It was like nothing you could possibly imagine; it was an image of hell. We stepped off the ramp waist deep in the sea, the waves bounced us around like corks. I was terrified, it was several seconds before I registered what I was seeing. The sea was red with blood, and the nearer we got to the beach, the redder it became. There were bodies everywhere, men floating face down. All along the beach, bodies were washed up like so much flotsam, those who were not dead were crying in pain for help.

The air was full of a noise that sounded like we were inside a beehive. It was the sound of machine gun bullets flying all around us. Those that hit the landing craft made the most noise, they seemed to echo right through your head. Those that hit the water did so with a zing. Most frightening were those bullets that hit your comrades, it was just a dull thump, as a life was snuffed out. I fully expected to join the others floating in the sea, and when I reached the beach, I expected to join those bleeding into the sand.

There was no cover on the beach, no fox holes we could dive into, it was just an open killing ground. As I came closer to the bluffs, you could hear the relentless drone of the machine guns above us. When we were stuck at the top of the beach, I looked back to see guys following the same route I had taken. I saw one after another crumple and fall. A friend of mine was close behind me, he only had to cover another couple of yards to reach some cover. As I willed him on, his head seemed to explode right in front of me. My last memory was the noise of men shouting, machine gun fire, bullets flying, artillery shells exploding. One of those machine gun bullets had my name on it, I expected it. I almost welcomed it, as it gave me the silence I was praying for."

I held his hand all the while, but he appeared unmoved by his account. He looked at me but seemed to be focused on some distant object. He was no more than a boy who was lucky to be alive, but I sensed it was going to be a long time before he got his life back. That was probably the case for a large number of those brave boys. Cairns and his team could put them back together again and grant them a new life, but he was unable to exclude their previous life. His harrowing account had a profound effect which has always stayed with me.

Either they turned a blind eye to my staying in the nurses'

quarters, or perhaps there was some behind-the-scenes tacit agreement. The result was that I stayed the week, and young Patricia claimed full credit for the success of her 'wizard prank'. It was Beverley, the nurse who persuaded me to sing, who really transformed my life that week. It started in Edward's ward, when I sang for the patients, accompanied on the piano by Ruth, who was an accomplished pianist. Very quickly, I realised my singing was raising the patients' spirits. Their gratitude seemed to be boundless, I was really making a difference. I'm not sure that any of them realised, but their appreciation and gratitude was as nothing compared to the immense reward they gave me. To see a patient smile for perhaps the first time during his stay in the hospital, was an incredibly humbling experience.

There was one extraordinary moment when a young man who had been in a coma for over a week recovered consciousness. Several of the doctors took an interest, even Cairns became involved. It might have been a coincidence, or possibly that my singing somehow roused that young man from his condition. They simply didn't know. There was much discussion about what kind of music might be best; someone suggested that perhaps the structure of some operatic arias might be particularly stimulating to the semi-conscious brain. When they realised I could sing those arias, they were enthusiastic for me to sing to a wider audience.

After Edward's ward, we progressed from one outbuilding to the next. The orderlies moved the piano with Ruth and me following, looking like a travelling circus. By the end of our stay, I had sung to every ward in the hospital. It was such a pleasure to be a part of it, to be instrumental in raising morale. Above all, knowing what those soldiers had sacrificed in Normandy, it was also a great honour. We'll never know if my singing helped even one single soldier's recovery, but we think it might have done. That possibility filled me with pride.

When Edward was in a fit state to go home, they asked me

to perform for them one last time. I immediately accepted, not realising what they had in mind. I was totally confident singing for them in the wards, being accompanied on the piano. When I realised what they had in mind for the last night of our stay, it filled me with dread. They asked me to perform a proper concert, accompanied by the piano and a string quartet. They rearranged the beds and trolleys in the reception hall, turning it into a concert hall. I had never sung in such a vast space before, and never to such a large audience.

"I can't do it, Edward, I'm going to make a fool of myself. They seem to think I'm a real opera singer."

"You must be the only confused person here, Lily. They already know you're a wonderful singer, why do you think they asked you to perform for them?"

"You don't understand, Edward, it takes years of training to project your voice sufficiently to fill a space that size."

"You don't need to, Lily. You have a heaven-sent voice which seduces anyone who listens to you. Every single person in that hall tonight will think you are singing personally for them."

"But I won't be, will I? I'll only be singing for you."

"In that case, you are already a triumph."

Edward could express the most heartfelt sentiment! I wondered what his reaction might have been if he had realised how much I wanted him at that moment. Then again, perhaps he felt the same? One way or another, I was committed to the concert, but I remained terrified. I didn't own up to it, but there were a limited number of arias I was really confident to sing. So when the time came, I said I would arrange the evening into two halves. I would sing popular songs for the first half, and then I would perform some arias to finish.

They created an elevated platform for us to perform on, which only made me feel more nervous. The string quartet was composed entirely of staff members, and they were superb. Ruth would accompany me on the piano. This really felt like something I'd never done before; this was a real concert. We attempted to rehearse in the afternoon, but it was impossible with the hall in full-time use. At least we knew what we were going to do, so they had their music ready.

One kind woman even lent me an evening dress. It was actually a fabulous gown which was a good fit, doing much to bolster my confidence. When the time came, I can't even remember walking onto 'the stage', I was so nervous. I suspect my first couple of songs might have been a bit shaky, but the audience was enthusiastic. My confidence grew slightly with each number, as I drew energy from the rapturous applause.

The only song we did rehearse beforehand was Cole's arrangement of Over The Rainbow. That obviously surprised the audience, their reaction was overwhelming, really boosting my confidence. When we came to the break, I looked towards the musicians for signs of approval and was met by five beaming faces. It seemed that we were doing well, they appeared delighted, but none more so than me!

An enthusiastic doctor offered us a glass of champagne each. That was something I didn't expect, but gratefully accepted. Edward sat in his wheelchair with a beaming smile, then he gestured with his hands and mouthed a word. I looked at him quizzically from the stage, and he mouthed the word again, 'sublime'. He would have been in no doubt about my reaction. Composure restored, we took our places once again, and I sang the first aria, 'O mio babbino caro'. I thought it went extremely well and continued to grow in confidence.

By the time I was to perform the last aria, I realised what I'd done. I had achieved a lifetime ambition. I had sung my favourite arias, in front of a wildly appreciative audience, in what amounted to a concert hall. Add to that the extremely talented musicians supporting me, and I knew I was living a dream come true. It was only then, close to the end of my performance, that my nerves allowed me to fully appreciate what I had done. I plucked up the courage to say a few words.

"Ladies and gentlemen, you have all been very generous with your appreciation, thank you. When I arrived here a week ago, I was a broken and terrified woman. I will leave you tomorrow filled with joy and hope for the future. You offer the gift of life to all the brave servicemen who enter here, and now through Lord Middlebourne you have extended that gift to me. How can Lord Middlebourne and I thank you? There are no words to express the gratitude we feel. All I can offer in return is to sing for you. If I've managed to lift a single spirit this week, then I feel privileged to have been able to make a small contribution."

I went on, "The last aria I would like to sing for you has special meaning for me. My grandmother had a truly remarkable voice, she was known as the voice of Middlebourne. I grew up to the sound of that voice and could sing almost before I could walk. She managed to persuade me to have endless tuition and voice coaching, and I did it all because I thought I was doing it for her. She knew otherwise, of course, and one day in my late teens, she introduced me to her favourite aria. She said, 'I shall know when you have grown into a woman, Lily, because that will be the day when you'll be able to sing this aria properly.' My grandmother gifted her voice to me, and now whenever I sing this aria, it is my gift to her. Ladies and Gentlemen, 'Un bel di vedremo' from 'Madame Butterfly'."

I would have given anything for Gran to have been there that evening, but of course in so many ways she was. From the moment the music began I was transported to another place. I was Cio-Cio-San, and when I looked toward my trusted maid Suzuki, it was Gran's face I saw. The occasion really inspired me; I don't think I have ever sung better. When the last note faded, the musicians immediately stood up and bowed towards me, completely overwhelming me. The audience wouldn't stop clapping, it went on and on. It was everything I dreamed a concert performance would be. Standing there before those people was one of the most memorable and moving moments

I have ever experienced. We took several bows, but still the clapping and cheering continued. It only stopped when I agreed to sing once more. I spoke with the musicians and was relieved to find they had the music for 'O Silver Moon' from Rusalka, by Dvorak.

When the concert really was finally over, I knew it had been an unrepeatable experience, a memory which would stay with me forever. I left the stage and went directly to Edward. He had instructions to stay seated in his wheelchair, and yet there he was standing up clapping like everyone else. I wanted to tell him off, but I couldn't. He was as caught up in the moment as I was. My head was so high in the clouds, I'm not sure if my feet were touching the ground. Edward effused, in language that only he would use.

"I take it then, Edward, that you approved."

"*Approve!* My darling Lily, the angels must be weeping. I have never heard anything like that before, look at all these people, you have touched their souls."

"Only you could say something as wonderful as that, Edward. I don't think I've ever sung better; that was something I'll never forget, and never be able to emulate. It would be nice to think I stopped singing at my best."

"I hope you don't mean that."

"I do mean it, Edward, I can never repeat this evening. My legs are really shaking, would it be terribly embarrassing in front of all these people if you held me for a moment?"

"What people?"

Chapter Nine
Edward's Confusion

William arrived in the car bright and early. I asked him to be there by twelve o'clock but I think he must have arrived at least an hour early. A small case of Edward's clothes had been prepared just as I requested; William handed it to me, obviously enjoying the moment. When Edward asked how we were getting home, I simply said I had it organised, but he became suspicious when I handed him the case.

"Did you think I'd allow you to leave here dressed in hospital pyjamas?"

"Well, certainly not, that would have been intolerable. I thought perhaps I might borrow something."

"There's only one way you're leaving here, Edward! Get yourself dressed properly, in a manner befitting the Earl of Middlebourne. Do you need help?"

"I can manage, Lily, thank you."

Saying goodbye to those wonderful people of St Hugh's Military Hospital was very emotional. We both especially wanted to thank Hugh Cairns, but predictably he was in surgery. The musicians, together with some of the doctors and nurses, came to the door with us, where several of the walking patients gathered. Edward is always such a striking figure dressed in his customary impeccably tailored suit, and I think his exit made quite an impression. Mindful of his ribs, he hugged the nurses very carefully and shook the hands of the doctors. I felt very emotional saying goodbye as they gave us a truly memorable send-off. William opened the door of the car.

"Good to see you looking so well, My Lord."

"It's good to be feeling well, Evans."

He stepped into the back of the Rolls-Royce, looking at me with a wry smile. We both waved continually until St Hugh's disappeared from view, but it would never disappear from our hearts. It was a long drive from Oxford to Middlebourne. Initially, our conversation was entirely about the hospital and Edward's wonderful treatment. Gradually, as we distanced ourselves from Oxford, Middlebourne progressively filled our minds. Initially, he was concerned about his mother, and even more concerned at the prospect that his sister might be coming home. By the time we reached Basingstoke, our thoughts inevitably turned toward Station M and the war. I knew the V1 threat was uppermost in Edward's mind, but he'd been reluctant to discuss it in the hospital. Even in the car with William sitting in the driver's seat, we had to speak in hushed voices.

"It was decided that Station M should remain operational, and we keep our agents. All the intelligence services need to pull together on this, Lily. We will only be a small part of the overall intelligence operation, but we have special skills to offer. Apart from that, it's become personal!"

"Well, I suppose getting yourself blown up by one is rather personal!"

"Let's just say it focuses one's attention. I want us to start on this first thing tomorrow, Lily. This is potentially a very serious threat. I just hope they've found my briefcase, it's full of classified documents about the V1."

"Are you sure you're up to it, Edward?"

"I have to be, and with your help, I shall be."

"Still more responsibility!" I joked.

"I'm afraid so. If this unfortunate episode has taught me anything, it is that my reliance upon you is actually a dependence which I have come to embrace."

"Is that a complicated way of saying you can't do without me?"

"Precisely."

I sat smiling at him. Anyone else with a bandage around their head would probably invoke immediate sympathy. In Edward's case, dressed in his immaculate suit and tie, he looked slightly ridiculous, though he wouldn't even have understood the concept of looking ridiculous. When we arrived at Middlebourne, he behaved as if everything was perfectly normal. The staff obviously anticipated our arrival. Within moments, they lined everyone up outside the Grand Entrance to welcome him home. Jennings stood at the front with a beaming smile and his head held high. Fiona came down the steps and stood at the back with the girls. Edward, being Edward, approached them with an air of 'what's all the fuss about'. I think he was secretly deeply touched by the warmth of his welcome, the staff genuinely cared about him, not least Jennings.

"Welcome back, My Lord, may I say you had us all quite worried there for a moment."

"Thank you, Jennings," Edward replied, "very kind of everyone to be concerned."

"Welcome back, My Lord."

"Thank you, Mrs Morgan. I have some wonderful doctors and nurses to thank for my recovery, and of course Mrs Heywood."

I followed behind him, and Jennings turned towards me. It wasn't a conscious decision but I just gave him a brief hug. There are no circumstances in which you should hug the butler, but it was too late, I hugged him. He attempted to look stern, trying to convey his displeasure to the rest of the staff. It didn't work, not even for a moment, I just smiled. I was so pleased to see Fiona, we walked into the Manor arm in arm.

"You need to thank Fiona, Edward. She's the one who found you in the first place, and then she organised everything."

"You have both been quite amazing during this little episode, and thank you, Fiona. I can't exist without either of you, can I?"

Just then, Lady Caroline approached us from across the hall; Edward embraced his mother in a tearful reunion. I walked on to our office with Fiona, where we finally sat alone together.

"I can't thank you enough, Fi, you were amazing."

"At least there was something I could do. I would have felt helpless otherwise. But really, Lily, was it as close a call as it sounded?"

"It was. It was a very serious incident, it killed one of the occupants in the car and goodness knows how many others. We can't even be sure he would have survived without being moved from St Thomas' for the operation at St Hugh's."

"Thank heavens you were there, Lily."

"It's been quite a week I can tell you."

Edward put his head around the door. "Would you ladies like to come and join me in the Drawing Room? It's not too early for a celebratory drink."

"You two go ahead, I'm meeting Johnny later," Fiona replied.

Fi had plenty of time for a drink with us, but she never missed an opportunity for me to be alone with Edward. I was also desperate to see Dotty, but following the events we had experienced, Edward and I did need to conclude the week together. I asked Fi to reconsider, but she insisted it should be a private moment between Edward and me, so I made my way to my bedroom. Florence followed me upstairs, unable to contain her delight.

"I knew everything would be fine if you were with His Lordship."

"It was touch and go for a while, we could have lost him, Florence."

"Well, thank God you were there. I couldn't bear the thought of you and His Lordship not being together."

"I've used everything you packed in my case, you thought of everything, thank you. All I need this evening is something casual."

It wasn't the right moment for me to comment, but I was sure I could see a bump. She was doing her best to cover it up, but some things in life are inevitable. If Florence felt anguish about the forthcoming baby, then she disguised it well. She unpacked my case, prepared my things, and quickly got me ready for the evening. In our own ways, we were both happy in our strange relationship. She acted as my lady's maid, but that never defined our relationship. I was never sure if we enjoyed a kind of substitute mother-daughter relationship, or perhaps we were just friends. When she wished me a lovely evening, her hopes were entirely genuine. We walked down the stairs talking together. Jennings greeted me as I entered the hall and escorted me into the Drawing Room.

"What can I fetch you to drink, Mrs Heywood?"

"What do you suggest, Mr Jennings?"

"May I suggest a glass of your favourite Bowmore single malt?"

"Perfect, Mr Jennings. You were absolutely right about the Islay whiskies. I've really grown to like the twelve-year-old."

"I was thinking of opening the twenty-five-year-old, Mrs Heywood. It has been sitting in the cellar for years, waiting for the right occasion."

"You're spoiling me, Mr Jennings."

"I am, indeed, Mrs Heywood."

He was grinning as he left, and I went into the Drawing Room. Edward immediately stood up to greet me, as if we hadn't seen each other for days. As we sat together, my feeling was that we had reached the end of a long journey. I slipped my shoes off as I liked to do and stretched my toes out into the pile of the carpet. Edward always smiled whenever I did that.

"Do you know, Lily, we haven't had a single moment to ourselves this last week. I've not had the opportunity to talk to you alone."

"You make it sound as if you have something important to say, Edward."

"Well, there is just the trifling consideration that you probably saved my life, and not content with that, you then filled that life with joy."

"You really don't have to thank me, you know. Do you remember that Christmas when we talked about you being my knight in shining armour? I'll never forget it. You said, 'that is something you can implicitly rely upon.' Only you would express yourself like that, Edward. Well, I can tell you, if your life ever needs saving again, or if there is joy that I can offer, then that's something you, too, can implicitly rely upon. You don't have to thank me."

It was a rare day when Edward was silenced by someone else's conversation. I revelled in my moment of triumph. It prolonged his silence as Jennings came into the Drawing Room carrying a silver tray with two glasses of the vintage Bowmore on it.

"I have taken the liberty, My Lord, of pouring you a glass of this rather special single malt. It is Mrs Heywood's favourite whisky."

Edward needed a moment to respond. "Oh, yes, I'm sure it will be fine. Thank you, Jennings."

Jennings left, leaving Edward still struggling for words.

"I do implicitly rely upon you, Lily, it's true, and I hope you feel you can rely upon me. Unfortunately, beyond my dependence, I also have to admit to being terribly confused. My life has been preordained, there is a clearly defined path laid before me. Everything in my orderly life was reassuringly correct and in its proper place until '39. There was even a time when I might have envisaged a future beyond the war. It would naturally be a future where once again everything fell back into its preordained place, and I would resume my expected course.

I was disabused of that comfortable notion some three years ago when a certain woman, dressed as a farm worker, walked into my office, turning my preconceived notions upside down. My confession, Lily, is that you are the source of my confusion. You see, at no time has my clearly defined path contained an adorable and wondrously gifted woman from the East End of London! You have removed all the waymarks; I have no idea where I am going any more. I'm not even sure in which direction the future lies, my only certainty is that my future is now shrouded in uncertainty."

Only Edward could say so much, when just three words would do. I so much wanted to tell him what those strange feelings were which so perplexed him, but of course that was Edward's torment, he already knew. I also understood all the commitments and protocol which dictated his life. As much as I wanted to say those words, I also knew he had to conform with all that was expected of him. The only option I had was to take part in the strange ritualistic dance which he felt obliged to perform. As long as Edward's life remained uncertain, so would mine. That evening was the first occasion when our simmering relationship finally boiled over the saucepan to hiss and crackle upon the stove.

Despite my uncertainty I was deliriously happy when Caroline came into the room. She looked magnificent as always, making me feel shabbily underdressed. I apologised for not making more effort and slipped my shoes back on. Caroline would hear none of it, she was just happy that we were both there. We had a lovely relaxing family evening together. All the while, Edward was unusually quiet, despite the almost constant smile he directed towards me. Halfway through dinner, Caroline announced that Lady Elizabeth was on her way across the Atlantic.

"Oh dear, this could be a disaster, Mother."

I felt for Caroline, this was her daughter Edward was berating. However disagreeable Edward found his sister, Caroline could only view the situation from a mother's perspective.

"What a coincidence that my beloved sister rushes back across the ocean just when she suspects I might be about to depart this mortal coil."

"She is concerned for you, Edward, as we all were."

"Elizabeth is only ever concerned about herself."

I stayed out of it, not offering a word. Inwardly I was very apprehensive about meeting Elizabeth. Edward hadn't painted a very attractive picture of her. I became much more involved when Caroline mentioned that Lady Beatrice was also coming to visit.

"Beatrice is coming to see you tomorrow, Edward, she has been dreadfully worried. I wasn't sure if you would be strong enough, but I simply couldn't delay her a day longer."

My hackles bristled as my heart simultaneously sank. I watched closely to see Edward's reaction. Had his face lit up at the news it would have devastated me, but instead he remained reassuringly indifferent. Caroline's comment, however, was much more illuminating.

"I didn't encourage her, Lily."

"Oh well, it's got nothing to do with me, Caroline."

She chose not to reply, instead placing her hand on my arm and offering me a kind expression. There was an undeniable closeness between Caroline and me. It was initially difficult for Edward to embrace someone like me, I was so far removed from his social world. For Caroline, coming from the previous generation, the social divide between us must have felt like an unassailable chasm. The fact that she saw something in me is a constant source of wonder and humility for me. It wasn't as if I could meet her halfway - I tried, but she took that giant stride towards me. Caroline's comment about not encouraging Lady Beatrice kept returning to my mind. Perhaps it was what I wanted to believe, but I was sure she was broadly hinting that she would prefer to have me as her daughter-in-law.

It was easy to forget that Edward had been sitting in a wheelchair earlier that day. His determination to soldier on was admirable, but as the evening wore on, we could see the tiredness flooding over him with all the certainty of an incoming spring tide. He was exhausted, his battle to keep his eyes open had been lost half an hour earlier. Caroline was concerned, but I assured her it was nothing more than tiredness. What followed was a conversation that I will never forget. It was quite unintentional, neither of us considered what we were saying. Caroline's reaction was simply wonderful.

"Poor Edward, he's completely exhausted, you must assist him, Lily. Would you like to take him up to his bed?"

"I'd be delighted to take Edward to his bed, Caroline."

There was a long silence between us. I raised my hand to my mouth in order to disguise the fact that I was desperately trying to hold my breath. She did much the same, I could see her cheeks were filling, and her eyes widening. When neither of us could hold our breath any longer, we both spontaneously burst into raucous laughter. The more we tried to control ourselves, the more we laughed.

"Oh Lily, what a thing to say, what was I thinking?" she was almost choking with laughter.

"And I wasn't thinking at all, Caroline."

"I wonder what Mr Freud would say?" she said, bursting into laughter again.

Disturbed from his slumber, Edward raised his head. "What on earth has caused all this hilarity?"

"Nothing for you to concern yourself with, Edward," I said. "I'll ask William to help you to your room."

Chapter Ten
Dotty's Back

The office door opened slightly. First, I could only see a hand holding the edge of the door. Some of the fingers were neatly wrapped in bandages. A smiling face followed the fingers, peering into the room.

"I told you I'd drag myself back by my fingernails, didn't I!"

"Dotty!"

I jumped to my feet and rushed towards her. Fiona, who was following a step behind her, was almost knocked over in my enthusiasm to greet Dotty. We hugged each other for ages. If I could have said something to her sooner I would have, but I just couldn't. I was so overwhelmed to see her again. Apart from her fingers she appeared to be fine, her beautiful eyes as radiant as ever, the tears only making them shine brighter.

"So, what's all the fuss for then, Lily? I thought you'd be pleased to see me."

"Pleased! I've never been happier to see someone return from the dead in my entire life. We thought we'd lost you, Fi and I have been to hell and back in a handcart. We must never lose each other again, we must make a pact, the three of us, we can't go through that again."

"Well, it's kind of nice to be back, I must say."

"I guess all of us have been to hell and back," Fiona said.

"I've heard all about Edward from Fi," Dotty said. "It sounds like a close one. Imagine that, one of those V1 things hitting His Lordship."

"It was a close call, Dot. I very nearly lost him."

"Well, that wouldn't do, would it? Fi tells me you dumped Greg."

"Oh, don't put it like that, Dotty. I had to. We just couldn't go on as we were."

"So it's official then, you *are* gooey eyed over Edward?"

"God, I've missed you, Dotty! Yes, it's official, I *am* gooey eyed over Edward. Now, enough about me, what have they done to you?"

"They messed up my nail polish! Can you imagine, of all people, they had to mess up *my* nail polish."

"Seriously, Dotty, what have they done to you?"

"Oh, it's nothing that won't grow back. They stick things down your fingernails, that's all."

"That's horrible, are you sure you will be all right?"

"Of course. I tell you what though, they made a terrible mistake," she said, holding up the unbandaged first finger of her right hand. "They left my trigger finger alone, that cost them dearly!"

"How did you get away?"

"It's all in the debrief report. Rob saved me; I knew he would. I just sat there waiting for him to come for me."

"How did you know he would come?"

"What did you do, Lily, when you were told about Edward? Nothing was going to stop you going to him, was it? Well, it's the same for me and Rob."

"We didn't know about you and Rob. Are you saying that you and Rob are, well, you know?"

"Don't sound so amazed, I am a bit of a catch. You can't blame Rob for being gooey eyed about me!"

"You're the same, aren't you?"

"Well yes, he's not so bad, is he?"

"Not so bad! He's lovely, why didn't you tell us?"

"Well, it was Operation Top Hat really, we didn't want to say anything. You know, one of us... Well, it was always possible that one of us might have … "

"You mean, one of you might have been killed," Fiona said.

"Well, that's right, best not to dwell on such things."

"We heard about a running street battle in Caen; they thought you were the invasion force."

"We did put on a good show! The thing was the French boys were hopping mad about what the Nazis were doing in Caen. Rob was hopping mad about what they did to me, and I was hopping mad about what they did to my nail polish. We were an angry bunch, and we gave 'em what for."

"You didn't think you would get out, did you?"

"The odds were stacked against us, but it's amazing what you can do when you've got nothing to lose and you're really mad. I'm telling you - we were *really* mad."

"You're amazing, you are, Dotty! I can't even imagine how someone can be as brave as you."

"Didn't think about it, really, we just did what we had to do."

"What about Operation Top Hat, did that go according to plan? Apart from getting caught, I mean?"

"Textbook operation, Mac says it will go down in the manual. I was sure Rob would do his job, and once I'd climbed in through the window without being seen, I knew I had him. We were a bit unsure about which room he'd be in, but I was dead lucky. I went to the room that faced the best view, and there he was, sound asleep."

"So you just shot him?" asked Fiona.

"Of course, what was I supposed to do, introduce myself?"

"Did you not feel anything? You took someone's life."

"That bastard was having innocent village people shot almost every day. If anyone had it coming he did, and the only thing I felt was 'mission accomplished'."

Edward came into the office, obviously late starting his day - I hadn't seen him at breakfast. The extra sleep had been good for him, there was more colour in his cheeks.

"Dorothy!" he said in surprise. "How lovely to see you back with us."

"It's lovely to be back, My Lord, and may I say how good it is to see you in one piece."

Edward then surprised us by putting his arms around Dotty. They were a well-matched pair, with her bandaged fingers and his bandaged head. Fiona and I stood with the biggest of smiles, knowing that only months previously, Edward wouldn't have dreamed of hugging Dotty like that. They stood together comparing notes about their injuries, like the couple of wounded soldiers that they both were. We all sat down talking and Dotty had to re-live her exploits once again. She dismissed it all in her usual flippant way, but that wasn't going to work with Edward. He asked to see the written report.

"Bravery above and beyond the call of duty only applies to His Majesty's armed forces. The valour which you and Rob displayed goes way beyond any call of duty. I intend to use this report as the basis for a recommendation to the Prime Minister. It will be my honour to advise him that I think you should both be awarded the highest civilian award there is, the George Cross. The recipients of this award wouldn't even fill a tea shop, and the female recipients would fit into a telephone box. You should rightly both take your place in that exalted company, and it will be a privilege for me to put both your names forward."

She always seemed incapable of taking herself seriously, but I had long since come to realise that her brash happy-go-lucky persona was Dotty's way of protecting herself. She didn't feel that her inner person was worthy of any achievement, much less praise. When Edward said those words, he inadvertently addressed the real Dotty, inviting that fragile little girl to step out into the light. It seemed to hit Dotty like a bolt of lightning and she just sat there. Her lovely big eyes could not have grown larger. Her only reaction was tears until she finally drew a long deep breath and spoke.

"Are you serious? You'd recommend me for such an honour?"

"Without hesitation. Do you not realise, Dorothy, you stand amongst the bravest of the brave, it would be the nation's way of paying homage to you!"

That was it for Dotty. She buried her face in my handkerchief and sobbed her heart out. Edward had achieved what the might of the German Army had failed to do. I suggested he leave Dotty with us. Poor Edward, he was unsure if he had caused offence in some way but I assured him he had done nothing of the kind, it was merely a situation best left to us ladies. He left us looking a little bewildered, while Dotty tried to regain her composure.

"I don't know what came over me," she said. "I've never heard such nonsense, recommending me for a medal. I'm not worthy of a gong, or anything else, I just did my job."

"Edward made you realise something about yourself, didn't he, Dotty?" Fiona said.

"Well, I mean, treating me like some kind of heroine. That's not me, is it?"

"That *is* you," I said. "You just caught sight of the person we know and love. You should get to know each other, Dot. That woman is the bravest person I've ever known."

She sat looking at us with those big brown eyes of hers. They say the eyes are the window to the soul, and with Dotty's lovely eyes she could hide nothing. She was a fragile person, but her extrovert alter ego was just as real. Fiona and I had seen glimpses of the fragile Dotty before, but perhaps that was the moment when she confronted that frightened little girl. Her experience in Normandy was enough to change anyone, but I believe it was Edward who inadvertently took that frightened little girl by the hand because Dotty changed after that.

She was still the Dotty of old, still the same larger-than-life audacious character, losing none of her sparkle, but she gained something else. Of all the people in the land, Dotty had nothing to prove to anyone, and finally she had realised that.

"Why don't we walk over to the canteen and have one of Brenda's bacon sandwiches," suggested Fiona.

"Bloody good idea," Dotty replied.

In truth, the rest of the day was lost. We were in such high spirits that it was difficult to come back down to earth. As the evening approached, the prospect that we would go our separate ways seemed implausible. Dotty suggested we all go to the pub, more as a statement of the inevitable rather than a question. Edward appeared at that moment and I asked if he would join us. His reply was game changing.

"I would enjoy that enormously, but unfortunately circumstances contrive to prevent me from doing so."

"Oh, I'm sorry Edward, what's happening?"

"The Strattons are coming."

"Do you mean all of them?"

"I do, apparently they asked and Mother felt compelled to agree."

"I'm sorry, girls, that means me as well."

"Not at all, Lily, this is a family commitment, you have no obligation to be there."

"I agree, but unless you would rather I didn't, I would like to."

I could tell that Edward was probably pleased at my insistence. He left saying that he'd see me later. Dotty immediately asked what was so important about the Strattons. I answered in two words, Lady Beatrice! They both understood immediately. I explained there was no way I was standing aside for Beatrice. If she wanted Edward, she had to go past me first. Dotty suggested she could help me with that and we joked about what she could do to her. Joking aside, they both understood and so I left immediately. I needed at least two hours to get ready.

Florence also understood my position, and between us there was nothing more I could have done to prepare myself. It was to be a formal evening so I wore my green evening gown, and all of my jewellery. I knew Beatrice would look fabulous. Unfortunately she would look fabulous whatever she wore. I used every second of my two hours, the time just seemed to flash by. I was as prepared as I could possibly be, but I entered the Drawing Room full of trepidation, knowing I was out of my depth and that everyone knew it. My heart sank the moment I saw her, wearing a wonderful dress and looking nothing less than radiant. It just seemed so unfair, she had it all. I doubted the man existed who wouldn't be swayed by her style and beauty. Having greeted Lord and Lady Stratton, I turned towards Beatrice.

"Hello, Beatrice, how lovely to see you again."

"Yes, it's been a little while. Edward tells me you were with him throughout his time in hospital."

"Yes, that's right."

"He tells me you might even have saved his life."

"I don't know about that, but it was a worrying time."

"I wanted to visit him myself but I was told he was unable to receive visitors."

"That's right, it was a military hospital."

"So why were you there then, Lily?"

"I was there in my capacity as His Lordship's Chief of Staff."

"I'm not sure that was the case, Lily. I should have been there."

"There were some very senior officials involved when the incident happened. I had to take care of several sensitive issues."

"And I suppose you were the only person who could do that?"

"That's right, I was the only person who was not lying in a hospital bed. I'm sorry if my presence offends you, Beatrice, but in matters concerning our work, I outrank you."

"Thank you for reminding me. I am not used to women outranking me."

"Maybe not, but it's a fact you will have to accept."

Caroline stepped in and changed the subject, and not before time. There were no raised voices, but I think everyone realised where our conversation was going. I was sorry about it afterwards but she just made me so annoyed. We were poles apart in every way except for Edward. Her manner was so superior, and by her definition I was so inferior. In truth, I felt inferior and that was why I behaved like I did. We clashed again once or twice more, albeit very politely. When the evening came to an end, she put her arms around Edward and kissed him before they all retired for the night. I waited to be alone with Edward and Caroline, so I remained in the Drawing Room.

"I apologise, Caroline, I behaved terribly. Can you forgive me, Edward?"

"I must say that was a very uncomfortable evening."

"I know, I've let myself down as well as you, I feel awful about it."

"I am surprised you allow Beatrice to goad you like that. I thought you would have risen above petty squabbles."

"If I have embarrassed you, Edward, I'm truly sorry."

That was the first time I had seen Edward cross with me. My self-confidence was fragile at the best of times - he made me feel wretched. Caroline could see the effect it had on me. She took me to one side and suggested Edward might retire and leave us to talk for a moment. He seemed perfectly happy about that and excused himself in the most dignified way. This left me alone with Caroline and I felt as if I had been sent before the headmistress.

"I know why you react to Beatrice, Lily, and why she reacts to you. I can assure you there is no need for it. You are two quite different women, you both excel in your own way, but it was unwise to antagonise her in circumstances where she excels. You place yourself at a disadvantage when there is no need for you to do so."

"I know, you're right, Caroline. Beatrice is everything that I'm not. She's young and beautiful and comes from one of the most respected aristocratic families in the county. You can't imagine how inferior she makes me feel. She's my constant reminder that I am as far removed from being a 'lady' as it is possible to be."

"There is far more to being a titled lady than just being competent in your social graces. Beatrice is a fine young woman, but in my opinion you are twice the lady she is, and I can tell you that Edward feels the same."

There was no-one whose opinion I valued more than hers. For all that we were poles apart, we shared an unlikely, yet close connection. She had restored my diminished self-esteem and we walked up the stairs together, going to our respective bedrooms. When we reached the landing, she gave me a lovely hug, and we agreed I should put the whole episode behind me.

Chapter Eleven
The V1 Threat

Edward's briefcase duly arrived at Middlebourne by special messenger. He greeted it like one might greet a lost child, lovingly concerned for its wellbeing. I stood with him in his office while he sifted through the documents. The look of relief on his face was palpable.

"It's all here, Lily, thank God. We shall never know if the police have been through it, but at least I now have it. Let's have a meeting in Hut 3 right now, we need to plan where we go from here."

"You feel fine, don't you? You can't wait to get back to work!"

"Finest convalescence there is, work. Get the brain engaged and the body will follow."

"Promise me you won't overdo it, Edward, you mustn't set back your recovery."

"You worry over me like an old mother hen, I'll be fine."

"I do worry about you, that's a part of my job."

He was irrepressible, the prospect of engaging his brain was Edward's life blood. We marched out of his office with a sense of purpose. Fiona looked up and smiled at the re-energised Edward. Then he did something he'd never done before, he offered me his arm. It was so unusual that it took me a moment to realise what he was offering. I linked my arm with his and we walked across the hall together. Florence saw us and her face lit up as our eyes met for a second and I smiled back. William greeted us, looking rather pleased with himself.

"Good morning, My Lord, Mrs Heywood."

"Morning, Evans, looks like a lovely day."

"It certainly is, My Lord."

It was a lovely day, the V1's that were now an almost constant threat in the skies above us were mercifully absent. The sky was clear with little more than the odd fluffy cloud. Most of the pre-war flower beds were long gone, but the gardeners maintained a few small beds to raise our spirits. They were not as elaborate as before the war, but the begonias, geraniums, and busy lizzies looked wonderful, gently swaying in the warm soft breeze. My spirits didn't need raising that morning. Instead, the wonderful display added something extra to an already beautiful day. I don't ever recall enjoying the walk to the intelligence section more than I did that day.

We walked together arm in arm, occasionally glancing at each other, he would smile at me, and I would smile back. Edward had taken another giant stride towards me but I knew that hundreds of years of tradition could not quickly be overturned. If our relationship was to progress at all it would have to progress at the pace he felt comfortable with. Walking with Edward by my side, I was simply enjoying being with him. If the war existed at all, it was in another place.

There were occasional moments when circumstances conspired to push the war from your mind, usually fleeting, with the return to reality often being painful, but while it lasted, those moments were sublime. That day walking with Edward was one such moment. When we arrived at Hut 3 and opened the door, my illusion vanished in a second, plucked from my hand like a cherished love letter, blown in the wind.

"Good morning, gentlemen, what's the latest V1 figure?"

"Morning, Edward. Morning, Lily," replied Woody. "We

received an update this morning, I have all the figures here."

There were no more pleasantries, we all sat down and our world became that of the V1. The boys were taking this very seriously, and I soon realised why. On June 15th, when Edward's car was hit, 244 V1's were launched, 73 of them hit Greater London, while 71 fell into areas outside of London. In just three days, another 500 were launched, and on the 18th of June, they hit the Guards Chapel at the Wellington Barracks. It killed 121 people with another 68 wounded. Those figures sent a deathly chill down my spine. The fact was that this deadly weapon was now raining down on the South East of England on a daily basis.

We understood enough even at that early stage to realise we were facing a very serious threat. How serious we didn't yet know, but the dreadful carnage at the Guards Chapel left us in little doubt that we should prepare for the worst. Edward distributed the intelligence paperwork from his briefcase. The boys were good at absorbing information and they instinctively distributed the paperwork between themselves. During the build-up to D-Day, they came together to form a well-oiled machine - that machine was now ready to spring back into action.

"Right," said Patrick, "let's get some background, when did we first find out about these things?"

"I think it will amaze you when I say that we have had an idea about them since early '42."

Edward continued to describe the work of the Polish Home Army intelligence unit, Armia Krajowa (AK). The Poles had a unique relationship with the British secret intelligence services throughout the war. Perhaps best known for supplying us with our first German Enigma machine, they were also our first source of intelligence about the development of both the V1 and the V2. The Polish reports were both numerous and authoritative.

"It's all here," said Rolo. "We have AK reports going back

to '42, and several reports about launch ramps, from a French field agent, Michel Hollard. And there is aerial reconnaissance."

"Let me see," said Maggie.

"It says a WAAF Flight-Officer called Constance Babington-Smith was the first to spot the ramps pointing out to sea," said Rolo.

"I heard about that at Medmenham," replied Maggie.

"What did we do about it?" I asked.

"Eventually we sent 600 bombers to Peenemunde and bombed the hell out of it," replied Woody.

"Well, it obviously didn't work, did it, Woody?"

"No, they moved all their research and production under the Harz Mountains, totally impregnable. And when launch ramps started appearing in Northern France at the Pas-de-Calais and Cherbourg, we bombed those as well, but they just rebuilt them."

"So what do we know about the actual V1 itself?" asked Maggie.

"We know quite a lot already, we've defused one," replied Rolo. "There's a detailed report from Bletchley."

He handed the documents around. While they were concentrating on the documents, we all suddenly stopped and instinctively looked at each other. The now familiar sound of an approaching V1 filled our ears. We were directly under the flight path between the launch sites and London. They were now flying over us regularly, but the sound of the pulse jet engine never failed to fill you with fear. Death had visited itself upon me several times in the past, with its cold grey hand silently reaching out towards me. On that day, it was announcing its presence loud and clear; *I am the bringer of death and I'm coming for you.* The message was clear as my heart rose up in my throat for the duration of the approaching sound. It invoked horrible memories of the Blitz.

When the sound receded and we knew that death had failed to find us, we breathed a collective sigh of relief. The bringer of death was still searching for victims, but this time, not us! What we would do if the sound suddenly stopped, I had no idea. Not knowing where it would fall, I supposed we would have just sat there looking at each other, waiting for our fate to unfold. During the Blitz, the air raid warning siren was the sound which first filled you with fear. As terrifying as it was, I now realised the siren was the messenger, not the assassin. The moment the current danger was past, our lives resumed as normal, as if nothing had happened - until the next time.

The boys absorbed the technical details like blotting paper. Edward was the first to comment on the fuse device, and they all instantly realised how fortunate we were to have recovered a reasonably intact V1. When I looked bewildered, Woody quickly explained that the fuse was a critical part of any bomb device. In this case the Germans equipped the V1 with three fuses! There was an electrical impact fuse, and another mechanical fuse which would allow for ground penetration. Finally, it had a delayed action fuse, set for two hours after launch. This was not as Edward explained a booby trap, the designers simply wanted to make sure that we didn't get hold of an intact weapon. The fuses would detonate 1800 lbs of Amatol.

I listened in awe as they discussed one technical issue after another. It was quickly apparent that it was one thing to have a warhead full of Amatol, it was quite another to deliver it onto a target. So a critical thing for us to understand was the guidance system. It seemed that we already knew quite a bit about that, courtesy of AK. It was in all respects an arbitrary weapon, a completely blind assassin. The orientation of its launch ramp determined direction; it was nothing more complicated than that.

"There must be more to it than that?" I queried.

Rollo looked up from his paperwork. "It's a simple auto-pilot, with yaw and pitch controlled by a pair of gyroscopes. It has a magnetic compass to control azimuth, and a barometric device to control altitude."

When they explained it to me, even I understood how it determined its range. It had a simple counter, driven by a vane anemometer mounted on the nose of the missile. Every thirty rotations of the propeller produced one click of the counter. When the counter reached its pre-set number, a series of automatic sequences came into effect to reset the elevator and rudder, putting the missile into a dive. A random number decided the fate of thousands of innocent individuals. In effect, it was a lottery. For those in the wrong place at the wrong time, their number was up.

They all found the engine design extremely interesting. The pulse jet was not a new idea, it had been patented way back in 1903 by a French inventor, but the Germans were the first to mass produce a reliable engine. Rapid pulses of fuel were injected into a simple combustion chamber and ignited. The expulsion of ignited gasses provided thrust, while incoming air provided oxygen for the next ignition. It was the buzzing sound of the pulse jet engine which gave rise to the names 'buzz bomb,' and 'doodlebug.' When that terrifying noise stopped, everyone cowered in fear, knowing only too well it meant the flying bomb was falling close by. Ironically, the additional level of terror which the sudden silence imposed upon its victims, was unintentional. The engine wasn't designed to stop, it was a design error which caused the fuel to cut off when the missile was sent into a dive. They later modified it.

"Right, it's an effective, arbitrary killer, so how do we stop it?" asked Patrick.

"We need to know speed and altitude," Woody replied.

"Initial estimates tell us it cruises at about 340 mph, at 2000 to 3000 feet," Edward said. "Anti-aircraft batteries along the Downs have not been effective."

"Not surprising, that's just above the effective range of our light guns," commented Woody.

"We can improve that," said Corky.

"There's a lot of development going on with gun-laying radar, and proximity fuses," said Rolo. "Bell Labs have got a new fire control system."

"We can do the calculations, it should be possible to shoot these things down," Corky said.

"What about aircraft?" asked Edward. "340 mph, we can do that."

"Yes," replied Woody, "a Mosquito has already shot one down. We need additional speed to catch up with one, but once we have, they're vulnerable."

"Right, let's get to work on the numbers," Edward said. "We can work out an optimal strategy for the fighters, and we need all the available technical details about the gun-laying radar."

"That's right," said Corky, "we need to know where they launch them from. Once we know that, combined with altitude and speed, we can plot the most likely interception points. Correctly placed anti-aircraft guns with radar guidance should prove very effective."

"We need reconnaissance," Edward said. "Rolo, give Maggie all the recon we have and let's get Johnny over there again as soon as possible. We need up-to-the-minute location of launch sites, and their research, development, and manufacturing sites."

"There's another consideration," Rolo said. "The arbitrary nature of the targeting means they're still trying to perfect it. So they need to know precisely where they are falling."

"Excellent, Rolo," said Edward enthusiastically. "They must have spies on the ground reporting back to Germany."

"Of course, well done, Rolo!" said Corky. "Misinformation, we can feed them misinformation!"

"MI5 has an operation called Double Cross," Edward said, "it has been incredibly successful at rounding up German spies. I'll put this to them immediately."

I sat smiling at them all, they simply thrived on problem solving. Give them a difficult challenge, make it a national emergency, and it was like a drug to them, they were all immediately motivated. Hut 3 had moved back into operational mode! This was not like the D-Day preparations, we weren't alone in this endeavour. My job was to coordinate with the other agencies and services. There was no point working on problems other people had already solved, and vice versa. This applied specially to sharing reconnaissance and intelligence. It represented a complete departure from our previous incarnation, where I always had to deny our very existence. We would need to integrate with the wider intelligence community.

They hardly noticed me leaving, only Edward raised his head. We smiled at each other as I opened the door. It was the same lovely day outside, the sun still shone, and the flowers looked equally radiant, the difference now being the war. As I walked in the direction of the Manor, my mind was racing with all the connections I needed to establish with the different services. Communication between SOE sections was notoriously difficult but communication with the wider intelligence community was even harder.

MI6 regarded us as enthusiastic amateurs at best. There was, however, a back channel, a little-known vital link which held us together. The saying that behind every great man there is an equally great woman was never truer than in the world of intelligence. There were four women at the heart of the British establishment. These women were all-powerful, and we formed a kind of sisterhood. I was in awe of the authority they wielded, my role at Station M was very minor in comparison. I quickly realised that together we were greater than the sum of our parts, a fact which undoubtedly benefitted me more than it did them. Strangely, I never actually met one of them in person, but despite that, we formed a close relationship based upon mutual trust and respect.

I quickly realised that Joan Bright was an extraordinary

woman. Her recruitment into the world of behind-the-scenes activity would probably sound implausible in a spy novel, right down to wearing a pink carnation in order to be recognised for an interview. What we shared in common was that we both became involved without knowing what we were getting into. She was recruited by secret intelligence and fell under the sphere of Lt. Colonel Joe Holland and Brigadier Colin Gubbins, who was later to be in charge of SOE. Joan later ran the Secret Intelligence Centre, which was in fact a room in the Cabinet War Rooms. From that all-powerful position, she moved to become personal assistant to General Sir Hastings Ismay, who was close to Winston Churchill. In 1946 when Joan was awarded the MBE she was described as, "Principal, Offices of the Cabinet, and Minister of Defence." Joan was all-powerful.

I spoke very regularly with Margaret Jackson, she was personal assistant to Colin Gubbins, head of SOE. Margaret graduated in modern languages from London University. Her sister, who worked at the War Office, heard that General Gubbins was looking for a French-speaking secretary. So at the tender age of just 23, Margaret joined Gubbins in Paris. Rather like Joan Bright, her obvious ability quickly propelled her to become Gubbins' assistant. She was at the very heart of SOE, nothing happened that Margaret didn't know about. She also was awarded the MBE after the war.

The woman I felt closest to was Elizabeth Layton, who was Winston Churchill's private secretary throughout the war. Elizabeth travelled with the PM almost everywhere. She was present when the PM visited America where she met President Roosevelt in the White House. She was a part of the British delegation to the Yalta conference, where Winston Churchill proposed a toast to Miss Layton at a banquet during the conference. My close association with Elizabeth provided me with almost direct contact with the Prime Minister. On occasions such as when Edward was fighting for his life after the V1 incident, the Prime Minister personally issued instructions to St Hugh's Military Hospital and I knew who to thank for organising that.

Vera Atkins was the only one of us who actually came from an intelligence background before she joined SOE. Born in Romania, she actually came to the attention of British Intelligence in her home country. She was recruited by British Security Coordination. One of her first missions was to get the Polish code breakers out of Poland with their Enigma machine. In February 1941 Vera joined SOE as a secretary, where like the other women her abilities quickly propelled her to the position of assistant to Maurice Buckmaster of SOE F Section.

As I walked back towards the Manor, I mulled over how best to deal with our new situation. With contacts right at the heart of the British establishment, I could have the ear of any of the Chiefs of Staff, or heads of SOE, not to mention the Prime Minister. When I asked for a top-secret X-class midget submarine during the build up to D-Day, I got it with just a phone call. I must admit the prospect of Station M being closed down had been a difficult outcome to contemplate, and like the boys I revelled in our new incarnation. I felt that we were still fighting back, that I was continuing to do my bit for King and country.

Whenever I reached the vantage point from where you could see the estate office, I would always turn and look to see if Greg was there. He was just going into the office, looking incredibly smart in his tweed suit. Without thinking, I turned and walked in his direction and he caught sight of me. He stood by the door watching me walk towards him.

"I've just got back," he said, "would you like a cup of tea?"

"I would, thank you."

We walked through to his kitchen, where I sat down. The moment I did so, I entered the world we used to share so passionately together. It was impossible not to think about how we used to be. Greg busied himself with the tea, but I guessed he would be thinking the same thing.

"How are you, Greg, it's difficult, isn't it?"

"I'm okay, now I can last nearly twenty minutes without thinking about you!"

"I suppose I'm about the same."

"So how is it between you and Edward?"

"I can't, Greg, it doesn't feel right to talk about it."

"No, you're wrong, you *can* talk about it. I've accepted the situation. If I can't have you then I want to know you'll be happy with someone else."

"You can't mean that, Greg? If you had someone else now, I'd be jealous of her."

"Do you remember that 'situation' I left behind in Scotland? Well, she's coming down south to see me."

"You told me that was over."

"It is. I have no idea why she's coming, but that's someone you can be jealous of."

"If she meant something to you, I would be."

"Oh, she means something to me all right, we were together for quite a while. I suppose in some ways we were like you, me, and Edward. The difference is I chose you."

"Do you hate yourself for doing that to her?"

"I do."

"I wondered about her. I assumed your 'situation' had been serious. What's her name?"

"Aileen."

"Isn't it silly, now I know her name, I'm jealous. But then a part of me wants you to go back to her."

"I'm not sure that's even an option."

"I'm not sure what will happen between me and Edward. I know he loves me, and I love him, so who knows. I can't explain any of it, but it doesn't mean that I didn't love you as well."

"I can't explain it either, but I understand."

"There's only one way that anyone could understand. You loved Aileen, didn't you?"

"I did, but I made my decision. I did to her what you did to me, so I do know exactly how you feel, Lily."

"I'm pleased you've told me and in a strange way Aileen brings us even closer together."

"You never cease to amaze me, Lily. You were right about Mary as well, she's an incredibly bright young woman. She asked if I thought she should become my full-time trainee."

"What did you say?"

"I asked her if she thought she was ready. She said it was what she wanted, but she also said she had to live up to your expectations, and there was no way she was going to let you down."

"Oh, bless her. She's a lovely girl, you won't regret it, Greg."

It had been an enlightening time with Greg. I always suspected his 'situation' in Scotland was a woman, but I was pleased that he'd now told me about her. I don't know why he chose to tell me then but was glad he had. I had no secrets from him, and now he had no secrets from me, it brought us closer. There's nearly always a difficulty between previous lovers. Jealousy or rivalry, or even downright hostility, can often prevent genuine friendship. While my heart would always be Edward's, I also wanted Greg to be a part of my life, as a friend.

Chapter Twelve
Lady Elizabeth

Towards the end of June 1944, I became ever more conscious of crossing out the remaining days on the calendar. We were only too aware of how vital it was that Allied forces broke out of Normandy, and it had been three weeks since D-Day. We pinned our hopes on Operation Epsom. The port city of Caen was strategically vital for the Allies, standing between the beachhead and the rest of France. The Germans realised this, so most of their armoured divisions were concentrated there. While this was helpful for the Americans pushing west towards Cherbourg, it ensured Caen would be the scene of a protracted battle.

Operation Epsom, planned for June 19th, was intended to break through the German front, skirting the city of Caen to the west and taking the bridges over the river Odon. The operation had to be postponed due to a storm which also destroyed two of the artificial harbours so vital for Allied resupply. The British and Canadians finally launched Operation Epsom on June 26th. With only the last day of June left on the calendar, Edward and I were desperate for news. We made our way over to Hut 3 first thing that morning.

"Morning, everyone."

"Morning, Lily. Morning, Edward," replied Rolo as he hurriedly made his way towards the communications room.

"What's the latest, Woody?"

"It's not good, I'm afraid. It's been a massive operation, involving 60,000 men and 600 tanks. The fighting was intense, ground has been won and lost, and retaken. The British and Canadian losses amount to over 4000 casualties with the loss of 150 tanks. German casualties are of a similar order."

"When you say it's not good, Woody, what do you mean?"

"We've only advanced six miles. I don't think Montgomery has had much of an option; he's called a halt to the advance."

"This is a terrible setback," said Edward. "Have we gained no advantage at all?"

"Operation Epsom is a strategic failure," replied Woody with an air of resignation. "Caen remains an immovable obstacle for the Allies."

"If there's anything to be said for this operation, it's that we have diverted attention away from the Americans," said Corky. "They've made fast progress towards the vital deep port of Cherbourg."

"Have they taken Cherbourg?" I asked.

"Yes," replied Woody, "but it was strongly defended. The victory came at an enormous price - 22,000 American troops either killed, wounded, or missing. The German losses are even more severe."

"This is really depressing," I said, "all those boys killed and we're still stuck in Normandy. Is nothing going in our favour?"

"We can take a little bit of credit for the way the V1 campaign is going," said Patrick. "The misinformation operation which MI5 put into effect is starting to show results. The Germans have fallen for it, obviously believing their flying bombs are overshooting London. They're resetting the counters to lower numbers. V1's have started to fall short of London. Many of them are falling harmlessly into the Kent, Sussex, or Surrey countryside."

"Even that's not entirely going our way," said Corky. "Southern Greater London is now receiving a disproportionate number of hits. The Croydon area especially is suffering enormously."

"Oh no, that's where my Uncle George lives," I said fearfully. "The only good news I'm hearing is from Vera Atkins. She tells me SOE agents of F Section are causing havoc with German infrastructure. In the vital first week of the invasion our agents and the Special Air Service really handicapped the German attempts to bring forward reinforcements and supplies."

"I agree, Lily," replied Edward. "Winston Churchill said he wanted SOE to set Europe ablaze, and so far his vision is proving to be enormously successful."

Edward was right about SOE operations, together with FR they were one of the success stories of the war. Set against that success, the strategic failure of Operation Epsom was a constant reminder that the prospect of an end to the war hung by a thread. Our V1 countermeasures were slow to take effect, but gradually we started to knock some of them out of the sky. At Middlebourne, sitting directly under the flight path of many of those V1's, each one reminded us of the urgency of our work. Every V1 which evaded our countermeasures and flew over our heads was potentially the bringer of death.

Amid all that increasing tension, Lady Elizabeth arrived. Edward received a telegram to say that she would arrive at Liverpool in two days' time - would he arrange to have her collected. The message came at a particularly difficult time. The V1 threat was growing more significant by the day. We were immersed in the technicalities of the new Bell radar-guided anti-aircraft gun system. Edward was very dismissive of her request.

"She probably expects Evans to drive all the way to Liverpool in order to pick her up."

"In the circumstances, what with petrol rationing and everything, that sounds a little unreasonable," I commented. "How would you like me to reply?"

"Tell her to catch the train like everyone else. I suppose Evans could pick her up at the station in London."

"Will you go with William to meet her?"

"Certainly not, far more important things to do."

Lady Elizabeth was my age, in fact she was just one month younger than me. I'd seen the family photographs of her, she was something of a dark-haired beauty. Her defining feature appeared to be her mouth and teeth. I don't mean that in a derogatory sense, her teeth were perfectly aligned, which, combined with her large mouth, gave the impression of a permanent smile. The broad smile within the context of the photographs painted a picture of a fun-loving if rebellious woman.

Perhaps Edward had already influenced my attitude because I thought the later photographs portrayed the very image that he described. Except for the formal family portraits, she obviously wanted to be seen as some kind of exalted socialite. She appeared to flaunt a mixture of flamboyant hats, long pearl necklaces, cigarette holders, and headbands. Her eye for fashion was obviously as extravagant as her allowance. I conjured up a mischievous image in my mind, visualising a woman looking like the reincarnation of a 1920s flapper.

Edward was so preoccupied with the V1 that he didn't mention the subject again. When Elizabeth finally arrived, Edward made what was for him something of a concession - he met her at the Grand Entrance. I obviously chose not to be involved with the family reunion. As the evening approached, I would have to confess to feeling uneasy, the prospect of meeting her filling me with apprehension. I suppose my fear was that she would disapprove of me, even worse that she would look down on me. Deciding what to wear for the evening was becoming a real torment, I really needed Florence to give me confidence. She was late coming to my room, which was most unusual, so as soon as she arrived, I immediately asked her what she thought I should wear.

"I know exactly what you should wear, because I have just had to dress Lady Elizabeth."

"Why, what happened?"

"She asked Mr Jennings who was going to be her lady's maid. She demanded someone, and there was only me."

"Oh, dear. So what is she wearing?"

"I've never seen so many clothes before, her wardrobes are full of them. She was really cross, saying I should have removed them all from the wardrobes a week ago to air them."

"So tell me, what is she wearing?"

"I thought perhaps she might be very formal, but she scoffed at the idea, and is wearing a cocktail dress."

"What kind of dress, what colour?"

"It's really lovely, it's red velour - she called it her crossover wiggle dress. It's quite low cut, I didn't think it was at all appropriate for a family evening."

"And jewellery?"

"Oh yes, everything."

"Did she ask about me?"

"You're the only thing she did ask about. She asked what I thought you might wear, I said I didn't know."

"What did she say?"

"She writes to Lady Beatrice so they obviously talk about you. She wanted to know what kind of person you are and did I think you had intentions towards His Lordship."

"Well, what did you say?"

"I said it wasn't my place to notice such things, but when she really pushed me, I said you were a wonderful lady. I made a point of saying, *lady*."

"Oh Florence, what a lovely thing to say. And what did you think of her?"

"Can I say?"

"Oh, don't be silly, of course you can say."

"She treated me as if I didn't really exist, and she complained about everything I tried to do for her. She's nothing like you at all, Mrs Heywood."

I left Florence sorting my clothes and made my way to the bathroom, all the while wondering how best to approach the evening. Having thought through a dozen scenarios, I suddenly realised I was being silly. I was allowing my demons to get the better of me for no reason at all. I always felt inadequate in the company of titled people, but what did I need to prove to Lady Elizabeth? My fear was letting Edward down, or Caroline, and I realised I would only do that if I allowed her to make a fool of me. When I returned to my bedroom, Florence had my clothes for the evening laid out for me. She had chosen my very best cocktail dress, the black one with the lace top.

"You obviously think I have to look my very best, Florence?"

"I do. I don't want her looking better than you, and she looks really striking in that red dress with her dark hair."

"Sounds like I'm not going to compete."

"You're twice the lady she'll ever be, she just doesn't know it yet."

"You're such a boost for my confidence, Florence."

"There's something else I need to tell you, Mrs Heywood."

"Something about her outfit?"

"No, it's Harry's parents." Her attitude changed immediately. "Harry's disowned me, and his parents called me a slut and told me not to bother them again." Her eyes welled up as she sat down with her head in her hands.

"Harry's disowned you! How *dare* he! He *can't* just walk away from his responsibility like that. And as for his parents, that's monstrous! I shall go and see them. I'm not having them call you that."

"I knew that's what you would say, Mrs Heywood, that's so kind, but they won't change their mind. They're not very nice people."

"I'll have words with them anyway, no-one talks to you like that. This is a real problem though, isn't it? Has nobody below-stairs mentioned it yet? That bump is getting harder to hide, isn't it?"

"Nobody has said anything, but what am I going to do?"

"I don't know, but I won't see you cast out on the street."

"I thought Harry loved me but he doesn't, does he?"

"I'm afraid that's obvious, Florence. I think you already know you have been a silly, misguided girl, but you're not the first, and you won't be the last. Everything will be all right, I promise."

The poor girl was so upset, I felt like crying with her. We talked some more as I tried to assure her everything would turn out for the best, but of course I knew her position was dire. Despite all her problems, she continued to fuss and worry about me, which in a way made me feel even worse. I had been in her position. I'd been that same silly, misguided girl, but my outcome had been very different. She insisted on finishing my hair and makeup. It was obviously a matter of pride for her that she really didn't want Elizabeth to cast a shadow over me.

When I finally received her stamp of approval, I left my bedroom feeling positively glamorous, while poor Florence dragged herself away looking forlorn. It really tormented me as I proceeded down the staircase. I felt sure William had been looking out for me, because as soon as I appeared, there he was, waiting outside the Drawing Room. He opened the door and announced me, which was something he wouldn't normally do. Edward jumped to his feet.

"Good evening, Lily, may I introduce my sister, Lady Elizabeth."

"Hello, Mrs Heywood," she said, looking me up and down. "I've heard a lot about you, I've been looking forward to our meeting."

"I'm delighted to meet you, Lady Elizabeth, how was your journey?"

"Bloody awful. Edward made me take the train. Can you imagine - it was full of foul-mouthed soldiers, utterly intolerable. I'll not forgive you for that, Edward."

She had a condescending tone of voice, and an exaggerated

manner. I assumed it was all an affectation, an attempt to make me feel inferior. I hugged Caroline, and we chatted together. Elizabeth was visibly agitated, sitting there looking critically at me. It was a relief when Jennings came to offer us drinks. Having taken Caroline's order, he asked Elizabeth.

"For you, Lady Elizabeth?"

"Manhattan, Jennings."

"Very well, My Lady. And what would you like, Mrs Heywood, I might suggest your favourite Bowmore, the rather excellent 25-year-old."

"You continue to spoil me, Mr Jennings."

"My pleasure, Mrs Heywood. And what would you like, My Lord?"

"You're right about the Bowmore, Jennings, it *is* excellent."

"Very well, My Lord."

Jennings departed, leaving behind an atmosphere that was not of his making. Thanks to Florence, I knew what to expect, and Elizabeth lived up to expectations. Her red crossover dress was stunning, and with her dark, almost black hair she looked equally stunning wearing it. Florence was also right about the low-cut front. She had plenty to flaunt, but this was decidedly not the right occasion on which to flaunt it. She was undeniably a woman who was used to making a big impression.

Perhaps this was the problem. None of that applied to her mother and brother, and it certainly didn't apply to me. Attempting to engage with her, I asked how the ocean crossing had been. By all accounts it was unspeakable, she would prefer not to think about it. Elizabeth seemed determined not to converse with me. I tried hard, but our conversation was more memorable for its silences than its engagement. Finally, after a lengthy silence, she said what was on her mind.

"I'm sure it is very nice of my family to ask you to join us for dinner, Mrs Heywood, but you must forgive me if I appear underwhelmed. When I was last in this house, we didn't dine with the staff. I can see there have been changes."

"You don't understand, Elizabeth," Caroline said. "We do not consider Lily to be a member of staff. I regard her as a part of the family."

"This is the very point I am making, Mother! You only have to listen to Mrs Heywood speak to realise she can never be a part of this family." She turned her disapproving gaze towards me. "Your job title, Mrs Heywood, is Chief of Staff. Is there some aspect of the word *staff* in that description that I am not understanding?"

I was completely wrong-footed. Nothing about her glamorous appearance could have prepared me for such an acerbic comment. My head was spinning and standing there in my beautiful cocktail dress and pearls, I felt exposed and vulnerable. Looking and feeling totally feminine was not conducive to being combative. I should have done my best to ignore her, but I couldn't.

"No, you understand very well, Elizabeth. As you are so keen to point out, I come from the East End of London, and I am a salaried member of staff. I'm not even allowed to tell you what I do here. All I can say is that my duties are many and varied, but you should know that my commitment to this family is absolute. I'm not sure that you understand what an unconditional commitment is, Elizabeth. It means there is absolutely nothing I would not do for this household. Your family recognises and respects my commitment. I am deeply honoured that they have extended the hand of friendship to me."

"This sounds to me as if you have weaselled your way into my family, and with what motive, I wonder?"

I looked towards Edward for support, but he just sat smiling. He gave me a lovely expression, as if to say, 'I told you so', while Caroline looked positively mortified. What was I to do? If I said nothing, it would seem to support her monstrous comment. If I argued with her, I risked creating a terrible rift between us. Determined not to make a scene, I counted to ten, very slowly, but it didn't work.

"You have totally misjudged me, Elizabeth, and may I say you misjudged your family as well. I cherish the wonderful relationship we share. I think perhaps your family cherishes it as well."

"You only support my contention, Mrs Heywood, and it is *Lady* Elizabeth, if you please."

"I'm afraid that is another delusion, Elizabeth. Your title is given to you as a courtesy, and courtesy is a mark of respect you have to earn."

"This is monstrous, Elizabeth," Caroline said. "You must both stop this at once."

"Mother's right," said Edward. "You know nothing about Lily, and as a result you're making yourself look ridiculous. Frankly, you are being an embarrassment. You have had a long and arduous journey, let's just blame it on that, and say no more about it."

"Very well if you insist, Edward, but I retain my opinion. I'm sorry if my assessment of the situation causes you offence, Mrs Heywood."

"Oh, no offence taken, I can assure you, Elizabeth. Why don't you call me Lily? There's no need for you to stand on ceremony, not for my sake."

She sat looking slightly wide-eyed. If I'm any judge of character, she was incandescent with rage, but to her credit she concealed it well. Jennings returned with our drinks, once again providing us with a welcome distraction. It had all been horribly embarrassing. I tried hard to make allowances for her, realising I had unwisely allowed myself to react, but her provocation had been inescapable. When we went through for dinner, I had the opportunity to speak to Edward.

"You're supposed to be my knight in shining armour, Edward. Why didn't you come to my rescue sooner?"

"I know my sister, and I know you, Lily. You didn't need my help. I just hope for her sake she doesn't push you any further."

I smiled; Edward's confidence reassured me enormously. Several drinks later, as she mellowed considerably, I started to see more of the outgoing socialite I'd been told about, but all the while she remained unforgiving towards me. Her attitude towards the war was also particularly infuriating as she seemed to regard it merely as an inconvenience. This was another obstacle to conversation because it was quite impossible for us not to mention it. She had no concept of being bombed, or losing loved ones, and even rationing and food shortages were an alien concept to her.

"Has it been bad then?" she asked. "The bombing, I mean."

"Do you not follow the news in America?" I asked.

"Well, I know about it, of course, but it all seems a long way away."

"During the Blitz, Elizabeth, over 43,000 people have been killed, and the Nazis have destroyed over two million homes."

"Oh, gosh. I didn't know it was that bad. Really, as many as that?"

"Yes, as many as that, Elizabeth! And the civilian death toll continues to rise. There's still bombing, and now it's the threat from the V1. That's the flying bomb which nearly killed Edward, while claiming the lives of nine other people. They were just innocent people walking down the road or standing in one of the shops."

We were accustomed to hearing the V1's fly over us, it had now become almost an hourly occurrence. She had no idea that the flight path placed Middlebourne directly in the line of fire, nor how initially the sound filled you with dread, and yet how quickly you become desensitised to the threat. As we were speaking, I could hear the distinctive noise of a V1 coming closer.

"Listen, Elizabeth, that's a V1 you can hear. If that sound stops while it's still approaching us, then there is every likelihood that it will kill us."

"Don't joke, that's hardly funny."

"Lily is not joking, Elizabeth," replied Edward. "In the event that the noise stops, get under the dining table immediately."

"Are you serious?"

"If it stops, you will see how serious we are."

Her expression changed immediately, finally the war was becoming a reality for her. We said nothing as the noise increased, growing louder and louder until it was directly overhead. Then, as the ghastly sound changed pitch, we knew it was moving away from us. Elizabeth was rightly frightened.

"It's going on to kill someone else, Elizabeth. In a few minutes, the bringer of death will complete its mission, delivering death and misery to some poor unfortunate family."

"Oh my goodness, I didn't know it was like this. What must it be like to have a bomb fall on you?"

"It's the most terrifying thing imaginable," I said. "You cling to the slightest possibility of hope for as long as hope remains, but when you know all is lost, something inside you simply accepts the inevitable. You let go of the struggle to survive, that last second becomes the most precious second of your life. There's no struggle important enough, and no fear great enough to separate you from it. You'll never give it up, it has to be taken away from you."

"I'm sorry, Lily, you're talking from experience, aren't you?"

"Yes, Elizabeth, I am. Death stared me in the face during the Blitz. My best friend was killed, as were her twin boys, they were all lying crushed beneath the rubble. When you witness the essence of a young boy's life ebbing away into the grey dust, that's an image that never leaves you. It's something that nobody should ever have to see. I was lying beneath that same rubble, it's nothing less than a miracle that somehow I evaded death's claim upon me.

Ever since that fateful day, there's something I've come to believe. I don't think I walked away because death spared me. During that last fleeting moment of calm before the bomb exploded, I grasped my final second. I held it so tightly in my hand, even death failed to tear it away from me. That final second is now mine to keep, I'll never give it up, because it constantly reminds me that every single moment of life is precious."

"When you told me about that awful experience, Lily, I'm not sure I realised how close to death you had been," said Caroline. "I so admire your spirit, my dear. Can you wonder, Elizabeth, that we welcome Lily into our family?"

"Forgive me everyone, I didn't mean to be so maudlin," I said. "It's listening to yet another of those V1's flying over. Every one of them reminds me of that night. And I'm not sure I'm over the shock of when I was told about you, Edward."

"Yes, I'm sorry, Lily, I'll try to avoid doing that in the future!"

"You'd better, I couldn't go through that again!"

"Edward tells me you saved his life, Lily, is that true?"

"He exaggerates, Elizabeth, I merely increased the odds of his recovery."

"Yes, you increased the odds from poor to excellent, I would call that saving my life. Lily stayed with me for the whole week, she was truly remarkable."

"It was awful for me knowing my son was lying in a coma but it must have been terrible for you, Lily, actually seeing him in that condition."

"It was terrifying, you were just a shell of yourself, Edward. It was as if you weren't there at all."

"I wish I had been there to see you sing to him, Lily. That must have been a wonderful moment when he opened his eyes."

"More than wonderful, Caroline. There was a moment when I had to let go of your hand, Edward. You'll probably think I'm being silly, but I wanted you to have my precious second so as our hands parted, I closed your fingers over your palm, and I left my second of time in your safekeeping."

Edward was reduced to silence, just looking at me adoringly.

His expression made me realise that I'd allowed Elizabeth to goad me into baring my soul. There was no necessity for me to demonstrate to her that I was worthy of respect, nor that Edward and I shared a special relationship. Even if Elizabeth had known my inner demon was the fear of rejection, she couldn't have done a better job of provoking me.

"It seems we have much to thank you for, Lily," Elizabeth said.

"We have much to thank the doctors and nurses for - they're the ones who really saved Edward's life. There's no need to thank me. Edward would do the same for me in an instant, he even has one of his little expressions for it." I continued with my best impression of Edward's voice. "That would be something you can implicitly rely upon, Lily."

We all laughed, including Elizabeth. "Yes, that sounds like Edward," Caroline said.

Edward smiled, accepting my mischief-making graciously. "I did say it, didn't I!"

One way or another, it was quite an emotional occasion. The imminent disaster which I assumed would befall the evening had failed to materialise. Elizabeth succeeded in goading me into a response which was both ill-advised and regretful. Perhaps, to her credit rather than mine, the evening wasn't a disaster as she seemed to choose to either tolerate or respect me, probably the former. My conclusion was that she was rather as Edward had described her, a spoilt brat with an enormous chip on her shoulder. Her title was indeed only a courtesy. She had nothing to pass on to her children and depended on the benevolence of her brother.

Before I came to Middlebourne Manor, I would have viewed her as an enormously privileged woman. I would have dismissed any talk of her 'unfortunate' position out of hand. But those three years had changed me, now I could see the world from her perspective. The hereditary system was almost as arbitrary as the V1, since her only sin was being born a woman with an older brother. The fact that Edward was incredibly capable as the beneficiary of the title, and she probably wasn't, was by-the-by.

The fact is, I ended up feeling sorry for her. She had all the attributes that the rest of us would die for. Firstly, she was beautiful with an amazing figure. Above all, I could see that in other circumstances, she possessed the same extrovert quality as Dotty. Her problem was that she channelled it in the wrong direction, allowing her bitterness to control her personality. By the end of the evening, I no longer saw her as an objectionable spoiled brat but as a sad and fragile person. Deliberately flaunting my relationship with Edward and her mother was not my finest moment. Neither was using every opportunity to put her in her place - I regretted it. When the evening drew to a close, I chose to leave the Drawing Room with her, and we walked together up the stairs.

"I'm sorry, Elizabeth, I've behaved badly this evening. You said some very unkind things, and I've spent the entire evening trying to make you feel sorry for it."

"I must say you have really surprised me, Lily, you're not what I was expecting at all."

"I won't ask what you were expecting!"

"Probably best not. Suffice to say you're quite a woman, I can see that, and I'm sorry about those unkind things I said. I don't know why I do that. This is very difficult for me, I'm sure you understand. This is *my* family, and yet I find you effectively taking my place in Mother's eyes, and it goes beyond that, doesn't it, with my brother. You have won my respect, Lily, now you need to win my trust."

"That's fair enough, Elizabeth, you've met me halfway. I *will* win your trust, I promise you.

Chapter Thirteen
Fiona's Unbridled Joy

I went with Edward to the hospital in Tunbridge Wells to have his dressings removed. This wasn't like St Thomas' and much less like St Hugh's. Built between 1932 and 1943, it was considered at the time to be a new 'modern' building and it certainly felt very fit for purpose. The long wards ran the length of the building. For the benefit of the patients, each ward had a sun balcony at the southern end. The most striking feature was that they were all joined by an external spiral walkway. I remember when they built it and we had a trip to Tunbridge just to look at it.

Edward had been suffering a series of headaches, and I was clinging to the hope that maybe the dressings were too tight. The staff were all very kind and helpful, the nurse in charge allowing me to sit with him while she unwound the bandage. It was only then when I realised how serious his injury had been. He had several stitched wounds, of which the worst was a horrible line of stitches above his left ear, I assumed these resulted from the surgery. The bruising was every shade of purple you could imagine, all the more obvious because they had shaved his head. None of that should have surprised me, but it did. My smile was the result of considerable effort.

"Well, how do I look, Lily?"

"Do you want my honest opinion?"

"Of course, what else?"

"You look lovely, you always do to me. He does, doesn't he, nurse?"

"He soon will. Your hair will grow back over that scar in no time," came the reassuring answer.

The nurse set about removing the stitches. Edward sat grimacing in pain as I sat doing the same in sympathy with him. We waited for the doctor to see him and perform some tests. After tapping his knees, elbows, and other reflexes, he tested his vision, before declaring all to be well. When I asked about the headaches, he thought that was normal for a patient at Edward's stage of recovery. When it was time for us to leave, Edward caught sight of himself in a mirror and stood for some seconds looking at the sorry reflection which greeted him.

"What on earth do I look like?" he said, rubbing his hand over the stubble on his head.

"You look like an escaped convict, Edward, shall I be safe in your company?" I joked.

"I'm surprised you want to be seen in my company!"

I placed my hands on either side of his face and kissed his forehead. "Don't be ridiculous, beauty is in the eye of the beholder, Edward. Would you think any less of me if I looked like a convict?"

"I can't imagine you could ever look like a convict, Lily."

Without thinking about it, I tossed him a barbed question. "You'd love me just the same though, wouldn't you?"

Typical of Edward, he didn't quite answer the question. "Well indeed, you could only ever be beautiful to me, Lily."

We stepped outside the hospital and set off arm in arm towards where William was waiting with the car. Just minutes into the walk, the sound of an approaching V1 filled the air. It was some way over to our right but was quite close enough. The receding noise was still audible when it abruptly stopped. We both instinctively crouched down, and moments later we heard the explosion, followed quickly by the residual shock wave.

There was no damage where we were, but the shock wave momentarily took our breath away. I noticed the net curtains in the houses opposite abruptly rise and fall in unison, as if an unseen hand had entered every building. I thought perhaps Edward might react badly, re-living his recent experience, but he coped with the incident well.

The V1 fell just on the outskirts of Tunbridge. We later found out that there was damage to one of the houses, though mercifully only minor injuries. Approaching the car, we debated if there was anything we could do. Within moments a police car rushed past us going towards the explosion. People were already running down the road as I convinced Edward that we should leave the locals to deal with it. Stepping into the opulence of the Rolls-Royce, it was easy to exclude the harsh reality just outside the car, but our minds were more occupied with the greater threat that existed from beyond our shores.

"We need to double our efforts, Lily, this threat is growing all the time."

"At least we're shooting some of them down now, but there are just so many."

"There are also reports from AK about a new kind of rocket that is being developed, I'm very concerned. This has the potential to change the war."

"What do you mean, change the war?"

"If the reports are correct, the new rocket has the potential to be orders of magnitude more deadly."

"You mean it is much bigger?"

"No, it may well carry a larger warhead, but it sounds like a ballistic missile. According to MI6 it doesn't look as if it's designed to fly like the V1, it follows a ballistic trajectory. If I understand that correctly it means it will follow a curved flight path, a parabola."

"You mean it goes up and down in a long curve, so it will just drop out of the sky."

"That's right, Lily. The first we would know about it is when it falls out of the sky. If that is the case, we shall have absolutely no defence at all."

"Oh, my goodness! So even now with the Allies in Normandy, if Hitler has enough of these, he could still defeat us."

"There are so many things we still don't know. It's obviously a race against time, because given enough time to develop the targeting, they may even be able to use them strategically against the invasion force as well as against us here."

"A weapon we can't defend against, that sounds like Armageddon."

"We have one defence - we need to find them and destroy them on the ground."

We talked about it all the way back to Middlebourne. I felt a fear that I hadn't experienced since the Blitz. D-Day was the start of a massive operation ultimately intended to defeat Hitler and put an end to the war. It was the first time since 1939 that we allowed ourselves to think such an end was in sight. The prospect of those hopes being an illusion sent shivers down my spine. Just talking about it had created a sense of urgency, and as we approached Middlebourne, Edward wanted to go directly to Hut 3. It took considerable persistence on my part to persuade him to see his mother and sister first.

William had inevitably overheard some of what had been said, and when we arrived he opened the door for me.

"You won't let that bastard Hitler succeed with this new rocket, will you, Mrs Heywood?"

"You're damn right we won't, William, not if His Lordship has any say in the matter." He smiled approvingly.

"Family must come first, Edward, they worry about you. Sit down and have a cup of tea with them, and then you can go to Hut 3. I'll go with you."

"I've never been ordered about before, not in my own

home. I must say, though, you have a gracious way of doing it."

"Oh Edward, I'm sorry, I don't mean to. It's just my way of taking care of you."

"I didn't say I was complaining."

Indeed he wasn't complaining, and I reassured myself it was a measure of how close we were now. I left him to see his family while I went straight to the office. Fiona's first words were to ask about Edward. I explained how everything had gone really well at the hospital and was just about to tell her about the V1 incident, when I noticed how excited she was. Her eyes were positively sparkling. I knew something was going on.

"What is it Fi, you look as if you're about to explode."

"Not about to, I have exploded."

"What is it?"

Hesitating for a second and then taking a deep breath, she blurted it out. "I'm getting married, Lily."

"Married! Oh my! Fi, that's wonderful. When?"

"As soon as we can, I'd marry him tomorrow if we could."

I was so happy for her, we hugged each other for ages and both had to dry our eyes before we could speak properly again!

"What's all the rush, you're not... you know?"

"I wouldn't care if I was, but no, it's nothing like that. It's the most wonderful thing, Lily, and I had no idea about it."

"No idea about what?"

Fi was right, she had exploded, barely able to speak as she did her best to relate the story to me, but without stopping for breath. I found I was holding my breath just listening to her.

"Johnny took me for a walk yesterday evening. We were heading towards the pub, you know, just before you get to Reg's farm. On the right there is that beautiful, thatched cottage, you know, the one that looks like Gran's."

"Yes, I know it, the one with the wonderful garden."

"That's it. Well, we stood in front of it, and Johnny asked

if I liked it. I said it was wonderful. He said he didn't think anyone was there at the moment and why didn't we have a walk around the garden. So we did, though it didn't seem right walking around someone else's garden, but it was so beautiful, and if no-one was there, maybe it was all right. Then he said, 'Oh look, the front door is open, why don't we have a look inside?' I said no, we can't do that, but he insisted. I felt really awkward, it just didn't feel right."

"Slow down, Fi, you need to stop for breath."

"I can't! You see, I followed him inside and there was a dining table with a bottle of champagne and two glasses. I just thought it was someone else's bottle, but then Johnny picked it up and opened it."

"Slow down, Fi, take a breath," but she ignored me.

"I didn't know what was going on, but he didn't stop smiling at me. I knew he was up to something, and then I noticed that the little box in the middle of the table was a jewellery box, and so I guessed what it was. Oh, Lily, it was the most romantic gesture imaginable."

She held up her hand to reveal a beautiful diamond engagement ring. Her excitement was so contagious, I could hardly speak.

"It's beautiful, Fi - it's really lovely. But why were you in a stranger's house?"

"I put the ring on and said yes a hundred times, and we kissed and kissed for ages. Then Johnny poured the two glasses and proposed a toast. You'll never guess what he said, Lily. He said, 'To us, my love, and our future together in this lovely house of ours.' 'What do you mean,' I said, '*this house of ours?*' And then he told me; he's bought it, it's ours, Lily, we're going to live in Middlebourne!"

We jumped up and down together like two hysterical schoolgirls. It must have taken fully five minutes for us to calm down. Moments of pure joy were rare during the war. Fi's moment eclipsed everything else, perhaps that's why we savoured every second.

"What about Johnny's father, the Air Commodore - is he still a problem for you?"

"No, I've listened to you and Dotty. And as Dotty would say, I don't give a shit."

We collapsed in laughter again, just as Edward appeared in the office.

"Have I missed something?" he asked.

"You have, Fi's getting married."

"Oh yes, I know about that," he said very calmly. "Congratulations, Fiona, that is wonderful news."

"What do you mean you know about it?" Fi asked.

"I knew the cottage was going to come up for sale, you see, so I informed Johnny."

"But did you know he was going to propose?"

"He did mention it to me."

"Do you mean you and Johnny planned the whole thing?"

"I certainly wouldn't go that far, but the second I found out about the cottage, I realised Johnny would want to be told. We all know your futures are bound together, so it was a bit like tipping over the first domino. I had to promise not to say a word."

Edward could contain his smile no longer, and he gave Fi an enormous hug. "I am so pleased for you both," he said. "I can't think of a more perfect couple, he's a lucky man."

"Thank you, Edward," Fiona said, "thank you for everything, it's just perfect."

Our celebration continued for an age. Fiona couldn't stop talking about their plans. It was the crest of a wave which both Edward and I wanted to roll on forever, but of course, like all waves, eventually it had to relinquish its energy to the sands of time.

"What do you think of Edward's prison haircut, Fi?"

"It's lovely, Edward. Your hair will soon grow back, but what happened to your striped uniform?"

"I had striped prison pyjamas at St Hugh's, but Lily insisted I came home in a suit."

Edward joking about his hair was a good sign. When we left Fiona in the office, our spirits could not have been higher. I knew where Edward wanted to be and could delay him no longer. As he was striding across the hall, Elizabeth appeared, coming from the Drawing Room. Having avoided her at breakfast, I was apprehensive. She wore a tight woollen jumper with trousers and looked fashionably casual although, with her hair tied back, her long pearl necklace and jewellery, 'casual' wasn't the image she presented. When her eyes met mine, I was looking for a sign of how she might receive me, but it was difficult to tell. Seemingly unable to conceal her sparkling dentition, she always appeared to be smiling. It was very disarming.

"Morning, Lily, he's a handsome brute, isn't he?"

"He soon will be, it will grow back quickly enough. What do you plan to do today?"

"I thought I would have a walk round; I need to acquaint myself with all the changes here. Where are all the staff, where is everyone?"

"They're mostly gone, I'm afraid," replied Edward. "The young women are being called to serve for the war effort. And you can't find an able-bodied man anywhere."

"Story of my life," she said, "I've been looking for an able-bodied man for years."

I smiled, and even more of her dentition smiled back. That at least was a promising start.

"You two seem to be bound at the hip, where are you off to now?"

"You will find out anyway," Edward said, "so I shall tell you, we have an involvement here with the intelligence services." He was being careful with his wording. "The military guards are on duty to ensure that no unauthorised personnel enter any of the restricted areas."

"Does that apply to me, Edward?"

"Unless you have written clearance, then yes, I'm afraid it does."

"You mean I am to be treated like a prisoner in my own home?"

"It's not like that, Elizabeth," I said. "Do you think for one moment that Edward enjoys sharing your home with a whole lot of military people? We're at war, we've been fighting for our lives here. No-one in this country is free to do what they might like to do, but we pull together. During the Blitz in London, we called it the spirit of the Blitz. Now we just call it the spirit of the nation, we're all in it together."

"I'm sorry, once again you have put me in my place, Lily."

"Oh no, please don't think that. I just didn't want you to think you're being victimised in any way, because you're not, I promise you."

"Well, can you tell me what is so important that you do here?"

"We had a critical intelligence function during the build-up towards D-Day, that's all I can tell you," said Edward. "Now we are involved with intelligence to do with those flying bombs you heard."

"If I were to mention anything to do with the work we do here outside of this building," I said, "I would end up going to prison. The same applies to any of us, you really do need to understand that, Elizabeth."

"Gosh! Does this apply to Mother as well?"

"Mother has stood shoulder to shoulder with us from day one. You haven't, Elizabeth."

"You obviously don't trust me, do you, your own family?"

"That's right, I don't!" replied Edward. "Give me reason to trust you, Elizabeth, because I want to."

Not knowing what to say, I said nothing. Elizabeth felt like a second-class citizen in her own home, I realised that, and felt sorry for her. Her ego was too big for the position in which she now found herself. We exchanged some small talk, but the substantive issue of how I might meet her halfway was not even on the agenda. There was no other option but to leave her to her own devices.

There was obviously a time when the young lady of the house would have improved herself with the aid of a book in the library, or perhaps enjoyed quiet contemplation while sewing in the Drawing Room. None of this applied to Elizabeth. Part of me wanted to support her, another part wanted to walk away. Edward was desperate to go to Hut 3, so we walked away. It was another lovely summer's day, but my mind was too full of concerns to enjoy any of it. I knew that the moment we arrived in Hut 3 our heads would be full of far more important issues, and I wanted to talk about Elizabeth.

"Can I talk to you about your sister, Edward?"

"Well, I warned you, didn't I?"

"She feels insecure in her own home, that can't be a pleasant feeling."

"What do you mean?"

"She's beautiful, isn't she, and she has that smile, it's difficult for her to look miserable. Before the war, did you ever do things with her outside of Middlebourne, perhaps with her friends?"

"No, her friends were all the same. You know me, Lily, I'm no good at these things where I have to make frivolous small talk."

"I know, I'm the same really. But Elizabeth is the opposite, isn't she? Extroverts like to be the centre of attention and that's something she can never be around you."

"What do you mean?"

"You and your sister are complete opposites. She tries to be the centre of attention by using her charm and charisma. But when she's with you, that doesn't work, does it? *You're* the centre of attention, Edward, your intellect fills the room, hers doesn't. You have the hereditary title, she doesn't. I suspect if she were a timid little woman, she would accept her role graciously, but she isn't, is she? All the airs and graces that she puts on, and all those affectations, I think it's just a misguided attempt to elevate her status. I think I might like the real Elizabeth if she was allowed to shine through."

Edward stopped walking. As we stood silently for a moment, I could see he was deep in thought.

"As you know, Lily, I've got a bit of a blind spot for this kind of thing. What you say makes sense - have I really been that blind?"

"It's just my opinion, Edward. You've always taught me to look beyond my own bias, to follow the evidence. Well, my bias tells me she is the spoiled brat that you told me she is. But if I put that to one side, I see an insecure woman, unsure about her own identity. She probably feels unjustly persecuted."

"Is this all my fault?"

"These things are never any one person's fault, there are always two sides to every story. The fact remains, however, that there's a longstanding rift between you and Elizabeth."

"You're right and if I thought I was the cause of our discord, I could never forgive myself."

"I doubt if either of you is the sole cause of anything, but you probably both need to give ground to the other."

"This is all unfamiliar territory for me, I feel rather foolish. Will I have your support, Lily?"

"You know you do. Can you remember when we arrived at the station on your way to London? I told you about all the memories that the station holds for me."

"Yes, I remember. You said they were sad memories, and I asked if you would share them with me."

"You're not unique, Edward. It's just a shadow which hangs over your family. My sadness doesn't even cast a shadow because it has never seen the sun. I haven't spoken about it to anyone, perhaps now is the time for both of us. Maybe one evening, we could both shine a light on our respective family issues."

Chapter Fourteen
The V2 Threat

Having witnessed the explosion of yet another V1, I felt a new sense of urgency, which in truth was the product of fear. Everyone was desperate for the conflict to end and the prospect that the new threat might prolong or even reverse the progress of the war was terrifying. That same sense of urgency was apparent when we entered Hut 3, the usual air of mischievous fun apparently almost absent. Needless to say, it was Patrick whose endless supply of humour lifted our mood from rock bottom.

"That's a fine haircut, Edward. You've certainly had your money's worth there!"

"It's what they call the St Hugh's special offer," replied Edward. "They throw in the stitches for free."

"Me Mammy likes a bargain. I must tell her."

The fun was short-lived as there were far more pressing matters. Woody gave us his customary report on the progress in Normandy and one of the key objectives – Caen - still hadn't been taken. Although Operation Epsom had failed, the German II SS Panzer Corps was badly depleted, and we had limited their operational effectiveness. Nevertheless, Caen remained a serious obstacle to the expansion of the bridgehead.

"What about the V1 countermeasures?" I asked. "One

exploded this morning on the outskirts of Tunbridge, we were only seconds away from it."

"There's some progress," replied Corky. "We've moved over 800 anti-aircraft batteries down to the South Downs, and there's a lot of work going on with the new radar guidance."

"We've contributed well," said Rolo. "Some of our calculations have proved decisive."

"Are we downing them?" asked Edward.

"We are, we've proved we can hit them, but many are still getting through so more guns are being deployed."

"Aircraft can shoot them down as well," said Patrick, "but the window of opportunity is small. We've got four fighters capable of catching up with them, the Spitfire, the Mustang III, Tempest V, and of course the good old Mosquito. There have been some successes but the barrage balloons appear less successful; it seems the weapon has a cable cutting leading edge to the wings."

"It seems that our countermeasures are working reasonably well," said Edward, "but I'm afraid we need to divert some of our attention to this new rocket threat."

"Are the reports about this new weapon credible?" I asked.

"Not just credible," said an irate Rolo, "MI6 have designated it the V2. It's already being tested and has been for a year or two. It's one of those ludicrous situations where we had excellent intel from the start, and it wasn't deemed credible."

"Why on earth not?"

"Intelligence didn't use its intelligence, Lily, the wrong people must have looked at it. The rocket AK described is over forty feet tall. Someone decided it was impossible for anything that size to fly powered by a rocket, because they didn't understand how any known fuel could develop sufficient power."

"It's the oxygen supply, Lily, nobody thought beyond an air-breathing engine," said Woody.

"If only we'd seen that intel, we would have worked it out. It carries its own oxygen, mixing liquid oxygen with a propellant, we think it's probably ethanol."

"Edward tells me it flies on a ballistic trajectory. So how high does it go before it comes back down to the ground?"

"We don't know yet, but we've done our own calculations, based upon liquid oxygen and ethanol, and its likely fuel capacity. The numbers are incredible. We think this thing can reach a speed of over 3000 mph - which means it could reach the edge of space."

"What - did you say 3000 mph?"

"That's right," replied Woody, "we wouldn't even know it was coming, much less defend against it."

There was total silence in the room. I knew how clever they were, I didn't doubt their estimates for a moment. The consequences were likely to be catastrophic if this new weapon should rain down upon us in any number. Maggie came into the hut at that point and picked up on the conversation.

"How much of this is speculation, and how much do we actually know?"

"We have some aerial recon, but nearly all of our solid intel comes from AK," Rolo said. "Most of the test flights are being done near Blizna in central Poland. When the rockets fall back to the ground, AK collects engine parts before the Germans can. Polish scientists have been studying them. We have solid evidence. This thing is well through its testing phase."

"There are many imponderables," said Edward. "How many are they capable of producing, how reliable will it be, and how accurate will it be? If the answers to those questions are all negative for us, then the outcome of the war becomes very uncertain. The more obvious questions are how long before the Allies overrun the launch and manufacturing sites, and in the meantime, how do we destroy them on the ground?"

"We think it's likely to have a considerable range, and they might be able to launch them from deep within Germany," said Corky.

"So the invasion force will need to advance over the Rhine before we get anywhere near them?" asked Maggie.

"That's right," replied Woody, "and we still haven't extended the beachhead beyond Caen yet."

"We have three courses of action," said Edward. "Reconnaissance plus intelligence, followed by bombing, but our success will be limited because the manufacturing sites are underground. Which leaves sabotage as probably our best option."

"But how do we get into heavily guarded underground sites?" asked Rolo.

"We may not, so we need to look at this problem from the German rocket engineer's perspective. What renders this weapon so technically advanced is its rocket engine and guidance system. We don't know precisely how it works, but we understand the principles, and therefore we can work out some technical issues which the German engineers and scientists had to overcome."

"I don't understand, Edward," I said. "How will trying to understand how they build it help us to destroy it?"

"Because, my dear Lily, the Germans have achieved a scientific breakthrough. They have harnessed a completely new technology, and to do that you need new materials, and new manufacturing techniques. For example, this new rocket engine requires a novel approach to fuel delivery. It's all about fluid dynamics. We don't have to know precisely how they have achieved it, but what would be very useful to know is what are the key components that have made such a technical advance possible."

"Brilliant, Edward," said Patrick. "A classic example of lateral thinking."

"What are you people talking about?" I asked.

"What Edward is saying, Lily, is that this kind of technical advance is being supported by specialist manufacturers. They must have components that are being manufactured outside of the underground sites."

"We can work through the basic design issues," said

Rolo, "and where we hit obstacles, that will be where *they* hit obstacles."

"That's right, Rolo," replied Edward, "and I have one good example. What is the principal problem of handling liquid oxygen, which is then multiplied a hundredfold if you have to pump it through a complicated system of pipes and valves?"

They all smiled in unison. "Corrosion," exclaimed Corky, looking as if he had just found the meaning of life.

"Will someone explain it to me?" I queried.

"Liquid oxygen is highly corrosive, and it's got a boiling point of -293 degrees F. It will, for example, destroy a conventional rubber seal." said a jubilant looking Edward. "The only material that might do the job is synthetic rubber, and I can only think of neoprene, so the seals must be manufactured to order by a specialist manufacturer. Find that factory, or find how they transport them, and we can cut off the supply."

The boys were ecstatic, they thrived on creative thinking, and here they were once again in their element. They threw ideas around like so much confetti. I didn't understand the science, but I understood the sheer brilliant simplicity of Edward's idea. The possibility that a shortage of something as small as a rubber seal might halt the production of this new weapon was a revelation. Rolo assured me they would find many more such items which would be vital for German production. This was now a new threat to deal with as well as the V1. The threat was entirely intelligence-driven; we hadn't seen one let alone suffered its consequences, but the V2 was soon to become a terrifying reality.

I left Hut 3 feeling frightened of the unknown but positively buoyed by their enthusiasm. My mind was racing in all directions. If we were going to pursue Edward's supply chain idea, then intelligence from all the agencies would be required. I would again need all my connections. As I walked towards the Manor, I saw Elizabeth strolling around the grounds where the ornamental garden used to be. She seemed a lonely figure, ponderously walking by herself. She caught my eye, and we waved to each other. It was difficult to be sure if she was pleased to see me or not, her perpetual smile was always so deceptive.

Our ears had become attuned to the sound of an approaching V1, and as I was walking towards her, I could just hear the distinctive sound in the distance. Like so many of them, it was going to fly directly overhead. Elizabeth didn't know what to do, her legs appeared to want to do one thing, while her body did another. I felt really sorry for her and hurried along the path.

"Don't worry, Elizabeth, it should pass over us."

"But what if it doesn't?"

"Just do what I do, lie flat on your face and hope for the best."

She was frightened, just as I was, but her reaction when the danger had passed was to be aggressive towards me.

"I won't delay you, Mrs Heywood. I'm sure you should be working somewhere."

"Please don't be like that, Elizabeth, and I would much prefer it if you called me Lily."

"I thought you should be on duty or something."

"Being terrified by something which may kill you is a very sensible response, Elizabeth. We are all just as terrified as you are, but we've had more time to get used to it. And yes, I am on duty. This is one of the things I do, I'm making sure that you're all right."

"I don't need a chaperone. I live here, for goodness' sake!"

"Have you met Fiona Robinson yet? She's my deputy, and one of my best friends."

"No, I can't say that I have, but then it is not my place to be introducing myself to members of staff."

"Why don't you come to my office and we can have a cup of tea together."

"Will you have me visit the kitchen next?"

"A cup of tea, Elizabeth, where's the harm?"

"Very well, lead the way."

We walked over to the Grand Entrance without saying very much, and I could see Corporal Harris standing to attention at the door. As we approached, his usual smile spread from ear to ear.

"Good afternoon, Corporal Harris."

"Good afternoon, Mrs Heywood. You must forgive me, I'm not feeling myself. Am I seeing double, or are these two beautiful women I see before me?"

"It's not your eyes, Corporal, which are in doubt, it's your judgement. This is His Lordship's sister, Lady Elizabeth."

"Oh, my goodness, forgive me, My Lady. I do apologise. Oh dear, I've done it again, haven't I?"

"Yes, you have, Corporal, and I'm really enjoying it."

Elizabeth didn't know how to react, so we left Harris to cool his cheeks while we went on our way. Florence was in the Great Hall and came over to me the moment she saw us.

"I removed that stain from your cocktail dress, Mrs Heywood, you can't see a thing. You won't want it tonight, will you?"

"No, that's fine. I'm very grateful, red wine can be a real problem."

"I'll bring it back this evening if it's properly dry."

"Thank you, Florence. Do you think you could fetch us some cups of tea in the office, or send Caitlin if you're busy?"

"Cook has just made some scones, she thought you might like some."

"Thank her for me, Florence, that's so kind."

I wasn't sure if Elizabeth was bemused or annoyed, she didn't say a word until we approached the office.

"You behave as if you are the Lady of the Manor, Lily, and the staff treat you as such. I know my brother trusts you, but let's be clear, I don't."

"I know you don't, and I understand why. I promise you,

Elizabeth, your fear is misplaced. We all need someone in our lives that we can trust, someone who is always there for us. My friend Fiona is one such person for me, and you'll come to find that I'm that person for you. As I've said to you, there's nothing on this earth that I wouldn't do for Edward, or for your mother, and my loyalty to this family extends to you, exactly the same. I don't expect you to believe it right now, but I will never let down any member of this household."

"That's quite a declaration, Lily."

"I don't make such a declaration lightly."

I opened the office door and noticed her reaction when she saw the magnificent room. She stood for a moment looking around; I realised that everything I was doing was adding to her mistrust.

"Lady Elizabeth, may I introduce you to Fiona Robinson."

Fi was still floating on a cloud somewhere way up in the stratosphere. Her eyes sparkled, she seemed to radiate happiness. Normally a stickler for protocol, I soon realised that protocol hadn't reached the height of the stratosphere.

"It's lovely to meet you, Elizabeth, please call me Fiona."

Elizabeth shook Fi's hand with an expression of resignation, which gradually subsided. Accents are important for some people, especially people like Elizabeth. Fiona's cut-glass accent was clearly met with approval. Trying to make conversation, I mentioned that Fi had just become engaged, whereupon Fiona could not be restrained from telling her romantic story again. Elizabeth smiled, how could she not!

"But you can't just walk into someone's home," she said.

"I know, it all felt so strange," Fi replied.

The story continued and Fi became as animated as she had been before.

"Oh my goodness, he set it all up?"

"He did, I only realised when he opened the champagne."

"Let me see the ring," Elizabeth said.

Fi raised her hand, and we all gazed at the beautiful ring as if a magic spell had entranced us, drawing us closer to it.

"I have never heard such a wonderfully romantic story. Who is this adorable man?"

"That's the best part, Elizabeth, he really is absolutely adorable."

"I can vouch for that," I said. "Johnny's gorgeous."

Elizabeth's wide smile filled the office. I used to joke about her teeth, but that was the first occasion when her smile really touched me. She had those little vertical creases at the sides of her mouth, and her brown eyes lifted at the corners. There was an innocent joy about her that seemed to coexist with the more troubled woman I had been introduced to. Fiona's happiness was so contagious, it was impossible not to be swept along by it.

When Florence came in with our tea, she couldn't avoid becoming swept along as well, just as we were. Fi showed her the ring, and they hugged each other. Florence left us with our tea and scones, and the three of us sat talking. Initially, Elizabeth asked more about Fiona and Johnny, and there was nothing Fi enjoyed more than talking about Johnny. When asked exactly what the Wing Commander did, Fiona was naturally hesitant. I thought about it and made a quick decision.

"The problem is, Elizabeth, Fiona is not allowed to tell you anything, neither am I. It's awkward, isn't it; it's not that we don't want to, but you have to be a member of the club, you see."

"What club are you talking about?"

"It's called the Official Secrets Act," I said, smiling, and appearing to make fun of it.

"Are you serious?"

"When I applied for a job here, Edward sat me down and explained in no uncertain terms exactly what my signature on that document would entail. It's a legal commitment, effectively a binding oath to King and country, that I will not divulge any information that my position grants me. This is deadly serious, Elizabeth. I would die before I disclosed anything of what we do here."

"I see," she replied. "You do take it seriously, don't you?"

"We do," replied Fiona.

"Should I sign it then?"

"I think you should, Elizabeth. We've all signed it, including Edward," I replied, as I removed a new copy from my desk drawer. "I want you to read it and understand what it means. You need to understand that the penalty for disclosing information is automatic imprisonment. And as Edward gleefully pointed out to me, if they consider your disclosure treasonous, the penalty is death!"

I hoped I was doing the right thing. I didn't intend to make Elizabeth a party to everything we did, far from it, but I wanted to draw her a little closer to us. She read it, and I was sure she had taken it seriously. She signed it thoughtfully, and when she looked up at us, I knew she had taken a step towards me.

"So then, now that I'm a member of the club, can you tell me what Johnny does that is so secret?"

Fiona looked at me with a smile. "He's our reconnaissance pilot. During the build-up to D-Day, he flew hundreds of sorties over France and took thousands of photographs."

"He then takes the film from the aeroplane," I said, "brings it here, where we have our own film processing lab, and our own photo reconnaissance analyst."

"So you are all a part of the government intelligence service?"

"We are, what we do here is really important - our decisions affect lives."

"I've made a bit of a fool of myself, haven't I, Lily? I'm telling you I don't trust you, and yet actually, it was always you who couldn't trust me."

"Why would you not trust Lily?" asked a puzzled Fiona.

"Oh, best if I don't say."

"Elizabeth thinks I've weaselled my way into Edward's family for my own advantage," I said.

Fiona laughed. "Oh, Elizabeth, you couldn't be more wrong!"

We sat looking at each other, Elizabeth wasn't sure if she was deflated or exhilarated. She was certainly confused. Here she was enjoying the company of not just one member of staff, but two! The question of trust was glossed over, and for what remained of the day we just chatted as three ordinary women.

"What we need is a night at the pub to celebrate my engagement."

"Great idea, Fi, when will Dotty come back from her training course?"

"End of the week, let's do it then."

"Who is Dotty?" asked Elizabeth.

"Why don't you come with us and meet her?" I suggested.

"I could, couldn't I?"

"Of course you can, but we'll have to warn you about Dotty."

"Why - is she dangerous?"

"Actually, Dotty is deadly dangerous," I laughed. "The thing is, I doubt you've ever met anyone like her. She's another East Ender, like me, but even more so. Dotty just says what she thinks, and often she doesn't think but still says it! There's this thing she does, where she can walk in through the door and instantly turn a light on in your life. Dotty's our best friend, we love her dearly."

"Wow, Dotty's a lucky lady having friends who describe her in such terms. I think I need to meet her."

"Good, it's settled then, but remember we warned you about her."

Chapter Fifteen
Gran's Bad Turn

July the 8th 1944 was a particularly beautiful day. The sun shone through a clear sky, and the still air was heavy with scents of the summer countryside. When a ghastly life-changing event thrusts itself upon you, the weather accompanying it is what you tend to remember. Fiona and I were busy working in the office when the internal phone rang. It was Private Thomson at the barrier.

"Yes, what is it, Private?"

"I've got a big bloke at the barrier, Mrs Heywood. He says he's your cousin, I didn't know whether to let him in or not, he says it's urgent."

My heart immediately leapt into my throat. Cousin Jim would only come to the Manor to ask for me if it was really urgent. Something must have happened to Gran, or Mavis. Fiona looked at me in horror, we were both thinking the same thing.

"I'll go immediately, Fi, you'd better stay here by the phone. Send Florence after me, I'll ask her to come back and report to you."

I literally ran as fast as I could all the way. Jim's broad frame quickly came into view standing there by the sentry box. I couldn't describe the expression on his face, but it confirmed my worst fear.

"What's happened, Jim?"

"It's Gran, Lily, she's had a bad turn, the doctor is with her."

"Oh, no! Please tell me she's not dead, Jim."

"She isn't, she's hanging on, but it looks serious."

My grandmother was the centre of my world, the prospect that she might not be there was something so unbearable that I had never been able to even consider it. Jim and I ran some of the way, and when I could run no more, I walked as fast as I could. It was only mid-morning but the temperature was steadily increasing as the sun rose higher in the sky. Beads of sweat ran down my face and dripped from my nose, my clothes clung to my body. We hardly spoke to each other, both breathing too heavily to form the words.

When we arrived, I burst through the front door without stopping and rushed up the stairs towards Gran's bedroom. The local doctor stood beside the bed holding her by the wrist. Mavis was sitting close by on one of Gran's uncomfortable splat-back chairs. Gran was so horribly pale and motionless that I immediately thought I'd lost her. The prospect was so terrible that something within me simply said, 'No, this is not happening, not to my Gran'. I then found myself speaking calmly to the doctor.

"How is she, Doctor Harrington, will she be all right?"

"I'm fairly certain she has experienced an apoplectic seizure. The next few hours are critical."

"How serious is it?"

"It's too soon to be sure, but your grandmother has not completely lost consciousness, her pupils react, and her heartbeat remains strong. I think there is cause for optimism."

The part of me which asked the question re-joined the part which was standing in terror. My legs buckled and I slumped onto the side of the bed. Her eyes opened momentarily, obviously recognising me but unable to respond. It was all horribly reminiscent of when Edward was lying in a coma, so

I instinctively kept talking to her. Mavis and the doctor stood up and left me alone, I think Mavis welcomed the chance of a break. She appeared completely drained, as if she'd shared the last vestige of her life force with her sister. Fiona must have sent Florence after me immediately, because she was less than half an hour behind me. The first I knew was that she was standing next to me.

"How is she, Mrs Heywood, is she going to be all right?"

"That's exactly what I asked the doctor, Florence, but we don't really know."

"He's sitting in the kitchen with your family, shall I make you all a cup of tea?"

"That's what we do in times of crisis, isn't it, we make tea. Please tell him I'll be down in a minute and I need to talk to him."

I raised my hand in a gesture of appreciation. "Thank you for coming so quickly. As soon as we have something to report I'd like you to go back and tell Fiona, she'll be worried sick."

"I'm just pleased I can help," she replied, holding my hand.

As soon as she went downstairs, I continued with my one-sided conversation, as if it were a perfectly normal situation. Every so often, Gran would open her eyes. She couldn't respond, but there was a certain look in her eyes that I recognised from my childhood. It was my memory of her welcoming smile when I arrived at the station. Had she been able, I knew she wanted to smile at me. I squeezed her hand and she closed her fingers around mine in response. In another situation, it would have been no more than an inconsequential movement. I knew my grandmother so well, her hand holding mine was not inconsequential, it was a defiant gesture of determination. She was telling me in no uncertain terms, *I'm not giving in, I'm not leaving you, Lily.*

"I know, Gran," I said, as if I had heard the words she intended. "You're going to be fine. I promise."

Mavis came back into the bedroom, carrying two cups of tea and looking desperately pale and distraught.

"How does she seem to you, Lily?"

"She's fighting, Mavis, there's no way your sister will give in, we aren't going to lose her."

"Oh my goodness, I hope so."

I had long since stopped calling her Aunty Mavis - we saw each other so often, she was just Gran's sister and closest friend, Mavis. Aunty Mildred remained 'Aunty,' probably because I didn't see her so often, but all three sisters were inseparable. If there was one thing that Gran did not lack, it was a family who loved her. I reassured Mavis that Gran was indomitable, I knew she'd find a way back.

"When did this happen, Mavis?"

"Must have been during the night, I found her like this first thing this morning."

"It must have been a horrible shock for you but thank heavens you were there."

"We never talk about it, but I suppose we look out for each other more these days."

"We have to let Aunty Mildred know. Jim should go over to her."

"He's already gone, Lily, I didn't have to ask him."

"I need to talk to the doctor, Mavis. Could you stay and have a chat with Gran, I'll be back in a minute."

Florence was obviously anticipating a long day. She made the tea using Gran's big, enamelled tea pot, the one with the extra handle on the front. The doctor seemed content enough sitting at the kitchen table. By the look of the crumbs on his empty plate, Florence had found the cake tin. There was another empty cup and more crumbs spread on the table.

"I see my cousin Jim enjoyed his cake, when did he leave?"

"He's only just gone, something about his Aunty," Florence replied.

"Thank you for coming, Doctor Harrington, what can you tell me about Gran's condition?"

Harrington was a kindly man, and although not far short

of retirement he was an enthusiastic, caring doctor. Whenever I had seen him, he always appeared to have been wearing the same old tweed jacket with leather patches on the elbows. The ink marks around the breast pocket were testament to the number of times his trusted fountain pen had leaked. His trademark bedside manner was facilitated by his gold-rimmed reading glasses. He would sit with a serious face, the glasses positioned low down on his nose. While he was listening to your problems, he would peer over them with his head bowed. When he finished making notes or had something to say, he would raise his head, lift off the glasses, simultaneously transforming his serious face into an altogether kinder smile.

"There's every reason to think she will survive this, Mrs Heywood," he said, taking off the glasses. "I'm afraid there will be some physical impairment, but the encouraging thing is that she is not completely unconscious and she has some movement."

"Is that good then, Doctor?"

"At this early stage, yes, it is. There are different kinds of apoplectic seizure, some more serious than others. In elderly arteriosclerotic patients, cerebral thrombosis is the most likely cause. The alternative is a cerebral haemorrhage, but I would not associate that with your Grandmother's degree of consciousness."

"Can you find out in any way?"

"Yes, if she goes to hospital they can test for blood in the cerebrospinal fluid."

"Would you recommend that?"

"Frankly, Mrs Heywood, no, I wouldn't. Moving her has its own risks and I'm reasonably confident this is typical thrombosis. How old is she now?"

"Gran is ninety-two years old, but you wouldn't have thought so."

"That's a wonderful age. She's a fine lady, your grandmother. I'm old enough to remember her singing at those open-air choral society concerts. To this day, I've never heard a voice like it, I'll never forget it."

"Yes, she was known as the voice of Middlebourne."

"Her singing days may be over but there's every reason to hope she will recover from this."

"You mean I can breathe again?"

"She's not out of danger yet, but yes I think you can take a breath, Mrs Heywood."

"Will she have any disabilities, as a result?"

"Almost certainly, I'm afraid. We shall not know for some time exactly what."

"If she stays here, what care will she need?"

"I can arrange for a nurse to attend her once or twice a day. She will need her bodily functions taken care of, and her progress monitored. I would also suggest a little later, a physiotherapist."

"Will you arrange that? I'll cover all the costs."

"Good, so you just keep on breathing, Mrs Heywood! Don't hesitate to call me back if there is any deterioration. I'll call in every day on my rounds to see her."

His air of confidence was really encouraging and he left with his usual reassuring smile, leaving me to ponder the future. I didn't know what Gran's outcome would be, but I knew she would need care of one kind or another. My mind was racing in all directions. I knew Mavis would offer to do everything for her, as would Mildred, but they were nearly as old as their sister. I sat looking at Florence washing the tea cups.

"I'm going to make a suggestion, Florence. Don't say anything until you've thought about it. You know Fiona is getting married, she'll want to move into their new home immediately. Dotty's away a lot of the time, and my grand-mother is going to need someone to look after her. You can't stay at Middlebourne Manor much longer, so we have to find somewhere for you."

Florence didn't allow me to finish. "I know what you're going to say, Mrs Heywood, and the answer is yes. And it's not just because I need somewhere to live. This is something I can do in return for all the kindness you've shown me. But what about when the baby comes?"

"I'm sure we can work it out between us, but are you sure, Florence? I haven't thought this through at all, and neither have you. I can't afford to pay you very much."

"*Pay me*! I'm not thinking about being paid to take care of your grandmother. You're offering me a roof over my head when everyone else would see me out on the streets."

"We trust each other, don't we, Florence?"

"Of course, you're the only person I've ever trusted."

"Okay then, I need to talk to my aunties, and to my Gran when she's able, and I need to talk to Dotty and Fiona. If everyone agrees, I think we can make this work. I'll pay you what I can, this has to be a proper arrangement."

I'm not sure that Florence had ever been given a break in her life. Her family background sounded as though it was a life of servitude. She had virtually no education, and with nothing to give her confidence to face the world, she had no expectations. Worst of all, it was clear to me that she was deprived of love and attention as a child. I speculated that her disastrous relationship with Harry had been motivated by that same need. She appeared overwhelmed, looking down at the floor.

"I'm so grateful, Mrs Heywood. I'll never let you down, I promise."

"I know you won't. Do you think I would trust the care of my Gran to just anyone?"

Seeing her standing there in Gran's kitchen, it did seem like the obvious solution to everyone's problems. I hoped I wasn't making a mistake - it had been such a hasty decision. There was no more time to discuss it because Fiona would be desperate for news and I had to ask Florence to go back to the Manor. I also needed her to ask Fiona to send a telegram to my parents. While I didn't want them unduly alarmed, I needed them to telephone me as soon as possible. It proved to be a very long day. I sat with Gran until the early evening when Fiona came home. When Fi was ready to discuss it, I mentioned Florence to her, and she was in complete agreement with the idea.

"Her situation will inevitably be met with moral outrage. There's no question that she has to leave Middlebourne Manor," I said. "Young women in service are quite literally thrown onto the streets, even nowadays. The situation has hardly progressed since the 19th century. 'Fallen women' in those days had few options, the principal one being the workhouse, where infant mortality was often as high as 90%."

"But that's dreadful, surely there was some alternative?"

"Not for girls without means. The only way they could stay in employment was to place the child into paid fosterage. They used to call them 'baby farms'."

"That sounds a much better idea."

"Not at all! I suppose some might have been loving carers, but history has a different view of them now. There was an old saying at the time which said, 'Remember not to plant 'em too deep, or they won't grow.' Either by neglect or design, most of the babies were planted in the ground."

"Oh, my goodness, Lily, that's awful. So what would Florence's options be today if you weren't taking her in?"

"I suppose one of the mother and baby homes that have come to replace the Magdalene Homes. Quite honestly, what Florence needs to do is to find some kind man who'll marry her and take on the baby. That's the only way she'll find respectability. It's so unfair isn't it, she's labelled an outcast, and the father remains totally unaffected."

"It's monstrous, and the stigma attaches itself to the child as well, doesn't it."

"It's really not right, but I'll make sure it doesn't happen to Florence. I don't know why I said I would take care of her, but I did, and so I will."

"Does she realise how fortunate she is?"

"Yes she does, but it works both ways, Fi. I have a friend for life in Florence, so I'm fortunate as well."

"I hope she'll also include me in that."

"Well, you're going to be living with her for a few weeks, so I hope so!"

"It'll be fine, I'm perfectly happy with that. She should be okay in the loft room during the summer, and I hope to be gone soon after that."

"Any news about that?"

"The banns have to be announced in church three Sundays before the wedding, and we did that last Sunday."

"That's awfully quick, can you organise it as fast as that?"

"Between you and me, Lily, we're desperate to move in together. We keep sneaking into the cottage pretending to be moving items of furniture. Besides, we only want a handful of guests. We couldn't have a big wedding now anyway, during the war."

"It's so exciting isn't it? You and Johnny living here in Middlebourne, what could be more perfect?"

"An end to the war would be good, and one way or another, I want Gran to be there."

"The doctor has given me confidence that she is going to recover. I know my Gran, she'll be there, I can promise you."

Chapter Sixteen
Collective Genius

Gran's predicament created a certain amount of urgency as far as Florence was concerned. I obviously had to inform the household. Telling Jennings would have felt strangely awkward, so I decided to tell Mrs Morgan by herself. I found her in the kitchen, with the two new girls and Jennings was nowhere to be seen.

"Can I have a quiet word, Mrs Morgan, in your office."

She looked at me apprehensively, her eyebrows came together and her forehead furrowed.

"Nothing serious, I hope, Mrs Heywood?" she asked as we went into her office.

"Well, it is really, it's about Florence. I'm sorry to say she is leaving us."

"I wondered when she would, it's not something you can go on hiding, is it?"

"You knew?"

"Of course, there's something about a woman who's expecting. We just know, don't we?"

"And there was me thinking it would be a shock!"

"Oh, don't think I'm not shocked. Now that it's out in the open, I'll give her a piece of my mind, silly girl. She needs to get married double quick before the whole village finds out."

"That's the problem, you see, she's on her own."

"Oh, no. Don't tell me the little tyke has run off."

"He has, and the boy's parents want nothing to do with it."

"This is worse than I thought. What on earth is going to happen to the poor girl?"

"I'm going to take her in. My grandmother needs care, so we can help each other."

Mrs Morgan stood smiling without a word passing her lips, it was some time before she ventured to speak.

"The fact that I'm not surprised speaks volumes doesn't it, Mrs Heywood, you really are the kindest person."

"Oh, come on, Elsie, you'd do the same thing."

"I'm not in a position to, though, am I? It's an enormous commitment, but I must admit I have a soft spot for Florence, she's a lovely girl. If there's anything I can do to help either of you, you know you only have to ask."

"That's kind, I might need to take you up on that. What about Mr Jennings? I can't face telling him."

"Don't you worry about Mr Jennings. I'll take care of him."

My meeting with Mrs Morgan went much better than I had imagined. Preconceived ideas about people can so often lead you astray. My dad phoned the office the next morning as soon as they received the telegram. I was able to tell them that Gran had a good night, and every hour that passed gave us reason to expect a recovery. Mum must have been beside herself, so I gave them as much assurance as I could. They would be down as soon as they were able to, they would stay with Mavis.

Despite everything that had happened with Gran, and by implication with Florence, I knew I needed to return to my duties. The war would not wait a day, not even for Gran. The walk over to Hut 3 served to clear my mind. Throughout the war, people struggled with sickness and bereavement, not to mention homelessness, and all the while everyone found the inner strength to continue. I knew I had to do the same.

As I approached Hut 3, it appeared strangely inactive. The boys were each sitting at their tables pawing studiously over documents, making notes. Edward was sitting at his usual table almost hidden from view, such was his pile of papers. I stood at one of the windows and made a funny face, as I often did. No-one noticed me, so I quietly stepped inside.

"You lot have just missed one of my best funny faces, what are you all so occupied with?"

Edward looked up; his eyes looked weary with concentration. The instant he saw me his tired expression was transformed as if he'd been wearing a masquerade mask. A delightful smile greeted me.

"Any progress on those V2 components?" I asked.

"There is," replied Edward, "but it's proving incredibly difficult to find the likely German manufacturers."

"What components are you concentrating on?"

Rolo looked up, squinting to re-focus his eyes, the red rims magnified through the thick lenses of his glasses. When he was thinking, he always had the habit of half closing one eye while staring towards the ceiling. I couldn't imagine how his prodigious mental processes worked, but when he was asked a question you knew a comprehensive answer would soon follow.

"We're concentrating on the V2 engine at the moment," he said in a matter-of-fact way. "The physics is fairly predictable."

"You mean you know how it works?"

"Not exactly," replied Corky, "but we know what's required to make it work."

"Come on, Rolo, I can see you're about to tell me."

"We've received far more intelligence from AK than we ever dared to hope for. They have engine parts and they have scientists studying the parts they collect. With everything they've told us about the size and weight of the rocket, we calculate that the engine must generate about 56,000 lbs of thrust. In order to achieve that, using an alcohol fuel and liquid oxygen as oxidizer, it's straightforward to calculate how much fuel it would need to combust every second in order to maintain that degree of thrust."

"Yes it sounds very straightforward, Rollo," I said with a mystified smile. "Is the amount of fuel a crucial factor?"

"It most certainly is, Lily," replied Woody, loosening his bow tie. "When Rolo calculated that figure, the technical issues the Germans had to overcome became perfectly clear."

They sat looking at me with an air of collective pride. Absolutely nothing gave the boys more satisfaction than the resolution of a mentally challenging task. I was even starting to think like them and reasoned that if their pride was commensurate with their mental achievement, then they must have achieved something very significant.

"Well, who's going to tell me?"

"Rolo, will you do the honours?" said Edward, wearing a smug expression as he joined the others.

"In order to achieve a combustion capable of producing that amount of thrust you would need to burn the fuel at the rate of 33 gallons per second! And all of it is forced at extremely high pressure through some kind of fuel injection system, in other words 33 gallons per second being forced through a series of nozzles."

"When you say forced, Rolo, you mean that it's pumped at massively high pressure and volume?"

"Your time spent in this hut hasn't been entirely wasted, has it, Lily!" said a beaming Patrick. "It's all left me Mammy far behind, but I can certainly see you're keeping up."

"I'm trying to, Patrick, but I won't even ask how you can work all of this out."

"Oh, there's more, Lily," said a jubilant looking Rolo. "Once you know how much fuel is required to produce the thrust, you can calculate the temperature generated in the combustion chamber. Would you believe it's between 4000- and 5000-degrees Fahrenheit?"

"Hot enough to melt steel!" added Corky.

"Right - I get the picture, incredibly difficult technical challenges, so I'm thinking from the look on your faces you've narrowed down some essential components."

"Come on now, Lily," replied Patrick, "you're not keeping up, even me Mammy can work this one out."

I thrived in their company. I couldn't hope to keep up with them, but like a one-legged woman entering a football team, I wasn't afraid to try.

"I'm guessing the critical factor is how to deliver such vast quantities of fuel, and oxidizer. They must have developed an amazing high-volume pump."

"That took you just long enough, Lily," said a mischievous Patrick, "any sooner and you might have sounded like a smart ass."

"Oh, bugger off, Patrick, what chance have I got of sounding smart amongst you lot?"

They may have been weary but their combined wit and enthusiasm was inexhaustible. The conclusion of their collective genius was that the Germans had achieved significant technical breakthroughs. The pumps delivering the fuel to the V2 rocket engine were like nothing we had ever seen before. They had to cope with extremes of temperature, minus 297 degrees Fahrenheit, in the case of the liquid oxygen pump. And they had to deliver vast volumes of fuel at high pressure.

They had also decided the combustion chamber must be cooled in some way, but even so it required special metal alloys. It was agreed that not all of this development could be going on beneath the Harz mountains. Specialist developers and manufacturers must be involved. Our job was to pinpoint those suppliers, with a view towards sabotage. And to think it all started with Edward's idea about a rubber seal!

-o0o-

I didn't know if it was out of respect for me or for Florence, but when she left her job at the end of that week, she didn't have to leave under a cloud. It was not at all uncommon for a servant girl to leave her employer with her head bowed in shame. Florence was at least spared that ignominy, all of the staff wished her well. I plucked up the courage to speak to Jennings about it after the event.

"I'm sure you must strongly disapprove, Mr Jennings."

"It is an appalling and degrading situation that the girl finds herself in. Without you as her benefactor, she would be destitute."

"I hope you don't think poorly of me, Mr Jennings."

"You must tread carefully, Mrs Heywood. Stigma has a way of attaching itself to anyone it touches. It is imperative that His Lordship does not become embroiled with this debacle."

"Why should His Lordship become involved?"

"I fear you have allowed your heart to rule your head, Mrs Heywood. You need to view this from a wider perspective, in fact you need to view it from the village gossip's point of view."

"I don't understand, Mr Jennings, what are you driving at?"

"Pregnant servant girl leaves His Lordship's employ in disgrace and is housed locally by His Lordship's Chief of Staff. There will be those for whom your action implies a certain connection to His Lordship."

"Oh, heavens! I didn't think of that, Charles. What can I do?"

"Gossip is like a stray dog, Lily, you never know if it will be friendly, or if it will bite you."

By the time Florence moved in at the cottage, it was clear that Gran was starting to make a recovery. It had been days of going into work really early, and then spending as much of the afternoon with her as I could manage. Progress was measured in baby steps. Both her sisters, plus Mum and I encouraged her every inch of the way. Any progress was greeted with joy, but with mixed emotions. The reality was that seeing my grandmother robbed of her dignity and self-reliance completely broke my heart.

It was typical of Gran that when I was at my lowest, it was she who had the strength to lift me up. It was the first occasion when she was able to combine a few words, simply knowing that she was going to be able to communicate again overwhelmed me. I held my breath and bit my lip, trying so hard to stay in control, but I couldn't suppress my reaction. When she smiled at me, she inadvertently opened the floodgates.

"Oh, Gran, you really frightened me, I thought I'd lost you."

What followed was a laboured and at times excruciating conversation. Eventually I understood well enough what she was trying to say, and I've never forgotten it. She said I would never lose her, I only had to look in the mirror and she'd be looking back at me. And when I sang, she would always be there singing with me, because she lived on in my voice. It was one of those treasured moments which never leaves you.

When I got back to my room at the Manor later that day, the first thing I did was to look at my photograph of her. Taken when she was in her early thirties, it's one of the earliest photographs ever taken. The scratched and faded image was recorded as a part of the history of the choral society. When I looked at that image, it sent a strange chill running down my spine, because I was looking at an image of myself from the past. As I got ready for bed I went through my singing practice routine which I often did to relieve the pressures of the day. I sang in half voice, and Gran was right that day, she's always a part of me.

Chapter Seventeen
Dark Secrets

Perhaps it was the long hours I was working, or perhaps it was just the emotional strain. Whatever it was, when I joined Edward in the Drawing Room that evening, I was exhausted. I imagine I entered the room as a shipwrecked sailor might enter a lifeboat, thanking God for my salvation! To be with Edward in that magnificent oasis of calm was precisely what I needed. He jumped to his feet the moment I entered.

"Good evening, Lily, how is she today?"

"There's progress again, it's only small steps, but it's an improvement. She managed to string a few words together today."

"Oh, that's good news, Lily. May I say you look completely exhausted. Sit down and do that thing with your toes."

I managed a weak smile and slumped into the Chesterfield armchair, doing exactly what Edward suggested. I kicked off my shoes and spread my toes into the pile of the carpet, allowing my arms to drop over the sides of the armchair. He smiled, as he always did. Jennings almost followed me into the room, standing next to me in all his usual calm sartorial splendour, hands hidden from view, shoulders back, and his chin raised.

"What can I get for you, Mrs Heywood?"

"You already have, Mr Jennings. Do you realise whenever you enter the Drawing Room, if I'm slumped in this chair, I immediately sit up straight?"

"I'm not sure that is one of my duties, Mrs Heywood."

"Oh, but it is, Mr Jennings. You bring order into my life."

"Perhaps I might also bring a glass of the 25-year-old Bowmore?"

"And with order came forth comfort."

"I assume that means yes, Mrs Heywood."

"Yes, please."

We smiled at each other. It seems almost inconceivable to me now that Jennings and I were once at loggerheads. I was never quite sure what our relationship was. Perhaps I viewed him as a kind of father figure, and maybe he regarded me in a daughterly way. But I suspect there was more to it than that. We were both East Enders who had left our respective pasts behind. The thing is, East Enders can never actually leave that heritage behind. It wasn't mentioned but I think that had a lot to do with the warmth we shared. He left amid all the splendour with which he had entered.

"You and Jennings have some kind of an understanding, don't you?"

"I suppose we do, something shared is something understood."

I doubted that Edward understood, but he did a good job of pretending to. His hair was growing back nicely by then. He still looked a little like a convict, but a more handsome and beautifully dressed convict you would never see. Our relationship was difficult to describe at that stage, it was entirely dictated by Edward. I regarded it as a strange courtship ritual. He was like a male spider tentatively reaching out to his Black Widow temptress, except it wasn't me that he was afraid of. It tortured us both, my anguish was as much for him as it was for me.

As always during our evenings, there was so much to talk

about, so much to distract us from ourselves. We needed to keep each other informed, and our evenings together were our time for doing that. He told me about the progress they were making with the 'V' threat and brought me up to date on the carnage from the never-ending rain of V1's falling on our capital city and surrounding area.

There was always that sobering moment each evening when we reflected upon casualties. It was how we assessed the course of the war, like a page from an accounting ledger, except the currency of war is dead and displaced people. If 'only' 320 Allied troops were killed in Normandy that day, that was positive news, because yesterday it was 900. If the rain of V1's killed 30 people today, that was a setback, because it was 'only' 10 people yesterday. It was never easy for me to view those numbers in any terms other than grief-stricken families and friends.

Like everyone, I just wanted it to end. We all realised that only the Allied troops in France could finally put an end to the war. D-Day offered us the hope of future peace, while defeat in Normandy offered us a prospect so dire, it tormented our every waking hour. Edward obviously saw the need to change the subject.

"Do you remember, Lily, when you came with me to the station, and you told me about the sad memories the place held for you. You said you would like to tell me about it one evening. Maybe this might be that evening?"

"It's a big thing for me, Edward, but I would like to share it with you."

"Then I would be honoured."

Almost at the very moment that I started to recall my childhood, Elizabeth came to join us. She looked lovely in a pair of black trousers and a white blouse. The heavy mascara, dark chestnut brown hair, and bright red lips were her signature look. I wondered what she looked like first thing in the morning but had to admit she never failed to impress in the evening. I was like a caterpillar next to such a butterfly! She was a little more accepting of me by then, but still held me at a distance. Edward asked if I wanted to continue, which of course prompted her to ask what he meant.

"Lily was going to tell me about her childhood."

I was really surprised he'd put me on the spot like that. Had anyone else done such a thing it would be downright rude, but he was incapable of being that person. I realised he must have had an ulterior motive. What he didn't understand was how significant such a moment would be for me.

"I can't imagine what life was like for a girl in the East End, I would be interested."

"I can't imagine what your childhood was like, Elizabeth. I mean what it was really like. Would you like to tell me?"

"No, I'm not sure I would actually, that's very personal."

"Precisely, my childhood was far from normal. It has affected my entire life, one way or another. I was prepared to confide in Edward, but as you say, Elizabeth, it's very personal."

Lady Caroline joined us, filling the room immediately with her regal presence. I slipped my shoes back on and adjusted my posture. Her resolute insistence upon dressing formally was admirable, and something I had enormous respect for. Despite our own casual dress, Caroline's presence never failed to make each evening feel like a formal occasion. She greeted Elizabeth first, and then me, but she treated us both exactly the same.

"Our discussion has been about childhood revelations," Elizabeth said, "or more correctly discussing why we should not talk about them."

"I hope I haven't interrupted you."

"Not at all, Mother," said Edward, in a considered tone. "Our opinion seems to be that such disclosures are altogether too difficult for a family discussion."

"Yes, I suppose you're right. This is why our childhood determines the rest of our lives. We don't always want to admit to those forces that shaped us."

"That's quite profound, Mother!" replied Edward. "What do you think, Elizabeth?"

"Well, you know me, Edward, I don't think, do I?"

"Perhaps you should try?"

I wasn't at all sure what Edward was up to, but that was the wrong response. Elizabeth didn't flash her eyes at him, like she was capable of doing to me. Instead, she seemed to diminish in size, sinking back into her armchair.

"That's a bit unfair, Edward," I said. "Elizabeth is eminently capable of speaking her mind."

"Not in this house, Lily."

"I suspect what you mean, Elizabeth, is not if it's a matter which concerns Edward?"

"That's right, I'm not supposed to think, am I, Edward?"

Edward was not good at family interactions, but I realised he must have an honourable motive for goading his sister. Without some good intention, it would have been totally out of character. He was about to say something else but I knew he wouldn't choose his words kindly, so I pre-empted him.

"Of course you're capable of thinking, Elizabeth. You also have the sensitivity to feel deeply about things," I said. "You can see what others perhaps fail to see, and feel what others are unaware of. But that gift comes with a cost, doesn't it, because when you touch the fire, it hurts."

She looked at me in such astonishment, I immediately assumed I had badly misjudged her, overstepping the mark. There was a tense silence before she responded.

"I'm not sure anyone in this house has ever realised that before."

"I know how sensitive you are, Elizabeth. Do you seriously think a mother doesn't know her daughter as well as she knows herself?"

"I'm afraid Elizabeth is talking about *me*, Mother, and I regret to say I am guilty as charged."

"What, my beloved brother is not perfect at something!"

"That's right, I sometimes fail to see what is obvious to most people - I realise this now, and I'm sorry, Elizabeth."

"This is you, isn't it, Lily – you've changed him. I've not known Edward to be wrong in my entire life. Maybe you're both perfect."

Elizabeth's eyes flashed at me, not at Edward. Stupidly, I felt I had to respond.

"I'm not perfect, Elizabeth, and neither is Edward. I reached out to touch the fire, and it hurt so much I screamed, and in my sleep I'm still screaming. My childhood is something I never want to think about, let alone talk about. You're not unique in feeling rejected, Elizabeth, it's what I lived with constantly. My parents had enormous problems in their marriage. There was a shadow cast over our house that no amount of sunshine could ever erase. The worst thing is that I was the problem!"

"Would you be prepared to tell us about it, Lily?" asked Caroline.

"I've never talked about it to anyone."

"Well, perhaps it's time that you did, my dear."

"You're probably right, Caroline, but it's so difficult. You see there were three people in my parents' marriage, my so-called Uncle George was the third member. We don't talk about this in my family - there's hardly ever been a word spoken, I had to surmise most of it. George and my Dad were friends almost from the day they both joined the army. During the last war, George was Dad's commanding officer. During the Battle of Passchendaele, Dad saved George's life, carrying him hundreds of yards across no-man's-land when George was wounded. That experience obviously created a very special bond between them. It didn't matter that George was Dad's commanding officer, they became inseparable. Even before the war, when my mum met them, she wouldn't have met one without the other.

Well, the fact is, I have no doubt that she had a relationship with both of them. I'm certain in my own mind that she loved them both. I don't know what happened next, but George married Ann, and Mum married Dad, but the thing was Mum was pregnant with me when they got married. George's marriage went on to be a disaster, sadly continuing like it for years. They would come to our house, or sometimes we would go to them, but mostly it was just George who came to visit.

I was brought up to call him Uncle George and always thought he was a member of the family. What I wouldn't have understood as a little girl was all the tensions existing between them. There were seldom raised voices while George was there, but the house was full of emotional undercurrents which I only came to recognise later. As soon as my parents were alone, those emotions would spill over. At best it might only be bickering, at its worst it would be shouting until one or other of them would storm off into the garden. I'd sit there crying, with them both shouting all around me."

"Oh, Lily, you poor child," said Caroline. "What an awful experience for you."

"Why did you assume it was your fault, Lily?" asked Elizabeth.

"Because they kept sending me away to live here with my Gran, I was sure I was the problem."

"But how could it be your fault, Lily?" asked Edward.

I sat for a moment unable to answer, in danger of crying and making a fool of myself, and I really didn't want to do that in front of the family. After a series of deep breaths, I told them my darkest secret.

"I'm not sure my Dad is my father! I think George is my father!"

"Oh, good gracious, Lily. You lived not knowing who your father was?" said an astonished Elizabeth.

"Please don't tell me your father was unkind to you," asked a very concerned Caroline.

"Oh, no. They're both wonderful. In so many ways, our house was full of love. They both loved Mum, and I'm sure she loved both of them. They each loved me, and my brother, but despite all that, it couldn't possibly work, could it? There were terrible jealousies. George couldn't stay away and just imagine how my Dad felt if he believed I might not be his daughter. And all the while their love triangle was too strong to break.

I was stuck in the middle, a constant reminder to them all that they were living a lie. They sent me away to Gran's for weeks and even months at a time in the summer. I even attended the local school for a while. I felt like an undelivered parcel that nobody wanted. This is my memory of the station, Edward, every time I arrived there, it was because I'd been sent away. My grandmother is the one constant in my life and that's why she's so important to me."

"I don't mean to pry, Lily," said Edward, "but why do you think George is your father?"

"The only thing I *am* sure of is that he treats me like his daughter in every possible respect. He's done everything for me, spending a fortune on my education, and giving me my career, teaching me everything I know. George would walk through fire for me."

"And I think you would do the same for him, Lily?" said Caroline.

"I owe him absolutely everything, so yes, there's nothing I wouldn't do for him."

"What happened to them, are they still all together?" asked Elizabeth.

"No, not in the same way, the tensions became too much. It cost George a divorce along the way, but finally he met Marcia. They are good friends now, the four of them, but that's all. Mum and Dad finally appear to be very happy. It seems that the unwanted parcel was the only thing permanently damaged. Rejection is a terrible thing; it scars you for life."

"Perhaps they were trying to protect you, Lily," Caroline said.

"I'm sure they were, they didn't want me to see the tensions in their lives but I was the source of all that tension. So yes, they wanted to protect me from it, but I'm sure they also needed to protect themselves from me."

"It's an impertinent question, Lily, so please forgive me," said Caroline, "but are you sure that a woman can actually love two men at the same time?"

I hesitated thoughtfully before I answered because I couldn't explain why I was so sure.

"Yes, as strange as it might seem, I have no doubt about that."

I gulped a large mouthful of the whisky Jennings had placed next to me. We sat in silence for an embarrassing moment, while I assumed they were all thinking badly of me but then Caroline stood up and walked over to me. She beckoned me to stand up, whereupon she put her arms around me and just stood hugging me.

"You are a truly remarkable woman," she said. "Your courage puts us all to shame."

I didn't know what to say. Caroline was so genuine with her affection; she lifted my spirit enormously. Edward was smiling, but I noticed Elizabeth diminished even further into her chair. Her mother's affection for me was unreserved, as was mine for her, and I suddenly realised this was yet another rejection for Elizabeth.

"I'm glad you encouraged me to do that, Caroline. It's only now when I'm relieved of that burden that I realise how heavy it was. Do any of you think less of me now that you understand my background?"

"I will not legitimise that preposterous question by offering you a response, Lily," replied an indignant-looking Edward.

"Is that your way of saying 'no', Edward?"

"Of course I don't think less of you. You have simply risen higher in my estimation."

"We are all the product of our past," said Caroline, "none of us can change that, but the future is shaped by what we do with our lives *now*."

"I would wholeheartedly agree with that," said Edward. "It's refreshing to hear you express such a profound opinion, Mother."

"Yes, it's quite liberating! I was brought up not to express an opinion, and your father never expected me to have one. I can thank you for this, Lily. I just wish my late husband were here today to meet you. I'm afraid he would consider you far too outspoken, and I'm not sure you would have approved of him either!"

"Sounds like a recipe for disaster, Caroline!" I replied.

"Well yes, but disaster for whom?" she laughed.

Poor Elizabeth hadn't spoken a word. I wanted to draw her into our discussion.

"Were you brought up not to express an opinion, Elizabeth?"

"Of course, Father would have been positively affronted to hear me express an opinion, even about the weather."

"I'm sure that's not completely true, but I know what you mean."

"It's worse, because when you're not expected to possess an opinion, no-one even asks if you have one. You could never understand, Lily."

"Do you seriously think that doesn't apply to me, Elizabeth? I worked in the docks - can you imagine a more male-orientated environment? When George considered I was ready to deal directly with clients, he just handed me the telephone one day. The ship owner asked to speak to George, and I had to assure him that I could deal with it. Can you imagine how difficult that was for me, to convince a ship owner that I wasn't just a typist or the telephone operator."

"Crikey, no, I can't imagine. I don't know how you do it, Lily."

"Is it the same in America?"

"No, I'm a completely different person over there. They love the British aristocracy, and everybody wants my opinion."

"So it's only here that you don't have an opinion. Perhaps you should explain that, Elizabeth."

"You're goading me into saying something I shall regret, Lily."

"I am, and I think you should say it."

"Very well, I shall," she said in a raised voice. "I've been a timid mouse all my life because that's what my father demanded of me. Then when I was older, I had to sit in your shadow, Edward. You're so damn clever, what could I ever say which could be of the slightest interest to anyone? And as you were so keen to point out, Lily, mine is only an honorary title. I'm not even the spare, I'm the also-ran, the timid mouse. Well, I'm *not* a timid mouse, and I *hate* my role."

She stood up and stormed out of the room. I was completely taken aback, as were Caroline and Edward. Elizabeth's overreaction was quite frightening to see, going from one extreme to the other in a matter of seconds. Edward and Caroline both instinctively stood up to follow her.

"I'm sorry - this is my fault. Might it be better if I go after her? I think she blames you more than she does me, Edward."

"You might be right, Lily. Go after her," Edward said.

I hastened into the Great Hall only to see her nearing the top of the staircase. Trying not to draw the staff's attention, I followed her to her bedroom, and went straight in without knocking. She spun around to face me, her eyes wide and burning into mine, mascara smudging onto her cheeks. The anger was real but it did nothing to disguise her vulnerability. Her distress was obvious to see.

"What do you think you're doing following me into my bedroom?"

"I didn't know what else to do, it was just a reaction to seeing you so distressed. I'd like to help."

"Part of your job, is it, Lily, to come running after me?"

"No, of course it's not! I'm here because I care about you, I'm not the enemy, Elizabeth."

"You goaded me into that outburst, we simply do not do things like that in this family. I've made a fool of myself."

"I don't believe you've made a fool of yourself because you're quite right and it needed saying. Your mistake was running away, not what you said."

"Do you really think so?"

"Why do you think I goaded you into it? I've seen how you and Edward react together and I understand why now. He can be insensitive, and he's hopeless at picking up those little signals that we all take for granted. I have no doubt he just followed your father's example and didn't credit you with an opinion. Can I tell you what I think?"

"You're going to anyway, so go ahead," she said in a raised voice.

"I think your family has treated you horribly, but Edward doesn't have a spiteful bone in his body, he simply does not realise how badly he has treated you. But you are also part of the problem, Elizabeth. Your response to Edward's insensitivity has been hostility and rebellion, and all you've managed to achieve is to hurt yourself. Just stop being angry and show him you're a lovely person who has an opinion worth listening to."

Raised voices one moment and silence the next. It was easy to overreact when faced with someone like Elizabeth and I hoped I wouldn't regret it. The silence didn't last, the raised voices returned.

"I'm always angry, Lily, why do I do that?"

"You're angry because you blame your family for everything, but it doesn't work, does it? You project your anger onto them, rather than face the fact that you're really angry with yourself."

"And why would I be angry with myself?" she shouted.

"Because you don't like that timid mouse you described. You despise yourself for being that person, it makes you angry. Those emotions hurt, so you direct them away onto someone else."

"How the hell do you know all this, Lily?"

"Night classes."

It was nothing more than an instant response, it was only after I had said it that I realised it sounded comical. There was another silence, but I could see the tension easing in Elizabeth's face. We stood looking at each other, and suddenly the absurdity of our situation became all too apparent. Her anger was replaced with a nervous smile.

"Night classes! You went to night classes to study anger?"

"No, it wasn't anger, it was psychology."

"Why did you do that? You said you worked in the docks."

"I wanted to go to a class on a Wednesday evening, but I was late applying, and that was the only course the Evening Institute still had available."

It did sound ridiculous when I said it like that, and our nervous smiles turned into laughter. The big smile and sparkling dentition were the real Elizabeth; the angry woman from moments earlier was her unwelcome intruder. She could no more instantly dismiss her feelings of anger than I could dismiss my lifelong fear of rejection, but Elizabeth took a giant stride that evening. The fact that I played no small part in that journey was a great sense of satisfaction to me. I persuaded her to re-join her family and to apologise for storming off. The prospect was daunting, but to her credit she did it. We entered the Drawing Room together to show a united front. I said nothing while waiting to hear the response from Edward which I was sure would follow.

"I shouldn't have stormed off like that, it was most unseemly, I apologise."

"I won't hear of it, Elizabeth," replied Edward. "You spoke in anger, but that did not detract from the truth of your sentiment. I have come to realise many things recently, among them is the realisation that the animosity between us has been of my own creation. This has been a salutary lesson for me, Elizabeth. The possibility that my insensitivities have caused you distress is an appalling realisation. I wouldn't ask that you extend your forbearance to the point of forgiveness, but perhaps you might give consideration to a fresh start."

"This is the first time I have ever heard you apologise, Edward," replied Elizabeth.

"It won't be the last, I promise you!"

Chapter Eighteen
Elizabeth Goes To Hut 3

Over the following days, my relationship with Elizabeth was improving but her hostility towards me was never far from the surface. Part of her problem was that she didn't understand the war, nor our part in it. Her life in America had distanced her from events. She had no concept of the day-to-day suffering of the people, or the true significance of events in Normandy. Having already managed to get her to sign the Official Secrets Act, I took a giant leap of faith. We were having breakfast together, both Edward and I as usual completely preoccupied with events, but we were constrained with what we could say in front of her. This only made her feel more isolated.

"Edward, I would like to introduce Elizabeth to the boys, do you have an opinion about that?"

He looked at me slightly askance. I knew full well he would be totally opposed to the idea.

"That would be very much against protocol, Lily, but I assume you have your reasons."

"Elizabeth has signed the OSA and if we are ever going to be able to speak freely in front of her, she has to know something about what we do here."

Edward looked at me and then at Elizabeth. One thing

was clear - in his parlance, I had bowled him a googly. For her part, Elizabeth didn't offer a comment. She might have been impressed that I wanted to take her into my confidence, but she probably anticipated yet another rebuttal from her brother.

"What is your opinion on this matter, Elizabeth?" he asked.

"Are you asking me out of courtesy, Edward, or do you actually think I might have an opinion?"

"Those days are gone, Elizabeth. I know you have an opinion and I would like you to share it with me."

"I do have an opinion, but I have also learnt a few things recently. I would like to hear you and Lily discuss this a little more first."

I was impressed, that was exactly what she should have said. Expressing an opinion when you are not in full command of the facts can be a disaster. I hoped my smile was received as a gesture of approval.

"As you know, Elizabeth," I said, "we're involved with military intelligence - that much is not a secret. Probably the most important and best-kept secret of this entire war was the date and whereabouts of the D-Day landings. No more than a dozen people knew that secret - it was *our* secret, Elizabeth! This is what we do here; D-Day is no longer a secret, but our involvement must remain unknown. We are now involved with the threat from Hitler's V weapons. I'm asking Edward to consider allowing you some inside knowledge of our activities. This is far removed from your personal differences. This is not about you as a family member, this is about you as a trusted individual."

"Lily is absolutely right," Edward replied, "the security of the nation cannot be dictated by personal issues, we must rise above that."

It was a big step for Elizabeth. Rising above her personal issues was not easy for her, but to her immense credit she took that step.

"I'm flattered that you're both considering taking me into

your confidence. You realise, Edward, that you have not once taken me into your confidence before, and neither did Father. This is quite a moment! I'm not the scatterbrain you think I am, your secrets will be safe with me. I can promise you that."

Edward really had been bowled a googly. I could see he was conflicted and understood why. I could not be certain if Elizabeth was to be trusted - my instinct told me yes, but like Edward, I would have liked more reason to be certain. The other consideration was the nature of our current work. It was top secret, but nothing was ever going to compare with the D-Day secret. Edward would have been thinking the same thing, but I still expected him to oppose my suggestion.

"Before I met Lily, absolute trust was not a concept I understood." Edward said. "Now I would trust her with my life without as much as a millisecond of thought. Absolute trust is a wonderful thing, Elizabeth. I have come to find it immensely liberating."

"It's not a concept I fully understand either," Elizabeth replied, "but I can see it between you and Lily, and I envy it."

I sat almost holding my breath - was Elizabeth prepared to put her animosity to one side and demean herself, in her eyes, by making a commitment to her brother?

"I don't suppose I'm clever enough to really understand what it is that you do here, but I would like to understand more so that I can be a support to you both. I do want to earn your trust, Edward."

"In that case, you have it, Elizabeth. When Lily suggests that we take you into our confidence, she will have sound reasons for doing so. I therefore share that confidence."

"And so, if Lily did not feel she could trust me, neither would you?"

"That is precisely the nature of absolute trust, Elizabeth."

"In that case, thank you, Lily, you've gone out on a limb for me, I realise that. I won't let you down, either of you."

"Good," I said, "I'll meet you in the Great Hall as soon as

you're ready after breakfast, and I'll take you to meet the boys."

"What should I wear?"

"You can see how I dress, something smart, but business-like."

"I don't have anything like that."

"Anything casual, but nothing that might distract them," I joked.

"What about what I wore last night?"

"The trousers are fine, but not that tight top, not with your figure! Wear a jacket."

When we went to our bedrooms I hesitated, looking for Florence, but of course she wasn't there. We saw each other most days when I visited Gran, but I greatly missed her company at the Manor. When I was ready, I went downstairs and was met by Mr Jennings in the Great Hall. I happened to mention how much I missed Florence.

"Yes, I've been giving thought to that, Mrs Heywood. In the absence of a more experienced woman, would you consider taking on one of the new girls as your lady's maid?"

"I can't believe you're asking me that, Mr Jennings. I'm not a lady, I should never have accepted Florence in that role in the first place."

"Not a lady, Mrs Heywood!" he replied indignantly. "Perhaps I should be the judge of that."

"Coming from you, Mr Jennings, I'm flattered, I really am, but I can manage. Besides, Lady Elizabeth will expect a maid, so perhaps you should suggest the same thing to her."

"Suggest what?" Elizabeth asked, as she appeared behind me.

"A lady's maid, someone to replace Florence for you."

"Yes, I need someone, Florence was very capable."

"We only have the two new girls, My Lady," replied Jennings. "It's highly unsatisfactory, but it's all we can have at the moment. All the experienced women are serving in the war effort."

"What about you, Lily, which one of these girls are you having?"

"I'm not, I can manage just fine without."

"So do you think I should go without?"

"Not at all, it's something you're used to, which hardly applies to me."

"Well, if I train the girl, don't go getting ideas about stealing her from me," she joked.

Elizabeth had heeded my advice to look a little more business-like, and she had been sparing with the makeup. She looked good in jacket and trousers as we set off together walking towards Hut 3.

"The thing to bear in mind about the boys," I said, "is that they are all incredibly clever. In fact, these are some of the brainiest people in Britain."

"Sounds like I need to be frightened of them."

"No, not at all, I love every one of them, I really do. It's just that some of them, like Rolo for instance, might appear to look right through you, as if you weren't there. And if you make a joke, he probably wouldn't understand. The thing is, he exists on a different level to the rest of us, he has to make an effort to think like us. And then there's Patrick, who you might be deceived into thinking was the complete opposite. Patrick's just as clever as Rolo, they all are, but he's more worldly, he's funny, and always flirtatious. Give him a hint of encouragement and his arm will be around you."

"Oh, heck, I hate men like that!"

"No, it's nothing like that, you have to remember they're not like other people. Patrick will never overstep the mark. He can appear outrageous, but he's an absolute sweetie. Besides, he's in love with Maggie, our aerial reconnaissance expert. Woody's a real gentleman, he's the only one who looks like a gentleman should look. Rolo has no idea about clothes, and cares even less, Patrick will only ever look sloppy but in an endearing way, while Woody always wears a bow tie and jacket. Corky sits somewhere in between Patrick and Woody. He can look and act like a gentleman, but mostly he can't be bothered. Take them all down the pub and Corky takes over, he's full of fun."

"You really do love them all, don't you, Lily?"

"I do, I really do. I've seen how they work, and what they're capable of. I feel honoured that they've accepted someone like me, and they treat me as if I'm one of them. We share that absolute trust that Edward was talking about. Just don't expect them to treat you any differently when I introduce you as Lady Elizabeth."

"And what about the aerial reconnaissance lady you mentioned?"

"Maggie, she's lovely, you'll like her. Incredibly sharp mind but keeps her feet on the ground."

Elizabeth looked slightly apprehensive as we entered the door to Hut 3. The boys were all so deep in thought, they hardly realised we were standing in the room. I coughed!

"My goodness, what is this I see before me?" exclaimed Patrick. "Not one, but two beautiful women."

"May I introduce Lady Elizabeth - this is Patrick, Woody, Corky, and over there is Rolo."

"Lily has told me so much about you all, it's a pleasure to meet you," she said.

"Did you say, *Lady* Elizabeth," Patrick replied. "What will me Mammy say when she sees me kissing the hand of a Lady?"

Corky stepped forward, and offering his best impersonation of Sir Francis Drake, he knelt on one knee and kissed Elizabeth's other hand. Woody, the only true gentleman, shook her hand showing a small degree of reverence. Rolo looked up from the other side of the hut.

"Hello," he said.

Corky followed his act of gallantry with, "So what do we call you then, do you like Liz or Beth?"

"Actually I prefer Elizabeth, if that's all right?"

"That's fine with me, darling," replied Patrick.

"Elizabeth has signed the OSA, so I thought it appropriate that she learn a little about what we do here," I said.

"You're honoured, Elizabeth," replied Corky, "we don't get many guests here."

"Certainly not beautiful women wearing trousers," said Patrick.

"Ignore him, Elizabeth," I said, "they're only allowed out of the hut once a year."

"It's a cruel life, Elizabeth," replied Patrick, "it's been more than eleven months now."

The banter continued and Elizabeth rose above it all admirably. It was quickly apparent that being the centre of attention was where she liked to be. Her generous smile appeared to make her an instant hit with the boys. The good-natured humour paused when we heard the sound of an approaching V1. The boys hardly reacted at all, other than quietly listening. We stood looking at each other until it was directly above us. The moment the sound started to recede, we all relaxed again.

"How many of those awful things are coming over?" asked Elizabeth.

"They're launching about 100 every day," replied Woody. "During the first few weeks over 2000 have been launched."

"What's the latest death toll, Woody?" I asked.

"Last official figures up to July 5th was 2500 killed."

"That's only the dead, Elizabeth, there will be thousands of injured and far more will be homeless as a consequence."

"I had no idea it was so bad, Lily," she replied.

"Thank heavens we're shooting down as many as we are," said Corky, "it could all be far worse."

"What's the latest news about Operation Goodwood?" I asked.

"What's that?"

"This is the latest offensive to dislodge the Germans from Caen."

"Is that important?" Elizabeth asked.

"Did you not get any news of the war in America?" I asked.

"Yes we did, I used to listen to things like Ed Murrow, we all knew the phrase, 'This is London calling.' But I'm not sure now that we listened intently enough. I just didn't realise everyone in the country is affected one way or another."

"When you ask if Operation Goodwood is important, I can tell that if it fails in its objective, it will put the whole invasion of Europe in doubt. Will you explain it, Woody?"

"The city of Caen is vital to our strategic plans, we hoped it would fall on D-Day. The Germans know how important it is, so they've massively reinforced the whole area. We have already suffered terrible casualties trying to liberate the city. Operation Goodwood is the largest gathering of armoured vehicles in this campaign. British and Commonwealth forces have nearly 1,300 tanks involved."

"And the ground assault has just started," said Rolo.

"You mean this is happening as we speak?" asked Elizabeth.

"It is," replied Woody, "there's just been an absolutely massive aerial bombardment. There's also a ground and naval bombardment going on, goodness knows how many shells will be fired."

"There's much more to this operation than just Goodwood," I said. "Our forces are going to bypass Caen towards the southern region. As far as we know, the plan is to make the Germans think this is the main push out of Normandy, so that they direct all their reinforcements there. This should leave the way clear for the American forces to advance out of the Cotentin Peninsula in what is called Operation Cobra."

"That fact is top secret, Elizabeth," said Rolo.

"Elizabeth knows that, Rolo," I said, "she's okay."

Elizabeth looked like a rabbit caught in the headlights. The war was suddenly terribly real.

"What happens if this operation fails?" she asked.

"It depends on how badly it fails," said Corky. "Ultimately, if we fail to advance out of Normandy, it will be a disaster. Hitler's army will regroup, the 'V' program will intensify, and who knows what the consequences will be."

"D-Day only had one objective, Elizabeth, that we would invade Europe in order to eradicate the scourge of the Nazi regime. There can never be peace anywhere in the world for as long as that ideology exists. We've heard terrible stories of atrocities coming out of Europe, especially from Poland. Some of the intelligence reports are so extreme we can hardly believe it. There is credible intelligence that they eliminate anyone they consider unworthy of life, which includes Jews, Romanies, people with disabilities, anyone they choose not to like."

"What do you mean, 'eliminate'?"

"The reports say they are transporting them from all over Europe into specially built concentration camps, with the sole purpose of exterminating them. There are even reports of smoke and ash rising out of crematoria and falling over nearby villages."

Elizabeth went pale. "That can't be true, Lily, surely that's just propaganda?" she gasped.

"That's what we all thought," said Rolo, "it doesn't sound remotely credible does it? The trouble is that the evidence is mounting all the time. Not only is this happening, but it also seems to be happening on a scale that we still cannot comprehend."

"The battle for Europe is not just about allowing us Brits to sleep peacefully in our beds," said Woody. "It's about eliminating an evil presence which has suffocated all of Europe and has no limit to its ambitions."

"I just didn't know, Lily, I feel completely stupid."

"It's not your fault, Elizabeth," I replied, "but now you know why everyone in Britain is glued to their newspapers and wireless sets. We're desperate to live without fear again."

Chapter Nineteen
Middlebourne On The War Front

While Elizabeth was still speaking, my attention was instinctively directed towards a faint sound in the distance. Despite our efforts now being directed towards the V2 we all remained vigilant to the sound of an approaching V1, instantly focusing on its noise to the exclusion of all else. This was the second one in less than an hour. The buzzing sound grew louder and louder - like so many of them, this one was going to fly directly over us. Everyone stood looking towards the ceiling, as if that might improve our hearing in some way. The sound became louder and louder as it always did, except this time it stopped!

There was a brief moment when you tried to convince yourself that it would start again, or perhaps you were just imagining the whole thing, but we weren't imagining it - the pulse jet engine had stopped. Elizabeth looked at me in abject horror. For several seconds, everyone stood motionless with eyes like saucers.

"Don't panic," said Rolo, "there was a distinct Doppler shift, it's moving away from us."

"What does that mean?" asked a terrified Elizabeth.

"It's what we listen for, Elizabeth," I said. "There's a difference in the sound frequency between a sound which is moving towards you, and one that's moving away."

Rolo was right, I had noticed the same thing, but the Doppler shift happened within seconds of the pulse jet cutting out. It was going to fall awfully close.

"Get down everyone, it's really close," shouted Patrick.

We crouched down on our knees and put our hands over our heads. Elizabeth copied what I did. It seemed to be an eternity, but in reality, it was just a few seconds before there was a terrifying explosion. It reverberated right through the hut, the floor shook beneath my knees. The shock wave followed almost instantly, violently rattling the windows. The entire building groaned as the roof compressed in reaction to the pressure wave. Objects clattered to the floor and papers seemed to momentarily float in the air.

The hanging lights swung back and forth as if dancing in the gimbals of a storm-stricken ship. Our ears and lungs reacted to the uninvited intruder. There was a collective sigh of relief and for a few seconds, none of us moved or said anything, just waiting for something else to happen. As soon as we realised it was over, the full horror of what had just taken place dawned on us. The village of Middlebourne had been hit!

"Come on everyone," I shouted. "Lock the door behind us, Patrick."

We ran outside and the first thing to greet us was a great cloud of smoke in the distance rising up from behind the buildings. It was not the Manor, nor Gran's house, but it was very close. Greg and two of the guards were running towards us. We all combined and started running towards the smoke. As soon as we had cleared the Manor buildings and were into the field beyond, it became obvious where the V1 had struck. On the far side of the field beyond the tall hedgerow there was a line of cottages. A great pall of smoke hung over where I knew the cottages to be.

We ran towards the smoke, all the while unable to see beyond the tall hedgerow. I quickly became aware of objects lying in the field. Initially, it was mainly broken roof tiles, but then lighter objects, some still smoking. I suddenly froze in my tracks, I stopped and picked up a scorched object. It was a child's teddy bear! Instinctively, everyone stopped running. We all looked down at the scattered debris. Everyday household items lay all around, pieces of splintered wood, roof tiles, and much, much worse, was to come. There were human body parts.

For those among us who had never seen such horrors, it had the effect of momentarily shutting down their senses. Several of them just stood frozen, as if incapable of movement. It isn't just the horror of seeing things that no-one should ever have to see. It's the assault upon the senses when you see those things in a surreal context while standing in the middle of a field. I was far from hardened to such scenes, but I had seen these horrors over and over again during the Blitz.

"Come on," I shouted. "We can't help them here."

As we ran towards the nearest gate, ribbons of smoke were snaking through the hedgerow, reaching out towards us. I tried to prepare myself for what I thought I was about to see, but no amount of preparation could insulate me from the scene which presented itself when we reached the gate. Virtually the entire row of cottages was razed to the ground. One solitary cottage stood defiantly at the far end of the road. Its windows were smashed and there were gaping holes in its roof. No other recognisable structures remained. The debris extended as far as the eye could see.

There were numerous small fires raging, thick smoke billowing from deep within the debris. The air was heavy with the smell of smoke as the soft breeze swirled it around us. One moment, it was reminiscent of an autumn bonfire, the next it was a toxic cloud making your eyes sting and your lungs heave. And all the while the acrid smell of oxidized Amatol violated our senses. The explosive left its tell-tale signature on everything it touched, as if to confirm a pride in its devastating achievement.

"Everyone spread out," I shouted. "Get as close as you can

and be quiet, listen out for survivors. People will be buried beneath the rubble."

Several more villagers came running towards us, we all scrambled onto the burning rubble to look and listen for survivors. There were some obviously dead bodies, and horrifically there were parts of bodies. Rolo stood looking down at the remains of one poor soul.

"Leave her, Rolo, you can only help the living," I shouted.

We quickly found two people, it seemed almost miraculous that they had survived at all. They were badly injured and had to be carried away. I recognised the expression on their harrowed faces. Covered in grey dust, unable to see properly, and deafened by the blast, they didn't know where they were or what had happened to them - lost souls detached from their bodies.

"Get these people away from the smoke," Woody shouted. "Lay them down here until the ambulance comes."

"Elizabeth, go with Patrick, search over there," I said.

We swarmed over the rubble like so many termites, listening, praying for a sound. I directed people towards any larger pieces of masonry or woodwork which might have shielded some poor soul beneath. In truth, the old cottages offered little resistance to nearly 2,000 lbs of Amatol. As time elapsed, I grew ever more desperate to find someone alive. We found bodies which initially raised a false hope, only to be dashed in the cruellest way possible. Greg suddenly shouted out that he had found someone alive, he had heard a sound. I was close by, so I ran to him and climbed over the rubble. We couldn't see anyone, but then I heard it as well, it sounded like someone trying to scream but unable to draw breath.

I shouted back, "Don't worry, we've found you, we'll get you out."

We both frantically set about the rubble with our bare hands. The more we heard the plaintive voice, the more frantic we became. Greg hauled away huge chunks of masonry, lifting pieces which should have been impossible for any human to lift. I clawed away everything I could manage to move. The person was lying deep beneath the rubble shielded by the remains of a staircase. We grew more desperate with every handful we moved.

The distressed sound coming out of the rubble grew fainter by the minute. This only added to our resolve. More people came to help us as we passed the rubble to each other in a relay. My hands were bleeding, but nothing was going to stop us from finding that victim. How Greg managed to lift what he did I shall never know, but somehow, piece by piece, we were gradually getting closer.

The voice diminished to a whimper, and by the time we found him, he was silent. I gasped an involuntary intake of breath when I saw him. His life was soaking into the grey dust before our eyes. About twelve or thirteen or years old, he was horribly injured, with one leg twisted away from his body at an alarming angle, a hand bent backwards almost touching his forearm.

"It's too late, Lily," Greg said.

"No, it's not, look at his leg, the blood's pulsing out."

The boy was wearing a belt; I ripped it off him and placed it around the top of his shattered leg, pulling it as tightly as I could. The blood stopped pulsing from his gaping wound. I pressed my handkerchief against it and the white of his bone stared back at me. Greg lifted the lad up from his premature grave, but he was completely lifeless. To my enormous relief, an ambulance appeared, and at the same time I saw Edward running towards me. I was covered in blood as was Greg - Edward must have assumed the worst and the look of terror in his eyes was horrible to see.

"I'm all right, Edward. This is not my blood."

"It is your blood, look at your hands."

I looked at my hands, and he was right. He grabbed me and clung tightly, but I could see Greg was struggling with the boy.

"I'm fine, Edward, really, leave me, get the boy into the ambulance."

Edward was so horrified at seeing me covered in blood, I thought he might freeze, but he didn't.

"Are you sure you are unhurt?"

"I'm fine, Edward, help the boy."

Edward immediately put his arms beneath the boy and took him from Greg, hurriedly carrying him towards the waiting ambulance. Greg could hardly move; he must have strained every muscle in his body. He put his arms out, and I fell into them. Reality came back that very second, my legs turning to jelly, and I found myself shaking violently. Greg groaned a mournful sound, he said he just had to sit down. The pair of us slumped to our knees in the rubble.

"You were wonderful, Greg, I don't know how you did that."

"Neither do I, but do you realise what you just did?"

More villagers appeared, and having seen the boy rescued, they started clapping. It was several seconds before we realised they were clapping for us. I had seen this before during the Blitz, but I'd never been on the receiving end of such an outpouring. When faced with death and destruction on that scale, people cling to anything that symbolises the good in humanity. A single life saved seems to override the horror of multiple deaths. Edward came back and stood for a moment clapping with the others, before helping me back onto my feet. Two of the villagers helped Greg.

"Is the boy alive?" Greg asked.

"He is," Edward replied, "you may have saved his life."

"I hope so, I hope it wasn't all for nothing."

"Whatever happens, Greg," I replied, "it wasn't for nothing."

"You need your hands tending to," said Edward.

"I'll be fine. If Mrs Morgan can't take care of it, Doctor Harrington will."

The rest of Station M were starting to gather. We made our way over to them, and we came together in a huddle.

"How many have we found alive?" I asked.

"Including the young lad, there are three badly injured, eight dead, and four unaccounted for," said Woody.

He looked completely incongruous. His bow tie was twisted round the wrong way, he was covered in dust and his face was blackened with smoke and soot. They were all covered in dust, Patrick had blood on his hands, as did Corky. I only found out later that it was not their own. Elizabeth appeared cautiously climbing down from the rubble. She looked to be in shock, her gaze fixed on some unseen object in the distance. Edward and I each put an arm around her.

"Are you hurt, Elizabeth, are you all right?"

"I'm not hurt," she said, "but I can't stop shaking."

"That's perfectly natural," I said, "look at my hands, I'm the same. It means we're alive. Those poor victims are not shaking, are they?"

"This is just awful," she said. "Those poor people, just ordinary men and women, not soldiers, and there were children among them. How can anyone do this, create this hell on earth?"

"That's exactly what it is, Elizabeth," said Edward. "I'm sorry you have had to experience it first-hand."

"You were incredible, Lily, just taking control like that! I just wanted to run away."

"But you didn't, did you! When the moment came, you did what you had to do. Look at all these people, Elizabeth; this is the spirit I told you about, nothing is ever going to defeat us, and you were one of those people."

"Well said, Lily," proclaimed Patrick. "This is as good an excuse as any for me to put my arm around you, Elizabeth."

It was just what she needed, there was not even a tiny spark of resistance. Edward wanted to make sure the villagers had everything they needed, reluctantly leaving me with Greg and taking charge of the remaining search operation. It proved to be a futile gesture, but it had to be done. The injured, including the boy, were rushed to hospital, while Edward made sure everyone who needed it would have a roof over their heads that night. The rest of us walked slowly away, clapped for our effort by each group of villagers we passed.

We said little as we walked back, our own haunting images of the carnage consuming each of us. Greg limped along with me, I wasn't sure if he was holding me up, or perhaps I was holding him up. The horrors lying in the field no longer held any terror for us, we walked past without a second look. Without realising, we left that part of our humanity amongst the rubble.

When we finally arrived, exhausted, back at the Manor, I asked them all to come into the Great Hall. Fiona and the staff descended upon us like a swarm of concerned locusts, Mrs Morgan immediately running off to fetch her first aid kit, while Jennings went to fetch some much-needed whisky and brandy. Each of us slumped into various chairs and sat staring into the distance. This was something else I'd seen during the Blitz. The rescuers are always conflicted between the lives they saved and those that they couldn't. I needed my glass of whisky as much as any of them, we all did.

"We did well today," I said. "Well done, everyone."

There was a half-hearted attempt to raise our glasses, but what could we toast? I said nothing. Mrs Morgan fussed around my hands with a bowl of water and Fiona fussed about with bandages while Mr Jennings calmly maintained the level in everyone's glass.

When he came back to me, he whispered. "There is some damage to the rear of the building, Mrs Heywood. Several windows are broken, including the stone mullions. The roof and two of the chimneys have sustained some damage."

"Was anyone hurt?"

"Nancy, one of the new girls, has received some superficial

cuts from the flying glass. Apart from that, we are all fine."

"How serious is the damage, will the weather get in?"

"It will, we are in the process of moving everything out of those rooms."

"I'll have someone here tomorrow, Mr Jennings. Whatever the damage is, we can fix it."

"That was His Lordship's view, Mrs Heywood."

"Excellent, we won't speak of it again. If anyone asks, tell them we've suffered a slight inconvenience. I will *not* allow those bastards to inflict more than an inconvenience upon us, do you understand?"

"Of course, exactly my own sentiment."

As far as it was possible, the spirit in our glasses restored the spirit in ourselves. We looked like a sorry bunch, but gradually we began to talk about it.

"I've never seen devastation like that," said Rolo. "Is that what the Blitz was like, Lily?"

"In many ways, yes it is, but in other ways, it's not. We used to see the bomb damage confined to just a few houses. Even the five-hundred-pound bombs only damaged three or four houses at a time. Why is there so much destruction, Woody?"

"It's a horrible weapon, Lily. We estimate the warhead to be about 1,800 pounds of Amatol. But it's not like a bomb that falls straight down and explodes in the ground. The V1 strikes at a shallow angle, and it has a contact fuse, so it explodes well above ground. The result is that all the force of the blast explodes outwards; it directs none of its energy into the ground. The blast radius is typically about five to six hundred yards in all directions. The air blast consumes the air creating a vacuum, and as soon as the shock wave extends outwards, the air rushes back in, creating a second shock wave."

No-one responded. With the full horror of the V1 so well explained, I suspect we were all thinking the same thing. What if it had fallen into the Manor? However bad it became during the Blitz, everyone ended up thinking the same thing: thank

God it wasn't me. I felt sorry for Elizabeth, the experience seemed to have hit her harder than anyone so I went and sat next to her.

"Are you all right, Elizabeth, you look as if you might still be in shock?"

"No, I'm not, how can anyone be all right after seeing that. I just had no idea, Lily! How can you live like this?"

"We live like this because the alternative is to give in, and we don't know how to give in, do we?"

"I'm not brave like you, Lily, or any of you," she said in a raised voice. "I can't do this."

I took hold of her hand. "During the Blitz, when I lived in the East End of London, they bombed us every night. Each morning, I came out of the Underground to find scenes like we saw today. Thousands of us were killed, and everyone said, '*I can't do this*'. But then the following night we did it again. Then we did it again the next night, until we said, '*we can do this*.' The moment you say that, Elizabeth, you're fighting back, you're saying they'll never defeat you, you'll never surrender. And when the whole nation says, *we will never surrender*, we become invincible."

Chapter Twenty
Operation Goodwood

First thing the following morning, I was on the telephone to Robert Fuller the builder, one of my trusted people. His secretary answered the telephone.

"Good morning, this is Mrs Heywood, may I speak to Robert Fuller please?"

"I'm sorry, he is really busy this morning, a V1 hit the village of Middlebourne yesterday, he's in great demand."

"Yes, I know about that, but nevertheless can I speak to him?"

"I don't like to disturb him, he's in the yard at the moment."

"I appreciate that he is very busy, but would you be kind enough to just ask him. Tell him it's Mrs Heywood."

"Very well, but he'll be too busy."

Some time elapsed before Robert came to the phone. "Good morning, Mrs Heywood, how are you all at the Manor?"

"We're fine, Robert, but that's more than I can say for the building."

"I guessed as much, you had no need to telephone me, Mrs Heywood. I'm just about to leave for Middlebourne. You were to be my first call."

"Bless you, Robert, I'm looking forward to seeing you. You know where to find me."

"Isn't he the man who designed this office?" Fiona asked.

"That's right, he's a lovely young man - we can rely on him."

Edward came into the office. "I'm going over to Hut 3, will you come with me, Lily?"

"Yes, of course."

I couldn't actually do very much at my desk, my fingers were too sore, so I welcomed the chance to walk with Edward. It was a delightfully warm day, so I could go dressed exactly as I was. He continued with his newfound habit of offering me his arm. As we walked across the Great Hall arm in arm, I never ceased to wonder how his strange code of aristocratic protocol was supposed to work. Everything about Edward's position and background placed demands upon him. I accepted that, for him, any overt display of affection towards me fell far outside of his normal parameters. And yet walking arm in arm with his Chief of Staff, smiling like a Cheshire cat, was somehow perfectly appropriate!

The staff obviously noticed, all smiling approvingly. By some sleight of hand, Edward was able to consign this into his 'socially acceptable file'. When Elizabeth appeared the situation was reversed, it was my turn to feel awkward and embarrassed. Elizabeth fell outside of my normal parameters. There was no sleight of hand available to me and I duly noted her disapproval. She had not appeared at breakfast, understandably the events of the day before were weighing heavily upon her.

"How are you, Elizabeth, did you manage to sleep?"

"No, I didn't. Do you just carry on today as if nothing has happened?"

"There is no option, Elizabeth," replied Edward. "The purpose of that V1 was to disrupt our lives and break our morale. Don't you see, if we do not carry on, it will have succeeded."

"Yes, Lily explained that to me. I'm sorry I'm so weak."

"Don't confuse decent humanity with weakness, Elizabeth," replied Edward. "You have to learn how to bear these things. Thank God it's not a natural human reaction."

"Thank you, Edward, that's a reassuring thing to say."

"Edward is absolutely right," I said, "never think that we don't care."

"I realise that. I must learn how to fight back."

"Would you like to join us now? We're going over to see the boys, to find out what's happening."

"If it's all right, I shall follow on later."

The moment William opened the doors, an influx of warm air greeted us. It was one of those balmy July days when it was difficult not to believe that all was right with the world. The sight of me walking arm in arm with Edward obviously met with Corporal Harris's approval. When I looked at him, the cheeky so-and-so winked at me! I immediately smiled, even though I tried not to. If I had any intention of registering my disapproval, my opportunity vanished along with my credibility. We walked on without me saying a word to him.

"I came to you as soon as I could yesterday, Lily, but I had to inspect the damage to the house, and to be sure everyone was all right."

"Yes, of course, I realised that."

"I saw you all running across the field. I could see you hadn't been injured."

"We could easily have been killed yesterday, Edward, a few seconds less, and that thing would have fallen on us all here."

"I know, I try not to dwell on that. There were some dreadful scenes yesterday."

"Yes, it was horrible."

"Can I ask you a personal question, Lily?"

"You can ask me anything, Edward."

"Do you have a relationship with Norton?"

My heart almost burst out of my chest as my legs wobbled. Edward obviously saw my reaction. I couldn't have broadcast my response any clearer. We stopped walking, keeping our arms entwined as I gripped his arm with my other hand. I didn't know what to say, this was my worst nightmare.

"I did have a relationship with him. If you ask me, I'll tell you everything, but I wish you wouldn't."

"Are you still in that relationship?"

"No."

"He was holding you in his arms yesterday, are you sure it's over?"

"I like Greg enormously, we are very close, but we no longer have a relationship."

"Can a man hold you in his arms like that and not have a relationship?"

"Yes, it's a measure of our friendship that we can do that."

"I apologise Lily, I'm behaving like a jealous schoolboy. I don't understand what has come over me."

"When Beatrice held you in her arms the other day, I felt exactly the same."

"But I have not had a relationship with Beatrice."

"I know, Edward, it's different with Greg."

"You speak very fondly of him, you have deep feelings for him, don't you?"

"I can't deny that, but please believe me, however deeply I care for him, I care for you more. Are you going to make me say it, Edward?"

"I'm not sure what you mean."

"You know full well what I mean, Edward. If you'd been trapped in that burning building yesterday, I would have died trying to save you. Had it been me in that position, I absolutely know you would have done the same. There's a word for what we share, Edward, a word you just can't allow yourself to admit, but that word is the reason why I no longer have a relationship with Greg."

Edward was completely taken aback. He had forced me to challenge the very foundation of everything he stood for. If he admitted he loved a woman from the East End of London, I think he somehow thought the whole aristocratic edifice would come tumbling down. His embarrassment and confusion were painful to witness but my guilt and embarrassment was equally painful to bear. If we continued that conversation, I didn't know how it might end.

"I'm deeply sorry, Edward, I so much wish it hadn't happened, but it did, and it's in the past now. Please, Edward, tell me we can put this behind us?"

I didn't know what else to say that wouldn't lead to some further confession. He was hesitant, wearing his damaged pride on his sleeve, and I couldn't blame him. I moved towards him, and for a second he moved away, plunging my heart to even greater depths. The possibility that we might lose each other was real - he moved back towards me when he seemed to realise that. We stood looking at each other, I was petrified.

"You're right, Lily, we need to put this behind us."

Did it mean he forgave me? Probably not, but it meant that I hadn't lost him. My worst possible fear had come true. All along, I dreaded Edward finding out about Greg. Now I tried to convince myself it was better that it was out in the open. Perhaps my guilt would somehow disappear. My doubts remained as I realised my hopes were the triumph of hope over experience. The sight of Elizabeth walking towards us meant that our conversation was over, for the moment at least.

"How do you cope so admirably in those situations, Lily?" asked Elizabeth. "You were amazing, I couldn't believe what I was seeing, I would have lost my head if you hadn't been there. When you shouted at me you were so calm, you made me feel that everything was under control."

"I wasn't calm, Elizabeth, inside I was petrified. Other people have the luxury of being petrified, but I have to conceal my fear and reassure everyone that I'm in control."

"I don't know how you can do that."

"I'm as frightened as anyone, but I'm even more frightened of letting everyone down, that's my greatest fear."

"No-one would ever know. Do those horrible memories ever leave you?"

"No, the images in your mind never go, but you learn to live with them."

"Did you find anyone else, Edward?"

"We searched for hours after you left, but it was to no avail," said Edward. "I lost count of the number of people who asked me to thank you and the boys for what you did."

"I hope the lad survives, I shall enquire at the hospital," I said.

When we reached Hut 3, my mind was full of my conversation with Edward, and images of the day before were flashing before my eyes. My inner turmoil was overpowering, I didn't know which way to turn. As we entered the hut, it was like entering another world where those past few minutes no longer existed. The war was like a disinfectant that could erase any emotional moment it came into contact with. The conversation in Hut 3 was as if nothing had happened the day before.

"Morning, Lily, Elizabeth. Morning, Edward," Woody said as we went in.

"Morning all, well done everyone yesterday, fine job." replied Edward. "What's the news about Goodwood?"

"Progress was slow, the problem was the three bridges across the Orne river," replied Woody. "It's an obvious bottleneck."

"There were mines as well," said Rolo. "The 11th Armoured Division was slowed down considerably."

"The Canadians took the village of Louvigny," said Woody. "And we have advanced nearly four miles towards Cagny."

"So what has been the German response?" asked Edward.

"They regrouped artillery and a Tiger tank on the high ground at Cagny," said Patrick. "They know our tanks are vulnerable to the 88mm guns; we lost 16 tanks in a few minutes; it was a bloody disaster."

"Did we fall back?" I asked.

"No, of course not," said a triumphant Patrick. "The Irish Guard attacked Cagny head on, while the 5th brigade of the Guards pushed east of Cagny towards Guilberville and Emieville."

"Patrick's right, the Irish fought a really decisive battle," said Woody, "but it came at great cost. The critical factor has been the superiority of the Tiger tank, we just can't match it."

"What *did* we achieve then, Woody?" I asked.

"Cagny has been liberated, and finally we can say Caen has been liberated, but we have advanced less than five miles."

"Do we know at what cost?"

"It's still early to say, but it looks like we have lost about 270 tanks, and possibly as many as 1,500 troops."

"That sounds dreadful, Woody," I said, "and this is only the beginning, isn't it?"

"I'm afraid it is. There'll be several more days of fighting ahead of us, before the Americans launch Operation Cobra. These are decisive battles, Lily, we have to break out of Normandy."

I understood the strategic importance of Operation Goodwood, that it was a battle we had to win. But we had lost 1,500 men for the gain of less than five miles of territory. It left me to wonder what defeat would look like. The thought that this was only the beginning was depressing. Set against the increasing threat of the V1 and soon the V2, I felt a heightened sense of urgency. Our only guaranteed hope of eliminating the V weapons was to overrun the manufacturing and launch sites. That we had advanced just five miles did nothing to calm my apprehension. With no other defence available our efforts to stop the V2 suddenly took on a new imperative.

"What news on the V2 operation?" asked Edward.

"We're stuck," confessed Rolo. "We established a list of vital components which we suspect will be outsourced, but we can't track down the likely manufacturers."

"What have you tried, Rolo?" I asked.

"I've got researchers at Bletchley looking at all of our known references. How did you get on with the Foreign Office, Edward?"

"Same thing, the problem is that so many established German manufacturers are relocated, or even repurposed."

"We need on the ground information," I said. "We know MI6 shares intelligence with the Poles. We also know AK has access to Polish scientists - most of our intel about the V2 came from them. Could we risk giving them our list of components, and asking them to track down the manufacturers?"

"I've considered that, Lily," said Edward. "They are the obvious people who might have that information, but it's a risk."

"If we can't find out without them, what is there to lose? At worst, we would inform the Germans about a sabotage plan that we can't put into effect, anyway."

"You're right, Lily, perhaps I'm being overcautious."

"Can MI6 communicate with them directly, or do we need to send over an agent?"

"Communications with AK are good," said Rolo. "Why don't we try it? We could give them one or two components at a time."

"Okay, let's do it, Rolo," replied Edward.

"We need to be aware of what agents we already have in the area," suggested Corky. "Can you find out, Lily?"

"I'll try, I can ask Vera Atkins."

"What's happening now in Normandy, Rolo?" asked Edward.

"The Germans have fallen back from Cagny, they're regrouping around the villages of Guilberville, and Emieville. They have the 21st SS Panzer division there. The Canadians are south of Caen, fighting what's left of the German infantry division."

"What about the 11th British Armoured division?" asked Edward.

"We're making some progress along the Caen-Falaise road," replied Corky. "They're up against the 1st SS Panzer division. 7th Armoured will be launching an attack against Bourguebus."

"How long will this be going on for?" asked Elizabeth.

"That's a good question," replied Patrick. "I'm not absolutely clear what the ultimate objective of Goodwood is. The weather is turning bad today, I have a feeling we aren't going to make much progress."

"I need to get back to the office," I said. "I've got the builder coming to see me about the damage."

"I'll stay here, Lily," replied Edward, "I shall let you know if there are any developments."

"Will you come back with me, Elizabeth?"

"Yes, I will."

This was a very tense time for us all at Station M. The 'V' threat filled our minds, and Normandy was ever-present. The V1 which brought death and destruction to Middlebourne was in some respects the final straw. We all disguised it well, but the tensions were there to see. Our reluctance to talk about what we had witnessed was just one manifestation. Elizabeth was traumatised, and for good reason. I felt an obligation towards her, so I was therefore totally unprepared for her comments as we walked back towards the office.

"Will you explain the nature of your relationship with my brother, Lily?"

"I don't have a relationship with him."

"For heaven's sake, you walk arm in arm with him! I can see there is a relationship between you."

"I'm not sure it's any of your business, Elizabeth."

"Well, I'm making it my business, he's my brother, and he happens to be the Ninth Earl. Whatever Edward does will affect this family. I can see how important you are around here, Edward relies upon you, and I respect your position as his Chief of Staff. I'm not asking about that; I'm asking about you and Edward. What are your intentions?"

"This is a really bad time for me, Elizabeth, is this conversation absolutely necessary?"

"Tell me, Lily," she demanded in a raised voice.

I replied in an equally raised voice. "All right, I will. I love Edward, and I'm quite sure he feels the same about me. I'm not interested in his title and wealth. I wish more than anything that he didn't have those things. It's that wretched title that's keeping us apart. I'm cursed by coming from the East End of London, and as you so kindly pointed out to me, Elizabeth, I'm not made of the right stuff to be the Countess of Middlebourne, am I? That leaves me with an enormous problem, because I can't live without him, so what the hell am I going to do, Elizabeth? Tell me that."

"You must put it behind you, we can't always get what we want."

"I can't, do you think I haven't tried? If Edward told me to go, there would be no option, but he can't do it either. We work so closely together, we share everything, we're a part of each other. He holds me at arm's length but he can't let me go, he's just as tormented as I am."

"Then I feel sorry for both of you, because it's not going to work, is it?"

I tried to calm down and drew a deep breath before I answered. "You're probably right! But you need to try to understand what that means for me. I couldn't leave even if I wanted to. Our work here is far too important, we have to see it through to a conclusion. So that leaves me working towards the most terrible heartache imaginable. That's the nightmare world I live in, Elizabeth. It's too painful for me to think about, so I just exist day to day enjoying every second I spend with him."

Her hostility seemed to drain away before my eyes. She looked at me with a sorrowful face.

"I'm sorry, Lily, these things build up inside me. I wish I didn't get so angry."

"So do I, because I really don't need reminding about how perilous my position is."

"I feel dreadful now, I thought the worst of you."

"Well, now you understand, so what are you going to do, are you going to make my life even more intolerable?"

"No, I'm not. How could I know you feel so vulnerable when you seem so confident?"

"Well, I *am* vulnerable, and when you say things like that it really hurts. You have the power to make my life a misery, Elizabeth. I just hope you will use that power with a bit of compassion."

"I've made a mistake, Lily. I'm sorry, and I'm not about to do it again."

"Can we say no more about it? Just let me live my dream. I'll wake up soon enough."

I didn't know it at the time, but that was the low point between us. Elizabeth and I managed to put our differences to one side, and from that day on we steadily grew closer together.

Chapter Twenty-One
Return From Arisaig

Dotty had been away for several weeks on a combat training course. It was something of a dubious honour for her. General Gubbins, head of SOE, had requisitioned an extensive property in Scotland, Inverailort House near Lochailort. Nearby stood another Victorian lodge, Arisaig. Nestling in a windswept location not far from the shores of Loch nan Ceall, it proved to be so remote, it was the place from where Bonnie Prince Charlie fled to France. For Gubbins, this was also the ideal location for one of SOE's most secret training establishments.

As with all things to do with SOE, recruitment could often be ad hoc. Mavericks, people with unconventional and often unrecognised skills, would suddenly find their particular ability recruited by SOE. There could be no more unlikely recruits than Eric Sykes and William Fairbairn. They arrived from the Far East and offered their special talents to the War Office. Both of them nearing retirement age, bespectacled and rather portly, they had very unconventional backgrounds. Sykes had worked for two American firearms companies in Shanghai, while Fairbairn worked for the Shanghai police where he became known as 'Shanghai Buster' Fairbairn.

They both had skills they'd honed to perfection and were

masters of close-quarters combat. When they offered their services to the War Office, they were considered so ungentle-manly, they were not seen fit to train British soldiers. What better qualification could there be to draw the attention of Colin Gubbins! Sent away to the remote shores of Loch nan Ceall, they created what amounted to a killing academy. In-verailort House became the endurance training centre while Arisaig became Sykes and Fairbairn's 'private school'.

Dotty and Rob had achieved immediate notoriety within SOE. Their exploits in Caen became folklore, but their names were only known by the chosen few - two of those chosen few being Sykes and Fairbairn. Although they had already jointly written a book called 'Self-Defence for Women and Girls,' Dotty was one of the few women to attend Arisaig. When she told us she was going, Fiona and I were apprehensive. Dotty, however, seized the opportunity with great relish, and her enthusiasm for learning how to kill people with her bare hands was disquieting. She let slip another motivation; due to the unconventional nature of Arisaig, Dotty had it in her mind that she and Rob would be billeted together.

Dotty and Rob came back from Arisaig towards the end of July 1944. An army vehicle dropped them off right outside the Manor. It was Fiona who noticed them arrive.

"Dotty's back," she shouted around the office door.

The pair of us went rushing out to meet them. Exhausted after a long and arduous journey, they both looked bedraggled. Dotty had no makeup on, both were extremely tanned and I hadn't seen her hair as short before, nor as unkempt. Rob was unshaven and they were both dressed in army fatigues. With no makeup and nail polish, I hardly recognised her, but the moment she saw us her big eyes flashed a smile. We hugged each other as if they'd been away for years.

"Come into the office and tell us all about it," I said.

"We will, but I must have a bath first, I feel foul," she replied.

"Are you going back to Gran's or to Hut 5?"

"Oh no, we'll stay here, just give us an hour."

Rob reported to Mac just as Dotty should have done but instead she appeared in the office looking much more like the Dotty of old. Despite many uncomfortable hours without sleep, her spirits were high. Something about her changed when she came back from Arisaig. Edward putting her name forward for the George Cross had obviously made an enormous impact on her. She finally found a reason to believe in herself and whatever they taught her at Arisaig had visibly built upon that new confidence.

The Dotty of old was brash and impulsive; she would think nothing of doing and saying the most outrageous things to gain attention. That Dotty was gone! The big smiling eyes and cheeky smile remained, her short hair and lipstick still projected the same sassy charm, but she had a new confidence which seemed to emanate like an aura around her. Apparently the centre of attention at Arisaig, her exploits went before her. I would imagine a woman with her unique abilities was probably quite a rarity, and a woman with those abilities who looked like Dotty was probably an even rarer commodity! I didn't wonder at her being the centre of attention.

"I've learnt to do things I wouldn't have thought remotely possible. It's been an amazing experience," she said, smiling as if talking about flower arranging.

"What sort of things?" I asked.

"You really don't want to know," she said.

"How did this differ from your basic SOE training course?"

"This is all at a different level. Everything that Bill and Eric taught us assumes the enemy has confronted you, and no quarter is given. The object is to completely incapacitate the person, if not kill them."

"And you can do that?" I asked.

"If you're in enemy occupied territory, the situation can arise where it's either them or you, and it's not going to be me again. Even if I don't have a weapon, provided the person gets close to me, I can disarm them and put them out of action."

"So you wouldn't fear someone with a knife or a gun?"

"No, if someone tried to attack me with a knife, they wouldn't have much of a chance."

She spoke in a very matter-of-fact way, neither smug nor boastful. It was quickly apparent that she saw this as an unfortunate but necessary part of her job. When I asked her how she could justify that to herself, she had a good answer.

"Look at any soldier on the front line, his job is to kill enemy soldiers. Look at a bomber crew, their bombs don't just destroy buildings, do they? Probably the best example is the fighter pilot. Look at Johnny, he's a Battle of Britain fighter ace. His sole purpose was to engage the enemy in combat and kill him. If the circumstances dictate, my job is exactly the same, the only difference is that we're up close and personal."

She was absolutely right. None of us thought of Johnny as someone whose job it was to kill people. We regard the Battle of Britain pilots as dashing folk heroes. I realised more than ever the enormous difference between people like Dotty, and people like me. She needed people like me, and I needed people like her. The difference is that she put her life on the line, I didn't.

"You wouldn't have heard any of our news, Dotty, but a lot has happened here. Gran has had a stroke."

"Oh no, she's not… you know?"

"No, not at all. She's recovering well, but I'm afraid she's not the same. Florence is living there and taking care of her."

"How did you manage that?"

"It's a long story," replied Fiona. "The silly girl's pregnant."

"Oh, for goodness' sake, she's only seventeen. Don't tell me, it's that young soldier she's been going out with, and he's done a runner."

"Absolutely right. I had to do something for her," I said, "so this works out well for everyone."

"Where is she sleeping, have we lost our room, Fi?"

"Well, you see, the thing is, I won't be needing my room soon."

Fiona held out her hand and Dotty's eyes fixated on the ring, following Fi's every movement.

"Well, about bloody time!"

There were more hugs before Fiona inevitably retold her story of Johnny's proposal. Dotty was captivated, sitting with an enormous smile on her face, a smile that didn't diminish - she clearly had her own story to tell.

"You're going to tell us something, aren't you?" I asked.

"I am, you're not the only one with a proposal, Fi!"

We enjoyed another wonderful moment. Rob had proposed at Arisaig, so we had a lot of fun making up scenarios, like he proposed while she held a knife to his throat. Rob was a card which Dotty had held close to her chest. We had all seen them together on many occasions, but none of us appreciated the true nature of their relationship.

Rob of course provided another reason for her newfound confidence. Dotty was in love. What a shame I had to break the spell by telling her about the V1. She was mortified, as we all were. The closer to home the war becomes, the more personal is the experience. The war in Europe had never felt more urgent. I told her about the prospect of Hitler developing ballistic rockets to use against us. She sat up in her chair with a very defiant expression on her face.

"What are you doing about it?" she asked.

Strictly speaking, Dotty didn't have clearance to share that intelligence, but we told her everything we knew. Her reaction amazed me. If sabotage became an option, she wanted to be a part of it. When I asked her why, she simply said the V1 which fell on Middlebourne might have hit us, or Gran - it had become deeply personal. She joked that Hitler had gone too far this time, but behind that smile, she was deadly serious.

Edward came into the office soberly, carrying some papers.

When he saw Dotty, his face lit up and he stepped forward quickly to greet her. He had changed a lot in the recent weeks, as had Dotty. Hitherto she always referred to him as His Lordship, and he only recently started calling her Dorothy, as opposed to Miss Archer. Edward put his arms out and embraced her.

"It's lovely to see you back, Dorothy, you must tell me about Sykes and Fairbairn."

"It's nice to be back, Edward."

I looked at Fi, and she looked at me. These were giant strides for Edward, while I don't suppose Dotty even noticed.

"Have you brought us news, Edward?" I asked.

"Yes, it's not awfully encouraging, I'm afraid. Operation Goodwood has ground to a halt."

"Everyone at Arisaig has been following the progress in Normandy," said Dotty. "Eric gets a report every morning."

"How bad is it?" asked Fiona.

"It's difficult to say. The Germans have fallen back from Cagny, regrouping around Guilberville and Emieville, including the 21st SS Panzer division."

"Have we reached any of our objectives?" I asked.

"Yes, we have reached Bourguebus. The Canadians are mopping up German infantry south of Saint-Martin-de-Fontenay."

"What about the 21st Panzer division?" asked Dotty. "The last I heard they were counter-attacking."

"That's right, we have pushed them back," replied Edward.

"So is it over, Edward?" Fiona asked.

"Not so much over, as ground to a halt. The weather is appalling, it hasn't stopped raining. I suspect there will be considerable debate about the outcome. We have only advanced about seven miles, and 3,600 men and 469 tanks have been put out of action."

"That sounds like a disaster to me," I said.

"I spoke briefly to the PM this morning," Edward replied. "The debate has already begun. There are questions being asked about the Goodwood objectives. If they intended us to break out of Normandy, then it has clearly failed. It has, however, succeeded in preventing a massive counter-attack against the Americans when Operation Cobra is launched, so perhaps we can say it's a strategic success."

"It's been over six weeks, and we're still confined to Normandy," said Dotty.

"Yes, it's not what we expected," replied Edward. "Let's hope Operation Cobra can capitalise upon the situation."

"When does that begin, Edward?" Dotty asked.

"The weather has delayed it - I expect tomorrow or the day after."

There were other events going on which we only heard about later. The first was that an Allied fighter plane strafed Field Marshal Rommel's staff car on the 17th of July, badly wounding him. It sufficed to put him out of action so he could no longer take command. Then on the 20th of July, there was an assassination attempt against Hitler. Claus von Stauffenberg planted a briefcase bomb during a meeting of Hitler and his Generals. Sadly for everyone, it failed in its worthy ambition. The resulting purge of high-ranking German officers ultimately resulted in Rommel being forced to kill himself.

My telephone rang, it was Mac asking if I had seen Dotty. I attempted to cover for her, saying she was on her way. We laughed as she hurried towards the door, muttering obscenities under her breath.

Her last words were, "What about a drink in the pub tonight after I visit Gran?"

"Great idea," I replied. "You ask Maggie and I'll suggest it to Elizabeth. Are you taking Rob?"

"I doubt he'll want to come if it's a crowd of women. Who's Elizabeth?"

"Lady Elizabeth is my sister, Dotty," replied Edward. "She has come back from America."

"We'll see you at Gran's, then," said Fiona.

"Will you join us, Edward?" I asked.

"No, thank you, I think this sounds like a ladies' evening."

I went in search of Elizabeth to ask her about the evening and found her just leaving the Drawing Room.

"Elizabeth, would you like to join us tonight?" I asked. "A few of us are going to the pub."

"When you say a few of you, who do you mean?"

"It's just Fiona, Maggie, and Dotty."

"Ah, this is the woman you warned me about."

"That's right, she can be a bit of a handful, but you'll love her."

"That sounds fun, Lily, thank you for asking me. I haven't been to the Forge for a long time."

"We'll be paying a visit to my grandmother's first, you must join us there as well. We can get a bite to eat in the pub. I'll meet you in the Great Hall at about 7 o'clock"

The difficult conversation Elizabeth and I shared about Edward had proved to be the nadir of our relationship. We were both moving towards each other, albeit in slow incremental steps. Elizabeth still regarded me as a challenge to her position in the family, her insecurity only fuelling her fears. For my part, I was trying hard - I felt it was imperative that we got along together.

Even with Dotty coming back and us having our night out to fill my mind, I was still worried about the conversation Edward and I shared. He was behaving as if everything was normal, but of course it wasn't. I was torn between letting sleeping dogs lie and speaking to Edward again. When he suggested a quick drink in the Drawing Room before I got ready to go out, I realised he also had something to say. I was terrified he was going to say something I didn't want to hear. My nervous response was to babble the first thing that came to my mind.

"I'm frightened, Edward. Goodwood hasn't gone well, has it? We aren't making progress against the V2, and that V1 the other day has really shaken me. Elizabeth was right when she said this is hell, it *is*. I try so hard to be in control of everything, but I'm not. Those poor people, it could so easily have been us. And all those boys killed in Normandy. I'm frightened; I never admit it, but I am… Edward, I'm not going to lose you, am I?"

"I've been terrified that I was going to lose *you*, Lily."

"This thing that I had with Greg, it's over, I promise you. I needed emotional support, I needed to be close to someone, Greg gave me that. It wasn't a sordid thing, he didn't take advantage of me, and I didn't take advantage of him. I can't make excuses for it, and I can't pretend it was something less than it was, it happened and I can't change it… What did you mean, worried that you might lose me?"

"I understand why you went to Norton. I wasn't there for you. You can't imagine how that makes me feel, Lily, but I know it was my fault. I am really struggling with our situation; I simply don't know how best to cope with it. There are decisions that I have to make, actions that will have consequences, there is so much for me to think about, and then there is Station M. We have so much vital work to do, you and I. The simple fact is, Lily, for the very first time in my life I have to admit I am not in command of the situation, and it terrifies me. How could I blame you if you gave up on me? That's why you went to Norton, wasn't it?"

"I suppose it was."

"That's why I am afraid of losing you, Lily. I can't expect you to wait for me."

"Is it any wonder that we're both frightened? We live in a world of uncertainty; we have no idea what the future holds. Whatever dreams we have are built on sand, we might be dead tomorrow. There's only one thing you can rely upon, Edward. For as long as I live, and for as long as you want me, I will always be there for you."

"Just know, Lily, I do want you. I want you so much, I can think of little else. I have no right to ask you to wait for me, but my hands are tied. There is no option for me but to walk the path destined for the Ninth Earl. Somehow I have to resolve my position in a way which honours the expectations placed upon me. What I shall never do is dishonour you in the process."

"Do you mean like I have dishonoured you by my relationship with Greg?"

"Absolutely not, our circumstances are totally different. My pain is that I drove you into the arms of another man. That is the heaviest cross I have ever had to bear."

I had never known Edward to step so far out of his comfort zone. Edward, with his incredible intellect, and all the heritage and paraphernalia shaping his life, was as emotionally frail and tormented as I was! It was something of a revelation, his image as the vastly superior human had a crack in it! I had broken his heart and I regretted it with every fibre of my body. Did he crumble and fall down to my level, or did he elevate me up to his? I shall never know, but that day we came together as two equally flawed people. The fact that we both loved and wanted the other was no guarantee that the future was ours to share. Edward's anguish became our anguish. We could see no future without each other, but that cold forbidding place might be our destiny.

Chapter Twenty-Two
Girls' Night Out

I was a little late meeting Elizabeth that evening. First my impromptu conversation with Edward delayed me, and then Robert the builder also delayed me. The work to repair the roof and windows had begun and he wanted to report his progress to me. He was such an intelligent young man, something about him immediately inspired confidence. Such self-assurance would normally belong to a much older person, not a young man in his early twenties. Add to that the fact that he was absolutely charming and rather good looking, and you will understand why I always had time for him. If I was to be delayed meeting Elizabeth, then Robert was a justifiable reason.

"I'm sorry I'm late, Elizabeth, the builder delayed me."

"That's all right, is it far to your grandmother's?"

"No, not at all, and it's a delightful walk."

She was wearing black trousers again with another of her rather tight jumpers, in a lovely dusky pink. Even if I had a figure like hers, I don't think I would want to flaunt it so blatantly, but Elizabeth was always intent upon making an impression and she certainly achieved it. Set against her pink jumper, the combination of her dark brown, almost black hair, pearl necklace and earrings, was striking to say the least.

It was only then that I realised how similar her features were to Dotty's. Her hair, while short, was not as cropped as Dotty's, but it was the same colour. They both wore red lipstick and had a large smile. Elizabeth's face was defined by her broad smile, while Dotty's defining feature was her beautiful big brown eyes. Above all, they both craved the limelight. I wondered what would happen that evening when only one of them could be the centre of attention.

Walking with her towards Gran's, I felt quite drab in comparison. I don't believe the guard at the barrier noticed me at all. We were enjoying our walk together when we heard that all too familiar sound of yet another V1 approaching. Instinctively I glanced around our surroundings looking for somewhere that would provide us cover. Elizabeth stood frozen to the spot, the awful events she witnessed had obviously left her badly traumatised. I understood and had every sympathy, having been in her position during the Blitz.

"You see that ditch over there, Elizabeth, if that noise stops I want you to run over and dive into it immediately."

I had to admit the muddy drainage ditch didn't look remotely inviting. I could see she was wrestling with conflicting thoughts in her mind. When the V1 passed over us on its way to kill someone else, she stood there shaking, so I took her in my arms.

"It will pass, Elizabeth, I promise, I've been where you are. There was a time during the Blitz after they destroyed my house when I couldn't stop shaking. It was horrible, then when we had another raid, I was so frightened, I peed myself."

"I can't imagine you being *that* frightened, Lily!"

"Well, I was! I've learned to control it, that's all. You'll be the same, Elizabeth, you can get used to anything, given the time."

"You've told me that before, Lily. I'm trying."

"I find it helps to imagine that ghastly little man with the silly moustache is looking at you. My reaction is not to give him the satisfaction of seeing he's frightened me."

She managed a half-smile, and we continued on our way. By the time we reached Gran's, she'd regained much of her composure, making me admire her determination. The front door was slightly ajar and as we approached it swung wide open with Spencer Tracy making a beeline for us. The silly dog was always overjoyed to greet me, but Spencer's generosity of spirit this time was also directed towards Elizabeth. She was alarmed and stepped back behind me. I made a fuss of him, but that did nothing to quell his enthusiasm, so I called for Dotty. That was Elizabeth's first introduction to Dotty as she stood at the door wagging her finger and shouting at Spencer.

"Come here, Spencer, you stupid dog," she shouted.

Spencer's ears dropped instantly. Employing his best 'hang-dog' impersonation, he went obediently to Dotty's side and sat down. She wagged her finger at him.

"Why are you so bloody stupid, Spencer?"

"What did he say, Dot?" I asked.

"He says he can't help it, he's a dog, and he's just plain bloody stupid."

I could hear laughter coming out of the cottage and Florence appeared.

"Sorry, Mrs Heywood, Lady Elizabeth. I haven't got the knack of controlling him yet, not like Dotty."

Florence had abandoned her attempts to conceal her bump, and I was momentarily taken aback to see the contrast. It was also pleasing to see her expression, she looked positively radiant. Relieved of the stress of not knowing what was going to happen to her, she had seamlessly settled into the household. I had already explained Florence's position to Elizabeth, but she nevertheless looked surprised to see her bump. She was also somewhat taken aback by her first impression of Dotty. I hadn't mentioned that they were very much alike in appearance. I confess I was fascinated to watch the outcome, because although they looked alike, they couldn't have been more different. Dotty came down the path and I introduced them to each other.

"This is Lady Elizabeth, Dotty."

"So you're Edward's sister, then. I'm Dotty, some say Dotty by name and dotty by nature, but don't you believe a word of what they've told you!"

"They've told me a lot about you, Dotty, and it's all good, I can assure you."

"Do I have to call you Lady Elizabeth, then?"

"That is the custom, Dotty."

"I can't see that working, can you?" she said with her cheeky smile.

"No, perhaps not," Elizabeth replied, appearing resigned to her fate.

"Come in and meet Lily's Gran, she's not what she used to be, but for my money she's still the best there is."

I couldn't help smiling at Dotty, she seemed to love Gran as much as I did and when she introduced them, it really showed. Gran was sitting in her favourite chair in the kitchen and Dotty put an arm around her.

"This is Lady Elizabeth, Gran, but I've been given special permission to call her Elizabeth."

Gran was left partially paralysed after her stroke, affecting her left side. She had very little movement in her left arm, but she was learning to walk again despite her left leg having lost some function. It also affected the side of her face and her speech, but we could understand what she was trying to say, and it was improving day by day. Her longer-term prospects were much better than we first feared. Gran would not countenance any break with tradition, saying she would refer to Elizabeth as Lady Elizabeth, and for her part, Elizabeth referred to Gran as Margaret.

Fiona and Florence made us all a cup of tea and we sat around Gran like so many courtiers paying homage to their monarch. I was very surprised how well Elizabeth appeared to fit in. Her world at the Manor could not have been further removed from Gran's kitchen, while as for Florence, she was coping with an even more difficult social transition. Sitting chatting with people like Lady Elizabeth was not just a world apart for her, it was hitherto unimaginable.

There was, of course, one very significant difference - Florence was no longer a housemaid, but she was also much more, she was an expectant mother. Elizabeth would normally have instinctively continued to regard her as a lowly maid but for women, pregnancy transcends the social divide. We talked about the V1 which hit the village, and Gran was mortified, knowing several of the people who had been killed. I worried that the almost constant procession of V1's flying above her cottage would frighten her, but not a bit of it, she was utterly defiant. We all sat smiling in agreement, even Spencer Tracy appearing to agree as he placed his head on Gran's knee.

"Are you comfortable enough in the loft room for the moment, Florence?" I asked.

"Oh yes, it's fine, but did you realise the roof leaks a bit?"

"No, I didn't. Did you know, Gran?"

"No dear," she managed to say. "We must get it fixed."

"I'll ask Robert Fuller to come round and have a look at it."

We spent an hour with Gran, she really enjoyed it. When Mavis came in, I thought it was the right time for us to leave them alone.

"This is my Aunty Mavis, Elizabeth," I said.

"It's very kind of you to come and visit Margaret, Lady Elizabeth," Mavis said.

"She's a fine lady, it has been my pleasure to meet you both," replied Elizabeth.

She was being decidedly pleasant, which delighted me. When we left, Spencer was firmly of the opinion that he was coming with us. Florence called him back, I sent him back, Fi shouted at him, all to no avail. Finally, Dotty grabbed him by the scruff of the neck.

"If you were a lady dog, Spencer, you wouldn't be so bloody stupid," she shouted at him. "If you don't do as you're told, I'm going to cut your balls off, do you understand?"

"What did he say, Dotty?" Fi asked.

"He says he's heard about that procedure and he's begging to be given one last chance."

We were all in fits of laughter. Florence came after us with his lead, and Spencer was spared his fate. As Florence walked him back to the cottage, he had his tail between his legs, and when he looked back at Dotty with his ears down, we were reduced to laughter all over again. It had been a pleasant introduction to my family for Elizabeth. I hoped it might help bridge the divide between us. When we entered the pub, we were already in good spirits.

Maggie was there waiting for us, having already commandeered our favourite table. The pub was bustling, with lots of locals, a couple of soldiers, and some airmen, the only thing lacking was a sailor. I could see Dotty had her eye on the RAF boys, but I didn't think that was a good idea.

"We can buy our own drinks, Dotty."

"I was only looking," she replied.

"This is Maggie, Elizabeth."

"Nice to meet you, Maggie. What did you mean, Lily, we can buy our own drinks?"

"Dotty usually shows us up in the pub by grabbing the nearest serviceman," Maggie replied.

"Well, how does that work, Dotty?" Elizabeth asked.

"I walk up to them and I say, 'I know what you boys want', and when they ask what, I say they want to buy us some drinks."

"You say that? And does it work?"

"Apart from the embarrassment," I said, "it works every time, but then we get stuck with them."

"To be fair," said Fiona, "this was how I met Johnny. Believe it or not, Dotty did this to a group of RAF boys, and now I'm marrying one of them!"

"The most embarrassing occasion," I said, "was when Dotty said it to Edward."

"You are kidding me?"

"She isn't!" laughed Fiona.

"It wasn't my finest moment," said Dotty. "I had a few too many to drink, well, far too many, really. You see, I didn't know it was Edward, and well, I've never been allowed to live it down."

"You have to tell Elizabeth what Edward said, Dotty," Fiona insisted. "It will be better coming from you."

"Well, it all got a bit out of hand, you really don't want to hear about it," Dotty said.

"Oh, but we *do*, Dot," I replied, "and it's much better when *you* tell it."

"You're rotten, you lot, do you know that!" she replied. "I was drunk, I might have said more than I should have. Edward told me I had made a serious misjudgement."

"What else did he say, Dot?" Fiona asked.

"All right, all right! He said, 'Madam, I can assure you, I would rather have Hitler as my father-in-law than be acquainted with you'."

We fell about laughing, Dotty took it all in good heart having accepted we would never let her forget it. When it was time to order a round of drinks, Elizabeth didn't understand why we all drank pints of beer. I explained the pub had some spirits but anything exotic like a mixer, or even more exotic like a martini, was probably out of the question. She had never held a pint of beer in her life, it was another first for her. When it arrived at the table, she sat gazing at it intently, as if it was a rare antiquity.

"You can drink *all* of this?"

"No problem," replied Dotty, "which is why I made a fool of myself with Edward."

It surprised Elizabeth how easily she drank that first pint. Even the second one didn't seem to present a problem. As her inhibitions waned, the extrovert in her started to emerge as she seemed determined to rise above Dotty, but that was always going to be a tall order.

"You must be pleased, Fi, there's two of you now that talk posh," Dotty said. "You're no longer outnumbered by us Cockney girls."

"Quite right, Dotty, it's a tremendous relief, I can tell you," Fiona replied. "At last now I can have a civilised conversation!"

"I did put you together with Johnny, though, didn't I?"

"You did, and I'm eternally grateful."

"I should think so, and when I told Edward he had to be kind to you, Lily, what did he say about me?"

"He said you were my very worthy friend."

"There you are then, he forgave me, didn't he!"

"Tell me about your fiancé, Dotty," asked Elizabeth.

"Ah, so Lily has told you about Rob. I met him during SOE training," she whispered, "and then they posted him here to us. It was fate, wasn't it! The first time I saw him, he came up to me as bold as brass, and said, 'I'm Rob Bartlett.' 'Yes, I'm sure you are.' I said, 'I'm Dotty, Dotty by name, dotty by nature.' He said, 'Yes, I'm sure you are, how about you and me getting together?' I thought, you cheeky bugger, so I said, 'Get together to do what?' And do you know what he said, he said, 'We've got the rest of our lives to sort that out'."

"Good heavens! Do you think he decided you were the one as quickly as that?" Elizabeth said.

"He says he did, he took one look at me and thought, this is it! But I mean, you can't blame him, can you, I'm a good catch."

"Why is it so easy for you people? I have to dance around in circles, seeing the right people, saying the right things!"

"Depends on what you mean by 'you people'."

"Oh, goodness, I didn't mean it like that."

"I know what you mean," replied Dotty, "you mean us working-class women who don't have any airs and graces."

"Well, I suppose I do, but I really don't mean it condescendingly, I can assure you."

"That's a big word, I must make a note of it."

"Actually, Dotty, I'm slightly envious," Elizabeth said. "If Rob said a thing like that in my circle, we would classify him as a rake, and he would be ostracised, and look what a mistake that would be."

"Isn't that what little Jewish boys have done to them?" Dotty replied.

"I hope not, but perhaps that would be a better admonishment. Tell me truthfully, Dotty, when Rob said that did you feel the same in that instant?"

"There was something about him. I could hardly sleep that night thinking about it, so I suppose I must have."

"Well, I think you're both very lucky."

"Wasn't that way for you, was it, Lily?" Dotty said. "The first time Lily saw Edward she came back fuming. You loathed him, didn't you?"

"It's true, I did."

"Then, of course, a couple of days later and she's all gooey-eyed over him."

"I'm sure Elizabeth doesn't want to know about me, Dotty."

"No, actually I am interested to find out about all of you."

"Well, I reckon you should have a word with your brother," said an increasingly mischievous Dotty. "Lily is absolutely crazy about him; she even gave up Greg for him."

"Dotty, please, that's enough," I said, feeling very awkward.

"And who is Greg, may I ask?"

"You would know if you'd seen him. He's lovely, I was told I shouldn't even look at him."

"Dotty, remember those occasions when you say to us, 'why did I open my big mouth'," Fiona said. "Well, this is becoming one of those occasions."

Dotty fell silent, her big eyes like saucers. "I've done it again, haven't I?"

"I can't recall a word you said, Dotty," said a very diplomatic Elizabeth. "So, Maggie, tell me how you met Patrick?"

"Well, I obviously met him here, but it wasn't like Dotty

or Fiona, it just kind of happened over many weeks. I just noticed he was always looking at me, and later he said I was always looking at him. You've seen Patrick, he kept putting his arm around me, and then before I realised what was happening, I'm in love with him."

"That is really lovely, Maggie, you are all so lucky," Elizabeth said.

"So what about you, Elizabeth?" asked Dotty. "I can't believe you're short of men!"

"No, I'm not short of men, but I'm very short of the kind of men you girls have found."

"Maybe you're looking in the wrong place," said Dotty. "Now take those airmen at the bar, I could get you one of those."

Elizabeth smiled; I thought for a moment Dotty was goading her a bit too far, but she didn't rise to it. She coped with Dotty far better than I imagined possible. For her part, Dotty just likes to feel people out, almost as if she wants to expose their weak spots. Having found their weakness, she would never exploit a friend. Dotty just needs to get the measure of a person.

"You say you met Rob during SOE training, Dotty; what were you training for?"

"Can we talk about this, Lily?"

"Yes, Dotty, Elizabeth is okay."

"I did all the SOE training courses. I've just come back from..." Dotty hesitated. "Somewhere in Scotland."

"So what do those courses teach you, then, Dotty?"

"Well, I can jump out of aeroplanes and creep around in occupied territory, that kind of stuff."

"Dotty is a field agent, Elizabeth," I said.

"Wow, have you done anything exciting?"

"No, just routine stuff."

"It certainly sounds exciting to me."

"Exciting makes it sound pleasurable, and no, it's not that."

Elizabeth continued to probe at Dotty. Perhaps she was genuinely interested to understand what attributes Dotty brought to such a role, or perhaps her interpretation of a field agent didn't match the woman she saw in front of her. Elizabeth had fallen into the trap that Dotty exploited so successfully. She concealed her special talents with all the dexterity that a magician employs before lifting a rabbit out of the hat. If Elizabeth was not taking Dotty seriously, then she was making a mistake. She pushed again, until uncharacteristically, Dotty responded.

"I don't know what you want me to say, Elizabeth. The work that me and Rob do is not glamorous or exciting. They train us to do everything we can to disrupt the enemy. That means we destroy things, and we kill people. Don't ask me anything else," she said firmly.

Elizabeth realised she had overstepped the mark. It might have caused a difficult situation but one of the local farmers we knew walked over to us.

"Can I persuade you to sing for us, Mrs Heywood?"

"Not tonight, Ron, sorry, I'm having a drink with my friends."

He left us muttering under his breath about how nice it would have been. Elizabeth looked at me quizzically.

"Do you sing here then, Lily?"

"Occasionally I do, yes."

"I didn't know you could sing, what sort of thing do you like?"

"Any of the popular songs, the kind of thing they like in a pub."

"Oh, I see. I've appeared in cabaret in America, did Edward tell you?"

"He mentioned it, so is it a career for you?"

"Yes, and no, really. It hasn't been that regular, but it's a difficult time, of course. You just do a turn in the pub, do you, Lily? It's nothing more for you?"

"That's right."

"What are you talking about, Lily!" said a seemingly indignant Dotty. "Lily has the finest voice I've ever heard. You can hear a pin drop when she sings here."

"Really, you're good, then."

I glared at Dotty. "Dotty is exaggerating, Elizabeth. I just sing a few songs and the locals sing along, that's all."

"Maybe I should sing for them," she said. "I could do some of my cabaret numbers."

The locals didn't realise who she was, it had been several years since she had been there. All they could see was a very attractive woman offering to sing for them. There was an immediate clamour of voices encouraging her to step towards the piano. I remembered what Edward told me about her apparently lacklustre cabaret career, and how she simply enjoyed the limelight.

The moment she stepped forward she became that woman. Someone volunteered to accompany her on the piano, and Elizabeth took over the pub. It became immediately apparent that she was a performer more than she was a singer. Her vocal range was probably no more than two octaves. But that didn't detract from her performance because what she did have was razzmatazz, and she had it in spades.

This was an entirely different Elizabeth. She moved with the confident poise of an accomplished dancer. Her interpretation of the songs was obviously practised, her timing flawless. She could reach out and engage the audience in ways that I could never dream of. It helped that she was such an attractive-looking woman, and her shapely figure was certainly not a handicap. When a farmer is confronted by something as exotic as Elizabeth, dancing around him and kissing his cheek, thoughts of his tractor take second place. The servicemen were all over her, and she was well versed in how to tantalise them while holding them at arm's length.

This was the side of Elizabeth I hadn't seen and could not

have imagined. Now I understood why she was so deflated in the presence of her family. She had total command of that pub audience, she had them eating out of the palm of her hand. If anything, she was too provocative; the servicemen especially had been drinking all evening. I doubt any of them had seen anything like Elizabeth in a long time. It wasn't a good idea to sit on the lap of one of the soldiers. Her performance had been wonderful up to that point, it was an unfortunate end. Things got badly out of hand and we could see she was distressed. I stood up, intending to help, but Dotty held my arm.

"I'll take care of this," she said.

Dotty stepped into the fray, and within moments it was over. The soldier was back sitting on his chair with a startled expression on his face, and everyone else stepped aside. The audience gave Elizabeth a tumultuous applause as she returned to our table. It was as if there hadn't been an incident. Dotty stood looking down menacingly at the soldier, almost willing him to stand up, an offer he was wise to decline.

"That was unfortunate, Elizabeth," I said. "You were fabulous until that stupid soldier spoiled it."

"It was my fault," she said. "I've had too much to drink, and I got carried away."

"Don't let it bother you," said Maggie. "You were great."

"What did you do to that soldier, Dotty?" asked Elizabeth.

"He's all right, drunks are easy to deal with."

"Thank you, that might have gotten out of hand."

I sat quietly, smiling to myself, knowing no harm had been done. Elizabeth had surprised us all, but I couldn't equate the performer we just saw with Edward's sister. Those two people appeared to be unrelated. The incident, however, was quickly forgotten, and we enjoyed the rest of our evening. It would be fair to say Elizabeth had risen considerably in my estimation, she was an intriguing woman. I had many questions for her, and after we left the pub, the walk through the grounds towards the Manor provided us with a wonderful opportunity to talk. It seemed that we both had questions to ask of the other.

"Can I ask, Elizabeth, where is the performer we saw this evening when you're with your family?"

"That person has never been allowed to exist."

"Has Edward seen you perform like that?"

"Of course not, it wouldn't be appropriate, would it!"

"I think it would surprise them."

"Well, I have no intention of surprising them, Lily. I would prefer it if you didn't tell them."

"Did you learn to perform like that in America?"

"Yes, of course, Lady Elizabeth only exists in private over there."

"So what did you think of Dotty, then? I told you she's a character!"

"She certainly is, I really liked her. There is a lot more to Dotty than my first impression led me to believe."

"I made that mistake the first time I met her."

"I'm sorry if she embarrassed you by mentioning that man, Greg."

"She has a habit of embarrassing me."

"She said you gave him up for my brother, were you close?"

"We were."

"Is Edward aware you did that?"

"Yes, and it's a difficult subject for us both."

"I understand, I'll not mention it again. You're being really nice to me, Lily, I appreciate that. I know I'm being difficult, and I'm trying not to be. It's just not easy for me to adjust to your relationship with Edward, that's all."

"And how do you think that makes me feel?"

"Yes, it must be difficult enough for you, without having me to contend with. I can't see a future for you and Edward, Lily, but can we put that to one side and be friends?"

"I'd like that, Elizabeth."

Chapter Twenty-Three
The Other Woman

The month of July saw Operation Goodwood grind to a halt. It had given the Allies a tactical advantage but was not the outcome anyone was hoping for. Everything now depended upon Operation Cobra. If the Allies couldn't break out of Normandy all would be lost, and after several attempts we knew this offensive represented our last best hope. The Americans launched Operation Cobra on Tuesday 25th July at 9:40am. We were all in Hut 3 listening nervously to the radio messages.

"What's the plan of attack, Woody, what do we need to watch out for?" I asked.

"It's already started with a massive air assault. If it goes according to plan it will be the largest carpet-bombing of the entire war, northwest of Saint-Lo. There will also be massive ground artillery fire. The Americans will launch their ground assault with six divisions that will follow the bombardment."

"What are the Brits doing?" asked Patrick.

"The British and mainly Canadians will launch Operation Spring, south of Caen," he replied.

The way Woody described it, the sheer scale of the offensive made the outcome appear inevitable, but of course in war there is no such assurance. The boys went about their usual work of analysing the V1 reconnaissance data, but all the while Operation Cobra dominated our concerns. The following three days were really tense. I would find any excuse to go over to Hut 3 and ask about progress. Each evening Edward and I talked about little else. When I went into the hut on July 28th it was immediately apparent that spirits were raised. I was greeted by smiling faces and Edward put his arms around me in front of everyone.

"The Americans have done it, Lily, they have broken through."

"The Bridge of Pontaubault is in Allied hands," said a jubilant Woody. "The road to Brittany lies ahead."

The significance of the breakthrough was not lost on anyone. After two months of savage fighting the Allies had won the battle for Normandy, our tenuous foothold in Europe now looked secure. Operation Cobra was a total success. July had been such a tumultuous month, I turned over the page of the office calendar to reveal a new month of hope and expectation.

On August 6th, the Germans launched a counterattack which they named Operation Luttich. What they were unaware of was that Bletchley Park had broken the German communication codes. The Americans were forewarned, and the German counterattack failed. On the 8th, the Canadians launched Operation Totalise. The Allied advance had created a pocket of German forces, known as the Falaise Pocket. It was another two weeks of intensive fighting before the Canadian and Polish forces joined up with the Americans. When I entered the hut one morning later in the month the atmosphere had changed.

"Is everything all right, you all seem quiet this morning?"

"I think perhaps we got a bit carried away, Lily," said Edward. "We allowed ourselves to ask when the rest of France would be liberated. The fact is we still have a very long way to go, and the V1's are raining down in increasing numbers."

"I thought the countermeasures were working."

"They are, Lily," replied Corky, "we're shooting down a lot of them but they're launching more. Hundreds are still getting through."

"We're also concerned about the threat from this new rocket, the V2," said Edward. "We know it's only a matter of time before the Germans start to launch them."

"I look at the latest casualty figures for the V1 and what sends a chill down my spine is that I read them as if they were a record of milk sales."

"I know what you mean, Lily," replied Edward, "we have just received the figures for casualties in Normandy, and it puts everything into perspective. The battle for Normandy has taken a dreadful toll. We have suffered 210,000 Allied casualties. Nearly 37,000 troops have been killed, and the air forces have lost another 16,000 men."

"Oh my God! That's a terrible price to pay. What about civilians?"

"This is even more sobering; between 15,000 and 20,000 have paid the ultimate price for a freedom they will not enjoy. Many say the figure is even higher. From what we know of the German casualties they too have paid a very high price. 200,000 German troops are now in Allied captivity, and 50,000 have been killed."

"Those numbers are horrific, Edward, is it going to be like this all the way to Berlin?"

"The Germans are a formidable enemy, Lily, they'll never willingly surrender even an inch of ground."

"What we must never overlook," said Woody, "is that so far, they have not been defending German soil, we can only expect ever stronger resistance."

That was a daunting prospect. I left them in a sombre mood and set off back to the office. The weather matched my outlook, with an overcast grey sky and a chill wind. I hurried along, but as I always did, I glanced over at the point where I could see the estate office. Greg was there, but he wasn't alone. A woman with a toddler grabbed my attention. I found myself standing still and looking at Greg as he took something out of the back of his van. Whoever she was, it was nothing to do with me but my curiosity got the better of me, I had to find out. When Greg saw me coming, I could tell from his expression that he felt awkward, but I realised that too late.

"Hello, Greg."

"Hello, Lily, may I introduce you to Aileen."

I instantly realised who she was but my reaction surprised me. My heart jumped. I was nervous! This was the woman Greg left behind in Scotland. She was poorly dressed, unlike the toddler she was holding, and she just stood staring intently at me.

"Hello, Lily," she said. "I know who you are."

Trying to change the subject, I asked the name of the little boy.

"Christopher," she replied, offering no other conversation.

"He's a lovely-looking boy. How old is he?"

"He's almost three. Lily, he's my son!" replied Greg.

If looks could kill, Aileen would have smitten me down there and then.

"I didn't realise you had a son, Greg," I said, hesitantly.

"I didn't know, Lily. We've just met for the first time."

"Well, that must have been quite a shock! I'd better go, you'll have much to talk about. It was nice to meet you, Aileen."

"I don't think so, Lily," Aileen said in a broad Scottish accent. "We need to talk, don't we?"

"I'm not sure we do, Aileen. What would you want to talk to me about?"

"Can we go inside, Greg?" she asked.

Greg looked as if he was trying to balance on a slack clothes line. He swayed from side to side, not knowing which way the wind would take him.

"Perhaps Aileen is right, Lily. Shall we go inside?"

I followed them in silence with my heart racing, but I wasn't even sure why! Greg took us through to his kitchen and set about making a cup of tea while I sat down with Aileen. She lifted Christopher onto her knee. I understood something of Aileen from what Greg had told me but being unaware of her until after Greg and I split up, I wasn't sure what she had in mind.

"Are you two still together?" she blurted out, as if choking on the words.

"No, Greg and I split up some time ago."

"You knew he left me for you, didn't you?"

"Not at the time, no."

I could only imagine the turmoil poor Greg was going through with his two former lovers sitting at his kitchen table. And to compound his torment, he now had a son that hitherto he'd been unaware of. If my heart was racing, Greg's must have been bursting.

"What is it you want from me, Aileen?" I said sharply.

"You ruined my life. I was supposed to follow Greg south, when he got settled. You're the reason that didn't happen."

"I knew nothing about you, Aileen. I'm not to blame here. And don't blame Greg either, we didn't plan what happened between us. I'll tell you something which you can choose to believe or not. I tried desperately hard not to fall for him. I had my own reasons for not getting involved, and we held each other at arm's length for two years. In the end, we both just gave in to it. Neither of us planned it. Sometimes these things are beyond your control."

"That's right, and I was left holding the baby."

"Why didn't you tell Greg about Christopher immediately?"

Turning to Greg, Aileen said, "You didn't want me, did you, so why would you want me with the baby as well?"

"If you'd told me, I would have come straight back, of course I would," Greg said.

"I could tell from your letters that something was wrong, but like an idiot I thought the Chief of Staff was a man."

"He definitely takes after you, Greg; he's a handsome young man, isn't he?" I said, trying to change the subject.

Greg stepped forward and took young Christopher from Aileen. He bounced him up and down in his arms, eventually walking off with him on a tour of his office. Aileen looked on with a tearful but proud smile, seeing her baby in his father's arms.

"I promise you, Aileen, what Greg and I had between us is over - this is no longer about me, it's about you two. You've never stopped loving him, have you? I can see that. I could always tell something was tormenting him and I realise now that you were always a part of him. Take my advice, Aileen, stop blaming everyone for your heartache and set about trying to repair it."

"I can't see him coming back to me."

"Then why are you *here*?" There was a long silence. "It's best if I go, Aileen, this is your moment, the two of you. Try to appreciate how Greg feels. He's holding his son in his arms, and you're back in his life. I don't think you ever left."

I was desperately sorry for her, for both of them. She would have to confront me at some time, so I suppose it was better to get it over with, but the quicker I left, the better. She didn't know how to respond to me. Part of her was still sticking pins in my effigy, while another part was relieved it was over. As I walked towards the door, I held out my hand and she took it in hers. It was only for a second, but she accepted it - it was a magnanimous gesture. I didn't look for Greg, I just left.

Stepping out into the chill breeze jolted me back into reality. What on earth had just happened? It was too much to take in, my heart was racing and I still didn't understand why. It was almost as if Greg and I had broken up all over again. I couldn't face seeing anyone, so I walked around the grounds for a while. Elizabeth must have noticed me from the house.

She said I looked like a lonely figure, slowly walking around with my head bowed, and so bless her, she came outside to join me.

"Are you all right, Lily? It's not like you to walk around the grounds like this."

"I've just had a shock, that's all."

"Well, tell me."

"No, it's a very personal matter."

"Sounds like just the thing you should confide with me about."

I raised a smile. "Maybe you're right, Elizabeth. I've just been confronted by Greg Norton's previous love affair. It's all been a bit emotional."

"Oh, my goodness, affairs of the heart! Were you the other woman?"

"I knew nothing about her, but yes, in a way I was."

"Ouch! That sounds like one of those excruciating moments when you'd like to disappear."

"You're so right, Elizabeth, it was just awful."

"I met Mr Norton the other day. He's not the kind of man you could easily leave behind, is he?"

"No, it was a very difficult time for me."

"Is there no way back for you now?"

"No, I made my decision, and who knows, he may welcome the mother of his child back into his life."

"Child, there is a child as well?"

"Oh, I didn't mention that, did I. Yes, it seems they have a nearly three-year-old son."

"And he failed to mention that to you?"

"Poor man, he didn't know till today about his little boy."

"Oh, my goodness, what a tangled web you've fallen into! I thought I was the only one who blundered into disasters like this. There's one infallible cure for these situations which has never failed for me. Let's sit in the Drawing Room, and I'll ask Jennings to fetch it for you."

Chapter Twenty-Four
Wedding Plans

Fiona was prepared to accept all the wartime economies, except for one. She insisted upon a beautiful wedding gown. Fabrics were a problem, especially in the quantity required for bridal gowns. Rationing restricted anything like lace or trimmings but - for those in the RAF - there was a solution. White parachute silk was perfect, and for those able to get their hands on it, a beautiful gown was only a seamstress away.

Lady Caroline's two young dressmakers were as excited at the prospect as Fiona was. When it was time for the fitting, Elizabeth, Dotty, and I insisted on being there with her, all four of us caught up in the excitement. I knew it would be perfect, those girls were so talented. It was no surprise to me that after the war they went on to be the driving force behind a well-known fashion house. We stood there like children on Christmas morning, anticipating what we were about to see, and when Fiona appeared, she was a sight to behold.

She didn't want to break with tradition, so it had the usual long sleeves, and full circle skirt which fell from the waist to the floor. It had a fitted ruched bodice, a sweetheart neckline trimmed with lace and the long sleeves were gathered at the shoulder. Most of the decoration went into the veil and headpiece. Looking at Fiona standing in the dress, it seemed almost incomprehensible that the shimmering material was intended for parachutes. She looked fabulous!

"Makes you want to get married, doesn't it, Lily?" said Elizabeth.

"It does! You look wonderful, Fi."

"It feels wonderful," she said. "You don't think it's too long, do you?"

"It's absolutely perfect," I replied, "don't think about changing a thing."

The girls fussed around her, but nothing needed adjusting. Fiona walked up and down, looking in the mirror, first one way, and then the next, as we all watched, thoroughly enchanted. We opted not to have special dresses made for us bridesmaids. Traditionally, we would all have dressed identically to confuse any malevolent evil spirit which might happen to be there, but that was not really an option in 1944.

Dotty, however, did require a special dress to be made, because she had nothing suitable for the occasion. She joked that her army fatigues would suffice, but her suggestion fell upon very stony ground. I'd never seen Dotty in a fabulous dress; even persuading her to have one made was a struggle. When we had all agreed that Fiona's dress was perfect, it was time for Dotty to try on hers.

"Do I have to do this now?" she asked.

"Of course you do, Dotty," I replied. "The girls might need to adjust it."

The fashion experts had decided upon green for the fabric because that would suit Dotty's hair, and then all the bridesmaids were at least wearing the same colour. It was a full-length dress not dissimilar to the first gown they made for me. She was funny, trying not to take it seriously, asking where she could put her concealed weapons. Dotty was a conundrum in so many ways, wonderfully attractive with her big brown eyes, always wearing red lipstick and nail polish, but paradoxically never really wanting to be feminine. I used to wonder if perhaps she saw her femininity as a weakness, especially then, when she existed in a male-orientated world. When she appeared wearing the new dress, we sat open-mouthed. She walked awkwardly in bare feet towards the mirror and the moment she saw herself, her jaw dropped and her eyes widened.

"You look absolutely beautiful, Dotty!" I exclaimed. "How does it feel?"

"It feels strange! This doesn't look like me, does it?"

"You're right, Dot, it doesn't look like you," Fiona said, "but you still look wonderful."

"Do you think so? Would I have to wear pearls or something with it?"

"Yes, of course you should," Elizabeth said. "I've got lots you can choose from and borrow if you want."

There was no escape for her, even though she pretended to wear it under protest. I remembered what Caroline told me when I had my first dress fitted by the girls.

"Trust me, Dotty, no woman can look as wonderful as you do and not feel good about herself."

It was a lovely morning and we talked of nothing else but dresses, jewellery, hair, and makeup. It was the kind of morning which seldom, if ever, existed during the war. We didn't mention rationing, the shortages or the war in France, nothing to spoil our wonderful time together. The lovely dresses had to go back into their boxes folded neatly between tissue paper, and Dotty had to report back to Mac. Elizabeth was having lunch with Caroline, while Fiona and I were going to Tunbridge to meet her parents.

Fiona's family had arrived the day before and were staying at a hotel in Tunbridge. It was the first time I had met them. They were exactly as Fi described them. Her mother Judith tried to be terribly well-to-do and awfully proud that her daughter was marrying the son of an Air Commodore. Her father, Dennis, was a self-made business owner who had done extremely well for himself. He was simply delighted with his daughter's choice of son-in-law. It seems that when they first met him, they had much in common and got on like a house on fire.

Younger sister Karen was delightful. She was so much like Fiona, I felt as if I already knew her. She was the third bridesmaid. Fiona had warned me about her mother, and she was right. Judith quickly decided that I was not standing on the appropriate rung of the ladder. Perhaps it annoyed her that I got on so well with her husband. Fiona raised her eyes towards the ceiling, smiling knowingly at me. I smiled back, quietly remembering that when I first met Fi, she was exactly like her mother! Nothing, however, detracted from a delightful afternoon and I was sorry to leave when William arrived to pick me up at 5.30.

It had been quite extraordinary, an entire day filled with pleasurable activity and absolutely nothing troubling to worry about. Was this a taste of peace, was this what we were fighting for? The only arduous decision of the day was deciding what to wear for dinner. When I was ready, I met Elizabeth at the top of the stairs, and we walked down to dinner together.

"How are you managing without a maid, Lily?" she asked.

"Do you know, I really miss having Florence."

"I'm not surprised, it must be miserable. Mind you, Nancy is a bit of a trial. She has so much to learn."

"Florence can do my hair much better than I can, and her skill with makeup used to amaze me."

"I think you should have a word with Jennings and see what we can arrange, you need someone."

"We didn't have lady's maids in Stepney, Elizabeth, I'm sure I can manage just fine."

"I know, you must think I'm terribly spoiled."

"I do! But then I really enjoyed having Florence, so I was spoiled as well."

When we entered the Drawing Room, Edward sprang to his feet as usual.

"Good evening, ladies, how did your dress fitting go?"

"We had a wonderful morning, didn't we, Elizabeth?"

"Yes, it's been so much nicer than listening to those V1 things."

"What are the latest numbers, Edward?"

I realised in an instant that simply by asking, I had stepped out of our fantasy world of wedding arrangements, dresses, and makeup, and stepped back into 1944. My illusion of peace-time tranquillity crumbled and crashed to the ground.

"The last 24 hours have been bad," he said, "with at least forty casualties, and it sounds like most of those are fatalities."

"This is happening every day, isn't it," said Elizabeth.

"Yes, and this isn't a particularly bad day," replied Edward.

"It's not just the killed and injured," I said. "There will have been hundreds of homes destroyed or damaged today."

"I understand why you are all so desperate for good news from France," she said.

"We have received one breakthrough today from AK," Edward said. "They have found us two important suppliers who we are reasonably sure are supplying key components for the V2."

"Oh, wonderful. How quickly can we put a plan into action?"

"Mac is working on that now. Polish resistance is best placed to carry out the sabotage with our people. Mac wants to follow the French model. We will parachute in sabotage equipment with our agents."

"When does Mac think we could be ready to do this?"

"He's been planning for something like this for weeks, so I think it's a matter of days, rather than weeks."

"If you're right about these vital components, Edward, this could make a real difference," I said.

"How serious is the threat from this new rocket?" asked Elizabeth.

"We don't know," I replied, "because they haven't launched one against us yet. The fear is that we'll have no defence against them."

Albert came over to us to ask what we would like to drink. I noticed Jennings watching his young prodigy from the side of the room. His face was so stern, I feared he might shout at the poor boy should he make the slightest mistake. But Albert didn't make a mistake and Jennings raised his chin slightly as he proudly followed him out of the Drawing Room.

Lady Caroline joined us, making me feel underdressed as usual. She was full of questions about the day's dress fitting and for a short time at least, we once again forgot the wartime issues of the day. It lasted until we were seated in the Dining Room, and a V1 flew overhead. I was prepared for Elizabeth's reaction. She was visibly nervous, as we all were, but this time she didn't react. I smiled at her, and she nodded back, effectively saying 'I'm getting used to this'.

Sometime later, Caroline casually mentioned that Lady Beatrice's family would like to visit again. I would like to have said, 'what *again*' but of course I didn't. Instead, it was Elizabeth who effectively suggested the same thing.

"Well, they can't come this weekend, we have the wedding. And you can see how busy everyone is here. Can we not put them off?"

"Elizabeth, that's not like you. You're great friends with Beatrice," said Caroline.

"Yes, we are, but I realise how important the work is here that Edward and Lily do. And if I can do anything to help, then I will."

"Well, I can try to put her mother off for a while, but it seems rather rude."

"I thought the V1 which struck the village the other week rather puts things into perspective," Elizabeth replied defiantly.

I could hardly believe my ears; this wasn't the Elizabeth of even a week ago! Edward didn't offer a comment, and neither did I. We enjoyed our dinner together with nothing more being said about it, not until Elizabeth and I were walking up the stairs together at the end of the evening.

"I thought it would please you not to be entertaining Beatrice," she said with obvious relish.

"Yes, why did you say that?"

"We all know what is expected of Edward so I thought you'd be pleased, Lily."

"Well, actually I am, but I didn't expect to receive your support."

"You know my opinion on this matter, Lily. I think the short odds are with the favourite, but there's nothing stopping me placing a small wager on the outsider!"

Elizabeth had taken my breath away. I was so surprised I hardly knew what to say.

"Thank you, I'm really touched that you said that."

"It's one of those quintessentially British characteristics that I missed while I was in America. We like to see the underdog come out on top. Goodnight, Lily."

"Goodnight, Elizabeth."

Chapter Twenty-Five
Fiona's Big Day

Saturday 12th of August 1944 was the big day. Fiona and Johnny were married in St Michael's, the village church. It was supposed to be a low-key celebration, as they all were during the war, but it turned out to be the opposite. On the morning of the wedding, the excitement was near to panic. I knew we had everything in hand, but we still worried. William drove me to Gran's in the Rolls- Royce. I was already in my fabulous green dress. He then waited to drive Fiona and her father to the church. Upstairs, Florence was putting the finishing touches to Fi's hair, while downstairs, Gran was not happy that I had arranged a wheelchair for her.

"If I had help, I could walk from the car," she said.

"No, Gran, this isn't the time to argue. You're not strong enough yet. Jim is going to push you."

"I don't want people seeing me in this thing."

"Gran," I said, pointing my finger, "for once, please do as you're told."

"I don't want to be a nuisance."

"Don't be silly, Gran, you'll never be a nuisance to me or to Jim."

Jim and Mavis appeared, looking wonderful, I hardly recognised Jim in a suit. Aunty Mildred was the next to arrive accompanied by my parents, who were staying with her, but there was still no sign of Dotty. When she finally came down the stairs, the entire house fell silent.

"What!" she said. "Haven't you lot seen a dress before?"

"Not like that, not on you, Dotty," said Jim.

"Don't make me feel self-conscious."

I didn't see Rob arrive. I just heard the voice coming from behind me.

"Dorothy Archer, is that you?"

"Oh, for goodness' sake, stop staring at me, Rob! Come and smudge my lipstick."

Rob didn't need telling twice, and we all gave a quick cheer.

"You lot are rotten to me!" Dotty said. "I'm no more dressed up than Lily is."

"Yes, but we've seen Lily dressed up before," said Jim.

"Come on, Dotty," said Rob, "let me see you do a twirl."

"You'd better behave, Rob Bartlett, or I won't marry you."

"Yes you will, give us a twirl, come on," he said, picking her up in his arms.

We had a lot of fun at Dotty's expense, but the truth is that she looked absolutely stunning. I think without the fun to lighten the mood, we might have been lost for words.

"We haven't met Rob before," Dad said.

"I'll introduce you," Dotty replied.

Dotty treated my parents as if they were her own, throwing her arms around them, making a point of planting two red lips on Dad's cheek.

"Dotty, you look lovely," he said.

"Well, you don't have to sound so surprised, Jack, you're as bad as this lot. They're all ganging up on me because I've got a posh frock on."

"What's all this I hear about you getting married as well?"

"That's right, this is the lucky man. Rob, this is Lily's Mum and Dad, Pam and Jack."

"How did you two meet, then?" Dad asked.

"We met at work, didn't we, Dot?" Rob replied.

"Do you work on the farm as well, Rob?" asked Mum.

"Was that where we met, Dotty?" Rob asked.

"Yes, that's right, at Reg's."

I left them to it before they asked me where they worked. I went upstairs to see Fi. There's something about seeing a bride in her bridal gown. She took my breath away and I just stood there silently, unable to say anything for a moment.

"Well, how do I look?"

"You're amazing, I'm just speechless, Fi. You look absolutely beautiful."

"Do you like my hair like this?"

Florence was clearly delighted with her efforts, standing there with a satisfied smile on her face.

"You can guess whose hair I've copied, can't you, Mrs Heywood?"

Fiona bore some resemblance to Ingrid Bergman and her hair only added to that resemblance.

"You're so clever, Florence, it's perfect. You couldn't look more lovely, Fi."

"Florence has been brilliant. I couldn't have coped without her this morning."

"I'm sorry I wasn't there to help you as well, Mrs Heywood. I've been worrying in case you needed me."

"Everyone seems to be worrying this morning."

"Are you walking to the church?" Fiona asked.

"Fi, stop worrying, everything is going to go like clockwork. Edward insists he'll pick me up in the Rover with Caroline and Elizabeth."

There was a knock on the door, it was Fiona's mother and sister Karen. Judith was in a flap. They were late arriving and everyone was checking the time.

"Don't worry about a thing," I said, "the church is only two hundred yards down the road. As long as the bridal party leaves in five minutes, we'll be fine."

"I didn't know you had organised a Rolls-Royce for Fiona," Judith said.

"Oh, yes, that's Lord Middlebourne's car and chauffeur."

"Lord Middlebourne?"

"Didn't Fiona tell you, Judith, we work for Lord Middlebourne?"

"No, I didn't know you worked for a Lord."

"We don't talk about it, Mother, best not mention it again."

Any association with a title was a matter of great pride for Judith. "Oh, of course, I won't mention it again," she said, smiling as if her daughter had just won a prize at school.

"It's time," I said. "See you there, Fi."

I could see Edward waiting outside in the Rover. It did seem rather ridiculous, driving me two hundred yards, but he was insistent.

"You must excuse me," I said. "Lord Middlebourne is insistent that I arrive with him."

"Oh, I quite understand," Judith replied, looking terribly pleased.

We arrived at the church only moments later. Johnny and his best man were there, along with another group of men in blue. They all looked so smart in their best uniforms. Although I had never met him, I assumed the older man with all the ribbons was Johnny's father, the Air Commodore. The parents had not had the opportunity to meet each other, which was a bit awkward, so when Judith arrived, I introduced her.

"I am delighted to meet you, Air Commander," Judith said.

"Air Comm*odore* actually."

Edward and I quickly stepped aside before we became embroiled in the confusion. Edward wanted to wear his tail suit, but I persuaded him not to. All the gentlemen who were not in uniform wore a plain suit, so he could see it was the correct decision. His hair had almost fully grown back by that time, back to his sartorial best. Caroline, of course, was dressed magnificently, and with the obvious exception of

Fiona, her regal presence seemed to cast a shadow over all the other women.

Elizabeth also struck an aristocratic presence. She looked really striking in a red dress, adorned with an abundance of jewellery, not to mention her sparkling dentition! The bridesmaids, together with the ushers, carried out our various duties, and we all took our places. Fiona and her father appeared at the entrance to the church. The organist struck up the bridal march, and she walked up the aisle with her father. It was absolutely magical and when it was all over, Johnny and Fiona walked back down the aisle and she was Mrs Albright.

As we stepped outside, the cool atmosphere of the church was replaced with the warmth of a beautiful August summer day. We gathered on the manicured grass between the church and its magnificent lych-gate. Confetti rained down like so many snowflakes and everyone was eager to kiss the bride and shake Johnny's hand. Family photographs were taken, and then more photographs were taken although even with our own processing laboratory, film was limited, and they had to make careful choices. There was one photo with us bridesmaids, then the RAF boys. Fiona then wanted a photograph with the boffins standing around them. Then she wanted one with all the staff from the Manor, everyone was involved. Karen was in tears, and Dotty pretended not to be. Everything was exactly as it should be.

The reassuring normality of the occasion was abruptly broken. I noticed the RAF boys checking their watches as they formed a line opposite the happy couple and held their hands in a salute. Then we heard the unmistakable sound of a Merlin engine. Everyone immediately stopped talking and looked into the sky to see an aircraft in the distance coming towards us. Probably like everyone else, I was slow to realise what was happening. Any aircraft coming towards you would quickly draw your attention during the war. As the aeroplane grew larger in the sky, I could see more appearing in the distance behind it. They were all approaching us at a low level and in a perfect line. It was a flight of Spitfires!

Everyone stood mesmerised, eyes fixated upon the lead Spitfire as it sped towards us. Then at the last moment as it approached, the pilot dipped the Spitfire's wings, first one side and then the other. Only when he was directly above us did he bank away to the left, soaring up into the sky. Our hearts soared into the clouds alongside him. The second Spitfire rapidly approached us and dipped its wings before banking off to the right. There was a third, and then a fourth, and finally a fifth Spitfire approached. This pilot performed a barrel-roll directly above us before joining his comrades high in the sky.

The combined roar of the Merlin engines reverberated through our bodies. We all, to a person, raised our fists into the air with a mighty cheer. For anyone who had lived through the Battle of Britain, it was a sight guaranteed to lift your spirit towards the heavens. Winston Churchill's speech to the House of Commons in August 1940 immediately came to mind.

*"Never in the field of human conflict was so much owed by so many to so few."

The wedding congregation were the 'many' and Johnny Albright was one of the 'few'! It was a magnificent moment that I've never forgotten, and neither has anyone else who was there. There was a buffet lunch at the village hall. Although it offered little in choice or quantity, we considered it extravagant at the time. Mrs Morgan had performed miracles, or perhaps one of her less scrupulous suppliers had! For a small family wedding, it was packed to capacity.

I asked one of the flyers if RAF Biggin had sanctioned the flight of Spitfires, and to my surprise he told me they hadn't come from Biggin. They came from RAF Hendon, Johnny's previous station. None of it was sanctioned, so it seemed that those pilots were going to be lucky to get away with it. As for there being five of them, there was a reason for that. Five was the arbitrary number of enemy planes a fighter pilot needed to shoot down to qualify as a fighter ace. Johnny surpassed that number, so given the occasion, there was no way his comrades at Hendon were not going to pay him their tribute.

We had the usual speeches, Johnny's best man was hilarious, and Fi's father, Dennis, said some heartfelt words. Johnny then told everyone how they met at the Forge pub. He described Dotty and me being there with all the other airmen, how noisy it was with everyone talking and laughing together.

"Suddenly," he said, "I could see and hear nothing else; there was only Fiona sitting in front of me. I knew in that instant she'd stolen my heart. If I was to have any hope of being a whole person again, I knew I had to spend the rest of my life with her."

He was met with rapturous applause. Johnny's father, the Air Commodore, was immensely proud of his son. I could see now why Fiona had been intimidated by him. Edward and I were chatting with him when Fi's mother, Judith, joined us. She seemed desperate to make Edward's acquaintance and I thought for a terrible moment she was going to courtesy. She then followed that by calling Johnny's father Air *Commander*, again! I waited for him to correct her, but he didn't bother. When Judith moved on, the Air Commodore made a cryptic comment which left me biting my lip and holding my breath.

"Who *is* that ghastly woman?" he asked abruptly.

I felt unable to speak, Edward had to come to my rescue.

"I'm afraid that ghastly woman is your son's mother-in-law."

"Oh, good gracious! Apologies, Middlebourne, and you, Mrs Heywood. Oh, dear, sounds like a foot in mouth job, do you suppose she heard me?"

"Is Mrs Robinson hard-of-hearing, Lily?!"

Unable to exhale, let alone speak, I shook my head. There was a period of enforced silence before Johnny's mother Barbara joined us. Having already spoken to her before, I could nod without speaking. Edward looked at me with the broadest of smiles as he turned towards Barbara.

"Your husband was just saying how charming Mrs Robinson is."

I lost it! I burst into laughter. There was nothing I could do to stop it. The Air Commodore also descended into uncontrolled laughter.

"Was it something I said?" Barbara asked.

"No, my dear, I'm afraid I've put my foot in it again. Both feet, actually - didn't realise that ghastly woman, Mrs Robinson, was our son's mother-in-law!"

For all that Fiona was intimidated by him, Stanley turned out to be a charming character with a wicked sense of humour. I hoped Judith hadn't overheard his comment, and later I introduced her to Caroline. She was, as I expected, embarrassingly enamoured of the Countess. What I didn't expect was that they would spend a considerable time together. Fiona noticed and came over to me.

"Is my mother boring Lady Caroline into submission?"

"Looks like it. She had an interesting exchange with the Air Commodore, or should I say the Air *Commander*."

"She didn't!"

"She did, but he made a joke about it afterwards."

"I warned you, didn't I!"

"It's just been the most perfect day, hasn't it, Fi?"

"It really has. Edward seems to have enjoyed himself, he's being very sociable."

"I think he's just trying to avoid your mother. I'll go and rescue him."

On my way towards Edward, I couldn't help but notice all the smiling faces in the hall. Dotty appeared to be everywhere, and Elizabeth insisted upon being introduced as Lady Elizabeth to all and sundry. Woody seemed to be engaged with one of the flyers, as was Corky. Patrick and Maggie were never more than an inch apart. Mac was deep in a conversation with Rob. Rolo was totally out of his depth - I think he might have been waiting for someone to ask him to explain what a logarithmic equation was, but needless to say, no one did! Gran was finally happy in her wheelchair. It delighted me that Lady Caroline also spent a lot of time with her. Greg was standing by himself, so I walked over and stood with him.

"Hasn't it been wonderful, Greg?"

"Yes, Fiona must be overjoyed. What a perfect day."

"Can I ask about Aileen? Just say so if it's a bad time."

"No, it's all right. I wanted to apologise for what happened the other day, but as you gathered, everything just happened at once."

"Yes, it was a difficult moment. Congratulations all the same."

"What do you mean?"

"It's not every day you become a father, and Christopher really is an adorable little boy."

"It's still sinking in, Lily, I still can't believe she didn't tell me."

"I have to ask… "

He quickly interrupted me. "It's something I have to think about, we both do."

"She still loves you, that's obvious isn't it?"

"Is it - how do you women know these things?"

"It's the way she spoke to me, she loves you all right."

"She was rather emotional. I thought you coped well."

"There's a part of you she's taken from me, and it hurts all over again. She knew that, and she was happy to throw it in my face."

"I know what you mean. When I see you with Edward, I feel the same. But we all have to move on, Lily."

"You'll make the right decision, Greg, I know you will. Just don't go back to her purely for Christopher's sake. In the long run, you would regret it."

I left Greg obviously deep in thought. He was probably the only person there that day who would have been happier somewhere else. I felt terribly sorry for him. Mrs Morgan and

Jennings came back into the hall, and for once neither of them was on duty. The sight of Mr Jennings in a plain suit was quite a revelation.

"Mrs Morgan," I said, "you've been brilliant at organising all this food, I won't ask how you did it."

"It would embarrass me to tell you, Mrs Heywood."

"I can assure you I know nothing about it," Jennings said, chin held high.

"Not sure I believe that, Charles, but well done anyway."

On my way towards Edward, I could see Mary talking to one of the RAF boys. I was immediately impressed with her appearance. Her hair was neatly pulled back from her face and tied into a bun. She was wearing a lovely skirt and jacket, in every respect looking like a young professional woman.

"Hello, Mrs Heywood," she said with great confidence. "Hasn't it been a wonderful wedding?"

"Yes, it certainly has. How are you, Mary? I haven't seen you for a while."

"I'm doing just fine, Mrs Heywood. Mr Norton has been marvellous. He's helped me so much I feel I'm doing quite well."

"That's exactly what he told me. You look and sound very confident, Mary, I can't tell you how pleased I am."

"I'm not really confident, but I'm trying to follow your example in everything I do. If I dress nicely and pretend to know what I'm doing, well, I find that's half the battle."

"You really *are* following my example, Mary! I'm incredibly proud of you, well done."

She was doing an enviable job, pretending to be confident. As I left her, I realised she'd already moved on from pretending. Edward was talking to Johnny, and when he saw me approaching, he put his hand out towards me, and I took it in mine.

"You must both be delighted, Johnny, it's been a wonderful day."

"We are, even the weather is perfect."

"Did you have any idea about those Spitfires?"

"None at all, it was a complete surprise."

"I shall never forget it, you must be so proud, Johnny!" said Edward.

"I confess, that was one of my proudest moments, ever. I just hope they don't sanction the boys for doing it."

The village band arrived and started to set up their instruments. It might have been extravagant to call them a band, the 'village players' may have been more accurate. They were talented individuals, and what they lacked in number, they gained in enthusiasm. Swing music was all the rage, and the moment the band struck up, the small amount of floor space available was full of dancing couples.

Edward obviously regarded swing as an aberration, a temporary manifestation of American populism. Other couples embraced it for the sheer fun and enjoyment it engendered. Of all the people on the floor, one couple captivated the audience. Elizabeth, accompanied by one of the RAF boys, was in a league of her own. She had all the moves and more besides. Dotty and Rob didn't possess Elizabeth's slick professional style, but they compensated for that with their outlandish improvisation.

When the band played a waltz, I stepped onto the floor with Edward. It was the very first occasion that we danced together. He had no idea about swing music, but to my surprise he was an accomplished ballroom dancer. We floated about the floor in perfect step and I noticed how many eyes were trained upon us. Edward, as the Lord of the Manor, was always something of a curiosity for people. I suspect as a couple we presented an even greater curiosity. One pair of those eyes were my mother's. It didn't take long for her to ask me about Edward.

"You seem to be extremely close with His Lordship, Lily?"

"Yes, we are."

"You didn't tell me about that in your letters."

"Tell you about what?"

"Your relationship with him."

"I don't have a relationship with him, Mum. I'm not saying I wouldn't like to, but we don't."

"I didn't mean to pry, luv, it's just that you look like a couple together."

"We can't talk about this here, Mum."

"No, of course not, just be careful, Lily, that's all."

Mum was just being protective, as mothers are. Gran's take on the situation was quite different when I spoke to her, she offered a totally different perspective.

"You and His Lordship make a lovely couple, Lily. Does he appreciate how lucky he is?"

"Maybe you should tell him, Gran."

"Don't you worry, dear, if I get the opportunity, I intend to."

I hugged her, my Gran knew and understood everything about me. Edward, Caroline, and Elizabeth had now met all of my extended family. While they may have been rough diamonds by their standards, they were *my* rough diamonds, my family, and it was important for me to share that part of my life with them. Both Edward and Caroline spent time with Gran though I never had the courage to ask what they had spoken about.

Above all, it was Fiona's day, and she was radiant. A more perfect couple would have been hard to imagine. She danced with just about every man in the room. Even Mr Jennings was forced to his feet, and to my surprise proved to be an accomplished dancer. Another highlight of the evening was Johnny dancing with our Queen of Swing, Elizabeth. When another ballroom dance was played, I said to Edward that I was going to ask Mr Jennings to dance with me. I also suggested he should ask Mrs Morgan. With their duties over for the day, most of the household staff came into the hall for the evening at Fiona's invitation. The sight of me dancing with

Mr Jennings was met with enormous smiles. They met the sight of Edward dancing with Elsie Morgan with wide eyes and disbelief.

It was a day of incomparable memories, moments none of us will ever forget. Fiona walking up the aisle, the flight of Spitfires, Johnny's wonderful speech, Fiona seemingly floating above the dance floor in her bridal gown, and Elizabeth showing us all how to dance 'swing'. And my enduring memory of Edward not only dancing with Elsie Morgan but doing so with a flourish.

Johnny was driving them somewhere for their honeymoon, but for their wedding night, they just wanted to be together in their new cottage. So when it was time for the couple to depart, we all said our goodbyes, as if they were going on a long journey. Everybody wished them much happiness for the future, and a wonderful honeymoon together, wherever that may be. They stepped into Johnny's car, amid the crowd of waving well-wishers, and then drove three minutes down the road to their idyllic cottage love nest.

Chapter Twenty-Six
The Telegram

Following the eventual defeat of German resistance
around Caen, the Allies prepared to advance towards
Paris. On the 15th of August 1944, a few days after
Fiona's wedding, a seaborne invasion of Southern France was
launched, called Operation Dragoon. This was another massive operation involving 800 Allied ships and 1400 landing
craft. It involved almost 4000 aircraft, including 1,300 heavy
bombers. Three divisions of American troops landed on the
beaches of the French Riviera between Toulon and Cannes,
and 5,000 British and American paratroopers landed to the
rear of the German defences to support them.

The German forces were concentrated in the north of
France, the south was not so heavily defended. The French
Resistance working with SOE harassed the Germans all over
the south of France. Communications, road, and rail transport were all disrupted. Against weaker forces, the invasion
was quickly successful. Within four weeks most of southern
France was in Allied hands. The southern ports were vital for
the Allied war effort; millions of tons of equipment, and over
900,000 troops would be landed over the coming months.

The moment that it became apparent that Operation
Dragoon looked likely to be a success, the boys in Hut 3

punched the air. There was the feeling that perhaps at last we were on our way to liberate the rest of France. I shared their enthusiasm, the talk was no longer if we would liberate Paris, I asked Edward when Allied troops would be standing next to the Eiffel Tower!

"We mustn't tempt fate, Lily," he replied, "but it looks as if the advance towards Paris is unstoppable."

Woody, always the realist, reminded everyone that the Germans were far from defeated.

"They're retreating, but don't forget, they're retreating in order to defend their homeland."

There was a mumble of agreement. The battle for Normandy had been hard won and Germany itself would be an even more formidable task. This had a direct bearing upon our proposed plan to sabotage the V2 programme. We delayed our operation, constantly reappraising the Allied progress in France. If we knew when the Allies would overrun the V2 sites, we would have a straightforward decision to make, but of course we were waiting for an answer that would not be forthcoming.

"We know more now that Dragoon has been successful," said Woody, "but that tells us nothing about the likely resistance within Germany. We have to assume there will be a big counterattack at some point."

Woody's comment only served to confirm that we needed to put our operation into action just as soon as possible, and thanks to AK, we were very nearly in a position to do that. The Poles had access to fallen test rockets but best of all with the collaboration of AK, British intelligence had the remains of a V2 spirited back to Britain during Operation Wildhorn. A Dakota FD 919 of 267 squadron on the 15th of April 1944 took off from Brindisi and landed in a beetroot field near Matczyn near Lublin in Poland. It was an impetuous mission, and right under the Germans' noses. Despite getting the Dakota stuck in the field, and against all odds, the remains of the V2 were successfully loaded into the aircraft and flown into the eager hands of MI6.

It provided us with invaluable information. To a degree, we were able to compare our theorising with the actual parts, albeit badly damaged. The boys worked out that the fuel and oxidizer pumps were in fact a twin-turbo pump which was independently driven by a steam generator. AK was able to confirm the power source for the generator was hydrogen peroxide using sodium permanganate as a catalyst.

The turbo pump itself was the key to the whole thing, and the more the boys understood it, the more the various essential specialist components became obvious. The breakthrough came when we realised there was only one specialist designer of turbo pumps in Germany, designing and manufacturing high-volume water pumps for the fire service. They were Klein Schanzlin Becker or KSB.

With pieces of the jigsaw puzzle slowly fitting together, other pieces became more obvious. With the help of the Poles, the boys were able to draw up their interpretation of the twin-turbo pump. They concluded that any number of crucial components were being made by specialist manufacturers. There was a final critical breakthrough which enabled us to pinpoint specific suppliers with absolute accuracy. The boys were elated and couldn't wait to tell me.

"Here's our list of specialist producers, Lily," said Woody, looking suspiciously smug.

"How have you arrived at this?" I asked in astonishment.

"Mathematical and analytical genius," replied Rolo.

"Well, tell me how you did it."

"Rolo's quite right, Lily, it was an act of pure genius," said Edward. "We gave the Poles a list of likely components to look for amongst their collection of crashed parts, while we looked at the components MI6 had recovered during Operation Wildhorn. Between us, we quickly formed a list of manufacturers."

"You make it sound easy."

"It was, we just made note of the manufacturers' marks on the components!"

"Are you telling me the manufacturers put their names on the parts? It's as simple as that?"

"There's a certain Irish logic to it," Patrick said. "We searched for the difficult answers and forgot to ask the easy questions."

"This is especially true of metal castings," said Edward. "Foundries always have a maker's initial inside the casting."

"Even better is the fact that the turbo-pump is made up of machined castings," said Corky.

"It's not just the body of the turbo-pump," said a jubilant Rolo. "There are several brass castings, like the oxygen nebulisers."

"And AK knows where these producers are?" I asked.

"Casting iron, aluminium, and brass, is very specialist. There are only a few foundries capable of doing this kind of work, and we have the list."

They deserved their moment of triumph. Just a couple of months ago, we knew nothing about the V2. Now we knew how it worked and had a detailed understanding about its most vital component. Not only did we understand it, thanks to the Poles, we even knew where vital components were being made! My admiration for the boffins knew no bounds, I felt six inches taller just being with them. For all their irreverent disregard of social norms, and their childlike pranks, I was always aware of being in the presence of genius.

"So, do we have enough to start planning?" I asked.

"I think we need to go ahead," said Edward.

"I agree," replied Patrick, "but is it possible to assess the risk against the reward, Mac?"

"This isn't like a mission in France," Mac replied. "Our agents can't rely on local support. This is much more dangerous."

"What about AK?" asked Rolo.

"Yes, we'll be working with them, but we don't have such established networks," Mac replied. "There's also an unknown element to this mission. Even if your assumption about these vital components is correct, we cannot know what the German stock level of that component is."

"You're right, Mac," said Edward, "we are dealing with the unknown, but AK has expanded the list of suppliers to four. It increases the odds that one of those supply chains is vital for them."

"Where are these places?" I asked.

"One of them is in the big industrial centre of Dusseldorf. There's one near Hamburg, in Pinneberg. Another is down in the south, a place called Furth. The last and possibly the most important one is at Frankenthal, near Mannheim. So we have one in the Ruhr valley, one in the north, and one in the south, and the most important target near Mannheim."

"So the targets are spread out," said Woody. "How many planes, Mac?"

"I think we need two. We can drop near Dusseldorf and go on to Frankenthal. A second plane could drop near Pinneberg, and go on to Furth, which is down near Munich, which does unfortunately give the second plane a long flight over Germany."

"Can we get aerial reconnaissance?" asked Maggie.

"It would be a big ask for Johnny," replied Corky. "These are industrial areas, plenty of flak, and the targets are probably not obvious from the air."

"What about the drop zones?"

"Should be okay," replied Corky, "but only if we can get an exact fix from AK. They would rely on torch signals at night."

"It all comes back to agents on the ground," said Mac. "Nothing gives you intel better than eyes on the ground."

"I agree," replied Edward, "but how risky do you rate this for our people, Mac?"

"We only have two fluent German speakers, so we would depend heavily on Polish resistance. But make no mistake, AK is very well organised and extremely capable."

"Are you saying the risk is acceptable?"

"We would be putting the lives of our agents in AK's hands, but I think that is a justifiable risk."

"Right, we go ahead," Edward said. "How will you plan it, Mac?"

"We coordinate with AK, and with the RAF, and we get our people safely on the ground over there. I'll designate one team to each of the sites. Phase two will be to assess the situation on the ground, and report back. Then we decide the next course of action. We can supply and coordinate whatever additional explosives or equipment they need. Phase three will be implementation, followed by phase four, extraction of our people."

"You make it sound easy, Mac," I said.

"It *is* easy for me sitting here, but any mission this deep into Germany is going to be dangerous."

"That's settled then," Edward said. "Rolo, you coordinate with AK, and Mac, you set it up. I shall inform General Gubbins and the PM."

I realised this would mean Dotty and Rob both being parachuted into Germany or Poland. My heart jumped into my throat, but I knew they were ready to accept the risk, and so it was my duty to do the same. I left the boys without a single screwed-up ball of paper being thrown at me, in a small way that was significant. Edward smiled at me as I left, but his shallow expression told its own story. He'd just made the decision to send our people into harm's way.

He willingly shouldered his responsibility, and I admired his strength of character, knowing such decisions weighed heavily upon him. With plenty of time for me to think as I walked back to the office, I imagined all kinds of disasters. I glanced over towards the estate office, but there was nobody in sight. When the Manor came into view, I could see Corporal Harris at the door and the corner of my mouth lifted slightly as I approached him.

"Morning, Corporal, how are you today?"

"Not so good, Mrs Heywood. I received a telegram from my mum this morning, her sister, my aunty, has been killed."

"Oh, Brian, I'm sorry. How did it happen?"

"V1 destroyed their house."

"Were you close to your aunty?"

"She and Mum were inseparable. She was a big part of the family."

"Is there anything I can do? Will you want some leave to go home?"

"It would be good if I could, yes."

"I'll arrange it, Corporal, consider it done."

I had become so used to Corporal Harris brightening my day, his terrible news really depressed me and I walked into the office in low spirits. Elizabeth was taking charge of the telephone for me. When I asked her if she would deal with the calls in Fiona's absence, the prospect delighted her. A sense of purpose was what she lacked in her life and she welcomed the opportunity to be useful.

"Any problems, Elizabeth?"

"No, I'm fine. This is a list of the people you need to call back. The two I've underlined insist on speaking to Edward. Mary in the estate office is asking if she can have the lease for one of the tenant farmers. Mrs Morgan wants Fiona's permission to increase her ration budget, and Mr Jennings wants your opinion about taking on another footman. Oh, and there is a telegram for you."

I regularly received telegrams, mostly just routine messages, and didn't give it a second thought.

"That's fine, Elizabeth, I'll start phoning these people back. Would you open that telegram for me?"

Elizabeth read the telegram and I noticed her expression as

she looked up at me. Her eyes widened and her defining smile had uncharacteristically vanished. With Corporal Harris' tragedy fresh in my mind, my heart leapt into my throat.

"What is it, Elizabeth?"

"It's from your father, you had better look at it."

I hardly dared to read it - it could only be the worst possible kind of news. My hands trembled as I held it. Being from Dad, I immediately thought it must be about Mum, but it wasn't. It simply read, "Sorry to inform you, Lily. Both George and Marcia were killed yesterday."

I put my head in my hands and cried. Elizabeth rushed over to me, she looked again at the telegram.

"This is your Uncle George that you told me about, isn't it?"

"That's right." I couldn't say anything else.

"I'm so sorry, Lily, your uncle means the world to you, doesn't he?"

I nodded my head as my tears became uncontrollable.

"What can I do, Lily, would you like me to get Edward for you?"

"No, I have to face this myself, Elizabeth. I'm going to go to my room."

Fiona would have known what to do for me better than I understood myself. I left Elizabeth in charge of the telephones and hoped beyond hope I didn't see any of the staff as I made my way towards my bedroom. As fate would have it, Jennings, Mrs Morgan, and Albert were all in the Great Hall. Elsie Morgan saw my distress immediately, and hastened towards me, quickly followed by Mr Jennings.

"What on earth is the matter, Mrs Heywood?" she asked.

"I've had terrible news from home. They've killed my uncle and his wife," I replied in a shaky voice.

Mrs Morgan and Jennings took charge of the situation. She put her arm around me and helped me towards my room while Jennings barked orders at Albert.

"I want a tray of tea and cake taken to Mrs Heywood's room immediately."

I felt faint as we walked up the staircase so Mrs Morgan carried more of my weight. Seeing us struggle, Mr Jennings stepped forward and took control just as Dad would have done.

"If you will excuse me, Mrs Heywood," he said, putting his arm around me.

They whisked me up to my room. Jennings naturally wouldn't step beyond the threshold, but Mrs Morgan helped me towards the armchair in the corner.

"Now, what would you prefer, Mrs Heywood? Would you like to sit here, or would you prefer to get into your bed?"

"I'll sit here, Elsie, thank you."

"In that case, I'll fetch you a blanket, we don't want you to be cold."

"I will be fine. I just need time."

"Death is no stranger to you, is it? It just doesn't seem fair, does it?"

"My uncle means so much to me, Elsie, why does death have to take everyone I love?"

"Not everyone, Lily."

"You mean His Lordship, don't you?"

"I do, I think you've both been spared for a reason."

"You don't believe in things like that, do you?"

"After all the things I've seen during this war, I do begin to wonder."

"I wonder sometimes as well. When they hit my house during the Blitz, I had the strongest feeling that I shouldn't have survived. Sometimes I have horrible dreams that death comes after me, to reclaim me. My nightmare is that if I evade him, he takes someone I love instead."

I have no idea why I confessed that silly notion to Elsie Morgan, but she appeared to be deeply moved by it. She held my hand and assured me it was only a dream which I should dismiss without a second thought. Jennings himself knocked on my door with a tray of tea and cake, and Elsie Morgan wrapped me up in a blanket, treating me like a sickly patient. I thanked them both from the bottom of my heart.

There's only one thing that can help the bereaved, and it's the one thing they can never have. In the absence of that miracle, the two of them had been the next best thing. Elsie was right, I was no stranger to death. You might say we shared a relationship based upon mutual antipathy. I knew my enemy; we shared a road well-trodden.

Elizabeth obviously decided I *did* need Edward, and she was probably right. His urgent knocking on my door made me jump. Being Edward, stepping into a lady's boudoir amounts to an inappropriate action, tantamount to instant disgrace. His concerns evaporated the moment he opened the door and he immediately took me in his arms.

"I am so very sorry, Lily. I am pleased you told me about George, now I can understand what you are going through. This is an awful day. Do you know what happened?"

"The telegram didn't say, but they're both dead, both George and Marcia, so it must have been a bomb or a V1."

"I see you have drunk your tea; would you like more?"

"No, thank you."

"I shall do my best to find out what happened. As soon as you are able, you must tell me what you would like us to do."

"*Us*, Edward!"

"Of course. Whatever you want to do, I shall be there to support you."

"That's kind, Edward, thank you."

Elizabeth must have told her mother as well because, the next moment, she also knocked on my door. Caroline appeared unmoved to find Edward in my bedroom, her only concern being to give me a hug. Between the two of them, their kindness achieved the impossible task of helping to raise my spirits.

Chapter Twenty-Seven
The Funeral

Allied troops did indeed stand next to the Eiffel Tower when the liberation of Paris took place on the 25th of August 1944. We greeted the news with a great deal of celebration. It was an important milestone in the battle for Europe, but it was a celebration in which I didn't take part. Dad telephoned me and confirmed my suspicion that a V1 killed George and Marcia. The circumstances of their death only added fuel to my recurring nightmare that death looked down on me, pointing a finger at all those I loved.

They were travelling on a bus in Croydon. They might have stepped onto any bus at any time, but they chose that particular one. It could have been a minute earlier, or later, but it wasn't. It appears that death selected them the moment they boarded it. The V1 was on a collision course with them, it seems that destiny is immovable. They died along with another nine poor souls whose destiny became aligned with theirs.

Neither of them had any close family. Marcia had a brother she hadn't seen for many years, and George had some cousins. Mum and Dad arranged the funeral to take place at Christ Church, West Croydon on Wednesday 6th of September. Churches and cemeteries were in high demand during the war. At the height of the Blitz, grieving families had to suffer the ignominy of their loved ones being interred in mass graves, now we only had to queue for a time to say goodbye. Edward drove me to the church himself, saying he wanted it to be a private moment we shared together. We met my parents outside the church and they appeared surprised to see Edward.

"We didn't expect to see you, My Lord," Dad said.

"Lily needs all the support we can give her at this time."

We hugged each other, and they shook hands with Edward, but I could sense an atmosphere between us. I dismissed it initially, assuming it to be no more than the gravity of the occasion. When the time came, we made our way into the church with the other mourners. Very appropriately, it was a joint funeral service. Marcia's brother and George's cousins were all there. The rest of the mourners were friends and colleagues, including a few old comrades from the previous war.

The service appeared slightly rushed. I didn't feel it offered them the dignity that they deserved. Dad said a few words, as did another close friend of the couple. Sadly I remember little of it, I just bit my lip and tried not to cry. The undertakers came in and carried the two coffins out, and row by row we dutifully followed on behind.

The interment is always the worst part. We all walked in a line towards the graves with heads bowed low. The overcast and dreary day seemed appropriate for the occasion. We stood around the two graves and words were spoken, none of which I really heard. I just remember that terrible moment when George's coffin was lowered out of sight beyond the world that I occupied. I remained completely in control until that point but became distraught as the coffin disappeared. Edward held me tightly in his arms. It was only later, after regaining some of my composure, that I noticed Mum was also in tears.

Eventually we moved away from the graveside in the same orderly procession of glum faces with which we had arrived. As we coalesced into groups, there was the usual attempt at small talk. Memories of the couple were recalled, and some folks discussed the progress of the war. I stood still and looked back at the graves. Now deserted, with no mourners, they looked like two insignificant holes in the ground. The apparent insignificance of the graves finally forced me to accept that they were gone. George, notwithstanding my dad, had been the single most important man in my younger life. There was nothing more important to me than the knowledge he took with him to that grave.

"I'm just going back to the graveside for a moment, Edward."

"Shall I come with you?"

"No, I just want to be alone with George, to say goodbye. Will you explain it to my parents?"

"Yes, I understand, I shall wait here. Just wave if you want me."

"I *will* need you, Edward, thank you."

Walking back, I became conscious of the sound of my footsteps. A tree in the corner of the cemetery rustled in the breeze, birdsong coming from within its branches. It all reminded me, these were the sights and sounds of my world, the simple things I took for granted, all the things George and Marcia were now denied. I approached the grave cautiously. For whatever reason, I didn't want to see the coffin lying there in the underworld. There was a pile of loose brown earth waiting to be George's eternal companion, the prospect of which made me shudder. At that moment, I wanted to believe he was not there, I wanted to believe he had transcended that place and he could see me, just as I could see him.

"Why didn't you tell me, George?" I said under my breath. "You loved me as a daughter, so why didn't you tell me? Am I yours, George, am I your daughter? Are you there watching over me? I need you to still be there, George, you've always been there for me. You told me I could do anything I put my mind to, all I had to do was to believe in myself. You gave me that belief. You said if others walked, then I could run. If others run, you said I could fly, and I can George, I *can* fly. I've done exactly as you told me, I only ever wanted to make you proud of me. I need you to tell me, have I made you proud?"

I slumped to my knees and put my head in my hands. Edward rushed over and lifted me to my feet.

"He's gone, Edward, he's gone without telling me."

"I think you know without him telling you. What's more, from what you have told me, I think you both lived with that same understanding."

"Maybe you're right, but I've lost the opportunity to hold him and call him Father."

"I wish I had known him, Lily, he sounds like a remarkable man. Of course I spoke to him once, didn't I. When I telephoned him about your reference - do you remember? His endorsement of you changed my mind. I shall never forget the immense pride in his voice when he spoke about you. He couldn't understand why you had applied for the job. He believed what I offered you was far beneath your capabilities. He made me feel utterly contemptible for offering it to you."

"Yes, that was George! He placed me on a pedestal so high, I became afraid to let go of his hand. I don't think I've ever let go, but now that it's been taken away, I feel so alone."

"You are far from alone, Lily, and you're so lucky, you have memories that few of us have. My father never felt such pride in me, not like George did of you. I was never good enough for my father, and I realise now how he treated Elizabeth. The relationship you had with George has made you the exceptional woman you are. Can you not appreciate the enormity of his pride, and the joy that you gave him in return?"

"I've not looked at it like that. I just wanted to make him proud of me, but I always needed to do more. Perhaps I didn't need to?"

"We had better go back to your parents, they will be wondering what has happened."

"Have you noticed how upset my mother is? She's very ill at ease."

"I'm not surprised, not if you're correct about George. What I can't understand, Lily, is why you didn't talk to George, or to your mother for that matter."

"It sounds silly when you say it like that. I suppose it frightened me to know the truth. I saw so much animosity between my parents as a child, and I knew it was about me. The whole thing feels like Pandora's box. I'm terrified of what will come out if I open it."

"You need to lay this matter to rest, Lily. You need to speak to your mother. Whatever is in that box, you both need to face it."

"You're right."

"Then do it today, this is as good a time as any."

"I can't, not with all these people here."

"There will always be a reason not to do it, but what better time could there be?"

Mum and Dad were waiting by the church. With Edward's advice ringing in my ears, we approached them. They were still visibly upset so I hugged them both. Dad said we should join the other mourners, that he had taken a room at a local hotel. It was only a short distance, and when we arrived there, I realised many of the mourners were from the shipping business. Many were faces I recognised but couldn't put a name to. They mostly recognised me, and to a person they offered their condolences. Even people that I hadn't seen before, said how sorry they were.

I looked at Edward as their collective sympathy really touched me, but equally it amazed me. As time passed, it became self-evident that there wasn't a person in the room that George had not spoken to in glowing terms about me. One shipping agent told me he found it impossible to have a conversation with George and Marcia without them talking about me.

He said, "They were so proud of you, Lily. You meant the world to them."

How had I been so blind that I failed to see what had been staring me in the face all the time? I could never allow myself to believe that I had done enough to repay his kindness. All the private education, the night classes, all the singing lessons, I thought I was doing it for George, or for Gran. I remembered not long after I joined the business, when I said I would do it for him. He said, 'Yes, make me proud, Lily, but always remember - you're doing it for *yourself*.'

The message from so many of the people in that room could not have been clearer. I *did* make him proud, and he was right all along, I did do it for myself. For the first time in my life I felt as if I had truly succeeded. My life's ambition had been to repay George's kindness, and to make him proud of what amounted to his life's work, which was me. With all those thoughts rushing around in my head, I suddenly felt terribly sorry for Mum. I didn't understand their relationship, but I had no doubt in my mind that she loved George.

They both chose to deny their past, and now poor Mum had to deny him beyond the grave. She had to grieve in isolation, while everyone commiserated with me. Edward was right about laying the matter to rest. I had always lacked the courage, or it was never the right occasion. That crowded room certainly didn't feel like the right place, but it was definitely the right occasion. I took a deep breath, and asked Edward to keep my Dad occupied. I wanted to talk alone with my Mum. The moment I said I wanted a quiet word with her, I could see the alarm in her eyes.

"I know what it is, Lily. I know what you're going to say."

"Then tell me, is George my father?" I didn't know how to go about it, so I just said it. She froze to the spot. I hadn't expected her to look so terrified. "It's all right, Mum. I'm not going to make a scene, but I have a right to know."

"Oh, my goodness, I've dreaded this day coming. I couldn't tell you, Lily, I'm so sorry."

"You mean he is?"

"Yes, George is your father! Can you ever forgive me?"

"I'm not sure how I feel about it. Does Dad know?"

"He has always suspected, but he doesn't know for sure."

"But why - how did you get yourself into that position?"

"You could never understand, Lily, that's why I couldn't tell you. No-one else could understand, it had to remain our secret."

"Try me, Mum. I might understand more than you realise."

"You won't, luv. You see, I loved them both, I couldn't help it. I was going out with George, who I loved dearly, but I realised I felt the same about Jack. They were both on active service but it was George who was called away. It couldn't go on, could it, so in the end with George away I had to decide. It was the hardest thing I've ever done in my life."

"I *can* understand, Mum."

She looked at me in astonishment.

"How can you possibly understand, Lily?"

"Trust me, Mum, I know."

"Then perhaps you can forgive me, Lily?"

"Understanding and forgiving are two different things, Mum. You came between me and my true father, you deprived us of our relationship."

"I know I did, and I hate myself for it. But don't you see, I didn't want anything to come between me and your dad. Oh, Lily, he knew about George and me, but when I found out I was pregnant I lied about it, I let him believe you were his. When George finally came back on leave I made him promise me that he would never mention it. I thought it was for the best. And so from that day on, I've had to live with that lie, and so has George."

Mum was so upset it became impossible for me to be cross with her. From what she had told me, it seems that Dad had chosen to believe what he wanted to believe, and I was certainly not about to disillusion him. After such an emotional day, neither of us wanted to pursue it any further. Common sense and duty told me it wasn't the time to fall out with my mother. We both needed time to reflect, time to live with the truth and to see how it felt. I hugged her, and she hugged me back. Edward looked at me from afar as I returned his smile.

"You look as if you could both do with a drink," he said.

Mum seized upon the opportunity to change the subject. "That sounds like a good idea, My Lord," she said with a nervous laugh.

"What about you, Lily?"

"Yes please, Edward, would you make it a large one?"

Dad came over and put his arm around Mum to comfort her, and no questions were asked. It left me reflecting upon our new truth. Very little had actually changed, everything had happened much as I guessed it had. I tried to see it from Mum's perspective, and to my surprise I found it wasn't that difficult. What would I have done had I found myself pregnant following my relationship with Greg? What would I say to Edward? Just the thought of such a tangled web filled me with the deepest dread. I can never go back and fully appreciate the turmoil in my mother's mind, but one thing is for sure, I would have hated to be in her shoes!

Chapter Twenty-Eight
The Briefing

August 1944 had been an eventful month, a mixture of pain and happiness. Turning the calendar over into September was accompanied by the usual mix of hope and fear. Hope that the Allied advance into Europe would continue apace, and fear of the unknown. Prominent among my unknown fears was our intended mission deep into Germany to sabotage what we hoped would be essential component supplies for the V2. One of the first things we always did was to give the mission a name. If nothing else, from that moment on, it was no longer a proposal, it had moved into the harsh realm of reality. Consistent with our system of using bird names during the D-Day build-up, we called it Operation Cormorant.

The targets were spread all over Germany, requiring four completely separate operations. Furthermore, it was decided we should coordinate all four to happen at the same time. We didn't want to give the Germans time to see the connection between them. Right from the beginning, we were aware of the logistical problems that such an operation presented. Mac wanted to avoid dropping our agents into four different locations, but the danger of moving our people long distances on the ground would only add another element of risk with every mile.

As with every operation, as it comes closer to reality, the doubts escalate into fears. The boys were frantically going back over all of their theorising and calculations. What if they got it wrong, what if the special component they thought was essential, proved not to be essential? It was always the same, as we worried ourselves sick with self-doubt. Mac was the only one who seemed capable of remaining detached, which was why he was such an incomparable planner. As the professional soldier, he went straight to the bottom line, while the boffins remained obsessed with all the detail along the way.

On the 7th of September, Susan received a message which sent a shiver down her spine. She rushed directly to Hut 3.

"I've just received this from Bletchley, a V2 rocket has hit Paris!"

"Oh, shit," exclaimed Woody.

"Oh, shit indeed," said Patrick. "So it's hit the proverbial fan."

"Did you expect this?" I asked.

"No, I can't say that we did," replied Woody. "We assumed a city, but not Paris."

"You mean London?"

"Yes, we don't think it can be accurate enough to hit strategic targets, so a nice big sprawling city presents an easy victim. The same approach we see with the V1."

"So does that mean we're next?"

"If I were a gambling man, Lily," said Patrick, "I would be looking for a bookmaker to give me good odds on one of those things hitting us today or tomorrow."

"So this is it, then," said Corky, "it begins."

"Let's not forget the V1's will also continue," said Rolo.

"Oh, heck, you're right, boyo, we can expect both at once!" exclaimed Patrick.

"We must tell Edward, and Mac," said Woody.

"I need to go," I said. "I can tell Mac and Edward."

Mac was unflustered, his plan would unfold in whatever

timeframe he deemed safe for our people. I really admired his consummate professionalism. Edward was equally resigned to the news.

"We knew it was coming, Lily," he said, "and here it is. This is not the time to be surprised, we shall be next."

"Patrick thinks later today, or tomorrow."

"I agree, but we shall just leave Mac to tell us when he decides."

When Fiona returned from her honeymoon in Cornwall she was suntanned and excessively happy. The news of the V2 did nothing to dampen her surfeit of delight. She waxed lyrical about their walks along the cliff tops, and the azure blue sea. They say love is blind, and I said nothing to prove the old saying wrong. I didn't even tell her about George and Marcia. She didn't know them, but I knew she would share my grief and take it upon herself. True lasting happiness was such a rare commodity during the war. What sort of person during rationing would take a bag of sweets away from a child!

"Elizabeth has been quite helpful, Fi. If you have any jobs for her, don't hesitate to ask."

"Oh, good, I hoped she would be."

"She's trying hard, actually, and it's been quite a turn-around. We've been getting on really well together."

"You must be relieved. I tell you what, if she could type, that would be really helpful. Why don't I give her some lessons?"

"Great idea, suggest it to her."

"I will. I went round to Gran's yesterday and Robert Fuller is doing all sorts of work there."

"I didn't realise, I thought he was just fixing the roof. I'm going to pop in to see Gran this evening, I'll see what he's been up to."

My internal telephone rang, it was Rolo. "Mac has called a briefing for the operation."

"When?"

"Now."

"Okay, I'll be there in ten minutes, thanks, Rolo."

As I was rushing to leave, Elizabeth came in. "Morning, Elizabeth. Fiona wants to teach you to type."

"That's a menial job, isn't it?"

"Only when you're very good at it, and I'm not sure the war will last that long!"

"I'd better get started then," she replied.

On my way to Hut 3, I was waylaid in the hall, first by Nancy, and then Albert. No sooner had I dealt with their problems than Mrs Morgan wanted me. I finally rushed out of the entrance to find Harris was back on guard at the door.

"Morning, Corporal, is everything all right at home with your family?"

"Yes, thank you, Mrs Heywood. We had the funeral the day before yesterday."

"I wasn't able to tell you, Corporal, I lost my uncle the day after you lost your aunt. We've not long had the funeral."

"I'm sorry, Mrs Heywood. I just want this all to end."

"Don't we all, Corporal!"

"I'd like to thank you for getting me leave. I don't understand how you can manage these things when you're not even in the army."

"It's all a case of who you know, Corporal."

"Well, I certainly owe you one, Mrs Heywood."

"Don't worry, I've made a note in my diary, I won't let you forget!" Despite everything that had happened to us both in the last few days, Harris stood there with a smile on his face. I guessed he was thinking of how he might repay me and being Corporal Harris it wouldn't be a box of chocolates. "Don't say it, Corporal."

"You surprise me, Mrs Heywood, a lovely lady like you, thinking thoughts like that."

"I was only thinking of you offering to do extra guard duty."

"Those very words were on the tip of my tongue."

I left him with a spring in my step. Grief was a peacetime preoccupation and we'd learned to regard it as an indulgence, something we were prepared to delay for that time when our lost ones could re-join us. I hastened my stride towards Hut 3. They were all there, including all eight of our field agents. I rushed in to find everyone sitting on chairs or tables looking like a bunch of attentive school children, with the headmaster standing facing them, pointer in hand. I gave my apologies, and saw that Mac had a large map of Germany in front of him as he began his presentation with an announcement which was news to me.

"This morning, the first V2 rocket has fallen upon London. It has caused widespread destruction in Chiswick. I don't believe we have the casualty figures yet."

"When did this come to us, Edward?" I asked.

"We heard about half an hour ago."

Mac had chosen his moment to announce Operation Cormorant with an unnerving sense of timing. It certainly concentrated minds. He went through the plan meticulously. They would fly the eight field agents to Germany in two Halifax four-engine bombers, departing simultaneously from RAF Tempsford in Bedfordshire. Tempsford was a part of the RAF Special Duty Service, the most secret airfield in Britain. It was the starting point for nearly all SOE operations involving parachute drops into Europe.

The operation was to begin during the night of September 14th. Mac confessed that the date was far from ideal. There would unfortunately be a waning crescent moon, giving the pilots and agents precious little night vision. The next full moon was not until the end of the month, and there was another complication, that we had only just been told about. A major Allied offensive was to be launched on the 17th, which would involve 40,000 airborne troops. Operation Market Garden would have implications for our own operations, especially in and around Dusseldorf. He chose the 14th because it was the first practical opportunity for us and it was before the 17th. Moonlight would diminish every day thereafter. Mac confessed he didn't like the sudden haste, but we'd only just been made aware of the pending Operation Market Garden.

"The two Halifax's are to be designated Alpha One, and Alpha Two," Mac said. "Alpha One will navigate directly to a drop zone west of Dusseldorf. Agents Dipper and Wren will rendezvous at the drop zone with AK. Alpha One will then continue to a drop zone east of Frankenthal, where agents Goshawk and Osprey will rendezvous with AK. Alpha Two will navigate to a drop zone north of Pinneberg, where agents Jay and Swift will rendezvous with AK. Alpha Two will continue to a drop zone southwest of Furth, where agents Woodlark and Swallow will rendezvous with AK."

I immediately whispered to Dotty, "Which one are you?"

"I'm Goshawk."

We all understood flying over Germany was extremely dangerous but parachuting out of the night sky into exactly the right place, guided by only a couple of torches, was also fraught with danger. The risks to be taken by the Polish resistance were equally immense. Getting our agents safely on the ground, and into the hands of AK, was one of the most dangerous aspects of the mission. The RAF would navigate the least dangerous route to avoid concentrations of ack-ack, but this remained a dangerous part of the operation. Dotty and Rob were on separate operations; Mac never knowingly allowed 'couples' to work together, calling it a conflict of interest.

Mac discarded the possibility of sabotaging the components in transit. He felt that the weeks of intelligence required would add too much risk. The aim of the operation now was to destroy the factories and each factory would represent a unique challenge. Our agents' task was to assess that challenge and come up with a plan to put them out of action.

There was an excellent precedent for such an audacious

operation. In 1942, the Pessac electrical transformer station near Bordeaux provided an essential power supply for the German submarine base in Bordeaux. RAF precision bombing had often proved itself to be more lethal for the flight crews than for the chosen targets. General Gubbins saw the opportunity to demonstrate the capabilities of SOE sabotage to his sceptical detractors. Four men cut through the wire perimeter fence in the dead of night and planted magnetic limpet mines against the eight enormous oil-filled transformers, destroying six out of the eight. The Germans assumed it must have been an air raid, and all four SOE agents returned safely to England. Known as Operation Josephine B, it set an example for future SOE operations, with an outcome that we wanted to emulate.

Mac went through the many sabotage options available to our agents, and the kind of equipment they could be provided with. Canisters would be dropped with the agents at each drop zone, containing basic armaments and explosives. Any additional specialised equipment that the agents deemed necessary could be dropped later. That part of Mac's briefing was probably for the benefit of the intelligence section, our agents understood precisely how to blow things up!

Dotty appeared enthusiastic about the operation, while I sat in stunned awe of all of them. The prospect of jumping out of an aeroplane high above Germany and plummeting down in total darkness was incomprehensible to me. Anyone who served on active service was a hero, as far as I was concerned, but agents for whom discovery would mean certain death or worse, were a different kind of hero, they were a breed apart. Their courage is without parallel.

-o0o-

I'd promised Gran I would drop by that evening, so arranged to walk home with Dotty. I found her outside chatting with Brian Harris.

"Don't trust this man, Dotty, he'll lead you astray."

"I don't think I *could* lead Dotty astray, Mrs Heywood."

"Well, I suppose you have a point there," I replied. "Doesn't stop you trying it on with me though, does it!"

"You'd best be careful, Brian," Dotty said. "If Lily gave me the word, I would have to remove your parenting prospects."

"What a way to go!" he said.

"Come on, Dotty, let's be on our way before Corporal Harris says something he'll regret!"

We had only walked a little way before Dotty said, "You're going to nag me about being careful, aren't you?"

"Yes, I am, you're right."

"I knew it, you're always nagging me, you and Fi."

"And why do you suppose that is?"

"I know, you worry about me, but it's no good you nagging."

"Do you not feel fear, Dot? When you go on these dangerous missions, why are you not terrified?"

"I *am* terrified, but you just have to control it. You don't understand how we deal with these things. What everyone is really frightened of is the unknown, so we turn the unknown into a series of probabilities, each of which we have a response to. In that way, the unknown isn't so frightening."

"Well, that's fine for you, Dotty, but for me and Fi, the unknown is what would we do if you didn't come back."

"I'll be back, don't you worry. The SS had a hold of me once and they ain't ever getting a second chance."

"Just make sure they don't, all right? So what has Robert Fuller been doing at Gran's, then? I've only authorised the roof repair."

"He's doing all sorts. I suppose Gran's given him the go-ahead. If you ask me, he's got the hots for our Florence."

"What do you mean?"

"Well, they get on so well, they seem to spend a lot of time with each other."

"But she's pregnant."

"So, that doesn't mean she's not an attractive girl, does it?"

"I suppose not. I'm just surprised, that's all. Robert Fuller is really going places, he's got his head screwed on."

"Florence isn't daft, you know. I get on well with her, we're mates."

"I'm not saying that; she's a lovely young girl, we're really close. I'm just surprised Robert is interested, considering Florence's circumstances."

"I understand what you mean, but he doesn't seem bothered. Florence invited him for dinner the other night. He's a bit of a dish if you ask me."

"He is, isn't he? You're only what, about four or five years older than him, a few months ago you'd have been all over him like a rash."

"I know, I'm reformed! Anyway, Rob would kill me."

Alerted by the barking, we looked up to see Spencer Tracy bounding towards us. Florence was standing by the gate with her hands on her hips and a look of resignation on her face. No amount of her shouting was going to stop Spencer. I braced myself for the inevitable slobbering affection from the silliest labrador in Middlebourne. Dotty took a step forward and pointed a finger at him, turning her head slightly sideways. Spencer applied the brakes just in time, and sat at her feet looking up as if to say, 'Am I not the smartest dog in Middlebourne?'

Florence and I burst into laughter. "How *do* you do that?" Florence asked.

"I threatened to cut his balls off once so he has respect for me now."

We walked into the cottage, still laughing, with Spencer snapping at our heels. Gran was in the kitchen, in her usual chair, her face lighting up when she saw us. Her recovery was progressing well for someone of her age. Her left arm had lost a lot of movement and was obviously not going to come

310

back. The same applied to the left side of her face, but she was speaking really well by then. Above all, she was stoical.

Her attitude was that she was still here, and she'd damn well make the best of it. While I hated seeing her handicapped, I so admired her spirit. Initially, she'd been resistant to having Florence there, helping her. It wasn't Florence, it was just anyone helping her but I noticed that had changed. Like everyone else, Florence called her Gran. I smiled to myself, seeing how well she'd fitted in. There was one silly problem - she would only ever call me 'Mrs Heywood'. Considering how close we'd become over time, it seemed ridiculous in Gran's cottage.

"Would you like a cup of tea, Mrs Heywood?" she said.

"For goodness' sake, Florence, call me Lily."

"All right, I'll try."

"So, tell me about Robert."

"What's Dotty been saying?"

"I'm told he comes courting!"

"No, I didn't say that!" said Dotty.

"He's been for dinner, that sounds like courting to me," I said, laughing.

"He's a nice young man," said Gran, "and he's done lots of jobs for me."

"He is nice," said Florence. "I like him."

"That's what I said, he comes courting!"

"Well, maybe," Florence replied with an irrepressible smile.

We had a lovely evening together, and Robert's name might just have been mentioned once or twice again. As I was leaving, Dotty had a last word on the matter.

"I think you're right, Lily, I think he *is* courting."

"Oh, he's courting all right," I replied, smiling at Florence.

Chapter Twenty-Nine
A Letter From The Grave

The 14th of September 1944 was another of those dates burnt into my memory. We hardly saw Dotty during the build-up to Operation Cormorant. As the aim was to destroy industrial production sites, they trained relentlessly, deploying every kind of explosive, using every type of fuse SOE offered. When they were not assembling explosive charges blindfolded, they were practising killing one another. I could see them from afar; one of them would play the unsuspecting German guard, while another practised creeping up on them, silently dispatching the unfortunate individual.

They were like cats approaching a mouse, both sharing the same deadly intent. The weapon of choice for their deadly game of cat and mouse was their fighting knife. A more sinister looking weapon I've never seen. Designed by Eric Sykes and William Fairbairn, it was nearly a foot long with a seven-inch stiletto blade, made by the Wilkinson Sword Company. Viewed from the victim's perspective, that knife in the hands of an SOE agent, or an SAS soldier, would represent your worst possible nightmare.

Our agents left us on the morning of the 14th. Fi and I only had time to say a brief goodbye. I realised the last thing Dotty or Rob wanted was us blathering on about them taking care of themselves. They would have hated tears even more, and while I could control the former, I had little control over the latter. The makeup and lipstick were gone, she wore authentic looking local dress for the area she would operate in.

Originally SOE tried to source genuine German or French clothes, but when that became too difficult, they had them made. A single seam produced in the wrong type of stitch could have proved disastrous, so they used immigrants and refugees to produce the clothes. Labels were taken from second-hand garments or reproduced exactly. The Dotty I knew had already left; the Dotty I hugged was another woman, calm, focused, and resolutely determined.

It had never happened before, but everyone was there to see them off. It annoyed Mac. He said this was a clandestine operation, everyone gathering to say goodbye was completely out of order. He was right, obviously. There was, however, something about this mission that none of us had experienced before. Never had all of our people been involved on the same mission, and never before had we sent our people so deep into an enemy country. Nobody said it out loud, but we realised the odds on them all coming back safely were not in our favour.

The army lorry carrying them to RAF Tempsford slowly moved away. I expected a wave from the back, but the tarpaulin just flapped open momentarily, revealing two rows of determined looking faces. We waved anyway, and when they were out of sight we dispersed with hardly a word being spoken. Mac was right, we shouldn't have gathered like that.

Back in the office, the atmosphere was subdued, and Hut 3 was probably the same. It would be the best part of twenty-four hours before we would know if they had dropped safely. Fiona and I did our best to keep busy, but it was difficult to concentrate on anything other than worrying about Dotty and Rob. However, there was a distraction waiting for me in the post, an inconspicuous envelope which had found its way to the bottom of the pile. It was late in the afternoon before

Fi handed it to me, a large plain envelope with a typed name and address.

Only half concentrating as I opened it, my attention was immediately drawn to the headed paper which I recognised. It was from the firm of solicitors we used for the shipping agency. The contents of the letter were relatively brief. It concerned George's last will and testament. The solicitor informed me that in the event of Marcia preceding George, or in the event that they both died together, he bequeathed his entire estate to me.

George had no other family, so I suppose, considering what my mother admitted at the funeral, I shouldn't have been surprised. Nevertheless, it was something I hadn't thought about. Rather than bringing me any consolation or joy, the news merely renewed my sorrow. The solicitor went on to say I should make an appointment with him to discuss the details. Finally, it said there was a second sealed envelope addressed to me. This envelope was apparently to be given to me only in the event of George's death. I recognised George's handwriting on the envelope and opened it nervously. It was two pages long.

My dearest Lily. If you are reading this letter, then we both know I am gone from your life forever. We also know there is something between us which has gone unsaid, something so important that I cannot take it with me. If I thought what I am about to tell you would be a terrible shock, I would seek a form of words to ease the way, but we both know this is not the case. The answer to the question that you chose not to ask, is yes, I am your father.

Your mother was the love of my life, there could never be a greater love for me. The day she chose Jack over me remains my darkest day. Strange as it may seem, I believe it was also the darkest day for her too. When she found out about you, it was too late, she had made her commitment. Your mother made me pledge I would never say a word about it. She said my pledge was for Jack more than it was for her. What you have to remember, Lily, is that I owe my life to Jack. He carried me to safety across no-man's-land. No man could owe another more than I owe Jack. A pledge made to him was a commitment I could never break.

Sometimes words cannot express what the heart feels. I know we both felt the same, which is why in your heart you always knew. I regret so much, but most of all I am sorry for what you were denied. You have given me so much, and I have given you so little in return, I hope you can forgive me. I watched that frightened little girl overcome her demons. I witnessed that inner belief growing inside you. It has been the greatest joy and privilege of my whole life to witness what that frightened little girl has achieved. No father could have greater pride in his daughter than I have in you, and be assured, no father could love you more.

I ask just two things, Lily. If I leave Marcia behind, take care of her, she loves you as I do. Finally, forgive your mother, she and Jack are the two finest people I have known. If you feel you have to tell them, be kind. If you decide not to, it would be kinder still. If in the future, the occasion is right, tell Pam I never stopped loving her. Goodbye my darling Lily, yours is the last face I will see, and our love is the only thing I take with me. Your loving father.

I put my head in my hands and sobbed my heart out.

"Oh, Lily, what's happened?"

"It's from George, I didn't tell you Fi, it was while you were on your honeymoon. George and Marcia have been killed."

"When, what happened?"

"It was a few weeks ago, I didn't want to burden you with it."

She rushed to my side, as I knew she would. In an instant, all her happy memories of the Cornish coast were dashed against the rocks, as I knew they would be.

"Let me see," she demanded.

She put her arm around me and read the letter.

"You were right, you said he was your father. I'm so sorry, Lily, but you must never keep something like this from me. I understand why you did, but we need to support each other. Now, tell me everything that's happened, you can cry on my

315

shoulder. Then I'll ask Jennings to get you a large whisky in the Drawing Room, and I'll tell Edward you need him."

"You're a wonder, Fi, thank you."

I read the letter several more times, I could hear George saying the words. To finally appreciate how much he and Mum loved each other was tragic, but strangely comforting. Fiona was wonderful, making me talk it through, and in the process allowing me to see it for the act of closure that it was. Perhaps that's what George intended. The afternoon was drawing in, already past five o'clock. Edward was still in Hut 3 and I heard Fi effectively summon him over the telephone. She also summoned Jennings. When he appeared in the office, Fiona dispatched me to the Drawing Room with a flourish.

"Mrs Heywood needs a comfortable armchair and a large glass of whisky, Mr Jennings. Would you escort her to the Drawing Room? His Lordship will join her there."

"With the greatest of pleasure, Mrs Albright."

"You're wonderful, Fi," I said, as I left with Jennings.

"Is everything all right, Mrs Heywood?"

"It is now, Mr Jennings. I've just had to contend with a difficult family situation, but I think the matter is finally closed."

"In my experience, Mrs Heywood, family matters can take their toll on you. Feel free to take my arm if you so require."

"Thank you, Mr Jennings, I will."

He led me to the Drawing Room and sat me down in my usual armchair. As always, his calm and dignified manner and his reassuring smile were a great source of strength. As he was leaving to fetch my glass of whisky, a very concerned Edward came bounding into the room.

"What's wrong, Lily, what's happened? Fiona sounded concerned."

"I'm all right, Edward, really. I've just had a bit of a shock, that's all."

I handed him George's letter, together with the solicitor's. He read both very seriously.

"This is a beautiful letter from your father, Lily. If my father had expressed sentiments even remotely similar to this, it would have meant the world to me. This must surely help you draw a veil over the matter."

"I think in time it will, but you can imagine what it felt like, reading those words for the first time."

"Indeed, I can, a letter from the grave. We are not in a position to pass judgement on the agreement he made, but I sense a man who has suffered heartache beyond anything I could imagine. I feel nothing but pity for the poor man. He lost his true love, and then that loss was compounded by the loss of his daughter. He must have been a completely broken man to make a pact with the devil like that. I might disagree with the decision he made, but I have to admire his principles. It speaks volumes about his strength of character and integrity that he remained true to his word. And yet despite everything, he remained determined to do his absolute best for you. I have nothing but admiration for him."

"That's a wonderful thing to say, Edward, if only he could be here now to hear you say that."

"I wish it too, Lily, it would have been an honour to meet him."

"He was wonderful to me. Isn't it crazy what love can drive people to do?"

"I agree, Lily. There are philosophers who say that what we perceive as free will is no more than an illusion. How much truth there is in that statement is not for me to say, but that there *is* truth, I think, is beyond doubt."

That was the kind of philosophical debate that Edward loved to dissect, and normally I would enjoy debating with him. Elizabeth soon joined us, having been to Tunbridge to buy some clothes, but it was quickly apparent that the trip was not entirely successful.

"I just don't understand how you manage, Lily, there is absolutely nothing in the shops. I will have to go to London."

"You may not find London much better, Elizabeth, it's called rationing."

"Well, I realise that, but I didn't think it would apply to nice clothes."

"It applies especially to nice clothes, I'm afraid."

"Oh, good gracious, that ghastly man Hitler really has to go."

She laughed and I was relieved she wasn't taking her own words seriously. I could never be sure with Elizabeth if she took the war, and our efforts, seriously enough, or perhaps Edward and I had allowed ourselves to become too consumed by it. For us every event, every twist and turn, had some significance, and it came to us like a daily ration of gruel. As un-sustaining as that gruel was, we had learned to survive on it, and when that was all you had, you became dependent upon it. Elizabeth was learning fast but she hadn't lost her sense of freedom and fun. I'm afraid for me 'fun' was something we remembered rather than enjoyed, something we occasionally snatched from beneath the shadow of war.

It was a difficult evening for me. When I wasn't thinking about George, I was looking at the clock. Edward put a brave face on it, but he too kept glancing at the time. Elizabeth knew the reason for our preoccupation with the time and was tactful enough not to mention it. Caroline, always the soul of discretion, didn't mention it either. Come the end of the evening, I apologised for being distracted, and having wished everyone goodnight, I wearily made my way up the stairs. It was to be a long and restless night.

At 11:06 that evening, September 14th, 1944, two Halifax bombers took off from RAF Tempsford. On board the two planes were eight SOE agents accompanied by canisters of weapons and explosives. They flew deep into Germany. Operation Cormorant had begun.

Chapter Thirty
Market Garden

The morning of September 15th was a difficult time for everyone. Our agents should have been in the hands of AK for five hours by that time. I was becoming increasingly nervous. We knew only too well that any radio message was potentially a dangerous beacon, directing the Germans to its source. I sat looking at the clock, Fiona was doing the same thing. Edward came back into the office and he too was looking at the clock. Just as I was about to admit my concern, the internal phone rang. It was Rolo, he just said one word, "August."

That was the code word which meant Alpha One's second drop had successfully liaised with AK. We all breathed a small sigh of relief, but that good news only made us more nervous about the other three drops. The telephone rang again. "October," Rolo said. That was Alpha Two's second drop successful. We didn't celebrate or even say a word, we just sat silently waiting. My heart was thumping in my chest; I kept taking a deep breath in the vain hope that it might slow it down. When an hour later the telephone rang again, I grabbed it in an instant, I could sense the relief in Rolo's voice as he said, "July and September."

"That's it," I shouted, "they're all down safe."

Edward leaped up with his fists in the air, Fiona came over and hugged us both. It was a wonderful moment. There was a lot of punching the air and jumping up and down. In retrospect, it was ludicrous to be celebrating at the start of the operation, but we all realised how dangerous the drop would be. The next phase of the operation necessitated radio silence, and we knew it might last for days or weeks, but it didn't make the waiting any easier. To add to Fiona's stress, Johnny was flying regularly over the Channel, photographing anything he could find which looked like a V1 launch ramp. It was the start of a long period of tension which seemed to build up day by day.

The number of V2 rockets striking the Southeast were increasing, adding a new level of fear for Londoners. While the V1 announced its presence in advance, the V2 offered no such warning. The first that the victims knew was when it was too late. That the V2 was a more deadly weapon than the V1 was quickly becoming apparent. Dropping out of the sky at supersonic speed, the V2 penetrated the ground before detonation, thus concentrating the explosion. The effect was like an earthquake, people reported things like cracked wash basins a quarter of a mile away from the epicentre. After all that had gone before, it was perhaps unsurprising that the morale of Londoners was at a low ebb.

We were all war-weary, just wanting it to stop, and always being aware of Allied progress only seemed to increase our weariness. Our planning for Operation Cormorant was still in progress, while Operation Market Garden was just about to begin. The war in Europe was entering a new phase. The battle for Normandy was won and the Allies were now advancing across France towards Germany. The German Siegfried Line presented a formidable challenge. Field Marshal Montgomery proposed a daring plan designed to bypass those defences. Three airborne divisions would drop by glider and parachute into the Netherlands. The plan was to seize strategic territory and more importantly, to capture the bridges over the Rhine which would enable Allied forces to cross the river.

The first phase began on September 17th, 1944. We all gathered in Hut 3, desperate for every crumb of news. The 101st Airborne had the task of capturing Eindhoven, and several other bridges near the town. The 82nd Airborne was to capture Nijmegen and an important bridge over the River Waal. 10,000 British and Polish paratroopers were charged with capturing the most northerly of the bridges, at Arnhem. As reports trickled in, it became obvious to us that some things didn't appear to be going according to plan. Woody was furious to hear that there weren't enough transport aircraft to fly all the British Airborne troops in one go. There had to be a second airlift the following day, and the Polish troops were even more delayed.

"This is not a good start," said an irate Woody. "It means we've lost the element of surprise and our second wave may become separated from the first."

More reports came in of poor weather, and then we heard that radios were not working.

"I don't understand," I said. "How can our radios not work?"

"They're in a wooded landscape," replied Edward, "plus, after the second drop, they're separated."

I could tell from their attitude that the boys had misgivings about the Arnhem aspect of the operation. The town was heavily fortified with ack-ack guns, and so the drop was eight miles away. Despite that, the 2nd Battalion of 1st British Airborne managed to reach the northern end of the bridge. The German defences were formidable, so they had no option but to hold the bridge while waiting for the relief force to arrive. This was when things started to unravel. The relief column had to advance along a narrow road and nine British tanks were lost almost immediately. They only advanced seven miles by the end of the first day.

"You're looking worried, Edward," I said.

"I don't like the sound of it, we are too stretched."

Woody and the others all agreed, so if they were worried, I was worried. The 18th of September brought us news from Operation Cormorant. One of our teams had a plan in place for the destruction of their target and would wait to coordinate the attack with the others. This was splendid news, at least something was going right. That same day, we heard that the relief column had covered twenty miles and had caught up with the 101st Airborne near Eindhoven.

Tension in Hut 3 seemed to grow by the day. We had the daily V1 figures coming in, and now of course there was another set of figures for the V2. It was a never-ending stream of death and destruction. Johnny was bringing back an almost daily trove of reconnaissance photographs, all of which had to be analysed. The battle in Europe intensified and Operation Market Garden was not looking favourable. And all the while, we worried ourselves sick over Operation Cormorant. Only one team had radioed that they prepared. When your list of concerns grows like that, the absence of good news becomes bad news. To our enormous relief, the next confirmation of readiness from Operation Cormorant came through on the 20th of September.

Troops crossed the River Waal that day, but they were still eight days away from relieving the embattled troops at Arnhem. Then came confirmation of a different kind. An Allied reconnaissance plane confirmed unequivocally that there were two German SS Panzer Divisions in and around Arnhem. When Woody heard the news, he sat with his head in his hands. We all reacted the same. There had been a lot of discussion among the generals about the reports of Panzer Divisions in Arnhem, but for whatever reason, they chose to ignore the possibility. Well, now it was no longer speculation.

"Those poor bloody troops on the Arnhem Bridge," said Patrick.

"I wonder if they know about the Panzers?" I enquired.

"To be sure, they soon will," he replied despondently.

On the ground, the advancing troops from Nijmegen were met with fierce resistance. And after five days of heroic combat, the final German assault upon the British brigade at Arnhem bridge had an inevitable result. Operation Market Garden came to an ignominious end when what remained of the British troops were forced to dig in at Oosterbeek until the 25th of September when they finally evacuated back over the Rhine.

Our Operation Cormorant had achieved its third state of readiness, but that good news hardly lifted our spirits. In the fullness of time, Market Garden achieved the liberation of much of the Netherlands, which offered the Allies some strategic advantage, but we were only too aware that it had been a costly mistake. For me, and for the war-weary British people, it confirmed that the much hoped-for end of the war by Christmas wasn't going to happen. I was really depressed. Come the evening, I was the first person in the Drawing Room, where I headed straight for my favourite armchair. My shoes came to rest several feet in front of me and I just fell back into the chair with an arm hung over each side. No-one knew I was there until Edward appeared.

"I wondered where you were, Lily."

"I'm sorry, I just felt so tired, I had to sit down quietly."

"Excellent idea, do you mind if I join you?"

"It depends on what bad news you're coming with!"

"You're right, I am the bearer of yet more bad news. Shall I leave you in peace?"

"Of course not, tell me."

"I have the final casualty estimates from Market Garden."

"Is it terrible?"

"Well, judge for yourself. About 10,600 troops made it north of the Rhine, and they estimate 7,900 were killed, wounded, or taken prisoner. Estimated casualties for the operation as a whole are about 17,000."

It wasn't just those horrific casualties, it was everything. It was George and Marcia, Mum and Dad, it was Dotty and Rob. The final news of all those casualties was just too much for me. No-one knew better than me the suffering of losing a loved one. I felt as if I was sharing the grief of every single one of those wives, mothers, fathers, sisters, and brothers. Edward took me in his arms, saying nothing, just holding me.

"I'm sorry, Edward, it's all getting on top of me at the moment."

"You have been a tower of strength despite everything which has been thrown at you. Perhaps it has come as a shock to find that you are human like the rest of us."

"It's been a bad time. I don't think I've really been able to come to terms with that letter from my father."

"I think you are starting to, Lily. You just called him your father and not George."

"Did I? I suppose I did. He was lovely, Edward. He did everything for me, he worshipped the ground I stood on. If only things had been different for us."

"It seems to me that you had a wonderful relationship anyway. I don't recall anyone waxing so lyrical about their father as you do about yours. It certainly does not apply to me."

"I do, don't I. There was just something between us, I always loved him. I feel so sorry for Dad now. He either knew or had a good idea. When I was a child, every time George came to the house I'd run to him and he would pick me up and spin me around. Poor Dad, what must he have been thinking!"

"I understand now why your family was so troubled, it's such a tangled web you found yourself in. It is an enormous credit to them and to your extended family that you grew into this amazing, beautiful woman. In many ways, your father was a very lucky man, and he must have been so proud of you."

"It could all be worse, I suppose, but I so wish I had a normal family, and a conventional upbringing."

"I believe it was the Victorian polymath Francis Galton who coined the phrase, 'nature or nurture' when considering heredity. You might wish for a conventional childhood but look what happened in its absence! You were gifted at birth with the voice of an angel and a determination to succeed. Then your father lifted you from the childhood you so despised and gave you opportunity. But you should be in no doubt, Lily, it was you who seized that opportunity with both hands. You are the product of that unconventional childhood. I for one would not wish to change a thing."

He did it again! He could be beautifully eloquent when he wanted to. I managed a smile, how could I not?

"How can you possibly know about this man, Francis Galton?"

"Oh, it's just one of those insignificant facts I retain."

"Well, I'm grateful to him, and to you, Edward. When I feel cast adrift, like today, it's you I cling to. If you weren't here, Edward, I think I might drown."

"You won't drown, Lily, I shall never allow it."

He was going on to say something else, but Jennings came into the Drawing Room.

"What can I get for you, Mrs Heywood, My Lord?"

"Mrs Heywood is in fear of drowning, Jennings. I think, subliminally, she is requesting a single malt whisky without too much water."

I smiled again, two smiles in as many minutes! Elizabeth soon joined us, coming in all bright and breezy, obviously unencumbered by the bad news about Market Garden.

"Hello, you two, I've hardly seen either of you today. What's been happening?"

Elizabeth had been in the office all day apparently, helping Fiona, and she had actually become extremely helpful.

"Not good news about Market Garden, I'm afraid," said Edward. "In fact it's not good at all."

"Oh no, I thought that might be the case yesterday when

you told me about it. What about Cormorant, any good news there?"

"Actually, I haven't told Lily yet. The last of our four teams radioed a coded message this evening. It seems they are willing to attempt sabotage but think the chances of success are extremely slim. They have offered an alternative for us to consider. If we can arrange a bombing raid, they will light up the factory to guide in the bombers."

"What a good idea," I said. "The Germans may think that the other factories were bombing raids too. It might give our agents a little extra time to get away. Do you remember the SOE sabotage of the Pessac electrical transformer station? The Germans assumed that was a bombing raid and the agents all got away and back to England."

"That's right, if this is possible, it will help all of our agents."

We discussed it for a while and it seemed to make sense on several levels. Elizabeth was fully engaged with us, having finally come to realise that the war even affected people like her.

"Listen to me! I'm becoming like you two, you're a bad influence on me," she joked.

Jennings came back with our glasses of whisky, and Caroline then joined us. I put my shoes back on and sat up properly. The war continued to devastate lives, but the evening meal at Middlebourne was like the ravens in the Tower of London. It would be a terrible harbinger of doom if either of them ceased to exist.

Chapter Thirty-One
Greg Norton's News

September 1944 had proven to be another very eventful month, and not always for the right reasons. The failure of Market Garden possibly added several months to the war. With the aid of hindsight, we now realise what a difference that could have made. The Russians were marching west. They were already in Poland. Had Market Garden succeeded, the post-war map of Europe may well have looked very different. East Germany and the Baltic States might not have fallen under the control of the Soviets.

The Nazis brutally put down the Warsaw uprising, while their garrison at Calais surrendered to Canadian troops. Allied forces landed on Crete, and Canadian troops crossed the border into the Netherlands. And all the while V1 and V2 rockets continued to rain down upon south-east England. Despite all that was going on for us, one event dominated the new month - our own Operation Cormorant would succeed or fail in the coming days or weeks.

I had difficulty giving my full concentration to all the other events taking place. The daily drone of V1's flying directly over our heads was a constant reminder of our own peril, and that of our agents in Germany. Operation Cormorant had reached its final planning stage. Edward went directly to the PM to ask for a bombing raid to be sanctioned against the factory in Dusseldorf. The PM gave his instant support, but there was opposition from Sir Arthur Harris. The establishment didn't always regard SOE favourably and 'Bomber' Harris was not disposed to be involved with us. Dusseldorf had been the subject of many bombing raids, especially during 1943, and our losses had been severe. We will never know how the disagreement was resolved, but it was the PM who got his way.

Coordinating everything with our agents was difficult with only minimal radio traffic. We had to consider cloud cover and the moon phase, and the whole thing became more urgent when we realised there was a full moon on Monday, October 2nd. The weather forecast for that day was cloudy, the next cloudless forecast was October 4th. This was not a full moon but would be sufficient on a cloudless night for both the bombers and our agents to have some vision. We had a final meeting in Hut 3. It was ultimately Edward's decision, but together we discussed every possible scenario. Our introspection went right back to basics, Edward even asking how sure we were that each of the factories was definitely producing vital components for the V2.

Everything was discussed, and the time came when we each had to commit to the operation. One by one, we agreed that our intelligence was sound, our agents were in place - we should go ahead. When it was my turn to speak, I felt the lives of each of our agents resting heavily on my shoulders. The responsibility was daunting and the prospect of sending our people to their death terrified me. I knew I wasn't alone in that fear.

"We go ahead," I said, disguising my anguish. "My only stipulation is that we bring them back. We can't leave them to make their own way back."

"I agree," replied Edward. "I'll inform the PM immediately."

The meeting was over, we were each deep in our own thoughts. Edward said he'd follow me back to the Manor, he just needed to discuss the latest photo reconnaissance with Maggie. It was getting late, so I left him there and made my way back. When I reached the point where I could see the estate office, I glanced in that direction as I always did. Greg was there, and so was Aileen. It looked as if they had just arrived. I had been under the impression that Aileen had gone back to Scotland, so I was a little surprised to see them together. He saw me and for whatever reason I found myself walking towards them.

Once again, Aileen's eyes flashed the moment she noticed me. The last time I saw her, she looked rather down at heel but not so on this occasion. She wore a lovely blue and white polka dot dress, her blonde hair was really attractive, and what I remember most of all were her eyes. Why I hadn't noticed them before I can't imagine, perhaps she had made more effort with her makeup, or perhaps I just didn't want to see. Her eyes were blue, noticeably blue, she was really lovely.

"Hello Greg, hello Aileen." Seeing her luggage and baby Christopher, I then said the first thing that popped into my mind. "Are you arriving or leaving, Aileen?"

"Aileen has just arrived, Lily," Greg replied.

Greg and I had been so close at one time, we still had that way of sensing each other's thoughts. My presence didn't embarrass him and if anything, he seemed pleased to see me. Aileen, on the other hand, was very defensive, but she wasn't hostile in the way she was the last time. I sensed from Greg that her presence was significant. Any man who was at ease with his ex-lover in front of his 'significant other', was a man confident in his position.

"I've got the feeling you're here to stay, Aileen, am I right?"

"I'm not sure that's any of your business, Lily," she replied.

"You're right, it's got nothing to do with me, but I would like to wish you both well, if you are staying."

"We've decided, Lily. I would like you to be the first to know," said Greg. "We're not just getting back together; we're going to be married."

The news took me totally by surprise, but I tried not to show it. My instinct was to put my arms around him, but I managed not to do that either. I put my arms around Aileen instead.

"Congratulations, Aileen, I wish you every happiness."

"Do you mean that, Lily, or are you just being polite?" she replied.

"It's time to put the past behind you, Aileen. Greg and I are in the past, let it go."

"I'd like to. Greg keeps telling me I should."

"You must; taking something like that into your marriage is a recipe for disaster. What are your plans, then?"

"This is not ideal, here," replied Greg, "but if it's all right with His Lordship, we intend to stay until the end of the war, as I promised, Lily."

"No, I agree, this cottage isn't big enough, is it? Are you keeping your eyes open for a house in the village?"

"I am, but I'll be honest, Lily, when it's convenient we intend to go back to Scotland."

"I understand. Do you have a home there, Aileen?"

"Yes, it's not much, but it will tide us over."

"When that day comes, I'll wish you every happiness, but it will be a sad day for the estate."

"I think it will surprise you how well Mary is doing. You were so right about her, Lily, the girl really works hard to improve herself."

"Perhaps she might be the estate's silver lining!"

"She deserves to be, if not soon, then later."

"How is Christopher? He's such a lovely little boy, he's going to break a few hearts when he grows up!"

"Like his father, you mean?" Aileen said cynically.

I diplomatically avoided her comment. "He takes after you, Greg, doesn't he? My father died only a few weeks ago, and there was so much between us that was never said. I'm really happy for Christopher that he'll grow up knowing the love of his father. He's very lucky and you're both very lucky to have him, and each other."

"That's a nice thing to say, Lily," Aileen replied. "What about you? Where does your future lie?"

"I'm sure Greg has told you. I hope my future is here at Middlebourne."

"I hope for your sake that it is."

"Can we try to be friends, Aileen? I can't avoid you if you're living here. Will you invite me in for a cup of tea one day?"

"Give me time, Lily, I'm trying."

I gave her another hug which wasn't returned, but neither was it rejected, so perhaps we could be reconciled. I hugged Greg as well and secretly kissed his cheek.

"I wish you love and happiness," I whispered in his ear.

His expression told me everything he couldn't express verbally. I suspected his decision was as much for the benefit of his son as it was for their happiness together. Aileen was a lovely woman. I could certainly see why Greg was attracted to her in the first place. A part of me didn't want him to leave the estate, but at the same time I really wanted him to be happy. I was experiencing strange mixed emotions. It felt as if Aileen had usurped me, when in reality the situation had been the exact opposite, but nonetheless that didn't quell my strange emotions. Walking away from Greg was hard enough but walking away in those circumstances made me re-live it all over again.

As I headed back towards the Manor, I had the weight of the world pressing down upon my shoulders. Dotty was in the heart of Germany with people she didn't know, risking her life by just being there, and I'd agreed she should now push that risk to its limits. Even Corporal Harris at the Manor entrance failed to raise a smile on my face. I continued on to the office with my thoughts somewhere else entirely. Elizabeth was there again helping Fiona.

"The decision has been taken," I said. "Cormorant has the go-ahead."

"I thought it would," replied Fiona. "How long do we have to worry about it?"

"They go on the 4th," I replied.

"I didn't really appreciate what people like Dotty did until now," said Elizabeth. "She's such a character, but it's difficult to associate the woman I met with what she's doing over there."

"We all feel the same, Elizabeth. Dotty's seldom serious about anything, but beneath the brash exterior she understands exactly the risk she's taking, they all do. That's what makes their kind of courage so humbling for the rest of us. She does it for King and country. I suppose we all serve as best we can, the difference being that she's prepared to give her life for what she believes."

"I hope she will be awarded the George Cross," said Fiona. "Surely nobody could deserve it more."

"Is that a high honour?" asked Elizabeth.

"Neither Dotty nor Rob have military rank so the George Cross is the highest honour this country can award for non-operational gallantry," replied Fiona. "It's equivalent to the Victoria Cross."

"Crickey, that would be something, wouldn't it?"

"Edward has nominated them both for the award," I said. "They so richly deserve it."

"I don't like to ask, Lily, but this operation sounds really dangerous," said Elizabeth. "How do you rate the chances of them all coming home safely?"

"Edward and I have discussed this endlessly. It's our responsibility, so if I thought it was a suicide mission or they had little chance of accomplishing their aims, I wouldn't send them. In practice, these things are never that black and white. Between ourselves, we don't expect them all to return."

"Oh my goodness, how can you send them knowing some of them may not come back?"

"I take my strength from Dotty. She has the courage to put her life in danger, I only need the courage to send her. Mr

Jennings is a wise man, he once told Fiona and me that Dotty hadn't failed in her duty, and he didn't believe that we would fail in ours."

"When I met you for the first time, Lily, I stupidly had a low opinion of you. I thought all sorts of ridiculous things. I'm not so silly that I can't see now how stupid I was. The work you and Fiona do here is amazing, I think what I'm trying to say is that I'm sorry."

"You've absolutely nothing to be sorry about, Elizabeth. This is your home and you came back to find an SOE station in its place. I think that would confuse anyone!"

"Well yes, it did a bit."

"We're all on the same side here, don't give it a second thought."

Chapter Thirty-Two
Operation Cormorant

October 4th, 1944, announced its presence inauspiciously. There was a slight mist forming over the fields opposite, the chill in the air left us in no doubt that autumn was rapidly approaching. The trees were just starting to adorn themselves with their autumn display. Middlebourne would soon be dressed in red berries, golden brown leaves, and early morning frosts, and then that all too brief period would soon be replaced by the skeletal remains of trees standing dormant, waiting for the miracle of spring. There was nothing out of the ordinary to make the date memorable, nothing except the intolerable stress of knowing Operation Cormorant would take place that night.

It was horribly reminiscent of D-Day. There was nothing we could do but wait, and the waiting was the worst part. Each of our teams in Germany had confirmed their readiness to go, RAF bomber crews were briefed and ready. Despite all the preparation, we knew absolutely nothing about the strategy our agents would deploy, in that regard they were completely autonomous. It was the not knowing that was so unbearable. It was going to be a long day, the hours hung heavily in the air as Fiona and I sat in the office achieving very little. Time and again we kept returning to the same discussion.

"Dotty will be going over her plan again," I said. "She'll check her weapons, even though she's already done it ten times. She worries a lot about fuses, they'll all come back out again for a last check."

"You're right, she will," replied Fiona. "I pity the Polish resistance who are working with her. You can just see her, can't you, analysing every conceivable contingency plan over and over again, rehearsing every escape option."

"I just hope she doesn't have to kill anyone. I've watched them training, she stalks them like a tiger with that horrible knife of hers."

"She told me that she puts on her makeup just before an operation. If she comes face to face with some unfortunate German soldier, she reckons that if she looks sexy, it gives her an additional two seconds to kill the poor sod."

"I don't doubt that she was serious, those two seconds can mean life or death."

"She *must* come back, we can't go through that again, can we?"

"You're right, I couldn't bear it again."

We did our best to carry on as normal, but it proved impossible. Come the end of the day the habitual calm elegance of our evening dining was not to be disrupted by anything less than a direct hit from a V1. Superficially, it was like any other evening, but scratch beneath the calm surface and each of us was struggling with our fears. Neither Edward nor Elizabeth mentioned Operation Cormorant. It filled our hearts and minds, but protocol dictated that its name may not be spoken at the dining table. The operation was to go into action at 1am our time. Germany operated on European time, which was GMT + 1 hour. Try as I may, I couldn't get to sleep that night. At 1am, I was wide awake knowing that Operation Cormorant had begun.

There was a one-word code for the success or failure of each of the four operations. We were able to receive those signals directly at Station M, but Bletchley was also on standby. The first of those signals could arrive at any time in the early hours of the morning. I probably snatched an hour of sleep before I was walking towards Hut 3. It was still pitch black dark but I could see several thin lines of light escaping from the edges of the blackout blinds covering the hut windows. In the stillness of night, I heard hurrying footsteps behind me. It was Edward. He clasped my outstretched hand, and we continued the last couple of hundred yards together.

Inside the hut only Fiona, Patrick and Maggie were absent, Rolo was in the communications room. Woody immediately shook his head, there was no word yet. Five minutes later, Maggie and Patrick arrived, quickly followed by Fiona. I shook my head and confirmed that we had received no word. Elizabeth was the next to arrive. It felt exactly like the morning of D-Day all over again, except this time it was *our* people, and our responsibility. Waiting helplessly, incapable of doing anything, was a torment like no other. It was another hour before the first signal came in. It was the success code for the Dusseldorf factory bombing raid. Our agents must have successfully lit up the factory, and the bombers had hit the target.

There was clapping and cheering, not to mention plenty of hugging and back slapping. We calmed down again, fully aware that from our agents' perspective, Dusseldorf was the easiest of the assignments. The RAF did the work of destroying the factory. The sun had just lit up the eastern sky, and the first rays of light picked out Rolo running towards us from the radio room. He burst into the hut, his face expressing what was unmistakably good news. Pinneberg was a success! There was another spontaneous release of tension. The hubbub had hardly subsided when Susan appeared at the door of the communications room, waving a piece of paper. Rolo sprinted out of the hut towards her. In the rapidly increasing light, we could all see him punch the air. That could only mean one thing, the celebrations started again. Moments later, he confirmed that Furth was successful.

I hardly dared to breathe. Three out of four of our operations were a success. This only left Frankenthal, Dotty's assignment. The next half an hour was nothing less than torture. My eyes ached with tiredness and my stomach seemed to be knotted in a permanent convulsion. Fiona and I kept looking at each other. Elizabeth was biting her lip and clenching her fist. Finally, the signal came through and Rolo appeared with both fists raised in the air. I didn't wait to be told, I jumped up with my hands held aloft. We all did the same.

The sudden release of tension and the accompanying outpouring of emotion was inevitable. Elizabeth was hugged by everyone, as we all were. Patrick, over-enthusiastic as ever, picked her up in his arms and kissed her. Edward took me in his arms with no regard whatsoever for appearances. The emotional release at a time like that is indescribable, pure spontaneous joy. As we all came back down to earth, Elizabeth especially could hardly believe her abandon. We each stood silently for a moment gathering our breath, and no-one had a broader smile than Elizabeth.

During the planning stage we regarded a 50% success rate as a good result. The fact that all four of our targets had been successfully put out of action was nothing less than a triumph. Mac was the one who pointed out the obvious; our celebrations were very premature. Our agents were now at their highest risk. The Germans would be fully alerted and looking for them. The last phase of the operation to get them home was possibly the hardest part of all. Our celebrations were indeed premature, we all knew that, but like an overflowing champagne bottle, we revelled in that brief moment of joy.

"How do we get them home?" asked Elizabeth.

"There are two options," I replied. "If all goes well and AK can move our agents around, we plan to send three Lysander aircraft over there to pick them up. The Dusseldorf agents will attempt to travel overland into Holland, which is largely in Allied hands. The others each have a designated landing site where, if all goes well, a Lysander should be able to pick them up."

"When you say, 'if all goes well', Lily, what does that mean?"

"The danger is that they may not get to the landing sites, or that those sites are discovered. If that happens, we might be able to try again another time, but if not, they'll be on their own."

"When might that happen?"

"161 Squadron at Tempsford is standing by tonight, but it's more likely to be tomorrow night."

"How on earth do they find the agents in the dark?" Elizabeth asked.

Edward stepped in to answer that question. "Exact navigation gets the pilot close to the designated landing strip. The pilot needs sufficient moonlight to see the field layout. When our agents hear the plane, they'll flash a coded signal, and the plane will flash back a coded reply. The agents then turn on three landing lights in a prearranged pattern. The Lysander can land on a strip about 400 yards long, so we only need a level field. Grazed pasture with firm ground will suffice."

"It's a waning moon, Elizabeth, every night is getting darker. I think it might be too late after tomorrow," I said.

"Do they know that?"

"Of course they do. This is why we went as soon as we did. Moonlight is very important. There's no detail that we haven't covered."

"The more I find out about the work you do, the more involved it becomes. People have no idea, do they?"

"If we do our job properly," said Edward, "people need never know."

"So what happens now?"

"We wait," Fiona replied. "We should wait in the canteen."

She was overheard and there was instant agreement. We didn't expect to hear from our agents again for some time. If it was going according to plan, they should all be travelling using some kind of transport which would appear perfectly normal should it be stopped. If the Germans had put two and two together following the destruction of four of their vital factories, there might be roadblocks and searches, which was the aspect of the operation that worried me the most. In the meantime, the canteen sounded ideal.

As we stepped outside the hut, the sun would have just been visible above the treeline, had it not been obscured by clouds. We could see our breath condensing in the chill air. None of us had dressed for the cold weather. The memory of warm summer days was still fresh in our minds, and the last thing any of us thought about in the early hours of that morning was the weather. There was an immediate rubbing of hands and pulling up of collars for those who had them. It wasn't far to the canteen, but we each arrived thoroughly chilled.

"Brenda, my love," shouted Patrick. "We're in need of the finest breakfasts your establishment has to offer."

"Sit yourselves down, then," she replied.

It was as if Brenda had rung the bell at an RAF fighter station. The kitchen staff scrambled into action. The previously quiet canteen now echoed to the sound of cups, saucers and frying pans. The ample figure of Brenda marching towards us with her enormous teapot was a welcome sight.

"Brenda, you're a vision of loveliness," said Patrick.

"You know what you can do with your Irish blarney, Patrick!" she replied.

"Do you mean that place where the sun never shines?"

"That's the place I had in mind," she quickly replied.

"I'm shocked, Brenda, you've cut me to the quick, and in front of His Lordship as well."

"Oh dear, I do apologise, My Lord. I didn't see you there."

"Patrick deserves all he gets, Brenda, don't worry about me."

If ever there was such a thing as the archetypal canteen lady, it was Brenda. Equipped with a teapot and a smile, she was the antidote to a bad day. Her banter with Patrick was a daily ritual as reliable as her cooked breakfast. That was the first time Elizabeth ever set foot in the canteen, no doubt thinking the word 'canteen' was interchangeable with second class, as in rail travel. The informality and lack of social grace was clearly something of a shock for her.

"I don't believe I have ever been in a canteen before, Lily."

"It's not as bad as you imagine, Elizabeth. In fact, after this morning's early start, I doubt you'll ever enjoy breakfast more."

Elizabeth seemed to think the prospect was highly unlikely. However, when Brenda presented her with a plate of eggs, bacon, fried bread, and mushrooms, her eyes lit up. Our conversation came to a virtual halt, to be replaced by the sound of knives and forks clattering against plates, and cups being joined again with saucers. There was the occasional smile accompanied by the appreciative sounds of satisfied diners.

"Tell me you didn't enjoy that, Elizabeth?"

"You're right, Lily. I've never eaten so much breakfast, it was wonderful."

We all sat back feeling replete - Brenda had worked her magic yet again.

"You look well satisfied, Woody," I said.

"That was exactly what the doctor ordered; I'm feeling highly sorensified."

"Tell me, Edward," queried Corky, "how did you get the RAF to fly three Lysanders into the heart of Germany? Most field agents have to make their own way home, or at least get some distance out of Germany."

"You're right, it wasn't easy. When I discussed it with the PM, I made it a condition of the operation that our people were picked up."

I squeezed Edward's hand. He didn't mention that I had

made it a condition. I knew it was wrong, I should never let sentiment affect my judgement, but I did! There was no way I could be a part of a mission which left Dotty trying to get home from the heart of Germany. Our agents were now spread out across that country. We tried to work out how they could meet up to form one or perhaps two collection points, but it was impossible. The Lysander can only take two passengers, so even if we could get our agents together, they would still need three aeroplanes. Between us, we had created a situation where three RAF pilots, not to mention the aeroplanes, were being placed in danger for the sake of our agents. The more I thought about it, the more I could feel the weight of that decision bearing down on my shoulders.

Breakfast over, the rest of the day was something of an anti-climax. Edward and the boys were gathering intelligence about the V1 and V2 strikes. M15's Operation Double Cross was working incredibly well, with intelligence being fed to the Germans, informing them that the vengeance weapons were not hitting their intended targets. In the case of the V1, they believed they were falling beyond London, and so they reduced the flight time, allowing a good many to fall into open countryside.

The misinformation campaign about the V2 was only just ramping up. The boys had pinned a large map of south east England to the wall, and every pin on the map with a green head marked the site where a V1 had exploded. A pin with a red head denoted a V2. Ominously, the red pins were increasing in number. Elizabeth stared intently at the proliferation of pin heads on the map. It was a sobering realisation for her to know that each pin in the built-up areas almost certainly represented multiple deaths.

"Come on," I said, "let's go to the office and leave them to their pins."

We set off together on a gentle stroll back towards the Manor. As usual, each of us was consumed by our own inner thoughts. One of the gardeners was tending the only substantial flower bed we had left. Arthur had been a gardener at Middlebourne all of his long working life. He was truly a man of the soil; it was his life. He was never separated from his flat cap, unlike his jacket which often resided on the upright handle of a fork or spade. He always wore what looked like the same old crumpled tie, loosely knotted around his crumpled and frayed shirt, the sleeves of which were permanently rolled up.

The only item of clothing he ever appeared to change was his waistcoat. I noticed when one was less threadbare than the other. His grubby old trousers had a leather strap just beneath the knees. He told me once it was to stop the mice running up his leg, and gullible me, I believed him. In point of fact it was to keep his trouser bottoms up out of the mud, and to stop the material gathering at the knee when he knelt down. He was an essential part of the Middlebourne landscape. I swear if we buried his feet and tied him to a stick, he would appear to be growing there.

"Morning, Arthur," I said, "your fuchsias are still looking lovely."

"Morning, Ma'am," (he called every woman Ma'am). "I need to know when this damn silly war is going to end."

"Why is that, Arthur?"

"I need to know if we're going back to flower beds, Ma'am. I can't catch up halfway through the year."

"You'll be the first to know, Arthur, trust me."

"Well, just make sure now, there are more important things going on than this war nonsense."

I smiled to myself as we walked on. "That puts everything into perspective, doesn't it!" I remarked.

"It certainly does," replied Fiona, "there's still a life away from the war, it's just that we can't see it."

"I'm ashamed to say that was me a few weeks ago," said Elizabeth.

"No need to be ashamed," I replied. "If the war doesn't affect you, I suppose it's difficult to appreciate what's going on."

"It was very easy in America to think of it as someone else's war, something which didn't concern us."

"I can understand, Elizabeth, and it explains why wars start in the first place. The only thing necessary for the triumph of evil is for good men to do nothing. That's as true today as it was two hundred years ago when Edmund Burke said it. Winston Churchill was almost a lone voice when he raised the alarm about Hitler re-arming. The last thing any of us wants to think about is something that disturbs our quiet peacetime existence."

"It's true, Lily. We all knew about the war, but the feeling was that it didn't affect us."

"It's only my opinion, Elizabeth, but I think if the Americans hadn't entered the European war, it might have proved to be a disaster for the USA. Imagine a scenario where Britain is defeated by Germany. If Britain as an island was lost, can you imagine Operation Overlord being launched from the east coast of America? The alliance between Hitler and Japan would mean America fighting on two fronts with no forward staging-post. We also know the Nazis are developing a long range V2 that might reach across the Atlantic, and the boys tell me they are working on a totally new kind of bomb. They say it would have devastatingly destructive power. Hopefully now that the Allies are in Europe, we can put a stop to these developments."

"Thank heavens for people like Churchill," said Fiona. "If he hadn't seen the need to step up the production of Hurricanes and Spitfires, we wouldn't be standing here now."

"Thank goodness indeed!" I replied. "It wasn't just us who were staring into the abyss."

Chapter Thirty-Three
The Agents Return

We had just two windows of opportunity for the Lysander aircraft to pick up our people. The RAF pilots at Tempsford were standing by on the night of the 5th of October. They stood down before midnight when no message was received. On the following night, the 6th, the tension was again unbearable. When there is no communication, it allows your mind to fill in the gaps with any and all of the disastrous outcomes that we knew were possible. The minutes ticked by and became hours. We all sat in Hut 3 staring at the clock. Initially, our conversation was positive, we knew that weather conditions in Germany were good. By 9 o'clock, doubts entered our minds, and by 10 o'clock we started to consider what to do next.

The RAF's deadline had come and gone by ten minutes when all three signals came through simultaneously. The code words said, 'go for extraction', with each landing strip being confirmed. Edward rushed into the communications room, and Susan didn't wait to be told, she had RAF Tempsford waiting on the phone. It was another of those moments when the tension surged through your body. Edward was gone for some time. I thought perhaps the deadline had come and gone and the RAF had already stood down. When Edward returned with a smile on his face, it could only be good news.

"They were beginning to stand down," he said, "but we were just in time, they will take off immediately."

Stupidly, we greeted the news with cheers and celebration. We didn't need Mac or anyone else to tell us that the most dangerous part of the operation had only just begun. Our celebrations were short-lived but provided us with a temporary respite. The flight time varied between the three sites. Once again, we had many hours ahead of us, with time for the tension to ratchet back up to unbearable levels. As the clock passed midnight, our planes would be flying over Germany, and our tension level went up yet another click. With time to fill we found ourselves having a philosophical discussion. It was Fiona who sparked off the debate.

"Now that Johnny and I have the cottage in the village, I can see a wonderful future. Everything is perfect for us but I feel guilty."

"What does Johnny say about that?" asked Woody.

"He says I'm being silly. He says it's what he's risked his life for."

"Maybe that's the difference," Woody replied. "People who put their life on the line feel they've won a right to enjoy the peace. We, on the other hand, put other people's lives on the line."

"You make a good point, Woody," I said. "I'm the same as Fiona, take the three pilots who are flying into Germany as we speak. They're risking their lives partly because I insisted they try to get our people out. If any of them doesn't make it, I shall feel as if I've stolen their future from them."

"You're talking about the burden which all great leaders have to carry," said Edward. "We must all remain focussed on the greater good."

"The road to hell is paved with good intentions," commented Patrick.

"You're right, Patrick," replied Edward, "but what we must never lose sight of is that Hitler and his degenerate band of followers have set about ridding the world of anybody who doesn't conform to their twisted ideology. The stories we are hearing about extermination camps are no longer just stories. The Nazis have descended into the darkest recesses of human depravity, creating hell on earth in their own image. This is the road you speak of, Patrick, where good intentions lie in unmarked graves. Nobody in this room should feel guilty about their actions. We didn't choose the road we are on. We chose to stand against evil, and this is how we have to confront it. The only alternative is the hell they offer us, and that we shall never accept."

The room fell totally silent for a moment. Edward had a wonderful gift for oratory, having the ability to motivate and raise our spirits with nothing more than some well-chosen words. On that occasion, we needed time to digest his words. I did have feelings of guilt about the people who may have been killed as a possible consequence of my decisions. The more we learned about Hitler's regime, the more it became a nightmarish vision of hell. It is probably a prerequisite of war that first the enemy must be demonised, but in Hitler's case, that wasn't difficult to do. The more we heard about the atrocities being committed by the Nazis, the more imperative became their destruction. I had to accept that whatever the cost, it was a price we had to pay.

The time was approaching 3am. This was when we might have expected to receive radio messages confirming extraction. Nobody said as much, but we all started looking at the clock again. We each had our own way of dealing with the stress. Woody always doodled with a pencil, which he would sharpen every five minutes. Patrick played with the cigarette butts in his ashtray, pushing them around, forming shapes. Rolo played with a pencil rubber, skilfully manipulating it in his fingers. I withdrew into myself and became ever more aware of the contortions my stomach seemed to perform.

In the dead of night, tiredness invades your body like an

unseen assailant, surreptitiously disconnecting your senses. When reality returns you to the conscious world, it does so in an instant, your heart races, and your muscles tense. This happened at 3.45am when the first coded message came through. Pinneberg extraction successful! A muted cheer filled the hut. Then just minutes later another coded message said, Frankenthal extraction successful, our Dotty was flying home! This time the cheers became louder; we allowed ourselves some celebration.

My heart raced as the adrenaline coursed around my body. The involuntary action of my eyelids closing had been replaced with a heightened sense of anticipation. Two out of three successful extractions had been an incredible achievement, but statistically the odds of all three being successful seemed unlikely. We all realised that, but as the minutes ticked by, no-one allowed a negative word to pass their lips. When Susan appeared holding a scrap of paper, I hardly dared to breathe. She handed the coded message to Rolo without saying a word. He received the half sheet of paper very carefully, as if handling a poisonous snake. Rolo remembered all the codes by heart. He took one look at it and his expression cut through Hut 3 like a scythe. There were three extraction codes from AK, successful, aborted, and compromised. Rolo solemnly announced the latter.

"What does that mean Mac, what's happened?" I shouted.

"It means exactly that; they have been compromised by the Nazis."

"Perhaps the plane couldn't find them, or it couldn't land," I replied.

Edward sat with his head in his hands, there was a deadly silence in the room. I knew what compromised meant, I just prayed someone would tell me it had another meaning.

"Any other failure would result in an abort signal, Lily," said Rollo, "this only means one thing."

"Could this not also be that German activity prevented our boys getting to the extraction point?" asked Corky.

"No, I'm sorry, Corky," replied Mac. "It's the fail-safe signal, it means the whole operation could be compromised because our agents are in enemy hands. If this signal had come before the other two planes had extracted our people, the whole operation would have been in jeopardy."

Mac, the professional soldier, had cast out any lingering hope I might have been clinging to. Edward received the dreadful news badly. He continued to sit with his head in his hands. With the exception of Mac, we weren't seasoned warriors, this was not something we could dismiss as yet another casualty of war. These were our people, they had risked their lives on our operation, and they had paid the ultimate price. Our collective grief was no less because it was shared, Hut 3 emotionally imploded. A dreadful silence embraced us all, it seemed to fill the hut like a physical entity. I sat next to Edward. I had never seen him looking so distraught.

"We all sent them, Edward, it wasn't just you."

"It was my responsibility; I knew the risk."

"You're missing the point," Mac said, "they knew the risk and they accepted it. I lost several good friends when I was in North Africa. Every raid the SAS undertook was high risk, but you learned to draw strength from your fellow soldiers' courage. For every man that we lost, those remaining grew stronger. The courage of our agents lives on, we are now stronger for their sacrifice. We honour them, this is not the time to question the decisions we made."

"Well said, Mac," replied Woody.

"They didn't fail in their duty, so we are not about to dishonour their valour by failing in ours," I said. "Mr Jennings said that when we thought we'd lost Dotty on D-Day. Thank you for reminding us, Mac."

"I know these people better than any of you," replied Mac. "Operation Cormorant has succeeded in its mission. We've destroyed each designated target. We must celebrate their success; they wouldn't thank us for anything less."

Perhaps the courage Mac described is shared by all combat soldiers. It was not something the rest of Hut 3 understood, but his conviction had the unmistakable assurance of sincerity. We supported each other throughout the war, we each had a strength to share. That was the day when we gained a collective strength. Our number had decreased, but the sum of our parts had grown larger.

We toyed with the idea of calling it a night, but it was a futile gesture. The Lysanders should start landing back at Tempsford by daybreak. No-one would get any sleep until our people had landed safely on the ground. Our bodies had become wracked with fatigue, and our spirits had suffered a dreadful blow, but we were not about to stand down. Elizabeth had been a part of it, this was her first experience of an operation.

"My entire body aches, Lily. Is this normal? I just want to cry."

"Absolutely normal, Elizabeth." I replied. "Sometimes when operations like this are over, I feel really sick."

"I think what has really brought it home to me is knowing Dotty. It's different when it's personal, isn't it? Did you know the agents we have lost?"

"Yes, I know them. They're both single men, though that doesn't make it any easier."

"I just don't know how any of you cope with this. I couldn't do what you and Edward do."

"You should spare a thought for Fiona, she has all this to cope with, plus Johnny flies on reconnaissance missions several times a week."

"Oh goodness, you're right. Fi never shows that she's worried."

"No, she doesn't, and that's because she's an incredibly strong person, putting her job before her own fears."

"I've learnt a lot about my brother as well. I used to think he behaved the same as our father. I watch him working now and realise he is actually an amazing person. That little speech he gave us earlier about not feeling guilty about our actions! He can really motivate people, can't he?"

"I'm glad you can see that, Elizabeth. What Edward has achieved here has literally changed the course of the war. You should be very proud to have such a brother."

"Actually, I am, and I'm not too proud to admit it. I also realise how important you are to him. As clever as my brother is, I don't think he could have done this without you, Lily, he completely relies on you. You work so well together! You make a formidable team."

"Thank you for saying so, Elizabeth, it means everything to me."

"Well I mean it. You have just lost two of your people, and they are people you know and work with. I can see you all struggling with it, but I can also see that collective strength Mac was talking about. I don't know where you get that strength from, Lily, any of you."

Coming home from a prolonged stay in America had proved to be a baptism of fire for her, she had to contend with a cultural change of seismic proportions. As well as being thrust into a war situation, she found an intelligence section had taken over her home. Little by little we were becoming closer together and that night proved to be another turning point for her. For the first time, she shared the personal experience of war and the humbling reality that someone she knew was risking their life for her, and men she didn't know had died fighting for her freedom.

Gradually the conversation in Hut 3 became quieter as dawn approached and the necessity for sleep made its presence known once again. The darkest hour is just before dawn. One moment, the night obscures the world around you and there seems no end in sight. The next moment, a faint glow announces its presence in the eastern sky. Then, as if in an act of surrender, the night retreats towards the western horizon, and our world is restored to us. Our tiredness belonged with the retreating night and the new day gave us all a temporary boost of energy.

We waited patiently until thoughts evolved into concerns. Surely they should have landed by now! Eventually at 7.15am the telephone call came. Susan, who had stayed on waiting for this one phone call, put it through to Hut 3. We looked at each other as the telephone rang, nobody rushed to lift the receiver. Fiona said, "You do it, Lily."

"Hello," I said.

"Is that you, Lily?" came the reply in Dotty's unmistakable voice.

"Oh Dotty, you're safe!"

"Of course I'm bloody safe! You didn't think I was going to stay over there, did you?"

"Is Rob all right?"

"Rob's fine. It's bad news about the Furth boys, I wonder what happened?"

"Did you get away with no problem?"

"I wouldn't say *no* problem, but let's just say it was a bigger problem for the Nazis."

"Did the third Lysander make it home all right?"

"Yes, it was a very sad moment. He landed with no passengers, that was when we realised what happened."

"What about the targets?"

"I've been talking to the others. It sounds like all that extra training paid off. The foundry we had to deal with seemed to be a really old building. It looked like a gust of wind would blow the roof off. You should have seen it, Lily, talk about a gust of wind, the whole bloody roof came down!"

Dotty was really on a high, sounding full of it. I could never imagine being in her position, but I guess the euphoria of landing successfully after all that she had been through must have been overpowering. How she and the other agents dealt with the loss of their colleagues was a lesson to us all. Mac's words resonated in my mind, we had to draw upon their courage. The day would come when we would honour their names with pride, but for the duration of the war, we had to put that aside. It was a difficult path to tread.

Chapter Thirty-Four
Pact With The Devil

Our people arrived back at Middlebourne later that day. They looked like a sorry bunch as they decanted out of the back of the RAF lorry. Dotty jumped down into Rob's arms and there she stayed. It was arguable which of their priorities would take precedence. They were tired, hungry, and looked badly in need of a bath. Mac took charge of their weapons. They should really have gone directly into debrief, but nobody, not even Mac, had the heart to tell them that. We decided that the first order of priority had to be a cup of canteen tea, and while they were there, one of Brenda's all-day breakfasts wouldn't go amiss.

We all went with them to the canteen, and it became immediately obvious that they were not as unscathed as Dotty had insisted. Rob had his hand bandaged, and Dotty sported a few bruises, as did the other two. Although they were enjoying their food, they gradually slowed down. It was like watching a pendulum clock running down, desperately in need of winding. They were absolutely exhausted, as was everyone else. We were desperate for information, but their closing eyes indicated a greater priority.

The following day after breakfast, when we had all finally caught up with some sleep, we assembled in Hut 3 for a debrief. The truly remarkable thing about their account was the fact that each of the targets remained unguarded. In each case, they had been family-run businesses with the specialist skills required to produce particular V2 components. In the case of the foundries, there were many more in Germany who could produce the castings, but the moulds were an essential part of the process, so it was very important that we destroyed them. The detailed drawings would have been duplicated and held at the main assembly works at Mittelwerk, so they could start manufacturing again.

Our sabotage only needed to slow down production long enough for the Allies to reach Mittelwerk, and crucially, the construction of new moulds would be a very time-consuming part of the process. Our teams had succeeded in destroying the essential equipment in each factory and they also understood the other crucial items to look out for. As far as we could evaluate, they succeeded on all counts. Although the agents from the Furth operation were not there to report, we understood that part of their operation was a complete success. In Dotty's case, the entire building had collapsed. Edward asked her why that had happened.

"We placed our charges in the critical places, as instructed," Dotty said. "Then I noticed the factory had a lot of structural steel to support the foundry equipment. They built it integral to the whole building. We had lots of C2 left over, and fuses, so I worked out where the heaviest load would be, and we placed charges against the girders. I must have got it right because the whole place came down."

"You weren't supposed to endanger yourself beyond the essential equipment," said Mac sternly.

"We didn't endanger ourselves, Mac, we endangered the building."

"You know what I mean!" retorted a slightly annoyed Mac. "It took extra time and put you both in additional danger of being discovered."

Dotty's attitude changed in an instant; she became very serious. "We understood exactly what dangers we faced, Mac. They only had two nightwatchmen patrolling the place, not German soldiers, just civilians. We took care of them. Inside, they had two night-workers who kept the furnaces fired up. We took care of both of them. Apart from the two night-watchmen, their security turned out to be virtually absent. We assessed our situation very carefully. We had no reason to think we aroused any suspicion, and so we decided to demolish the building. Don't think for a second that we made a spur-of-the-moment decision, Mac. It *was* the right call!"

That was a side of Dotty I hadn't seen before. Even in that highly stressful situation, she could calmly calculate the likelihood of discovery, and was equally capable of clinically working out how to demolish the building. Mac happily conceded the point. Then they described how later that night they were confronted by a totally unexpected German checkpoint. Dotty calmly told us that there had only been two guards on duty, which they had to silence. My jaw hit the ground, realising that 'silenced' in Dotty-speak could only mean silently killed.

As the debrief continued, I learned more and more about her, about all of them. The courage that Mac had spoken of was clear to see among them. They had lost two of their colleagues, and yet somehow they managed to rise above that. They spoke of them in dispassionate terms while all the while they each had to contend with a painful void in their lives. I met a lot of amazing people during the war and would include among them all of our agents. Men like Rob who routinely risked their lives for King and country. Airmen like Johnny Albright, who placed himself in danger every day as he flew over enemy-occupied countries. But of them all, none stood taller than Dotty. My admiration for them all was boundless. Each team had destroyed their target, I had to view it as nothing less than an outstanding achievement.

I noticed throughout the debrief that Dotty carried a shoulder bag with her. Looking rather like a school satchel, the leather bag bore the marks and scuffs of a long and interesting life. When the debrief concluded, Dotty opened the bag. Its contents would not have been more devastating had it contained high explosive.

"We spent all of our time over there in the hands of AK," she said. "I'm sure the other teams will agree when I say that, to a person, they were magnificent. This wasn't like working with FR, where you have to constantly look over your shoulder. I didn't know about the atrocities that have been committed against the Poles. They hate the Nazis, and I soon understood why. Their resistance movement is the largest in Europe, and every single one of them is prepared to die for their country. You won't find many German sympathisers in Poland. The Poles work with us and MI6, but they don't understand why we seem not to act upon what they provide us with. They told me they informed us about Peenemunde early in '42. They also say they've given us evidence of atrocities, against which some of them say we should have taken action."

"This is true about Peenemunde," replied Edward. "We have been slow off the mark. We didn't bomb Peenemunde until '43. As for the atrocities, there has been a constant stream of information, but it has been mostly unsubstantiated. I think the general view has been that it is not all entirely credible."

"When they told us about the scale of the concentration camps, at first I didn't believe it either," said Dotty. "But AK can't understand why it isn't public knowledge in Britain. I asked them if they had any evidence, and this is what they gave me." Dotty pulled a handful of documents out of the leather satchel. Contained among the papers were several photographs. She put them down and just stood with her hand on them. "I've seen some terrible things during this war and I've had to do terrible things, but when I looked at these documents, it left me speechless. Nothing could have prepared me for this. I felt revulsion, and horror, but most of all I felt ashamed to be a member of the human race. I just didn't realise that human beings could descend this low."

I had never seen Dotty like that before. From the moment they returned to Middlebourne, she appeared to be preoccupied, and I wrongly assumed it was the loss of her comrades. She stood with her hand pressed firmly on the papers, almost as if she couldn't face revealing the contents. When she did, the atmosphere in Hut 3 changed abruptly. The moment is seared into my memory, my attitude towards the war from that day onwards was never the same.

Dotty told us that right from the start of the German invasion, the Poles had been treated dreadfully. Nazi ideology had conditioned its forces into believing their Arian superiority meant that the Poles, and especially the Jews, were effectively sub-human. They committed unspeakable atrocities, simply rounding people up to shoot them. As the Occupation consolidated, the arbitrary killing became more organised. The Jews, especially, had been rounded up and taken to execution sites, such as Babi Yar in Ukraine. Some were sealed in the back of lorries and gassed by the vehicle exhaust, while they marched others into open trenches and shot them.

As the number of victims grew, the very scale of the barbarity reached practical limits. Local people had become only too aware of what was happening. Even the German execution squads became revolted by the hell they had created. This was when the Nazi regime signed its pact with the devil. They deemed the mobile killing units inefficient and not good for morale. It would be more efficient to concentrate the killing in centres specially equipped for the purpose.

As Dotty was telling us this, I still had doubts in my mind that it could be true. Surely it couldn't be possible that man's inhumanity to man could extend to such obscenities. Dotty lifted her hand from the documents, but she did so in such a way that made it clear to us, something awful was about to be unleashed. She read the names of the extermination camps which the Nazis had built in Poland. At the time these names didn't mean anything to us, but they were destined to become names which sent a chill down our spines.

Auschwitz, Belzec, Majdanek, Chelmno, Sobibor, and Treblinka. AK had a file on each one, containing statements from many witnesses, with detailed drawings of the layout of the camps together with photographs. The Poles had photographs of the train station at Auschwitz-Birkenau. We could see endless lines of victims being herded away. Dotty said AK estimated from their observations at the train station that many thousands of people were being killed each day. The trains kept coming, and every carriage left the station empty. No-one ever left Auschwitz.

It stunned us into silence. The photographs taken at the station were compelling. The scale of the camp was unimaginable. The drawings detailed the whereabouts of gas chambers. I looked at the photograph containing tall chimneys with some puzzlement. When I compared the drawing with the photograph, I realised the smoking chimneys belonged to crematoria. The implications became so horrendous, I felt afraid to admit that it could be true. I thought of what Dotty had said about being ashamed to be a member of the human race and understood then what she meant. If fellow human beings were capable of doing such abhorrent things, what did that say about the rest of us?

As Dotty went through the paperwork, the cold, calculating horror of it became even clearer. Upon arrival at Auschwitz, they sent fitter people in one direction to be used for slave labour. All others went directly into gas chambers. They considered those used for slave labour to be expendable and the moment they became unable to work, they were condemned to the gas chamber. Majdanek was another slave labour camp. Treblinka, Belzec, and Sobibor were used for the sole purpose of killing people. Dotty stood in silence, and none of us spoke for some time. Eventually, Woody asked a question.

"Do the Poles have any idea how many people have been killed?"

"Millions," Dotty answered.

"Did you say millions?"

"Yes, they're quite sure, the numbers run into millions."

"Are you in *any* doubt about these figures, Dotty?" asked Edward.

"You only have to work with these people for a day to realise that it's true. They're traumatized as a nation. The Nazis consider every single Pole to be a second-class person. They kill anyone who aspires to be more than second-class. They kill people like priests or well-educated people like teachers or university professors. The Nazis use the Poles for slave labour. Anyone who rebels in any way is killed. The penalty for harbouring a Jew is death."

"So the Poles helping you and the others placed themselves at enormous risk?" said Patrick.

"It was so different from working in France, they may be traumatized, but they're not broken. To a person, they've lost loved ones or people they knew. They're united with a common cause, they hate the Nazis, and will do anything which might help defeat them, including risking their lives."

"Why did the Poles share this information with you, Dotty?" asked Edward.

"They told us about the camps, and then they asked if any of our teams could get the evidence to the right people. I said I could."

"I shall make sure that the Prime Minister sees this," said Edward.

Dotty had now achieved what they'd asked her to do. She slumped back into her chair, looking, if not pleased, then satisfied. It was not an ending to the debrief that any of us expected. We should have been elated that our people had achieved such startling success. Instead, we each sat with our heads held low, struggling with mixed emotions. We all looked at the evidence

Dotty laid before us; it was unimaginably horrific. Everyone felt the same; it was as if the smoke from those crematoria chimneys had enveloped the hut, leaving a noxious presence that we could never erase. The image of those poor people being herded towards their death at Auschwitz-Birkenau still haunts me to this day.

Dotty and Rob would both be sharing those same emotions, so I suggested we went to the pub that evening. Dotty agreed, saying she needed a drink and something to distract her mind. The moment the arrangement became known, everyone else said they would come as well. We all struggled with the images in our mind, none of us wanting to be alone with their thoughts that evening. Edward felt the same, he would come with us. It wasn't what I had in mind at all, having envisaged a quiet evening, but I quickly realised this was something we should deal with together.

Later that evening, we arrived at the Forge as quite a crowd. Roger, the landlord, appeared delighted to see how many pints he was about to sell. It wouldn't be one of our fun evenings, despite consuming many of Roger's pints. Instead, the evening turned into one of introspection, ably assisted by the alcohol. None of us wanted to talk about what Dotty had told us, but we had to. The Poles wanted the British public to know about it, yet we felt compelled to talk in hushed voices. Woody confirmed that genocidal massacres were not a new phenomenon, but the industrial scale of the Nazi 'solution' certainly was. None of us wanted to admit it, but our view of the enemy had changed irreparably. Edward made a good point, saying it was important that our own forces didn't descend into unbridled savagery.

"We owe it to the victims to make sure those responsible are held to account," said Edward.

"We only have the right to do that if we ourselves maintain the moral high ground."

Dotty remained quiet, which was completely out of character.

"Are you all right, Dotty?" I asked. "This has affected you badly, hasn't it?"

"It has. I'm not sure I can do this any more."

"Do you mean us here, talking about it?"

"No, I mean working as an agent."

"Get it off your chest, Dot, tell us what you're thinking."

"When we drove into the German checkpoint, I did something terrible. I completely lost control, I placed everyone in danger."

"What did you do?" asked Mac.

"I did the opposite of what I've been trained to do."

"You mean to stay calm and assess the situation?" said Mac.

"I just saw red, he was a Nazi soldier, and all I could see were those images. I didn't warn the others, I acted alone. The moment he stood next to the car, I stepped out and stabbed him, I must have stabbed him ten times. The other guard would have shot me had it not been for the AK driver of the car, who acted quick enough to shoot him before he had time to react. The shots alerted some nearby troops, and we were really lucky to get away with it. I placed everyone's life in danger."

"That was stupid, Dotty, you know that." said Mac. "But don't let one mistake undermine your confidence. You just over-reacted, you won't do it again."

"How can I be sure, Mac? I can't let people down like that."

"Lessons learned in stressful situations like that are the ones you never forget. You won't act without a plan again, and you certainly won't waste your time stabbing someone ten times."

I sat listening to the two of them talking about killing people which coupled with the dreadful information from Poland, left me feeling really depressed. Edward obviously saw my expression and leaned over and whispered into my ear.

"This is why we do what we do, Lily. We are fighting for a world where it is *not* normal to talk about such things."

"It can't come soon enough for me, Edward. I really don't belong in this world."

"Neither do I, none of us does, that's why it takes such courage."

Rob comforted Dotty, who was desperately trying to hold back tears. I speculated that the secret of their close relationship resided in the fact that they understood each other in a way that nobody else could. As close as I had become to Dotty, I could never comprehend how killing someone had affected her. Rob did, and the two of them were each twice the person together, and half the person apart. He understood exactly how Dotty felt and comforted her in terms that only they understood.

"When we rescued you in Caen," Rob said, "the moment I saw what they'd done to you, my anger took over. I didn't just want to kill them, I wanted to tear them limb from limb. I lost control, Dotty, and you were the one who told me to calm down."

"I did, didn't I?" she replied.

"After what we saw in Germany, what kind of person would *not* loathe and despise them? That unfortunate soldier represented everything that's evil about Hitler's Third Reich. You overreacted because you despise what he represented. The difference is that we have a moral compass to guide us so in the cold light of day, you regret your action."

There was unanimous agreement. "Well said, Rob," replied Woody.

Dotty half smiled. "Thanks everyone, you're not a bad lot, do you know that?"

Chapter Thirty-Five
Westminster Bridge

E dward came into the office through the adjoining door and asked me a question which seemed rather strange. "Where was George's shipping agency based, Lily; which dock?"

"Victoria Dock, why?"

"I've got the DG of MI5 on my green phone, Sir David Petrie. Would you have a word with him?"

I followed Edward back into his office, feeling intrigued as I picked up the telephone.

"Hello, this is Mrs Heywood."

"Hello, Mrs Heywood, this is David Petrie. I've taken Lord Middlebourne into my confidence concerning a matter of national security, and from what he tells me, I believe you may be able to help me."

"I'm intrigued, Sir David, how can I help?"

"What I am about to tell you is top secret, Mrs Heywood, and is not to be mentioned beyond Lord Middlebourne."

"Of course."

"The Nazis have been forging British five-pound notes. Our belief is that the objective is to debase our currency and cause financial chaos."

"How far advanced is their operation?"

"This all started in 1940. At first, the notes were not terribly convincing but subsequent notes have improved enormously, up to the point where now, quite frankly, we have enormous difficulty telling the forgeries from genuine notes."

"Are there enough of these notes in circulation to actually debase our currency?"

"We don't think so, not yet, but that is all about to change."

"Where do I fit into this, Sir David?"

"I understand from Lord Middlebourne that you used to run a shipping agency, based in the London docks."

"Yes. That's right. Our office was right next to Victoria Dock."

"We believe the Nazis intend to smuggle a large quantity of forged notes into the country concealed amongst the cargo of a ship."

"And you think this will happen in the London docks?"

"Our intelligence is inconclusive, but there is reason to believe the ship will set sail from Narvik."

"Is that all you have to go on?"

"We have sketchy details from MI6, but nothing conclusive. What do we usually import from Narvik, Mrs Heywood?"

"Nothing now, not since the German invasion, but Norway's chief exports used to be fish and aluminium. The port was also used to export Sweden's iron ore."

"What type of ship would carry iron ore?"

"That would be a ship specifically designed to carry loose cargo like iron ore or coal, they're called bulk carriers."

"So a cargo of iron ore from Narvik would be very unusual in the London docks?"

"I imagine it would, yes."

"So tell me, Mrs Heywood, if you had a ship full of iron ore, how would you bring it into the London docks without drawing attention to it?"

"Well, if it came from Narvik that would certainly draw attention, so the documentation would need to be falsified to make it look as if the cargo came from somewhere else."

"Who would normally do that initial paperwork?"

"That would be the freight forwarder, and the custom house broker would require that documentation at our end."

"What about the details of the shipper?"

"Yes, all those details will appear on the movement card, which is something the government brought in during 1939."

"You know your stuff! This is all extremely helpful. I will confess I am concerned about this threat, and so is the Prime Minister. He has requested to see me in order to discuss the matter. I need your expertise, Mrs Heywood; could I impose upon you to attend that meeting?"

"Where and when is it, Sir David?"

"It's the day after tomorrow, in the Cabinet War Rooms."

I put my hand over the telephone handset and quickly outlined the details of my conversation to Edward.

"The PM also wants to discuss our V2 operation, so that will fit in fine, Lily, we can go together."

"Hello, Sir David. Yes, I've spoken with Lord Middlebourne, and that will be fine. We have other business to discuss with the PM, so it will fit in well. What time do you want us to be there?"

"The PM commanded me to be there at 10am sharp, so better not be late. Don't want to incur the PM's displeasure!"

"I certainly wouldn't want to do that, Sir David."

"Good show, Mrs Heywood, I look forward to seeing you then, goodbye."

"Well, that's a strange twist of fate!" I said to Edward, putting the phone down. "Imagine that! Me advising the PM about shipping!"

"Who better, Lily? How many people with your clearance do you know who have been shipping agents?"

"I suppose that's true, and I'll get to visit the War Rooms."

"It will be a disappointment, I'm afraid, it's a bit of a dungeon."

"I suppose I'd better make sure we will have a pass to get in?"

"Oh, thank heavens you thought of that! Yes, it would be a problem otherwise."

"I'll telephone Joan Bright. She'll get it sorted for us."

I was looking forward to it. Surely it was just a case of me giving the intelligence people a little bit of advice about shipping. Or so I thought! Edward had to brief the PM on the progress of Operation Cormorant, and so I spent most of my time making sure he would have everything he needed in his briefcase. When the morning arrived, I was quite excited. William drove us to the station in plenty of time to catch the 7.30 train. All the while, Edward was adamant that the 8 o'clock train was early enough, but I wanted us to have plenty of time.

We had the first-class carriage all to ourselves, and Edward continued to assure me that the 8am train would have been fine. I argued for the earlier train on the grounds that we might be held up, he argued that the 8 o'clock train was quite early enough.

"Edward, do you realise we're squabbling like an old married couple?"

He thought for a moment before bursting out laughing. I thought he might have said something like, 'I suppose we *are* like an old married couple,' or, 'perhaps this is a vision of our future.' But being Edward, he didn't let his guard slip.

"That would never do, would it, Lily! A gentleman should never disagree with a lady, so I shall quietly agree with you and wait to see if we are held up sufficiently to justify your caution!"

There we were bickering like a married couple, and not finding that prospect remotely disagreeable, I smiled contentedly at him. He had a lovely expression on his face and I wanted to believe he was thinking the same thing. There was a brief hold-up while they stopped the train at a signal, and so I immediately claimed justification for my argument. Despite the hold-up, we still arrived at Charing Cross at 8.50. When Edward kindly pointed out that it was only a ten-minute walk to Whitehall, I put my arm in his and we both laughed.

"I've got an idea, Edward. Why don't we go to St Thomas' Hospital and say hello to the staff who were so helpful when we were there?"

"I have no memory of St Thomas' so I would be interested to see it."

We decided to take a taxi to the hospital, and then later we could walk back over the river via Westminster Bridge. It was all so reminiscent of my first taxi ride to the hospital. Along the way I spotted a lady with a flower stall, something I hadn't seen since the start of the war. I asked the cabby to stop so that I could buy two bunches of flowers to take with us.

Having been unconscious during most of his previous visit, it amazed Edward to see the extent of the bomb damage. That St Thomas' was still functioning was a great testament to the determination and courage of the hospital staff who weren't prepared to be defeated. We went in through what sufficed to be the main entrance, only to be met by the same disagreeable woman at the reception desk. Fortunately, knowing the ropes this time, I could easily circumvent her.

"Good morning, I'm here to see Mrs Riley. I know where to go."

I pulled at Edward's arm and hastened him on before the ghastly woman had a chance to disagree with me.

"Now don't forget, you're Edward Sinclair here."

"I don't even remember telling them that."

We found Evelyn in her office, buried beneath all the filing cabinets and cardboard boxes. She was genuinely pleased to see me, but of course she didn't recognise Edward. When I introduced her to Mr Sinclair, she was somewhat taken aback.

"It's lovely to see you looking so well, Mr Sinclair. When Mrs Heywood telephoned me to say you were making a good recovery, I was so relieved. I'll never forget that day. You were in very safe hands, Mr Sinclair, nothing was going to prevent Mrs Heywood from doing what she needed to do!"

"Rest assured, Mrs Riley, had I been conscious and able to

nominate someone to fight my corner, I would have looked no further than Mrs Heywood!"

We talked for several minutes and she became quite emotional when I said one bunch of flowers were for her. Realising our time was limited, she offered to take us to see Matron. We walked together down the stairs towards the underground ward. It intrigued Edward to see how they had utilised the basement, turning it into wards and an operating theatre. I still found it strange seeing a hospital environment amongst the pipes and ducting. When Marion spotted us her face lit up, promptly marching towards us.

"Lily, how wonderful to see you again."

I didn't expect to feel so emotional but it was like re-living that day again. We hugged each other.

"It's lovely to see you, too, Marion. That day is burnt into my memory."

"And mine, Lily. Evelyn and I often talk about it when we're alone. And this must be Edward?"

"I am, indeed, Matron. I understand I have much to thank you for."

"Not me, young man, you need to thank this remarkable lady. I see a lot of concerned relatives, wives, and husbands here, but I've seen nobody like your Lily before! She was prepared to move heaven and earth for you, absolutely nothing was going to stop her. You're an incredibly fortunate man to have this woman by your side."

"I do realise that, Matron."

"Well, just make sure you do! I know you must be terribly important, but you might not be here today if it wasn't for Lily. So, tell me about St Hugh's."

"They were marvellous, Marion," I said. "It's a military hospital that specialises in brain injury. I've no doubt they saved Edward's life. We were there for a week, and it was such a memorable week!"

"I'll certainly never forget your day here. Do you know,

within an hour of you leaving us a private ambulance arrived? Men in suits and hats came marching into the ward and insisted we move your people out into their ambulance. Dr Wisniewski didn't say a word! Whatever you said to him, Lily, it obviously worked."

"I was horribly rude to him, I felt bad about it afterwards."

"I'd love to know what you all do for the country. I know you can't tell me, but I was so pleased to help."

"We are just backroom people, Matron," replied Edward. "Nobody knows what we do, I even wonder myself, at times!"

"After what I've seen, I don't believe that for a moment! But you just carry on doing whatever it is."

"These are for you, Marion," I said, handing her the flowers.

She was so pleased that it was several seconds before she hugged me again. I explained we were on a flying visit, and we had to go to an important meeting. When she made a joke about it being with the Prime Minister, I didn't deny it and Marion just smiled knowingly. We left her holding the flowers with a beaming expression on her face. Marion was a wonderful lady. One moment she was the archetypal authority figure striking fear into the heart of every nurse on the ward; the next moment she was everyone's lovely grandmother. I turned at the ward entrance to wave goodbye only to see her pointing a finger at a junior nurse who appeared to be frozen in terror.

"What a lovely lady," Edward said. "It was quite disarming how she kept smiling at me."

"I wonder why, perhaps it was something I told her about us."

"And what might that be?"

"You were in a coma, Edward, that was between Marion and me."

He accepted my explanation, and so we made our way towards the hospital entrance. We walked away from St Thomas' and towards Westminster Bridge. With Big Ben always in our view, we walked towards the Houses of Parliament. I paused on the bridge to look at London, my home town, which had never looked finer in the morning sunshine.

For those who chose to see it, there was bomb damage everywhere, but for me London looked magnificent. The Thames flowed beneath our feet, as it always did. The glittering ribbon of water extended upstream to where Lambeth Bridge spanned its banks. The sun shone down on the Palace of Westminster and it had never looked finer, Big Ben standing there as defiant as ever. A red London tram trundled across the bridge in the other direction, while two army lorries drove past us. The guard in the sentry box gestured to the army drivers. People walked in both directions over the bridge enjoying the sunshine. I just stood smiling at what for me was the most magnificent sight in the world.

"What are you so happy about?" asked Edward.

"This is what we're fighting for, Edward. We've taken everything Hitler has thrown at us, we didn't surrender, London carries on as it always has. Look at it, look at these people, isn't it wonderful?"

"You're right it is. I shouldn't take it for granted."

"No, you shouldn't. Don't you feel proud, Edward? I do, this is my city, I'm a part of it, and it will always be a part of me. People are giving their lives to keep London standing like this, I'm so proud to be a Londoner."

"I am proud, Lily, I'm proud of you."

"Me, why are you proud of me?"

"I shall never forget what Winston said that day at Middlebourne. Do you remember, you had just told him in no uncertain terms that Hitler made a terrible mistake if he thought he could break the will of the British people. He reacted strongly, do you remember he said, 'Hitler has unleashed a mighty spirit, I can see it sitting here before me now.' Winston was quite right, Lily, you are a mighty spirit."

"Is that a compliment?"

"It's a statement of fact, Lily."

"Not the way you're saying it, it sounds more like a compliment!"

His face lit up with the most beautiful expression. He reached out and held my hands as we stood looking at each other. I didn't know what to say, I don't think he did either. Still holding my hands he drew me closer, I'm quite sure his intention was to kiss me. The look in his eyes was unmistakable, in that moment there were only three words he was desperate to say. But those words always come with a commitment, and when that realisation dawned, I could see the sadness writ large across his face. I felt his anguish as if it was my own, and I shared the burden of his sadness in equal measure. Ours was truly a love that must not mention its name.

"So, it was a compliment! I *told* you it was," I said light-heartedly, trying to lift the mood.

"There is not a compliment I could pay you which could do you justice. You burst with pride when you talk about London, I burst with pride when I talk about you, Lily."

He might not have said in words that he loved me, but in his own way, he had gone as far as his five hundred years of tradition would allow. I realised more than ever that Edward was a deeply emotional man. His wonderfully expressive eyes left him with little option but to wear his heart on his sleeve. Somehow his towering intellect and strength of character could coexist with his warm heart, combining to make him the very exceptional man that he is. It took me quite a time to respond.

"I'll never receive a greater compliment, will I? I don't know what to say, Edward, I'm overwhelmed. That was such a lovely thing to say and made all the more lovely because I know what lies behind those words, thank you."

"Perhaps we should continue towards our appointment."

"You're right, Edward, but I'm taking this moment with me. Do you ever have that feeling that a moment is so precious, you'll never forget it?"

"I do, and I shall never forget the sight of you standing on Westminster Bridge bursting with pride!"

Neither of us has ever forgotten that day. Edward did so much more than cross over the river, he crossed something much wider than the Thames. He took another giant stride across the social divide which stood between us. We were like two sticks dropped from the bridge, each swept away by the swirling current, but always together.

Chapter Thirty-Six
Cabinet War Rooms

It was only a short walk along Great George Street and then right into Horse Guards Road. Edward then steered me towards the Office of Works building. I thought he was joking, but he wasn't. The entrance was surrounded with sandbags, some of which had been used to build a pillbox. Marine guards were very prominent. They escorted us inside the government offices, and we were then confronted by more armed guards. There hadn't been time for me to get official passes before we left home, so we were reliant upon the guard having been informed about us. I knew Joan Bright wouldn't let me down, so I confidently announced to the guard who I was. They asked for our identity papers and one of them thumbed through his records. Sure enough, we were there on the list, although I still breathed a quiet sigh of relief.

Two armed guards then escorted us down some stairs and into what Edward had described as a labyrinthine dungeon. The corridor that we eventually stepped into seemed to extend forever in both directions. There were ducting and girders overhead, cupboards and filing cabinets seeming to occupy every recess in the white painted brick walls. People would suddenly appear coming out of one door, only to then disappear behind another door. The guard didn't say a word so it felt as though we were being escorted to face a firing squad.

Then we saw a group of people coming towards us. I instantly recognised some of them. There was Clement Attlee, the Deputy Prime Minister, Lord Woolton, Minister of Reconstruction, Ernest Bevin, the Minister of Labour. Edward appeared to know them all, Attlee addressing him as 'Middlebourne'. They were coming from a meeting of the War Cabinet. We continued on our way until we reached yet another door. The guard opened it and finally spoke two words. "Wait here." But just as we were stepping into the room as instructed, another voice shouted, "Come through."

There was a man beckoning us to continue even further down the corridor. Edward led the way and I followed. Another door appeared, and they instructed us to go through it. Once again, I followed Edward, expecting to find another cell-like room. Instead, I walked into a much larger room, with Winston Churchill sitting at the head of a large square of tables and chairs, most of which were occupied. I froze on the spot, realising there were no other women in the room. I was used to meeting generals and important people, but nothing like this. There is 'feeling out of your depth', and there's feeling like you've sunk to the bottom of the ocean! This was way above my head.

Edward shook hands with people he obviously knew. He was the smartest dressed man in the room, he just looked so confident. He was about to introduce me to someone when the Prime Minister caught sight of me. He rose to his feet to greet me. I didn't know what to do, but seeing my unease, he beckoned me around the table, and proceeded to put his arms around me!

"Lily, my dear, what an unexpected pleasure it is to see you."

"I'm pleased to be here, Prime Minister."

"Not as pleased as I am, I can assure you. So what good fortune has brought you here today?"

"Well, sir, to my amazement Sir David Petrie has asked me to come here to offer you advice about shipping."

"Intelligence people move in strange ways, Lily. I do not yet know why I need such advice, but rest assured, I am delighted to be in need of it."

He was absolutely charming, sensing I was ill at ease, and he couldn't have been warmer or more generous.

"Silence please, gentlemen," he shouted. An instant hush descended upon the room. "It is my very great pleasure to introduce you to Lord Middlebourne's Chief of Staff, Mrs Lily Heywood. Mrs Heywood is here today in her capacity as shipping advisor to the War Cabinet. On the first occasion that I had the pleasure to meet Mrs Heywood, she lectured me about the reasons why Hitler will never break the will of the British people. She was quite right, and I have never forgotten that occasion. So I can assure you, Mrs Heywood, I shall listen to your advice intently. Allow me to introduce you around the table.

Sir David Petrie, you know, MI5. Sir Stuart Menzies, MI6. The Foreign Secretary, Mr Anthony Eden. Home Secretary, Mr Herbert Morrison. Chief of the General Staff, Field Marshal Sir Alan Brooke. The Chancellor of the Exchequer, Sir John Anderson. The Financial Secretary to the Treasury, Mr Osbert Peake. Sir David and Sir Stuart will introduce these other gentlemen if so required. And for those who have not met him before, this is Lord Middlebourne. So take a seat, Mrs Heywood, and to work, gentlemen."

I sat down next to Edward, and I've never been more desperate to do so. My legs were shaking. I was petrified that I was going to be asked to speak in front of all those luminaries. Menzies nodded to one of his underlings and the poor man, who was obviously as nervous as I was, introduced himself and stood up to present a report. He produced a handful of five-pound notes and passed them around the table. I looked at one, touched it, held it up to the light, and as far as I could see it looked completely genuine. The notes, he assured us, were forgeries, and then he gave us the history of the Nazi plan to debase our currency.

They called their plan Operation Bernhard. It all started in 1942 and was created by the Sicherheitsdienst (SD) which was the SS intelligence agency. The forgeries were very good; they even produced a very similar rag paper to the British notes. It seemed, from what we could gather, that there were internal frictions within the SD because they shut the unit down. It was later revived, but rather than the SD producing the forgeries, prisoners were selected from various concentration camps, presumably all known forgers, and they sent them to Sachsenhausen concentration camp.

We knew little about the camp inmates nor their methods of production, but we were looking at the results. The forgeries continued to improve although there were problems duplicating the rag paper precisely. Bank of England experts could tell them apart by using ultraviolet light. By 1943, even that problem had been overcome, and a larger printing press allowed for four notes to be printed from each sheet of paper.

The Nazi plan was to use the currency to finance all of their intelligence operations. Our own latest intelligence showed that production had now been dramatically increased. It seemed that their plan had gone back to its original intention of debasing our British currency. His presentation over, the official sat down and looked pleased to be doing so. Menzies nodded to another official, who looked rather more composed as he stood up and confidently told us his name.

"Anthony Cuthbert," he said. "We have agents on the ground trying to get information about German operations. It's very difficult, Sachsenhausen concentration camp is just north of Berlin. We spent many months developing a contact within the camp, only for that contact to be lost. However, our last information was that the production of British five-pound notes has been stepped up to unprecedented levels. We're told that large quantities are being packed into crates and are being transported. There is another piece of information from a source with access to Berlin Tempelhof Airport. We understand there's a warehouse within the airport perimeter which is receiving and storing sealed crates."

Mr Cuthbert sat down, and the Prime Minister thumped his fist down on the table.

"Is that it? Is that all we know? But this amounts to nothing!"

"Not quite all, Prime Minister," Menzies said.

"Well, damn it, man, tell me, what else do we have," growled the PM.

Menzies looked as if he wished he hadn't raised the subject, the PM seemed about to explode but nonetheless, he continued.

"Our source believes those sealed crates come from Sachsenhausen concentration camp."

The PM sat back in his chair and appeared displeased. "I see," he said. "What use is this if we do not know where the forged notes are going?"

"I agree, Prime Minister, our information is incomplete," Menzies said. "However, there is also a report from Norwegian resistance. They report suspicious activity in and around Harstad Airport. Security is being stepped up, and troop numbers have increased. Our last piece of information comes from Ultra intercepts. A very sharp analyst at Bletchley Park has noticed a pattern with some recent transmissions. He noticed an Enigma-coded message from Narvik port authority. The message was a routine security check. What alerted the analyst was just the fact that it was an Enigma message. There had never been one before, so an Enigma machine indicates a military presence."

"We need more than just suspicion," the PM said.

"There *is* more, Prime Minister. Suspicion alerted, the analyst then checked to see if there was any other coded radio traffic mentioning Narvik. It seems there has been coded communication with both Harstad Airport and the railway depot, both of which are in Narvik. We initially saw none of this as a priority because the messages refer to what we might interpret as normal activity. However, our latest intercepts from Narvik port authority are particularly interesting. A message from Berlin asked about sea time. In response, the reply refers to five days sea time to London for a Massengutfrachter. That has been translated as a bulk carrier. The latest intercepts now confirm the analyst's suspicion, each message coming under the code word heading of 'Untergraben' or 'subvert'."

"I see," said the PM, obviously deep in thought. "What would be the implications of these crates full of forged five-pound notes finding their way into the British financial system?"

Sir John Anderson, the Chancellor of the Exchequer, said it would be disastrous. Our currency would become worthless. Even if we could change our currency, the repercussions would be far-reaching. The Chief of the Imperial Staff, Sir Alan Brooke, pointed out the rather obvious fact that America was funding much of the war effort. Our creditworthiness would never be more important.

Everyone sat waiting for the PM to make a pronouncement. His presence in that small room was totally dominant. Nobody else I had ever seen could command a room full of people by sheer force of personality alone, let alone the kind of people who were in that room. Winston Churchill was simply awe-inspiring. We all sat attentively waiting for him to speak. Eventually, after much deliberation, he spoke again.

"Let us assume for the sake of argument that your guess-work is correct," he said. And then with enormous gravitas he added, "So what are you going to do about it?"

"We should step up our surveillance in Norway, and Bletchley is listening for anything which might be useful. 'Five' will instigate surveillance here at the London docks."

Sir David Petrie said he had spoken to me because I had been a shipping agent, and he would like everyone to hear what I had to say. My heart lodged itself firmly into my throat,

I was petrified. Edward squeezed my hand. I didn't stand up because I thought I might fall over. I had no notes, and my mind went blank. The PM looked at me, his eyes like car headlamps and I felt like a frightened rabbit trapped in his gaze. He looked at me expectantly, but seeing my mind had gone blank, he came to my rescue magnificently.

"Mrs Heywood, before you give us the benefit of your expertise, do I have your permission to share an anecdote with these fine gentlemen?"

"Of course, Prime Minister."

"Mrs Heywood and I share a long-running bon mot. After much deliberation, we remain undecided if our conversations are to be viewed as an honour or as a pleasure. And so, may I say what an honour it is to have you here with us today, Mrs Heywood, and what a pleasure it is for me to be in your company once again!"

"You're very generous, Prime Minister, thank you. It is an unexpected honour for me to be here today. May I reserve judgment on the other matter until after I've advised the meeting?"

"Touché, Mrs Heywood, I eagerly await our next encounter! I must not delay you any further, pray continue."

He had seen I was out of my depth and his generosity of spirit, which always so inspired me, had lifted me up. I drew a deep breath and started my presentation.

"From what you tell me, if our intelligence is correct, and if our assumptions are right, then there might be a ship laden with counterfeit five-pound notes arriving at the London docks. If that's everything we have to go on, then all I can offer you is my best guess as to how the Nazis might go about doing this. First and foremost, we assume from the intercepts that the ship is a bulk carrier. Secondly, the Nazis need to disguise the fact that it comes from Narvik. Since the German occupation, there *are* no ships coming from Narvik to Great Britain.

So if the ship is not to raise suspicion, it will have to present falsified documentation. There are two important documents which come with any ship. There is the movement card, and there is the documentation from the freight forwarder. These would both need to be falsified. It cannot sail directly to London from Narvik, as that would raise suspicion. The sea time mentioned might indicate that it is sailing via the Faroe Islands and entering our waters by the western approaches."

"Excellent, Mrs Heywood," said Menzies, "can you hazard any guesses about the type of cargo?"

"I think we probably can. For this ship to enter any port without raising suspicion, it must carry normal cargo. Furthermore, to be sure not to raise suspicion if it should be inspected en-route, it would need to be a cargo which would normally come to us via the western approaches. If you ask me to suggest a likely cargo, I think your intelligence may have already told us. If the railway depot at Narvik seems to be connected with Operation Untergraben, then I suggest the cargo might be iron ore."

"Why do you draw that conclusion, Mrs Heywood?" asked the Foreign Secretary.

"Sweden has long exported its iron ore to Germany from Narvik; it has the advantage of always being ice-free, and there's a direct railway link. Such cargo has another advantage because we import most of our iron ore from Bell Island, Nova Scotia. Ships from Bell Island would normally come via the western approaches. Such a ship with correct documentation would not raise suspicion."

"What kind of ship would this be, Mrs Heywood?" asked Petrie.

"A bulk carrier, a ship especially designed to carry loose cargo."

"So, we are talking about a big ship," asked Menzies.

"Yes, fairly big, about five or six thousand tons gross, capable of about ten knots."

"Why would the Nazis want to hide a few crates of counterfeit notes in a bloody great ship full of iron ore?" he replied.

"When I worked in the shipping business, smuggling was always an ever-present problem. Either that, or some cargo simply going missing. The lesson you quickly learn is that the best place to hide something is in plain sight. If I were advising the Nazis, I would tell them to put it on a big ship with ordinary cargo."

The PM smiled, and they all started talking amongst themselves. I hoped my contribution was over, that I could finally sit back and notice the room we were sitting in. Edward was right about the dungeon. Above our heads were some massive iron girders, painted pillar box red as if they were regarded as a decorative feature. There were electric cables running up and down the walls, and ducting hanging from the ceiling.

Despite that, all those terribly important people gave the place enormous gravitas. Not to mention Winston Churchill, sitting as he was at the head of it all, like a giant Colossus. There was a large map of the world on the wall behind him, which seemed to hint towards the extent of his powers. Just as I was thinking my contribution was over, Petrie asked me another question.

"Mrs Heywood, how far in advance is the paperwork for a shipping consignment prepared?"

"It can be weeks ahead. Things like port time have to be organised weeks in advance."

"So the paperwork for this supposed ship may already be here?"

"It's possible, yes."

"Another question, Mrs Heywood. How do you suppose they intend to go about unloading these crates without raising suspicion?"

"Yes, I've been thinking about that. It's not unheard of for a ship like a bulk carrier to also carry a few crates amongst the cargo. So they might enter them on the movement card as some innocent commodity, but they would risk running foul of the custom house broker. The alternative is that they're spirited away from the docks."

"You need to explain, Mrs Heywood."

"Well, there's always been a criminal element in the docks. Smuggling is a big problem, but if that were the case, it would imply that the criminal element is collaborating with the Nazis."

Petrie asked if I thought that was likely. I said it wouldn't surprise me. He then asked me if I knew any of the criminal elements.

"I lived in Stepney, Sir David. My late husband worked in the docks and I know these people. The docking system effectively promotes criminal behaviour. Dockers usually work as gangs, and often a gang is based upon a family who might have been working the docks for generations. The man in charge of a gang is called the ganger, and he holds a lot of power. He will work with either the shipping company or a contractor and he will organise dockside logistics. The dockers are totally reliant upon the gangers and contractors for their work, so you can imagine the system is rife with abuse."

"That might be extremely useful, Mrs Heywood. Would you object if I were to call upon your services again in the future?"

"No, of course not, but what exactly are you thinking?"

"We've given much thought to how the Germans intend to circulate these notes. The simple thing would be to drop them like confetti from a bomber. The problem we can see with that is that it would alert the public to their operation. People would know they are forgeries, and also many of the notes could be lost or ruined. We suspect they intend to circulate them covertly, and following our Operation Double Cross, it seems very unlikely that there is an agent network capable of this scale of operation. It all points towards collusion with the criminal underworld."

"If that is the case," said Edward, "there is little incentive for the criminals to cooperate with the Nazis. If they debase our currency, they also debase their own spoils."

"That is quite right," said the First Secretary to the Treasury. "Armed with such knowledge, however, these people could exploit all manner of black-market goods, as well as investing in gold bullion."

"The country has never been in so much debt, this all points towards financial ruin," said the PM, looking incredibly serious. "You had better put a stop to it."

"I have a suggestion," I said. "Could we have people posing as some kind of government official, going into all the shipping agents, and demanding to see their books? There's a possibility that the paperwork for the consignment may already be in place."

"Excellent idea," said Petrie. "We would need someone who knew what they were looking for. Do you have any suggestions, Mrs Heywood?"

It was a few seconds before I realised what he was implying. "I'm not a field agent, Sir David."

"I do realise that, Mrs Heywood, but you are supremely qualified for such a role. Quite frankly, it would take weeks to train field agents to recognise all the nuances of the shipping industry which you have so adequately described."

I knew he was right but was uncomfortable about it. Being known in the docks could be a tremendous advantage, but equally I could draw attention to myself. There were many people in the room looking at me with that reassuring, you-can-do-this kind of smile. There seemed to be no other option for me.

"If Lord Middlebourne can spare me, then it will be an honour to serve my country in any capacity."

"Well said, Mrs Heywood," replied the PM. "Remind me, when this matter is concluded, to ask you if your task was indeed an honour, or perhaps your success might prove to be a pleasure!"

"I will look forward to that conversation, Prime Minister."

"Leave this with me, Mrs Heywood," said Petrie. "I shall furnish you with the necessary documentation. We had better use your correct name, I'm afraid, you will be some kind of designated government Customs official."

Petrie said he would keep me informed over the coming days, and then that part of the meeting was adjourned. Now it was Edward's turn to bring the PM up to date with Operation Cormorant. One or two of the attendees left the room, and one or two more took their place. Edward briefed the meeting with his usual command of detail and eloquence. It was well known that the Chiefs of Staff and MI6 did not share the same confidence in SOE that the Prime Minister did. At the end of Edward's presentation, the PM sat back with a very satisfied smile. Nothing was said, but the silence spoke volumes. The success of Operation Cormorant was equally a success for SOE.

When we left the War Rooms, we had to be escorted off the premises just as when we arrived. Climbing the stairs back into the government building was like entering a different world. I wasn't sure if I was entering normality or stepping away from it. The guards escorted us out onto the street beyond and instantly turned their back on us. Their job was done, we were just two more people standing on the pavement. We walked a few paces, and I realised the War Rooms were just beneath our feet. It seemed to me that the subterranean world below us was where true reality existed. We were standing in an alternative place, waiting for reality to find us.

Chapter Thirty-Seven
MI5

The tremendous success of our Operation Cormorant was well received in all the various branches of power. General Gubbins, always pleased to demonstrate the effectiveness of his 'Baker Street Irregulars', was particularly pleased about it. Our credibility as a 'semi-independent section' was greatly enhanced. It was noticeable that the flow of expense queries from the War Office slowed to a trickle after Cormorant.

We maintained the contact we had gained with AK, particularly regarding the 'V' programme. It was a tough time for them since the Nazis crushed the Warsaw uprising. The Allies badly served the Polish Home Army, Warsaw was a disaster for them. There was little left to support the Polish government in exile, effectively allowing the Soviets a free hand in Poland. Our immediate concern was to demonstrate that our operation had slowed production of the V2. The Poles were more concerned for the Allies to overrun the German underground production site at Mittelwerk near Nordhausen, and they had good reason.

The Mittelwerk V2 production site was next to the Dora concentration camp. Many of the camp occupants were Poles, and thousands of them were forced to dig the tunnels which made up the underground works. The slaves were housed in these tunnels, their number increasing to as many as 19,000. They were worked to death, and every second day a truck would load up as many as 250 corpses, transporting them to the crematorium ovens at Buchenwald. It is thought that 26,500 died in that way.

Attitudes at Station M inevitably hardened after all the recent revelations. Edward was at pains to ensure that morale was maintained. Our reconnaissance flights continued with Johnny flying over Germany two or three times a week. We were looking for launch sites for both the V1 and the V2. The month progressed in what for us was fairly routine, until on the 21st of October 1944 the Americans captured the German city of Aachen. This was the first significant intrusion into German territory and a big psychological blow for the Nazi regime.

Towards the end of the month, I received another telephone call from Sir David Petrie. It was about the Nazi five-pound notes again. "Our intelligence is patchy, Mrs Heywood," he said, "but it's beginning to look as if you might be right. Our analysts agree that iron ore is the most likely cargo for a bulk carrier coming from Narvik."

"Oh good, I'm pleased I was of some help."

"We would like your help again, Mrs Heywood. Your suggestion about inspecting the books of the shipping agents turns out to be a sound idea. I wouldn't ask you, Mrs Heywood, if we had your kind of expertise, but I'm afraid not one of our people understands the first thing about it. Would it be asking too much if I suggested you come and join MI5 for a day or two?"

"Well, I suppose I could, just for a day or two. When would you like me to start?"

"Would this afternoon be a bit of a rush?"

"Yes, it certainly would! What about my cover story?"

"Yes, everything is in hand."

"What if I had refused to do this, Sir David, you seem to assume a lot?"

"Forgive me, Mrs Heywood, I *am* assuming a lot, but I'm also sure that I do not underestimate you. Our information is that a cargo, possibly of iron ore, is being prepared. We can be sure that the Nazis have set up this elaborate operation in order to destabilise our currency. This is an urgent matter of national security."

"It seems I have little option, then. Tell me what my cover is."

"All the paperwork is prepared. You are one of His Majesty's Inspectors of Customs & Excise. We have concerns about your name. The fact that they know you in the docks is very much to our advantage, but we don't like our people to be using their actual name. So, we have come up with a compromise, you are now Mrs Lily Hawkins. This, of course, is your married name for the benefit of those people who recognise you. All your paperwork is prepared."

"Where do I go to receive my identity and instructions?"

"Do you know St James' Street?"

"Not especially."

"Will you come by train?"

"Yes, I imagine so."

"We will meet you at Charing Cross station. Can I say you will be on the 8.45am arrival?"

"Yes, that will be fine. How will I recognise who I am meeting?"

"Don't worry about that, my man will find you."

"Very well, I'll be there."

"Good show, Mrs Heywood, I shall look forward to seeing you tomorrow."

I put the phone down in something of a daze. What on earth had I just agreed to?

"What's that you've just agreed to?" asked Fiona.

"Can you believe it? I'm going undercover as an MI5 agent."

"Really? You're not kidding?"

"Well, all I have to do is pose as a Customs inspector and look at some shipping agents' books. It's just paperwork, but I'll be working for MI5, wait till I tell Dotty."

We laughed about it, and we decided to tell Dotty that I had become a field agent. When I told Edward over drinks that evening, he took it far more seriously.

"I'm sure you're right, Lily, about it just being paperwork, but do not forget my background was with these people. You may joke about being an agent, but that is what you will be."

"Should I be concerned then?"

"Maybe not. Promise you will telephone me each day. Let *me* be the judge if you should be concerned."

"Sounds like a bit of fun," said Elizabeth.

"Take Edward's advice, Lily," said Caroline. "Do make sure you keep him informed."

We had a lovely evening together. Cook had prepared an exquisite Boeuf Bourguignon, with Jennings and Albert serving us in grand style. I noticed Albert appeared to be particularly happy about it.

"Albert looks to be pleased with himself this evening, Mr Jennings."

"Yes, Mrs Heywood, there's rather a lot of the Bourguignon left over."

"How did Cook acquire the beef, or should I not ask?"

"I asked the same question, Mrs Heywood. Cook advised me not to ask on the grounds that it might incriminate me!"

"Sounds like excellent advice if you asked me, Jennings," said Elizabeth.

"Quite so, My Lady." Jennings then spoke quietly into my ear. "I couldn't help but overhear Mrs Heywood. You will take care tomorrow?"

"I will, Mr Jennings, you can rest assured."

I had no apprehensions at all until everyone started telling me to be careful. Sitting in bed that night, I made notes of all the shipping agents I could think of and wondered how much the docks had changed since I was last there. It was almost an afterthought to realise I would need somewhere to stay overnight. That was when it annoyed me that my parents didn't have a telephone. I asked Fi to send them a telegram first thing in the morning, because it seemed like an ideal opportunity to stay with them.

Next morning the train was exactly on time, and William placed my case in the first-class carriage for me. I had plenty of time to thank him and settle myself down.

"Thank you, William, that was kind of you."

"My pleasure, Mrs Heywood. Whatever this trip is for, Mrs Heywood, you will take care, won't you?"

"Yes, I'll be careful, William and tell Mr Jennings he didn't need to ask you to say that!"

At Sevenoaks, a terribly smart elderly woman joined me. Any other time she might have been delightful company, but I'm afraid I grew increasingly tired of her never-ending stories about her grandchildren.

"Do you have children of your own, my dear?"

"No, I'm afraid not."

"Oh dear, you really must, you know, the sooner you start the better."

"Yes, I'm sure you're right."

"I wouldn't want to pry, obviously, but I do hope there isn't a problem there. There are lots of things they can do these days, you know."

"There is one slight problem."

"I can always tell, I was only just saying, wasn't I? I do hope you don't mind me mentioning it."

'Actually, I do mind you saying, you're a really irritating woman and you are driving me nuts with your incessant baby talk.' No, I didn't say that, but I would have liked to. I was slightly more polite.

"My slight problem is that I'm not married."

"Oh, good heavens, what must you think of me? Of course, I shouldn't have said a word. How tactless of me."

I sat there longing for Charing Cross to relieve me of the woman. When the train pulled into the station, I breathed a sigh of relief.

"Goodbye," I said cheerily, "it's been lovely talking to you."

I walked along the platform looking at the crowd of people standing in the concourse. One of those strangers was my escort. I felt rather silly looking at every man expectantly. I'm sure one man thought I was making a pass at him, because he started to walk towards me. As he approached, another middle-aged man dressed in a suit and bowler hat stepped straight in front of me.

"Mrs Heywood, how delightful to see you," he said. "I was only saying to Sir David yesterday that I was looking forward to your arrival."

"Yes, it's lovely to see you, do you have a name?"

"Collins, Mrs Heywood, just call me Collins."

"Very well, Collins, I'm in your hands then."

We walked together as part of the movement of people spilling out onto the street. In contrast to my fellow passenger, he said very little. He marched along with an upright posture, a rolled-up newspaper under his arm, obviously an ex-military type. His car was parked in a side street, and he politely opened the rear door for me.

"I assume from your accent that you know London, Mrs Heywood."

"You assume correctly, Collins."

He offered little in the way of conversation, which was fine by me. It didn't take long before we were in St James' Street, where we pulled up outside an empty-looking building with a 'To Let' sign outside. I didn't say a word, just following him inside. We walked into an empty room where he pressed a concealed button. Moments later, a door opened and we continued into a hallway. Halfway down it, he knocked on another door. A smartly dressed woman answered it and invited me in. I turned around and Collins had gone. The room was quite large, with a window which would have looked out over the rear of the building, except the glass was obscured. It was clearly a functional room with telephones and filing cabinets, ordinary in every respect. Sir David was sitting behind a desk.

"Come in, Mrs Heywood, I hope you had a pleasant journey?"

"Yes, fine, thank you, Sir David. So this is MI5?"

"Yes, it's not very impressive, is it? Do sit down."

There were no pleasantries, he just got straight down to business. The smartly dressed woman offered me a cup of tea, which I gratefully accepted. Another younger man joined us, and between them they bombarded me with information. They didn't know which London dock the ship was destined for, but somehow they were sure it would soon be on its way. The disturbing part was the list of names they suspected as possible collaborators in the operation. It was a gangland Who's Who. When I asked which of the names was their prime suspect, they didn't have one.

The assumption was that only one of those names had the wherewithal to distribute such an enormous amount of cash. When I pressed them, they told me Jack 'Spot' Comer was a likely candidate, as was Charles 'Darby' Sabini. I didn't know these people, but like most people who lived or worked in the East End, I had heard of them. They had people watching these likely villains but had seen no connection to the docks. I explained that the docks were regarded rather like personal 'thiefdoms' by the gangers who dictated which docker would unload or load which ship. If outside criminals were involved, they would have to go through the gangers if they wanted to avoid a Customs inspection.

"Do you think the gangers themselves could be the sole collaborators?"

"No, I wouldn't think so," I replied. "They are all-powerful in the docks, but I was never aware of their reach extending beyond the dock."

"But you are sure it must involve them at some level?"

"That would depend. I assume that the crates or boxes, whatever they are, would have to avoid a Customs check? If that is the case, then yes, you would need the cooperation of the ganger. He would almost certainly not be aware of what was in the crates, other than it was some kind of contraband."

"Excellent, Mrs Heywood, your first-hand experience confirms our guesswork. If you can find out where this ship is docking, we shall put an end to the whole thing."

"You make it sound relatively straightforward, Sir David."

"Yes, it appears straightforward, that is what's bothering me. All we can do is follow the scant information we have."

It was all extraordinarily low-key, and seemingly haphazard, but it wasn't. They had excellent information at their fingertips. They gave me a relatively short list of all the shipping agents in and around the London docks. Collins was my driver for the duration and had I not insisted upon staying with my parents, they had accommodation arranged for me. I was to report any progress through Collins, and they gave me a phone number I had to memorise. It all sounded like great fun, and best of all I had a uniform to wear with the rank of Senior Prevention Officer. They showed me to another room where I was asked to put it on to make sure it fitted. Clever, I thought; it fitted perfectly!

When I presented myself suitably equipped with my uniform, there were smiles all round. They gave my identity papers to me as well as ration cards. I was Mrs Lily Hawkins, and they were thorough to the extent of giving me a typed sheet containing everything I needed to know about my 'husband', Mr Hawkins. Based apparently upon a real but now deceased man, I was advised to learn it off by heart before destroying the sheet of paper. It was all becoming terribly exciting. I found myself looking forward to it. When every detail had been covered, Sir David declared me ready for duty. I should start as soon as possible.

Chapter Thirty-Eight
Active Duty

When it was time for me to leave, Collins miraculously reappeared, as if he'd been standing behind a curtain the whole time. They obviously wanted me to get on with it, so with no more ado I prepared to leave. They wished me good luck and it all seemed quite normal, as if I was going shopping.

"Where to first, Mrs Hawkins?" asked Collins.

"I suggest we start with Mackinnon's. I know them well, that will get my foot in the door."

Collins put a tick next to the name, and we set off back the way we had come. The car was right outside, with maps on the front seat which he briefly consulted, and then we were off. Collins hardly said a word, so I spent my time reading about my 'husband'. As we drove across London, I could see my city was battered and bruised, but it still stood defiantly. People walked without even a second look as they went past huge gaping spaces where shops had once stood. There was one bomb site which looked much more recent. Here the people looked around, concealing whatever emotion it was they were feeling. There was an enormous crater in the ground with people staring down into it.

"That was a V2," said Collins.

"I guessed it must be. The damage is enormous."

We just drove on. The closer we came to the East End and the docks, the more extensive the damage was. Vast tracts of terraced houses in East Ham were levelled. The landscape no longer looked like London and yet, even there, people appeared to be going about their business. There were a couple of vegetable stalls operating, a cheery Cockney shouting "Fresh apples, lovely fresh Cox's apples."

"You have to admire these people, don't you, Mrs Hawkins?"

"It goes way beyond admiration, Collins, these are *my* people."

As we drove into the Royal Dock area, I was speechless. The entire landscape had changed. The tall red brick Victorian dockside buildings were either missing or damaged. I directed Collins towards where I thought my office had once been. On the way, I saw the most wonderful sight, there it was, sitting totally defiant with the buildings on either side missing - the little tea shop was still standing! Where my office had once stood, there was rebuilding going on, I didn't recognise any of it. Mackinnon's, the shipping agents were still there. Like the tea shop, lady luck had been kind to them.

Collins parked the car well away from the building. I stepped out of the car really looking forward to seeing them. I didn't feel remotely like an MI5 field agent, it felt more like a fancy-dress prank. I marched into Mackinnon's office expecting to see Ann at the desk. I didn't recognise the young girl who went into an immediate flutter and called me Ma'am.

"I was expecting to see Ann, has she left?"

"Yes, I'm sorry, it's me now. Is there something wrong?"

"No, not at all. Is Mr Mackinnon here?"

"Yes he is. Who shall I say wants him?"

"Mrs Hawkins, Customs and Excise," I said without a flicker of hesitancy.

She lifted her telephone and spoke to Mackinnon. "There is

a Customs officer to see you, Mr Mackinnon, Mrs Hawkins."

The young girl said he would see me now and she would show me the way.

"That's all right, thanks, I know the way."

I knocked on John's door and marched straight in, bearing a big smile.

"Lily, what on earth is this, you're with the Customs?"

"Yes, who'd have thought it?"

"Mrs Hawkins, you got married again?"

"I did, he's a naval officer, and here I am in uniform."

We chatted for some time. He asked a few more questions than I would have liked about my 'husband' but I didn't slip up once. What was difficult was that he didn't know George had been killed. It was ridiculous really, me lying to him. I was convinced he was no more caught up in fake fivers than I was. Sir David was adamant, though. Never ever blow your cover, he said, so I didn't. I can't say that I was comfortable about it with someone I knew so well. I spun him the line that I needed to see his books because we had been tipped off about some contraband goods coming in hidden in a bulk carrier.

I immediately realised I shouldn't have said that about the bulk carrier, not that it mattered with John, but it was a quick lesson. What became obvious was that understanding the business would be invaluable. I could imagine how an outsider would have struggled. I asked to see his movement tickets, which were introduced to guard against smuggling. I was looking for something like iron ore, possibly coming from Nova Scotia. John knew off the top of his head that he didn't have any iron ore listed. We chatted about the old days, probably more than I should have done, but it was a pleasant way to start my assignment. I thanked him for his help, went on my way, and found Collins looking rather bored.

"Where to now, Mrs Hawkins?"

"You have the list, Collins. Let's just go round in an orderly fashion, shall we?"

The next shipping agent was another that I was familiar with, and it was very much a repeat performance. Like an actor rehearsing a role, I was getting better at playing my part so that when I visited agents that I had not seen before, I found I played my part even better. As a Customs officer, I could demand to have sight of documents, and people jumped to attention. I was looking for any kind of anomaly between the various documents. People seemed to be quite taken aback when I asked for things they didn't expect me to know about.

For instance, I used to keep a separate account of cargo type correlated against the dock where it was unloaded. Hauliers would often phone up and ask which dock they needed for the dried meat, or New Zealand apples. It was easier to ask me rather than wade through the documentation that they rarely had.

What was quickly apparent was that no-one had iron ore from Nova Scotia, or anywhere else. I could only recall a few occasions when I had dealt with iron ore, it was usually shipped to places like Port Talbot. I wanted to take Collins to the tea shop for lunch, but he rather put me in my place.

"You need to take this more seriously, Mrs Hawkins, they must not see us together."

"I'm sorry, Collins, I'm new to this."

"You can go by yourself or we can share a sandwich. I also have a Thermos flask of tea."

"You know how to live in MI5, don't you, Collins!"

If you've never had an MI5 sandwich, I thought, it's not something which would encourage you to join the service! We shared a memorable lunch, parked next to a bomb site. Collins' conversation was as thin as the corned beef in his sandwich. I welcomed getting back on the job where I thought I had a better chance of being offered a proper cup of tea. My uniform commanded a good deal of respect wherever I went and if I demanded something I usually got it.

By the end of the day, my confidence in Mrs Hawkins had

grown considerably. I entered strange offices without batting an eyelid. I remembered how some of the top military brass had entered my office at Middlebourne. They were so damn superior, everything about their language and appearance was designed to intimidate you. It was all terribly exciting to start with and I was expecting to find a bulk carrier full of iron ore at any moment. Unfortunately, it was a triumph of hope over experience as I didn't find a thing. I trudged back wearily from the last agent, looking for Collins.

"When do you go off duty, Collins?"

"When you do, Mrs Hawkins."

"Good, I'm going to expand my remit, Collins. I want you to take me to the pub."

"That is a terrible idea, if I may say so."

"Why is that? Don't Customs officers go to the pub after work?"

"No, not in dockland dressed in uniform."

"Very observant, Collins. Drive somewhere like our delightful lunchtime venue, will you. I'll get changed in the back of the car."

Collins seemed adept at finding bleak and desolate places, it suited his character. He politely handed me my case from the boot of the car and walked some distance away. I was impressed!

"You can come back now, I'm quite decent. I didn't have you down as the perfect gentleman, Collins, you've gone up in my estimation."

"Where are we going, and what is the reason for this diversion?"

"There's a pub on the Isle of Dogs, if it's still there, called The Pelican. Every rogue and villain from around the docks drinks there. I'm not intending to stay there long, but I thought it would be a good place to pick up any gossip. I'll be all right for half an hour. I know how to deal with dockers. In fact, I'll probably be acquainted with some of them."

For all my bravado, I wasn't looking forward to it. As we drove through Poplar to get there, I was having second thoughts. When the pub appeared, I was sorry it hadn't been blown to smithereens. Even the bombs didn't want to go there. I had on some casual clothes, but I would still stand out because my 'casual' was a bit posh for The Pelican. He dropped me off, and I walked towards the pub with a good deal of apprehension.

Once inside, I could see that it hadn't changed a bit. It was still the place the low-life frequented because they enjoyed the company. I walked up to the bar as if I meant it and ordered a pint. Even before the pint arrived, there was a comment from a crowd in the corner. Why didn't I join them? Without giving it a thought, I reverted to the Cockney East End girl I used to be. I hadn't even noticed that I had cultivated a different accent at Middlebourne.

"In yer dreams, pal."

"You can be in my dreams any time, darlin'."

"Sorry mate, your dream would be my nightmare."

"Bloody hell, that's you init, Lily?"

"Who are you, then?"

"You remember me, I worked with Gerry."

"Oh yes! I remember you, Freddy, init?"

"That's me, luv. I was sorry about your Gerry, I ain't seen you since."

"Well, that's right, all the bombing and everything. I cleared off out of it."

"He was on the Hood, wasn't he, and we lost his mate, Alan. What ship was he on?"

"Gloucester, he went down within days of Gerry."

"You still working on the shipping, then?"

"Yes, kind of. I got a job with Customs."

"Hide yer baccy, lads, there's eyes about!"

"Don't have to worry about me, Freddy. I'm not going to grass on Gerry's mates, am I!"

"That's my girl! Where you workin', then?"

"I'm all over, I do spot checks on the agents."

"What you looking for, then?"

"Oh, you know, the little scams the agents get up to. I turn a blind eye to most of it. What's the harm in the odd crate of apples?"

"You was always a good girl, Lily. I'll be honest, I thought Gerry was a lucky bastard havin' you."

"That's exactly what I told him."

"What you doin' in this dump, then?"

"I just needed a pint and a bit of a chinwag with some old mates, you know."

"They were good days before the war, Lily. Do you remember those crates of champagne that went missing?"

"I remember Gerry turned up pissed as a rat. Silly bugger dropped his boxful. There were only two bottles not broken. I didn't 'alf give him a bollocking."

"I can imagine. Why don't you come and join us?"

"I'd love to, but I've got to go. It's been good meeting up with you, Freddy. I might come back to this dump again."

"Any time, Lily, we even welcome Customs people when they're made of the right stuff!"

"Don't you tell my guvnor, Freddy, I need this job."

"As if!"

"See you then, fellers."

I walked out onto the street, wondering where that woman in the pub had come from. Did I really mix with people like that? I suppose I must have, but never in The Pelican. It was lovely to get away from them and their cigarette smoke. I didn't enjoy it there at all, I felt really threatened. Collins appeared pleased to see me, and surprisingly, I was pleased to see him.

"How did it go?" he asked.

"I hated it, but I was right. I worked here for a long time, I thought I might recognise someone and I did."

"Any useful gossip?"

"I didn't stay long enough to find out, but the way is open for me to go back. If they know anything, they might just be daft enough to tell me about it. I think it's worth me going back tomorrow, but I can tell you, I'm not going alone."

"Very sensible, we'll find someone to go with you."

"Yes, I can just see one of your lot in The Pelican! You'd stand out like a pork pie at a bar mitzvah. I need a genuine East Ender who I can trust with my life, and I know just the person."

"This is a matter of national security. I'm afraid you can't just take anyone with you."

"I'm not talking about just anyone, I'm talking about a highly trained SOE agent with security clearance."

"Oh well, if you're *sure* about this person."

"Oh yes, I'm sure all right. I need to stop at a phone box so that I can organise it."

Collins found me a phone box well away from the docks. We sat in the car for some time before he pronounced it safe for me to use the telephone. His obsession with security seemed rather ridiculous to me, but as time went on, I found I was doing it. I got out of the car, looking in all directions. Even as I stepped into the phone box, I looked up and down the road. The silly thing was, I had no idea what to look for. Jennings answered the house phone and seemed pleased to hear from me. I had to assure him again that I wasn't in any danger. Edward came to the phone. His first question was about my wellbeing.

"I'm fine, Edward, I don't understand why everyone is worrying about me."

"Have you found anything?"

"It's been a long day, and nothing yet, I'm afraid."

"Is it the same again tomorrow?"

"Yes, I've got this driver called Collins who goes everywhere with me but must never be seen."

"Is he a dependable chap?"

"I think that describes him well. He says precious little, but he's always there. What I need though, Edward, is someone to come to the pub with me."

"What? What do you mean?"

"I'm thinking like an MI5 agent, Edward, you should be proud of me. I've just dropped into a notorious dockland pub to see if I could pick up any gossip and I've struck lucky. I met a docker I used to know. I think I should go back tomorrow and see what happens."

"Absolutely not. What are you thinking of, Lily, I should be worried sick!"

"I thought I'd take someone with me."

"In that case, I shall come up to London and go with you."

"Now that really is a silly idea. You would stand out like a sore thumb where I intend to go. No, what I need is someone who wouldn't look out of place, and who can protect me. Who do we know, Edward, who can look and act just like a girl from East Ham?"

"Yes, of course, and I would feel that you were in safe hands. I'll tell Dotty immediately; you will need to speak to her."

"Tell her to have clothes ready for a couple of days. We can both stay with my parents. I'll telephone the office at lunchtime. If she catches the afternoon train, I'll meet her at the station."

"It sounds as though you have it all organised. Just promise me you will take care. If you did get anywhere near the people behind this conspiracy just remember, they would stop at nothing!"

"I'm not brave, Edward, if anything like that happens I'll run a mile."

"Good, make sure you run fast."

"I'll speak to you tomorrow and don't worry. Bye, Edward."

"Bye, Lily."

Chapter Thirty-Nine
No Place Like Home

Collins drove me to Stockwell, to my parents' house. I just hoped that the telegram had got through, that they were expecting me. It had been a long time since I'd been home. When Collins stopped the car outside, I became strangely emotional. He kindly carried my case to the front door and immediately retreated to the car. He sat outside the house as I knocked on the front door. It was quite sweet really; he didn't drive away until my mother appeared. My first words were, did she get the telegram? It was an enormous relief when she said they did.

They were both so pleased to see me, it was the first time since George and Marcia's funeral. I was initially concerned that perhaps the conversation we had that day was unfinished. George's words in his letter to me were quite clear that he didn't want Dad to know. I didn't want him to know either. As long as there was the possibility in his mind that he was my father, then I thought it was a kindness for it to remain that way.

They fussed over me as they always did, and we immediately had a cup of tea. I could smell something delicious cooking in the kitchen, and just knew that despite all the problems of rationing, Mum would produce a lovely evening meal for me.

Everything was exactly as it should be. There's much truth in the saying that there's no place like home. Dad lit the fire, making everything feel cosy and warm. If only home could have been like that when I was a child, how different my life might have turned out. We'd never talked about it, not then and not since, it had been an open wound for such a long time. Even then when it had healed, it remained too painful to touch.

Dad produced a couple of bottles of beer, and Mum had a glass of sherry. That was pushing the boat out for them! It made me realise that my visit had become something of an occasion. The meal I could smell cooking was a steak and kidney pie with a suet crust pastry. They pretended it was everyday fare, but it wasn't. Rationing had got tougher as the war progressed. That pie represented many days of rations, assuming Mum could get it on ration, which was unlikely. It no doubt cost them dearly, but I had to admit there was something about black market produce which made it taste better!

That pie has never left my memory, it was absolutely wonderful. We certainly had our differences when I was a child, but one thing remained constant. My mum was the best cook in the world! We finished the pie between us, our plates so clean they hardly needed washing up. We had the usual ritual when Dad commented on how delicious it was and Mum said it was just something she quickly put together. It was always the same, the immense pride in her smile giving her away every time.

"What was all the rush to come and stay then, Lily?" Mum asked.

"Yes, I'm sorry it was a rush."

"What are you doing in London?"

"This will sound really strange, but I can't tell you."

"You can tell us anything, Lily, you know that."

"I wish I could."

"This is all to do with what you do at Middlebourne, isn't

it? We're not daft, Lily, if you're working for the government in some way you can tell us *that*."

"Okay, but you must not repeat a word of this to anyone. I mean it, this is really important. I work for Edward, but it's the government who picks up the bill. We're a kind of government department, but it's all hush hush. I can't tell you any more than that."

"I told you, didn't I, luv," Mum said to Dad.

"Yes, we guessed as much, from what your Gran and Mavis have said."

"Yes, but please say nothing."

"We won't, I promise. Is it really important work?"

"And you mustn't ask questions, because obviously if it's secret it must be important."

"And what about His Lordship, you seem awfully close to him. Is there something we need to know about that?"

"What is this, the Spanish Inquisition?"

"You're everything we've got, Lily, we care about you."

"Well, yes, it's true, I *am* close to him."

"You can guess what I'm going to say," Mum said. "Be careful, luv, he seems to be a lovely man, but he's a lord, and you're...well, you know what I mean."

"I know, and you may be right, but I can't help myself, he means everything to me."

"I'm sure you know best, luv. I bet you get to meet some important people in that place."

"I do, I'm really not the same person any more, Mum, it's changed my entire life. Would you believe that I've met the Prime Minister?"

"Not Mr Churchill?"

"I've had lunch with him, he calls me Lily."

"Really, you had lunch with Winston Churchill! What's he like?"

"I've met no-one remotely like him. His personality just fills the room. When he speaks, you just want to hang on to every word, because every word seems to be so important."

"My goodness, you really are a changed woman, Lily!" Mum said. "You're not my little girl any more, are you? Imagine speaking with Mr Churchill. Whatever you do at Middlebourne, it must be *really* important. We're so proud of you, luv!"

"I can't believe it myself at times I just wish I could tell you more about what we do. You would approve, I can assure you of that."

"Whatever you do, luv, it's obviously got something to do with the war," Dad said. "So when do you think it will end?"

"I fear it's still some way off yet. My guess is some time next spring or summer."

"What about the doodlebugs?" Mum asked. "When are they going to stop?"

"You're asking me as if I know about these things."

"If you had lunch with the Prime Minister, I think you *do* know, luv."

"I can tell you we're doing everything we can to stop them."

"Only last week one fell just down the road," Mum said. "Everyone is really frightened, Lily. It's not like the Blitz; you could set your watch by when they arrived but we can't take shelter now because we don't know when one will come over."

"I know, believe me, I do. They're mostly being launched now from northern Germany, but the flight path still takes them directly over Middlebourne. We see and hear them every day."

"Oh good heavens, any one of them could fall on you!" Dad said.

"One *has* fallen in the village, killing eight people."

"I'll not stop worrying now!" Mum said.

"We just live with the threat like everyone else. I can tell you though, the efforts being made to stop the V1, and the V2, are paying off. There would be hundreds more hitting London otherwise."

"Best change the subject, luv. I've made a nice apple tart if you'd like some."

"Yes, please. The other piece of news is that I've invited Dotty to stay with us for a couple of nights, I hope you don't mind."

"Oh, it would be lovely to see Dotty again, but what's she doing here?"

"I can't tell you that either, but let's just say she's coming because I need her."

It must have been strange for them, me being unable to tell them what I was doing. They seemed to accept the situation, putting their trust in me, and I was grateful for that. Our conversation steered clear of George. We managed to avoid all the old wounds. Ian was in my mind, with the photograph on the mantelpiece a constant reminder, but that was another wound we avoided. I broke the news to them that I would come down for breakfast wearing a Customs uniform.

"But you're not a Customs officer?" Dad said.

"No, but I look like one," I replied, hoping they would not need to pursue it.

They were very good, they must have been dying to ask, but didn't. I assumed they'd put two and two together. I slept well that night, safe in the knowledge that the Blitz was over. My memories of rushing outside into the Anderson shelter were vividly fresh, as if it had been yesterday. I could still hear the wail of the siren in my head as I went to sleep.

I appeared in the morning looking crisp and smart in my uniform, seeming to impress them. They were desperate to ask me, but obviously interpreted my expression correctly. When Collins arrived, Dad spotted the car outside and asked who it was. I simply said he was my driver, which made Mum want to offer him a cup of tea. Trying to explain that Collins did not socialise was difficult.

"I'll be back later tonight, Mum, and Dotty will be with me. Now don't worry, I'll be okay."

She drew in her bottom lip between her teeth, a sure sign that she was worried. I reassured her, waving goodbye as cheerfully as I could. Collins, ever the gentleman, opened the car door for me.

"There's hope for you yet, Collins! You can be a proper gentleman when you put your mind to it!"

He mumbled, "Good morning," and sat back behind the wheel. Collins wasn't communicative, but he was efficient. The shortest route between shipping agents was already worked out and he knew exactly where he was going. By lunch time, we had visited four different agents. I was becoming rather convincing in my role but it was all to no avail, nothing was amiss and nothing was suspicious.

As it approached lunchtime, I asked him to stop at a telephone box, so that I could phone the office. Fiona was concerned about everything, while Dotty thought it sounded like great fun. I explained exactly what was happening. She wasn't remotely phased at the prospect. Her confidence rubbed off on me and our conversation gave me a lift. I needed something to brighten my day, after what had been a dull morning. The highlight proved to be our lunchtime sandwich, enjoyed in the splendid environment of a bombed-out cul-de-sac.

"You certainly know how to impress a woman, Collins, is this one of your regular haunts?"

"You really *must* take this more seriously, Mrs Hawkins. It is imperative for your cover that we are not seen together."

"Is there a Mrs Collins, Collins?"

"There is."

"Does she call you Collins as well?"

"You're a trial, Mrs Hawkins. There's no need for you to be concerned about Mrs Collins."

"You're smiling, Collins, be careful now!"

I poked fun at him, but he was reassuringly reliable. We finished our delightful corned-beef sandwich, and thermos flask tea, and set off towards the next agent. On the way, I poked a little more fun at him, complaining about the sandwiches.

"It's the rationing, Mrs Hawkins, it's the best Mrs Collins could do."

I wondered if he had deliberately set out to trap me, because obviously it made me feel terrible.

"I apologise, Collins, if I'd realised Mrs Collins was going to the trouble of making me a sandwich, I would have appreciated it more."

He left me to stew in my own ineptitude. I quickly changed the conversation towards Dotty.

"When you first meet my friend Dotty this evening, or Miss Archer if you prefer, you might be misled into assuming she's not suited to her role. I can promise you, Collins, that would be a mistake."

"I am suitably advised," was his only comment.

So far, being an MI5 field agent proved to be much more like the daily grind of a Customs officer. My second to last visit in the afternoon was to a shipping agent I had been acquainted with, and where I received a warm welcome. After hearing what I was looking for, he immediately shook his head, no iron ore. The only bulk carrier he had on the books carried a cargo of grain. I went a little outside of my remit, asking if he'd heard any rumours of anything going on, and again there was nothing. The Nazis damaged the docks so badly during the Blitz that trade had never picked back up to previous levels. All the shipping agents I visited knew what ships they had on their books because there were relatively few destined for the Port of London. I walked back to Collins a little despondent.

"Not a single iron ore shipment," I said. "How many are left tomorrow?"

"There are only three left, but they're all further out."

"Will you have a word with head office, or whatever you call it? Ask them how certain they are that the cargo is iron ore, and London is the port."

"Will do," replied the efficient Collins.

We set off to Charing Cross station with plenty of time to meet Dotty. I talked all the way to Collins about the lack of any leads. It seemed strange to me that there hadn't been a hint of a suspicious ship. He was suddenly very erudite and well-informed for a driver.

"You're not just a driver, are you, Collins, what are you really?"

"I'm just your driver, Mrs Hawkins."

I didn't believe him but if he needed to keep up that pretence, who was I to argue? When we arrived at Charing Cross, Dotty was standing outside. She was wearing a blouse which was only half buttoned up beneath a jacket, high-heeled shoes, and a rather tight skirt. To say that she had an arresting appearance was understating it. The open blouse left little to the imagination.

"That isn't your friend, is it?" Collins asked.

"That's her. Now, I warned you, assume nothing."

I stepped out of the car to greet her and was met by her usual cheeky smile.

"How do I look then?" she asked. "I'm thinking, East End pub, full of randy dockers."

"They *will* be when they see you! Could you fasten just one more button?"

"Who's the chap in the car?"

"He's the one I told you about, Collins."

Dotty being Dotty walked up to the car and said hello.

"Hello Colin, I'm Dotty."

"No, he's not Colin, he's Collins," I said.

"That's not a proper Christian name, why do you call yourself that then?"

"If you prefer, Miss Archer, you may call me Mr Collins."

"No, don't be daft, what's your name?"

I could see he hadn't met anyone like Dotty before, he was flummoxed.

"Collins will be fine," he said.

"Well, all right, bloody silly name if you ask me. So where is this pub then, Collins? Where are you taking me?"

To his credit Collins took it all in good humour, having obviously taken to heart what I'd told him. We drove back towards the Isle of Dogs and all he would have heard was Dotty going on about how exciting it all was. I was in no doubt that he was trying to assess her from a professional point of view, while I was still trying to assess him. He wasn't just a driver, but I wasn't quite sure what he was.

When we arrived at The Pelican, it really looked like a forbidding place. I wondered if Dotty might have had second thoughts, but she didn't. She made the concession of buttoning up one of her blouse buttons. This was the point where the other Dotty stepped forward as she asked me exactly how I wanted to approach the men in the pub, how far I wanted to go with the charade. Collins was not as pedestrian as he made out, obviously observing the change in Dotty's attitude and I could see it met with his approval.

"I am informed, Miss Archer, that you are SOE. May I ask to which level you have been trained?"

"Most of it. I finished up at Arisaig with Sykes and Fairbairn."

"Really? That *is* impressive! Are you carrying any weapons, Miss Archer?" he asked nonchalantly, as if asking about her lipstick!

"Why do you need to know, Collins?" asked Dotty.

"I'm charged with the task of watching over Mrs Hawkins, and if you are to carry out the same function, I need to be sure how competent and well-equipped you are."

"You don't have a very high opinion of SOE, do you, Collins?" I commented.

"Perhaps not, MI5 is a professional organisation. I'm not used to dealing with irregulars."

"We may be irregulars in your view, Collins, but do not make the mistake of thinking we are any less professional."

"For everyone's sake, let's hope you are. I am assuming you *are* armed, Miss Archer."

"Of course. I have a fighting knife concealed inside my jacket, and a 45 calibre semi-automatic handgun in my handbag."

"That's a very noisy handgun," he said.

"Exactly, frightens the shit out of anyone who hears it."

"What is it?"

"Ballester-Molina, one of those South American things."

"Good, a sensible precaution," Collins said. "Organised crime frequents this pub. You should not underestimate the danger. I would remind you that these people are not German soldiers so you come under civil law here. I suggest you try to avoid discharging your weapon. I shall observe from a distance and will only intervene if it is absolutely necessary."

Dotty wasn't concerned, while it terrified me. All the talk about organised crime and guns was not what I had in mind at all. We agreed to use my connection with Freddy if he was there, otherwise Dotty would ingratiate herself with whatever crowd I thought appropriate. We also agreed it was a shame I told Freddy I was working with Customs, but my concern was that they would see me in uniform, in which case it would be even more suspicious if I hadn't told him. We agreed that we would just have to work with it.

I hadn't enjoyed the previous evening, but it didn't terrify me. As we went inside, my heart was racing. I looked around and Freddy was there; I caught his eye immediately, and he waved us over. He was with a crowd of undesirable looking types, absolutely the last people I would normally want to be sitting with. Dotty just went into her 'tantalise the men' role. She played them like a violin; it seemed that in Dotty's hands they could be made to dance to any tune. I looked on in wonder as she spun her web around them.

They bought us a beer each and Dotty made sure they also had another one. Her next tactic was brilliant, getting up to go over and have a quiet word with the barman. Her story was that we both loved a particular cocktail, and she needed to be sure the barman could make it. In reality, it was nothing more than Ribena and lemonade, and the barman was told in no uncertain terms to remain quiet about it. She called the cocktail a 'passionflower', with the emphasis on the 'passion'.

When the cocktails arrived at the table, we both downed them quickly. Naturally we then wanted another 'passionflower' which would entail the men having another beer. Dotty dictated how much they drank with consummate ease. An hour into the evening and they were already well drunk. When she deemed they were just ripe for picking, Dotty handed them over to me like a basket of apples.

"I had a nice earner a couple of weeks ago, Freddy. There were some crates of sugar where the paperwork had got mixed up. You know how easy that can happen. Well, naturally I agreed it was just a mix-up, and provided I got the going rate for one of those crates, well, it was something we could overlook."

"Well done, Lily, you always had a good eye for these things," Freddy replied.

"Yes, I was pleased with that. It would probably surprise you what a crate of sugar fetches these days. You got anything on the go, Freddy?"

"Only small stuff. Between you and me, Lily, there are some big players getting their nose into the docks these days. You probably know that."

"Yes, Jack Comer's becoming a bit of a problem. Comes to something when a hard-working docker can't get the odd little perk."

"Didn't I tell you fellers? Lily's all right!"

"Are you boys losing much to Jack?"

"Well, I can't say too much," said Freddy. "You do a bit of work for Jack, don't you Thumper."

"Thumper? How the hell did you get a name like that?" asked Dotty.

"How do you think?" said Freddy.

"Do you do much for Jack, Thumper?" I asked.

"I do the occasional little errand, you know, there's sometimes one or two down the dock I need to have a little word with."

"Any other of Jack's boys here tonight?"

"No, they've all clammed up, something's going on if you ask me," said Thumper.

"Well, it's a shame you don't know what it is, I could do with a warning. Last thing I want in my job is getting involved with a lot of paperwork. If I knew where, I would steer well clear."

"You're all right, Lily. Word is it might not be the docks."

"Thank heavens for that! I just want a quiet life."

One of them started pawing over Dotty. I was less concerned about Dotty, and more concerned for him. She fended him off, pretending to be drunk and it worked for the moment, but I was sure he'd be back. I pumped them some more about Jack Comer's activities, but it was clear that they didn't know. One useful piece of information, however, came to light. Jack, or at least some of his boys, would be in The Pelican the following evening. I thought we'd got about as much information as we were likely to get, so I suddenly remembered why we needed to leave. Dotty's admirer was all over her like an octopus and although she managed to prize herself away, the ghastly man was convinced it was his lucky night.

"I tell you what," I said, "we'll see you lot again, tomorrow is a good night for us."

The situation with Dotty appeared to become increasingly problematic. I looked on as she handled it with consummate ease.

"You don't have much style, do yer?" she said. "Not in front of this lot, what are you thinking? Outside, come on, I'll give you a treat."

We left in a hurry, Dotty's admirer salivating at the

prospect. She got him outside and led him into a dark recess at the side of the pub. There was a bit of a commotion before they reappeared. He had his arm over Dotty's shoulder as she supported most of his weight. They struggled back to the pub entrance where Dotty announced that the silly sod was so drunk, he fell over and banged his head. They all laughed and helped him to a chair and we walked off double quick. Some distance from the pub, we turned into another road. Collins reliably followed us.

"May I say you handled that situation admirably, Miss Archer, extremely professional."

"I'm glad you approve, Collins."

"Now the thing is, did you get any information, or is that man suffering a concussion for no reason?"

"Not for nothing, no. I think we have a significant piece of information," I said. "The feeling among the dockers is that something big is happening, but it may not be in the docks."

"Not in the docks!"

"I just heard an echo, Lily," said Dotty.

"It's interesting, isn't it, Collins," I said. "Perhaps you need to ask the 'powers that be' how confident they are with their intelligence."

"This is indeed an interesting development," he said. "If not the docks, then why is it known to the dockers?"

"I've already had a think about that, Collins," I replied. "If it was something being parachuted into the wilds of Kent, then why on earth would the dockers have wind of it. I suspect your intel may be right about it coming by ship, but perhaps you're wrong about the docks or the cargo. Maybe it's being unloaded somewhere else, and somehow one or several of the dockers are involved."

"That sounds like a sensible hypothesis, Mrs Hawkins."

"That's a good word, Collins, I must make a note of that," replied Dotty.

"Is there any way you can follow up on this?" he asked.

"We could go back to the pub tomorrow when some of Jack Comer's gang will be there."

"I take my hat off to you ladies, you've done remarkably well. It was well worth that unfortunate man's concussion."

"I thought so, Collins," said a mischievous Dotty. "Not bad for a pair of irregulars!"

Collins decided not to rise to the comment. The next stop was Mum and Dad's in Stockwell. All the way there, we discussed what we had gleaned so far. It sounded like a good lead, but we all agreed I should continue checking the remaining agents' paperwork the next day. There were only a handful left, and those were all further afield.

The possibility remained that it might be a shipping agent from another part of the country. Hoping a local agent would have the information we wanted was always a long shot. We were looking not so much for a needle in a haystack, more like a length of straw floating on the ocean. I asked Collins to stop the car at the end of the road so that I could use the telephone box. To my immense relief, it was working, and Jennings answered the phone.

"Is everything all right, Mrs Heywood?"

"Yes, I'm fine, Mr Jennings. I just need a quick word with His Lordship."

Edward came to the phone sounding extremely concerned. I assured him there was no need to worry and told him exactly what had happened. I asked him to convey every detail to the boys in Hut 3. I reasoned that, being as we had some of the sharpest brains in Britain, then we might as well use them. Edward agreed and said he would also have a word with his old colleagues in MI6. He thought it was likely that they knew more than they were letting on, to which I was inclined to agree.

Chapter Forty
An Evening With Jack Comer

I t was fairly late when we arrived home, but Mum had kept something warm for us to eat, just in case. Considering that Dotty had only met them a few times, I never ceased to wonder at how she had adopted them. We had a wonderful, albeit brief evening together, but I confess our minds were elsewhere. The following morning, Dotty was as impressed with my Customs uniform as my parents were. She kind of gave it away to them when she said it was all cloak and dagger stuff.

"I understand you can't tell us about it," Dad said, "but I want the pair of you to promise to be careful."

"Don't you worry, Jack, I'll take care of Lily."

"Who's going to take care of you, then?"

"You don't need to worry about me, Jack, the Government has spent months training me to take care of myself."

I glared at her! "Oops, you didn't hear that, Jack," she said hastily.

"Can you just assure me you both know what you're doing?" pleaded Dad.

"Seriously, Jack, we know precisely what we're doing," Dotty replied. "We're just gathering information and in another day or two we'll be finished."

Dad seemed to be a little happier after that. Then, just as we were preparing to leave after breakfast, a V1 flew by, which put things somewhat into perspective; we were all in danger, every day. Collins arrived exactly on time and sat in the car outside. Mum and Dad hugged us both, almost as if they believed we wouldn't return. Collins was still Collins, continuing to regard us as a couple of irregulars. I didn't feel the need to convince him otherwise, but Dotty didn't miss an opportunity to goad him.

We spent a lot of time in the car that morning, driving long distances between the remaining handful of agents. Not one of them had an iron ore cargo on their books. It was theoretically possible that a shipping agent might be in collusion with the Nazis. However unlikely that might have been, I had to satisfy myself that they were telling me the truth. I could see why Menzies wanted me involved, coming from the industry gave me an enormous advantage. When I left the premises of the last agent, I was quite convinced that none of them had a suspicious cargo on their books.

"This doesn't seem right to me, Collins," I said. "I know it could be a shipping agent from somewhere else, but shipowners tend to use agents local to the dock. I haven't picked up even a hint of anything suspicious. If it's possible, I'd like to go back to St James' Street and discuss the whole thing again."

"I'm afraid you can't just demand a top-level meeting, Mrs Hawkins."

"I was under the impression that this was an extremely grave matter of national security. At a meeting in the Cabinet War Rooms, the Prime Minister himself was fully behind it."

"You attended a meeting with the Prime Minister?"

"Yes, I did."

"I didn't realise you were so well connected, Mrs Hawkins."

"What *do* you know about me, Collins? What did they tell you?"

"They only informed me you were SOE, and therefore an irregular."

"Did they tell you I have considerable experience as a shipping agent?"

"Yes, that's all I've been told."

"We're all on the same side, Collins, this departmental mistrust is absurd. I think you need to telephone them and tell them we're coming in for a high-level meeting. I expect you'll find them cooperative."

After that slightly sharp exchange between us, Collins mellowed. We stopped at a telephone box and he did as I suggested, returning with a smile on his face.

"You were right, Mrs Hawkins, they granted you your meeting."

"I don't suppose you could drop this ridiculous Mrs Hawkins nonsense, could you Collins?" said Dotty.

"No, best not."

The last agent had been in Finchley. Their dockland premises had been bombed, and they moved as far away as possible. This left us with a drive across London to get to St James' Street. It proved to be an eventful journey. We hadn't travelled far, still on the Finchley Road, when we ground to a halt. The traffic was stopped in all directions, and several police officers were rushing about trying to turn the vehicles around. An ambulance rang its bell in the vain hope of trying to get to whatever had caused the delay. Dotty got out of the car and ran over to one police officer to find out what had happened.

She made a sign with her fingers as she came back, it was a V2. It had struck in Golders Green. We had no option but to turn back. Collins was a capable navigator, overcoming the problem by driving through Highgate and we duly arrived at St James' Street, albeit a little later than we planned. There was no delay, they were already waiting for us in a large meeting room. Sir Stuart Menzies was there as well as Sir David Petrie. Besides them, there were three other men, all looking terribly serious. Dotty and I walked into the room as directed, only to find that Collins had vanished. I asked immediately why he wasn't there.

"I would assume he doesn't have high enough clearance," replied Petrie.

"This is rather silly, Sir David. Collins knows everything about our activities."

"Yes, of course," he said. "Someone fetch Collins back here."

Collins appeared looking slightly overwhelmed by all the top brass. As he entered the room, I wondered why they hadn't questioned Dotty's clearance so I introduced her, assuming they were in the dark about who she was.

"Gentlemen, this is my colleague Miss Dorothy Archer."

"We know all about you, Miss Archer, it is a pleasure to meet you," said Menzies.

Dotty was somewhat taken aback. "You say you know all about me, sir, that sounds rather ominous," she said nervously.

"I am sufficiently well informed, Miss Archer, to know that you have been put forward for the George Cross," replied Menzies. "It is an honour to meet you."

Dotty didn't know what to say. She was completely nonplussed and sat down without saying another word while Collins appeared equally dumbstruck.

Menzies continued. "I spoke with Lord Middlebourne this morning. He was insistent that you should be told everything, Mrs Heywood. Having discussed this matter with him, we agree."

"Good," I said. "I've failed to uncover anything even slightly suspicious among the shipping agents. I know these people. I understand exactly how they work and am confident that there is not an iron ore shipment coming into London during the next two weeks. So the question is: how reliable is your information?"

"This is always the question, Mrs Heywood. There continue to be Enigma coded messages being sent from Nazi military headquarters at Narvik, to and from the airport, and the railway. They are all connected by the code name 'Untergraben'.

It looks increasingly likely that they have flown the forgeries from Berlin to Narvik. What the connection is with the railway, we are only speculating. Our analysts confirmed your idea, Mrs Heywood, that the cargo is most likely to be iron ore."

"I'm afraid iron ore is now looking rather unlikely," I said. "If we're sure the vessel is a bulk carrier, then it would be sensible to consider alternatives."

"We can be sure of nothing," replied Menzies. "We know something is going on which connects Narvik port with both the railway and the airport. We also have the intercept which refers to a bulk carrier in association with the word 'Untergraben'. It's suggestive, but nothing more than that. Norwegian resistance has the port under surveillance, but there's a heavy German presence."

"What about the intelligence you have obtained, Mrs Heywood?" asked Petrie.

"It may just be hearsay, but the feeling among some dockers is that something big is happening. The important information is that whatever it is, it may not be happening in the London docks. It also sounds likely that Jack Comer is involved."

"That would make sense," said Petrie. "Comer has control of a lot of the race tracks, the ideal place to distribute counterfeit money."

"We're going back to the same pub tonight," I said. "We're told some of Comer's gang will be there. I am also assuming there must be a German agent involved. I can't imagine Comer having direct contact with Germany."

"Yes, I agree, he is already under surveillance," Petrie said. "We have been very successful in rounding up and turning German agents with our Operation Double Cross but I agree, there must be one we have missed. This is not without danger, Mrs Heywood. You had better go with them, Collins, but keep yourself separate."

"Yes, sir," was all Collins said.

"Thank you for doing this, Mrs Heywood, and you, Miss Archer," said Menzies. "My gut feeling is that we are on the right track."

The meeting was adjourned, and so I availed myself of a private room to change out of my uniform, and to telephone Edward. We left none the wiser. I had assumed they knew more than they were telling us, but it appeared not. In reality, we had nothing more than scraps of information, and some imaginative guesswork. Collins was quiet as we made our way back to the car, we were each in our own thoughts. My thought was that, after the coming evening, we would have done everything we could and we would leave it to MI5.

As we were walking back to the car, Dotty said, "That wasn't how I thought MI5 would look, I was expecting a grand building."

"And me," I replied. "I understand there *is* a grand building they use at Blenheim Palace."

"It seems I owe both of you ladies an apology," said Collins.

"What have you done?" asked Dotty.

"I assumed they had given me a job with a couple of amateur irregulars. The way the top brass received you - well, that's not the case, is it?"

"We like to think we know what we're doing, Collins," I said.

His attitude changed from that moment on and now we were working very much as a team. We decided that when we arrived at The Pelican, Dotty and I would go in and he would stay in the car for an additional hour before coming in himself. We were early, and it was likely that the dockers weren't there yet.

"I'm pleased you're coming in with us, Collins," I said. "I don't like the sound of these gangsters."

"I would like you both to be careful. If it gets at all unpleasant, just leave. That would be much better than using your firearm, Miss Archer."

"For goodness' sake, call me Dotty, like everyone else."

"I didn't like to presume. It's Raymond, friends call me Ray."

"You have friends?" Dotty replied.

"Not many!"

He parked the car some distance away from the pub while Dotty and I made our way there. I didn't feel comfortable about any of it. Dotty told me not to worry, but I didn't share her confidence. We found it almost empty except for a couple of old stalwarts propping up the bar. It really was a drinkers' pub and nothing else, what my Dad used to call spit and sawdust. The walls were almost entirely bare except for a couple of posters. There was the inevitable Guinness Pelican poster where the bird's bill is full of bottles, and another for Bisto Gravy. The floor was bare boards and after decades of spilt beer, the smell was better imagined rather than experienced. The original gas pipes which supplied the lighting were still there, though the lights were now electric bulbs hanging from the ceiling.

Dotty asked for two of our 'passionflower' cocktails. She asked me if I wanted a sandwich, to which I responded with a look of horror. I agreed to a packet of Smith's crisps. The pair of us sat there looking at each other, wondering what we'd let ourselves in for. It must have been fifteen minutes before the dockers all came in together. We realised we'd made a mistake sitting opposite each other as we ended up with men sitting on each side of us. While they were sober, they were reasonably well-behaved, but I could tell that wouldn't last for long.

When Collins appeared walking up to the bar, I realised we had only been in there for an hour although it felt like a lifetime. He asked for a pint and made himself comfortable on a barstool with his feet resting on the rail. I looked away from him, and he avoided eye contact. The docker who 'bumped' his head the previous night was sporting a nasty bruise on his forehead but he didn't question his accident at all. That was when another group of men came into the pub.

They walked in, each looking decidedly unpleasant. A much smarter man wearing a suit and tie beneath an overcoat followed them. It was Jack Comer! They came directly to our table where all the seats had been taken. To my horror, he wanted to sit next to me. Initially, I didn't think he looked like a gangster. He had a pleasant enough face but that was only until he required the docker sitting next to me to vacate his seat. His expression left no doubt about his intention. The men on either side of me became immediately compliant and offered their seats as if they'd always intended to.

They bought more drinks, and the men became more rowdy while I became more uncomfortable. Comer had made a point of sitting next to me, but at first he didn't talk to me other than a few words. I said nothing out of place, I just waited to see if anything was mentioned. I didn't have to wait long!

"Freddy tells me you work for the Customs, Lily, is that right?"

"Yes, that's right, Jack."

"Freddy says you're a good girl, you know which side your bread's buttered."

"I don't understand what you mean, Jack."

"He says you were married to one of his mates, says he's known you a lot of years."

"Yes, we go back quite a few years."

"He says you can be trusted, but how do I know if that's true?"

"You don't need to know, so I shouldn't worry."

"What if I needed to know, Lily? What if I needed something you could do for me?"

"I'm sure I don't know what you mean, Jack."

"Would you be interested in knowing what kind of thing you could do for me?"

"That depends, if I like the sound of it, maybe."

"I could use a tame Customs officer, could that be you, Lily?"

"It could be; depends what's in it for me."

"Do you get any say in where you're assigned?"

"In theory no, but in practice yes. I can usually wangle myself into where I'd like to be. I assume you'd like me to turn a blind eye, Jack. Perhaps you might like me to tip you the wink about some interesting consignments. Is that the kind of thing you've got in mind?"

"That's right, Lily. All you need to do is look the other way, easy money."

"How much easy money?"

"Depends, could be as much as a monkey."

"For five hundred quid, Jack, I can't see a bloody thing."

Everyone laughed, I was obviously putting on a good act, but inside I was shaking.

"Freddy said you were all right. What about this friend of yours, what's your name, luv?"

"You can call me Lorraine. Friends call me Lolly."

"Can I now? Do you come with a reference, like Lily here?"

"No, you have to take me as you find me, Jack."

"If I need to come looking for you, darlin', I'll find you all right."

"So Lily's got a blind eye and I've got a deaf ear?"

"That's right, is that going to be a problem?"

"What did you say? I'm deaf!"

"You're a bit too clever for my liking."

Comer moved his eyes towards his henchman who was sitting next to Dotty. He indicated an instruction with an imperceptible movement of his head. The man stood up and grabbed Dotty by her jacket lapels. As she rose to her feet, the man bent over double and groaned in pain, letting go of her lapels immediately. Dotty then casually pushed him back onto his seat. It was an alarming situation. Violence was the answer to everything for those kinds of people. Dotty remained standing with her hand inside her jacket. If one of them really threatened her, I had the horrible feeling that she would produce her fighting knife, and there would only be one way that would end.

"You need to teach your gorilla some manners, Jack," she said.

Comer appeared to be furious. He sat looking at Dotty with a frown which reduced his eyes to slits. People like him expected others to fear them and when that didn't happen, he didn't know how to respond. Gradually his expression changed. He wouldn't admit it, but in his world, Dotty had gained a grudging respect. He indicated with his hand that his 'gorilla' should remain seated and I breathed a sigh of relief. If Comer wanted to see fear in someone, he only had to look at me.

"If you want me to do you the odd little favour, Jack," I said, "upsetting my friend is not the way to go about it."

"Do you trust her, Lily?" he asked.

"Of course I bloody do, she's got me out of quite a few scrapes, she takes care of me."

"How do I contact you, then? Where do you live?" he asked.

"I was in Stepney, but I'm just moving to a place in East Ham. I won't have a phone, but if there's a monkey in it for me, I'll damn well get one. In the meantime you can always leave a message here at The Pelican."

"Good girl, if you get a phone, give the number to Freddy or Thumper."

"I will, Jack. Have you got anything for me now?"

"No, not right now."

"Oh, that's a shame. Times a bit lean on the river, are they, Jack?"

"You've got some nerve, like this friend of yours, I admire that. As it happens, I do have something on the go, and the beauty of it is that it doesn't involve Customs."

"No Customs, ah, that's convenient. How have you arranged that on the river then?"

"You don't need to know that, Lily, your opportunity will come."

"You be sure and ask for me, Jack, next time you've got a job on the river."

"I will, Lily."

They had stretched my nerves to breaking point. I had pushed my luck further than I dared to imagine and I wanted to leave as soon as possible. Perhaps Dotty was reassured by the gun in her handbag, but I wasn't. Telling him it was time for us to go was a dreadful mistake. I was wearing the watch Edward bought me for Christmas. It was a fundamental mistake that neither Dotty nor Collins would have blundered into. Comer took hold of my arm and looked at the watch.

"That's a very expensive watch, Lily, what's a girl like you doing with a Patek Philippe?"

"What do you mean, a girl like me? That's a bit of an insult, Jack. It didn't fall off the back of a lorry if that's what you're thinking. It didn't get as far as the lorry!"

Everyone laughed, including Comer, but he maintained his grip on my arm. Dotty put the strap of her handbag over her shoulder and came and stood behind me. It was an extremely tense moment. The watch impressed him, I thought he just might have ideas about taking it off me. I pulled my arm away.

"I'm very attached to it, Jack, you can take your eyes off it."

"You're a piece of work, you are, Lily," he said, nodding to the unpleasant character sitting on the other side of me. He immediately grabbed my arm and obviously intended to remove my watch. Dotty took hold of his arm with her left hand.

"It's not polite to take a lady's watch," Dotty said, "I should leave it if I were you."

The man immediately stood up. Whereupon Dotty, without a moment's hesitation, hit him in the throat with an open hand. He gasped and fell back in his chair struggling to breathe. It was a desperately serious situation. One more escalation and people were going to end up dead! I was petrified, but I had to think of something to say.

"I told you, Jack, my friend Lolly takes good care of me! I can't afford to take chances, I've got a nice little earner going on around the docks, and I can't have it ruined by idiots like this bloke of yours. Now, the reason I'm looking at my expensive watch is because I have to go. There's no need for you to be broken-hearted, Jack, I'll be back. Now you know me and Lolly can take care of ourselves, so when you need me, you know I'll get the job done."

I stood up and waited for Comer's response, either he would show us a grudging respect or all hell was going to be let loose. They normally traded in a currency of violence and intimidation, but Comer was unsure how to react to a pair of women. It appeared that my usefulness took precedence in his mind, obviously seeing me as a potential asset.

"You really are a piece of work, both of you. Where did you learn to do that, Lolly?"

"East Ham, Jack, would you like me to show you another little trick?"

He finally managed a smile, at least Dotty had gained a mark of respect. Seeing his friend gasping for air, Comer's other henchman felt there was a score to settle, and he made his intentions known.

"Sit down, you idiot," said Comer, "Lily's right, this can be a nice little arrangement."

"Good," I replied. "As long as your gorillas don't upset my friend again, I think we're going to get on just fine, Jack. I'll see you all in here again soon, then."

I immediately turned towards the door. Collins was looking very tense. I quickly looked away from him. Dotty followed close behind me, watching them like a hawk. My instinct was to run, but Dotty remained completely calm and prevented me from taking to my heels.

"I'm looking forward to working with you, Jack," she said. "Sorry about your man there, I'll be kinder next time."

"I think he'll be more polite next time."

"See you then, fellers."

The moment we were on the other side of the door, I was determined to run, but again Dotty restrained me.

"Just walk slowly and talk normally," she said. "One of them might follow us."

To my immense relief I was outside in the fresh air, I could breathe again. I felt as if I had just run a marathon. My heart was racing and my legs were shaking, but I was so relieved to be out of there. We walked to the next sideroad junction and Dotty quickly pulled me by the arm to follow her. As soon as we were out of sight from the pub, she stopped.

"What are we doing?" I asked.

"It's only been two minutes; we wait for another two just to make sure nobody follows us."

"Why? Do you think they will?"

"Probably not, but it's just standard precaution."

When Dotty was satisfied no-one was following us, we walked on to the road where Collins picked us up the last time. Five minutes later, he appeared in the car. I'd never been so pleased to see him. I puffed up my cheeks and let out a long breath of air.

"Thank goodness that's over, I'm never going back to that pub again, Collins, that's it!"

"I've really got to hand it to the pair of you," he replied. "You were brilliant."

"Really? I thought he would see through me at any moment."

"No, Collins is right, Lily, you were amazing, especially when he saw your watch. I had my hand in my handbag."

"I saw you do that, and when you hit that man I was terrified, I thought you were going to shoot him."

"I was!"

"Well, thank heavens that didn't happen," said Collins. "It would have been a disaster at this stage. So tell me, did you get any information?"

"I think we almost got the Crown Jewels, Collins. Comer admitted he has a job coming up, and he more or less admitted that it was a job on the river. Best of all, he said he didn't need me as a Customs officer, he didn't need one at all."

"So when you say he more or less admitted it was a job on the river, he didn't actually confirm it was an inbound ship. He also didn't say where or when."

"That's right, but that was the impression I got, didn't you, Dotty?"

"Yes, but he might equally have just been saying that."

That was how our conversation continued, all the way to Stockwell. We were definitely onto something, but we just couldn't be sure what it was. One thing was for sure, my nerves wouldn't survive another trip to The Pelican. We'd gone as far as we could and Collins agreed.

"I agree, Mrs Heywood, your experience made you the perfect candidate to examine the agents' books, but we didn't intend you to become an active field agent. You mustn't put yourself in harm's way again, either of you."

"I don't intend to, Collins. I suggest you take us to St James' Street in the morning and they can debrief us. We can catch a train to Tunbridge just as soon as everyone is satisfied."

We stopped on the corner of the road so that I could phone Edward. He was delighted to be told we were coming home the next day. I told him the information we had gleaned and asked him to share it again with the boys, perhaps they could make sense of it. It pleased Mum and Dad to know that there was to be no more 'cloak and dagger' stuff going on. Everyone was happy that we were going home, and none more so than me!

There wasn't much left of the evening to spend with Mum and Dad, but what there was proved to be difficult. The events of the evening filled my mind to overflowing, but we couldn't share any of it with them. I suspect they both realised we were preoccupied, but I felt rather guilty. I hadn't seen them for a little while and it probably appeared that I was ignoring them. I promised to make up for it on another occasion.

The following day in St James' Street they welcomed us like returning heroes. Sir David Petrie was there, as well as an assortment of other people whose function they didn't make clear. We all gathered in the same meeting room where we had met before. A secretary sat recording verbatim everything that was said. Petrie sat behind a desk, as did the secretary and two of the other men. They arranged the desks in a line and Dotty and I sat on chairs facing them. It might sound intimidating but we were so well received, I felt reasonably comfortable.

For all that the building and appearance of the occupants might hint at a chapter from "Tom Brown's School Days", the reality was the opposite. They analysed our account of events methodically. Petrie appeared delighted with the information we had gleaned. None of it was conclusive, but it was much more than they had before. They considered our direct contact with Jack Comer to be something of a triumph. Comer saying that Customs were not involved with his 'job' was a tantalising lead.

We debated the point. It could have meant he had his own people posing as Customs officers or, what we believed more likely, was that they would spirit the forgeries away from right under Customs' noses. In gangster parlance, that would qualify as Customs not being involved. Intelligence from Norwegian resistance was also inconclusive. The heightened security was causing them considerable difficulty around the port. They reported goods coming into the railway station as usual, noting iron and aluminium ore, as well as coal, military supplies, and grain.

Petrie remained confident they were getting closer. He had Comer and his henchmen under surveillance. They would have people watching the London docks, as well as a man in The Pelican pub. The threat from the forgeries was considered so serious that RAF Coastal Command was flying reconnaissance missions over the North Sea and Western Approaches. They had at least two Sunderland's in the air during daylight hours, seven days a week. Against that background of intensive effort, Ultra intercepts also showed heightened Nazi activity. It certainly felt as if the whole thing was coming up to the boil.

It was nice to know that we had contributed usefully. When I handed back my Customs uniform and identity papers, my brief career as a field agent came to an abrupt halt. I may not have covered myself in glory like Dotty, but I can fairly say that, during the war, I served as an active field agent! I might not have been in an enemy occupied country, and it was only for three days, but nevertheless, I had been an agent. When we left, Petrie made his gratitude quite clear, and to my surprise, Collins had a pleasant side to his character.

"It's been a pleasure to work with you both," he said, shaking my hand. "If all of SOE are like you and Dotty, perhaps you're not a bunch of amateurs after all."

"My, my, Raymond, steady on now, that sounds like a compliment!"

"It does, doesn't it! May I give you both a ride to the station?"

"That would be very nice, thank you."

The journey to Charing Cross served to remind us that the war raged on. We passed two recent impact sites where a V1 had brought death and destruction to the already war-weary Londoners. It provided a sobering reminder that the forgeries were but one small part of the German war effort. We both shook Collins' hand at the station and thanked him for taking care of us. I could see he had warmed towards us, just as we had towards him. He drove away and disappeared from view, and it seemed somehow appropriate that an MI5 agent should simply melt away into the crowd.

Chapter Forty-One
The Memorial Service

William met us at Tunbridge Wells West Station, where Dotty was hugely impressed to be met by a Rolls-Royce. She sat in the back practising her royal wave, much to William's amusement. Upon arrival at the Manor, we both went our separate ways and I walked straight to the office. Fiona had obviously been worried and was really pleased to see me. Edward heard me arrive and came through from his office. He put his arms around me and kissed my cheek, holding me just as long as protocol allowed.

"We have both been worrying about you. It's a relief to have you back safely," he said.

"I'm not sure that I was ever in real danger, not having Dotty with me."

The welcome I received from both of them was heart-warming. They were desperate to hear all about it, and I started to tell them, but quickly realised I would have to go over it all again in Hut 3. Edward agreed, so with no more ado, we set off together for Hut 3. A nasty bitingly cold wind seemed to go right through me. We each ended up running with our hands up under our chins. I was pleased to see smoke being blown away from the hut chimney, knowing the stove would offer us a warm embrace.

Edward had briefed the boys each day, and apparently they had been giving the matter considerable thought. Having just come back from a similar meeting in St James' Street, it fascinated me to compare the two different approaches. MI5 were meticulous in their analysis of every word being said. The boys concentrated on certain keywords, looking for hints that might fit with the scenarios swimming around in their collective brain. When I had told them everything I could think of, they each sat back with a satisfied smile.

"What have I said that's made you smile?" I asked.

"Whatever you say makes me smile, Lily," replied Patrick, "it's just the sound of your voice."

"Come on, tell me," I said, smiling back at him.

Patrick was the first to tell me. "Well, you see, me Mammy said when you go to buy a hat, you have to try them all on before you find the one that fits, the one that sits just right."

"So what does your Mammy say about these fivers?"

"She said fivers are the same as hats!"

"Is there anyone here who can tell me what the hell Patrick's Mammy is talking about?"

"We put ourselves into the shoes of the Nazis," said Corky, "or should I say hat."

"Don't tell me, we are now looking for hats?"

"Well, in a way, Lily, yes," replied Edward. "We worked out what the perfect hat is from the Nazi perspective."

"That's right," said Rolo. "We worked out every possible scenario, from the sublime to the ridiculous. Then we had to wait for you to tell us which one is likely to be correct."

"Have I told you, then?"

"Probably!" replied Rolo. "You said Comer didn't have to worry about Customs, and you just confirmed what the Norwegian resistance says is being loaded at Narvik. If a shipment of iron ore is looking increasingly unlikely, we should look at the other possibilities that we know are being loaded. When we do that, Lily, it makes one of our scenarios statistically highly probable."

"You've lost me, Rolo."

"Do try to keep up, Lily," teased Patrick.

"What's the best way to avoid a Customs check?" asked Rolo.

"Well, there might be several ways, but all highly risky," I said.

"Precisely," said Edward, "so why risk it when there's a class of consignment which requires no Customs? Answer, a ship leaves one British port destined for another British port - no Customs required."

"What is the one cargo which routinely leaves a British port in a bulk carrier destined for another British port?" asked Corky.

"I can't think, so which one of you clever clogs is going to tell me?"

Each of them put a hand up, looking like a bunch of schoolboys including Edward. The lovely smiles on all their faces confirmed again that deep down they had never ceased being schoolboys.

"The magic ingredient," replied Edward, "according to Norwegian intelligence, was in the last list of goods being moved through the rail depot. It was coal!"

"This is how it works, Lily," explained Woody. "They load the ship with coal and fake fivers at Narvik. It sets sail at night when the North Sea is blanketed in fog. It steers directly towards Newcastle before heading south along the coast towards the Thames estuary."

"The last part is the best bit, Lily," said Rolo. "Your dockers hinted at the 'job' not being in the docks, and why would it be? The docks are full of officials and Customs people, not to mention the gangers who would know if something didn't look right. A bulk carrier is a big ship. It needs to go somewhere away from the glare of the Port of London. It also needs to go to a place where it would be inconspicuous. Why not take the ship to where most bulk carriers go? The obvious place is Beckton Gas Works! It's in Gallions Reach, just west of Barking Creek, and the gasworks are the only thing for miles around. This is the largest gasworks in Europe, bulk carriers full of coal routinely dock there, a lot of them bringing coal from Newcastle."

"It's perfect," I said. "You *are* a clever lot!"

"It's also the perfect time," said Edward, "because there is a thick fog forecast for several days."

"I must telephone Sir David immediately. They need to know this. It's only a best guess scenario, but it's really compelling."

"*We don't guess*, Lily," retorted a very indignant Rolo. "We base our scenario upon statistical probability."

"However you do it, it's brilliant! I'll tell them."

I really enjoyed that phone call. I spoke to Sir David himself and made it abundantly clear that the scenario resulted from an SOE intelligence unit's statistical analysis. He was gracious enough to ask me to pass on his appreciation. I had it in the back of my mind to comment upon the often-mentioned MI5 opinion that we were a bunch of amateurs, but in the event, he was such a gentleman, I deemed the comment inappropriate. He assured me that whatever the outcome of the forgery threat, he would keep me informed.

From our point of view at Station M, it all provided a distraction from our usual line of work, but it proved to be a memorable distraction for me. As with all these things, the return to the daily reality of war was a harsh wake-up call. The coloured pins on the map denoting 'V' strikes were merging together into areas of uninterrupted colour. Our disinformation campaign against the Nazis was bearing fruit. The red-coloured pins denoting V2 strikes were no longer concentrated in and around London. Believing that their rockets had been falling well to the southwest of London, they now directed many of them further northeast into largely unpopulated Norfolk. The V1's, which had a shorter range, were being misdirected further south. They spared London, often at the expense of people living in the London suburbs, people like George and Marcia.

The effect of Operation Cormorant became difficult to assess. The boys produced charts of everything, and the number of launches charted against days provided the critical one. Our analysis clearly showed that what had previously been a rising graph, had now flattened. We didn't stop the V2's, but the evidence showed that we substantially slowed down production for many weeks, perhaps more. That might not sound much, but it equated to hundreds if not thousands of lives. We only had to slow production long enough for the Allies to overrun the manufacturing site. Working on that basis, Operation Cormorant had been a complete success.

Our other significant success was confirmed just six days later. Sir David Petrie telephoned personally to inform me that the latest German operation to flood Britain with forged five-pound notes had been foiled. At 10:45am on November the 22nd, a bulk carrier seemingly from Newcastle docked alongside Beckton Gas Works with a cargo of coal. They unloaded five crates of forged five-pound notes into a lorry before being intercepted by MI5. Petrie remained convinced that Jack Comer had been involved, but he had no evidence to connect him. There was also no evidence pointing to the suspected Nazi agent who he was sure must have acted as the go-between. In the end, only a handful of people were charged. Those included the captain and crew of the ship, and four London dockers, one of whom was Freddy.

It might have been an MI5 operation, but we decided to take a large share of the credit for ourselves. There had been precious few reasons to celebrate, so we enjoyed our moment. Our success with the V2 manufacturing sites combined with our intelligence contribution towards the forged five-pound notes, were seen as a massive triumph for SOE. There might even have been a brief period when we allowed our success with Cormorant and the forged fivers to go to our heads.

We continued our work plotting and predicting where the V1's were being launched. The RAF would bomb the sites and the Germans would rebuild them somewhere else. It seemed to be a never-ending cycle. The V2 rocket launches proved to be even more elusive. The concept of the mobile launcher was being developed. With our constant airborne surveillance, the boys in Hut 3 had worked out exactly how all of this operated. They were unable to transport the V2 in a ready-to-launch condition, so a typical trailer-mounted rocket would have to be accompanied by a retinue of support vehicles.

This would include a launch-table trailer, mobile crane, propellant vehicles containing liquid oxygen and alcohol, with the warheads being carried in another truck. In all, as many as thirty vehicles were involved, and hundreds of specially trained troops. Field stores of rockets were set up and the mobile crews would collect their rockets before driving to the launch site. Finally, the firing crew made the rocket ready. It would be aligned and fuelled, and they would set the electronics and gyros. The mobile crews could prepare the rocket for firing in about 90 minutes. The RAF mounted several raids to counter the threat, but by their very nature the mobile crews always stayed a step ahead. However, Operation Cormorant had significantly slowed production, giving us vital extra time for the Allies to advance upon the production sites. However, if we were ever tempted to feel slightly complacent, those thoughts were quickly erased towards the end of November.

The village organised a memorial day for the six adult and two child victims of the V1 which fell close to the Manor. Almost everyone from the Manor attended, along with the rest of the village. The weather reflected the solemn occasion, being cold and grey with a heavy mist hugging the ground. Most of the trees had shed their leaves, their skeletal branches reaching for the sunshine which wouldn't return until the spring. There were damp leaves underfoot, and the smell of decay hung in the air. The church quickly became full to overflowing, with even more people outside.

Edward, as an honoured guest and also as one of the readers, had seats reserved near the front. He asked me if I would like to read something. I didn't like public speaking, it terrified me, but because I had been so involved when the V1 had struck, rather felt obliged to. I opted not for a Bible reading, but for a favourite poem. Johnny and Fiona sat with us, together with the rest of the family. The vicar read a eulogy for each of the victims, which was followed by personal tributes from the surviving family members. It was very easy during the war to see victims as a statistic, each one a tragedy, but a faceless, nameless one. One after another, close relatives and friends told us about their loved ones. I found it harrowing, gripping Edward's hand as tearful people related their personal tributes.

A young woman stood up and had to be helped to the rostrum. She was a really pretty girl of about fifteen or sixteen years old. I didn't know her name, but I'd seen her before. The poor girl was distraught which, combined with being nervous about speaking in public, made it almost impossible for her to say anything. She stood at the rostrum with tears rolling down her face. It took her an age to say what she wanted to say, but to her eternal credit, she managed it.

"My name is Barbara Blackmore," she said. "Gloria Blackmore and Kenneth Blackmore were my mother and father. James Osborne was my adopted brother." The poor girl broke down, but she remained determined to continue. The congregation was behind her, to a person. We would have sat there all day if that had been what she wanted. Eventually she continued. "Jimmy came to my family as an evacuee from London in 1940. In 1941, both his mother and father were killed during the Blitz. When we found out his only remaining aunt and uncle had also been killed, my parents adopted him as their own. He was so special; he could play the piano and the violin. But most of all, he was my brother, and I loved him."

She had intended to say more, but she had said as much as she could. They helped her back to her seat in the front row of pews. No-one said a word for what felt like an eternity. Barbara had passionately exposed the true price of war, she laid bare the futility of armed conflict. So many lives cut short, so many promising futures lost. Edward had the unenviable task of following her with his reading. Barbara's words had moved him as they did me, but he delivered his reading faultlessly.

"Romans 8:35 37-39.

Who will separate us from the love of Christ? Will hardship, or distress, or persecution, or famine, or nakedness, or peril, or sword? No, in all these things we are more than conquerors through him who loved us.

For I am convinced that neither death, nor life, nor angels, nor rulers, nor things present, nor things to come, nor powers, nor height, nor depth, nor anything else in all creation, will be able to separate us from the love of God in Christ Jesus our Lord."

It was my turn next, and I made my way to the rostrum. The poem I had selected suddenly became overpoweringly personal. My close association with death came back to haunt me, not that death is ever far away. I stood there trembling, quite unable to read the verse. I first looked at Barbara, the young woman who had so courageously said her piece, and then at Edward who, seeing my distress, indicated that he would take over from me. I intended to accept Edward's help, feeling completely incapable of continuing. He was just about to stand up when young Barbara, who I had never spoken to before, spoke to me from the front pew. "You can do it," she said. That young woman's strength so inspired me that I did manage to do it.

"I don't know who wrote this poem, but I think it is very appropriate for the children of this tragedy," I said.

"Tear drops, slow and steady, the pain so real and true,

God took another angel, and that angel, dear, was you.
Angel's wings, upon the clouds, your body softly sleeps,
Hush now, little angel, no more tears you have to weep.
Little prayers are sent to you, the short life that you led,
Your family will never forget you, so rest your little head.
I know God will look after you, now you are truly alive,
Your spirit soars beyond the moon, your legacy will survive.
You're beautiful, you're endless, now stretch your wings and fly.
You're loved by so many it will never be goodbye.
Close your pretty eyes, no more tears, just go and rest,
Let your soul lie peacefully, we know you did your best.

Barbara thanked me. I wanted to say much more to her, but I just couldn't, and sat down with my head in my hands. The vicar finished the service and while not meaning any disrespect to the dead, I just wanted to go outside. Edward and I stood together and lots of village people thanked us for our efforts on the day of the tragedy, as well as our words in the church. There were far more people outside the church than there had been inside. I think nearly the entire village attended the service. We walked together to what remained of the site of the explosion.

There was nothing left standing where once there had been houses. The rubble had been stacked into piles and anything not reusable had been removed. What remained was even more poignant for being absent. The village stood in a three-minute silence, each of us in our own thoughts. Barbara's little adopted brother led a short life, and the poem I chose had probably been written for a child, possibly one just like him. When we dispersed, I found Barbara and spoke to her.

"Where are you living now, Barbara, who is taking care of you?"

"I live with my Aunty, here in the village."

"You know who I am, don't you? I'm Mrs Heywood from the Manor. Lily Heywood. Will you promise me something, Barbara, if there is ever anything you think I could do to help you, I want you to come to the Manor and ask for me."

"That's very nice of you, Mrs Heywood, but I have to manage on my own now."

"No, you don't, Barbara, you'll never be alone in this village. The war wrenches us apart, but the community pulls us back together again. We all need help from time to time, and I imagine right now, you need all the help you can get."

"I won't forget, Mrs Heywood, thank you."

Everyone from the Manor gathered together. Greg and Aileen were there. I went over to them and Aileen spoke briefly, but pleasantly enough.

"It was a terrible day when this happened, Aileen."

"I know, Greg's been telling me. He says between you, you saved someone's life."

"Yes, I believe we did. I can't imagine how the poor boy had survived beneath the rubble. It was Greg who found him."

"You did well to read that poem, I didn't think you were going to manage it," she said.

"You're right, I wanted to hand it over to Edward. Wasn't that young woman amazing? She put me to shame. Have you got any further with your wedding plans?"

Greg looked at Aileen and replied. "We're not in a rush. We're still looking for somewhere more suitable to live."

Edward joined us and I immediately felt very awkward.

"This is Greg's fiancé, Aileen," I said.

"Nice to meet you. Congratulations, Norton, and when is the big day?"

"I was just telling Lily, My Lord. We don't have a date yet."

"These things are difficult just now, I think many people are putting off all such arrangements, waiting for the war to end."

"You're right, My Lord, I think we all feel that way. The future for most people means the time when there's no longer a war."

"Insightful comment, Norton, I quite agree."

We walked on with Edward and Greg sharing a thoughtful

conversation together, while I chatted to Aileen. It all seemed so normal, but at the same time it was terrifyingly abnormal. I remained in fear every second that Aileen would say the wrong thing, or even Greg might re-ignite past regrets. When we arrived back at the Manor unscathed, I breathed an enormous sigh of relief. The memorial service had the same effect on all of us, putting names against the numbers was painful. It allowed matters to become personal which, for anyone involved in the war's conduct, was ill advised. There is only so much pain anyone can withstand which was why the news released the very next day hit us so hard.

On the 25th of November 1944 at 12:26pm, the single most deadly V2 attack took place. A V2 fell directly into the Woolworths department store in New Cross. The store had been full of people and the rocket exploded among them with devastating effect. Rolo got a detailed report from the local police and fire service. We all saw the remains of people in the aftermath of the V1 which hit the village. As horrifying as that was, it helped us to visualise what the emergency services had to deal with in New Cross. 168 people had been caught directly in the blast and a further 123 people were injured. A tram just happened to be passing, and they found all the passengers dead in their seats. Bodies lay everywhere, and they found remains far and wide.

The highly confidential report which Rolo obtained was explicit in its detail. The public had been denied much of that detail because it was considered bad for morale. We could understand the reasons for that decision. With no advance warning and no defence, people lived in constant fear of obliteration. The human side of the catastrophe could undoubtedly have caused some civil disruption because the report made clear that the store had been especially crowded. It was a Saturday, and Woolworths had obtained a supply of saucepans. It seems almost incomprehensible now that something as mundane as a saucepan would attract a larger crowd of people than usual. So many people died just because they needed a new saucepan.

Chapter Forty-Two
Baby George Arrives

I turned the calendar over, happy to consign November into history; a new month always offered fresh hope. There were few things during the war that you could predict with absolute certainty, we seemed to live in a world full of random events. A V2 rocket might fall on you at any moment, the Allied advance in Europe could be six steps forward or six back. There was just one thing in our lives that we were sure of, and that was life itself. Florence was fully nine months pregnant. Gran couldn't run and fetch the midwife, so I had Jim and Mavis on standby. One of us - Fiona, Dotty, or me - would go to see her every lunchtime, and each evening.

We were all rather slow to realise that the relationship between Florence and Robert Fuller had developed into something permanent. He visited her every day and between us all, Florence had an army of people looking after her. In amongst all the horrors of war, the prospect of a new-born coming into the world was an uplifting prospect. Florence had changed out of all recognition, and I don't just mean because she was the size of a battleship. The shy and timid Florence had vanished, and the young girl who saw no future for herself had been replaced by an outgoing confident young woman, soon to be a mother.

The village midwife had retired some time before, and I hadn't met the new woman who took over from her. I expected to see someone rather like Marion, the matron at St Thomas', a worldly-wise lady with years of experience, a jolly smile, and a safe pair of hands. The woman who came to check up on Florence was in her twenties, crisp uniform, with her hair tied up in a bun. When she had finished with Florence, I offered her a cup of tea, and tactfully asked how many births she had attended. I braced myself for the worst, expecting her to say two or three. She politely informed me she became a qualified midwife in 1936, soon after the new Midwife's Act when she was eighteen years old. She had lost count of how many babies she'd attended. I drank my tea!

Jim rushed to the Manor on the morning of the 8th of December. Corporal Harris at the barrier told him to go straight through. Jim told William, who ran to tell me. There was no need for any of us to rush about, everything was progressing normally, but of course we rushed about. Fiona and I ran to find Dotty, and Edward and the boys in Hut 3 all wished her well. When we came back past the Grand Entrance, most of the staff were there, wishing Florence well. Corporal Harris passed on his best wishes. When we arrived at the cottage, everyone was there, with Spencer Tracy obviously beside himself, barking at everyone.

"Anything happened, Mavis?" I asked.

"No, but everything is progressing well."

"Is the midwife with her?"

"Oh yes, I just hope she knows what she's doing, she's only a child herself."

"I think you'll find all midwives are getting younger, Mavis. Where's Robert, I'm sure he would want to be here?"

"He's here! He's in there with Florence. I don't know, whatever next! We didn't have men in attendance in my day."

I smiled and asked Jim if he would be kind enough to put Spencer in their house. Gran was sitting with a look of anticipation on her face, obviously looking forward to holding the new baby. In amongst the crowded kitchen, the teapot was continually being topped up. We drank tea until it was coming out of our ears, and we reduced Gran's biscuit and cake tins to crumbs. Spencer suddenly made a reappearance, having escaped via Mavis' back door. Dotty shouted at him, and despite all the distractions, he instantly sat at her feet. I didn't have the heart to send him away again.

At 1:45 in the afternoon, Florence gave birth to a lovely baby boy. We were all desperate to see mother and child, but the midwife had complete charge of the situation. Only when she deemed it to be the appropriate time were we allowed to see her. Jim helped Gran up the stairs, she would be the first to hold the baby. Florence was a picture of happiness and a joy to behold. There were too many of us standing around her, it must have been overwhelming. Suddenly, I belatedly realised that Robert Fuller and Florence intended to share their future together because it was immediately obvious he had adopted the baby as his own. It was Robert who handed the baby to Gran.

He certainly was an adorable little boy, and inevitably memories of my miscarriage momentarily filled my mind. When he was placed in my arms, it was easy to see why Robert felt like that about him. I looked down at him with his flushed cheeks and matted hair, his tiny fingers grasping at the air. He had to be almost prized away from me as reluctantly, I had to part with him and Fiona took him from me. I put my arms around Florence and hugged her.

"Thank you, Lily," she said.

"I told you it would all work out fine, didn't I?"

"You did, but you didn't tell me it would be *this* fine!"

"You caught me by surprise with Robert, I didn't see that coming! I'm delighted for you, for both of you. Are you planning to get married?"

"We are, I'm just so lucky."

"Have you got a name for Baby yet?"

"Yes, we're going to call him George after Robert's father."

"That's my father's name as well, isn't that a coincidence?"

"Then it's even more perfect, isn't it?"

I congratulated Robert. He was a young man who was really going places in the world. I couldn't have been happier for them both. Poor Florence hardly saw her baby for about twenty minutes, we seemed to have embarked upon a game of pass the parcel. Dotty surprised me; she never seemed to be the mumsy type, but she was besotted with little George. When he was finally handed back to his mother, we all drank a toast to young George. It was a toast with cups of tea, but that didn't detract from our heartfelt good wishes.

Things were never to be the same again. When a house has a baby in it, everyone looks towards the future. When we returned to the Manor, the staff were desperate to hear the news. There were so many people who cared about Florence. Some six or seven months earlier, there had been a moment when she could have ended up destitute, a single mother, one of society's cast-offs. It was Greg who said you can't go through life without disturbing the grass, and when we look back, we can all see where we've been. When I look back, I see moments of great joy, as well as great sorrow. There are things best left behind, and things that fill me with pride. The greatest of those joys are the ones which travel through the decades with you, a single moment in time which continues to bring you happiness. Helping Florence in her hour of need was one of those moments.

Chapter Forty-Three
Battle Of The Bulge

D ecember 1944 proved to be a pivotal turning point in the war in Europe. The Allied advance towards Germany had not exactly stalled, but as winter set in, it lost momentum. We knew at some point the retreating German army would regroup. Our most likely scenario was that they would throw everything they had into a last-ditch attempt to reverse the entire course of the war. Come the beginning of December, the expected German counteroffensive had not taken place. For us at Station M, and probably in the Cabinet War Rooms, it felt as if a very slow fuse had been lit.

Johnny's flights over France and Germany were primarily to identify V1 and V2 launch sites. It was not within our remit to reconnoitre German troop movements, but Johnny did it anyway. The weather was quite extreme, with snow and fog, the worst possible conditions for reconnaissance. Johnny was only able to get photographs on the occasional day, and then he was flying dangerously low at treetop height. Ultra intercepts, combined with what aerial reconnaissance we could get, all showed a considerable build-up of German forces in the Ardennes region.

We passed our intelligence on to the Joint Chiefs of Staff, as a matter of urgency. The question remains why our intelligence, as well as many other reports, was largely ignored. One reason for the failure of intelligence was that the Allies had become ever more dependent upon Ultra intercepts from Bletchley Park. For whatever reason, the German forces in the Ardennes used their telephone network in preference, and so they denied us some vital communications.

The German army was still a mighty force to be reckoned with, but the Allies had nearly complete dominance of the skies. Aware of that disadvantage, the Germans timed their counteroffensive to coincide with a period of severe weather, when Allied air power was unable to take to the sky. Temperatures were below freezing and the heavy snowfall and fog that had prevented Johnny from getting better photographs, were providing the German advance with ideal cover. Add to that, the cover provided by the Ardennes Forest, and the Germans used the element of surprise to great advantage.

The German Generals wanted to break through the Allied front in a decisive counterattack which would reverse the course of the war. In preparation, they dropped German paratroopers behind the Allied lines. They spoke English and were dressed in American uniforms. Their aim was to disrupt and cause confusion. They changed road signs and spread misinformation. It almost sounded like an extract from the SOE manual. We largely rounded them up, but not until they had succeeded in some of their objectives.

The long-awaited German counteroffensive began on the 16th of December in the Ardennes Forest. Thirty German divisions, containing 200,000 men and 1000 tanks, launched a ferocious attack. They achieved almost complete surprise. The consequence was that the Germans took the American Forces totally by surprise, immediately pushing them back. American losses were huge. The area of land conceded to the German advance formed a defensive line on the map that resembled a gigantic bulge. This became known as the Battle of the Bulge.

At that point, the situation looked grave. Whatever the

outcome, it would prove to be a critical turning point in the war. Neither side could afford to lose. The battle was to last for six more brutal weeks, and it proved to be the second costliest battle ever fought by the U.S. Army. The battle raging in the Ardennes Forest was of such critically strategic importance, it dominated the thoughts of everyone involved. It was our constant reminder that the fortunes of war can go in either direction. The scale of the German counteroffensive left us all in a state of shock. The consequences of such a reversal were too dreadful to contemplate. The fact that Christmas was nearly upon us had escaped everyone's attention. Edward mentioned it one evening before dinner.

"Do you realise how close Christmas is now?"

"I dared not mention it," said Caroline.

"I felt the same," said Elizabeth. "With all that is going on in France, it almost seems wrong to contemplate it. I can see how worried you and Lily are."

"It is a troublesome time," Edward replied, "but when I actually think about it, are we not admitting defeat by *not* talking about it?"

"You're right, Edward," I said, "but to talk of celebrating Christmas seems disrespectful to those soldiers who are fighting and dying for our freedom."

"Yes, I feel that too," he said, "but you might also argue that if we abandoned Christmas altogether, then we also abandon the very freedom for which we are fighting."

"Yes, I can see that as well, Edward," said Elizabeth. "When you told me how Londoners were determined never to surrender during the Blitz, you clung to your freedom, didn't you, Lily?"

"Yes, we did. Even in 1940, it wasn't a normal Christmas, but we did what we could, out of sheer defiance."

"Perhaps that sums up this Christmas," Caroline said. "Perhaps defiance can also be a mark of respect?"

"You're absolutely right, Mother," replied Edward, "we *should* go ahead."

"I don't know what I'll do," I said. "My grandmother can't cope with a full house now."

"You must bring her here."

"That's a lovely offer, Edward, but she's never had a Christmas without her family."

"Then bring them all here."

"Really, Edward, that is so kind, but I think my family would feel out of place here."

"I have spoken with your grandmother more than once," Caroline said. "Margaret is a fine lady. I shall never forget the famous concert the choral society performed in the Tunbridge Town Hall. There were some thirty or so people in the choir and four soloists, but only one voice that the audience heard. Margaret was simply sublime, I have never heard a voice like it, we clapped until our hands were sore."

"I didn't know you had heard her sing."

"I'm afraid I didn't realise until recently that the wonderful voice and your grandmother were the same person."

"It's wonderful to know you have that connection with my family!"

"All the more reason for her to join us here for Christmas," said Edward.

"It's all of my immediate family, I'm afraid, and recently it has included Fiona and Dotty as well. It's not going to work, Edward."

"Will you try, Lily? I mean it, they are very welcome."

"I'll ask them, but you would all have to make allowances for them."

The subject wasn't mentioned again that evening, but I knew Edward's offer was very genuine. I decided to ask them and discussed it with Fiona the following morning. She felt a little awkward because Johnny wanted them to go to his parents. Dotty hadn't thought about it, she just assumed she and Rob would be at Gran's. Jim was happy with the idea, but Mavis thought it was preposterous.

"The likes of us don't go swanning about with the Lord of the Manor," she exclaimed.

Mildred took the same view. If anything, she was even more vehement than Mavis. Gran was the one who really surprised me.

"I know how important this is for you, Lily, so of course I'll go, and so will Mavis and Mildred, you leave them to me."

"Lady Caroline is a big fan of yours, Gran, she attended that concert you did at the Town Hall in Tunbridge."

"All the more reason I should see her again, then. I must say, she was very nice the last time I spoke to her."

My parents, of course, met Edward at George's funeral, as well as Fiona's wedding. They didn't feel comfortable about it, but they agreed. It seemed like an enormous step to me, realising that Edward was reaching out to me through my family. It was a magnanimous gesture on his part, I had to accept. My fear, if I'm honest, was that they would embarrass me. They would use the wrong knife or fork, or they would do or say the wrong thing.

The first thing I worried about was what to wear. The three sisters wouldn't have fabulous evening dresses. When I shared my worry with Elizabeth, she immediately agreed we should break with convention and wear cocktail dresses. I was sure Caroline would dress as she always did. The usual strict dress code at Middlebourne was abandoned almost as soon as we created Station M, but despite her own preference, Caroline had never objected to Elizabeth nor me breaking with convention.

I thought the men should get themselves attired with black tie and dinner jacket; they would look hopelessly out of place otherwise. They could be hired, if necessary. I worried about everything. I was especially concerned about my parents, but we were unable to discuss it properly because when Mum telephoned me, she ran out of coins. I effectively informed them via letters. I had one eye on my family, another on our constant effort against the V rockets, and overshadowing everything was the raging battle in the Ardennes.

With only days to go before Christmas, Edward informed me that Lord and Lady Stratton would also spend Christmas with us. It was a long-standing tradition that the two families spent Christmas together. Long-standing in aristocratic language means extending back more than one generation. The other complication was that their daughter Lady Beatrice would be there. My heart sank into uncharted depths. Edward meant well by inviting my family, but the prospect of the Strattons meeting them filled me with dread. As for Beatrice, she was still convinced that she was the only marriage contender. I was still not sure if Edward would eventually agree to what they expected of him. With just a few days to go, my head was spinning, I felt sick with worry and spoke to Jennings.

"Can I have a private word with you, Mr Jennings?"

"Of course you can, how can I help you, Mrs Heywood?"

"His Lordship has invited my family to come here for Christmas."

"What a wonderful gesture, you must be delighted."

"I am, but I'm also worried, my family will be out of their depth."

"Yes, I see what you mean. How can I help?"

"I don't know, I just thought I should warn you."

"Leave it to me, I'll watch over them."

"Thank you, Charles. I'm very stressed at the moment and this is becoming a genuine worry for me. I don't want my family to make fools of themselves."

"I will instruct the footmen accordingly. I can assure you, regardless of how your family enters this building, they will leave as royalty."

I breathed a tremendous sigh of relief. Jennings always had such a calming influence on me. He was the central pillar of the Middlebourne establishment. I had never seen him in a flap, nor at a loss at what to do. I drew strength from him like drawing water from a well, and now I needed every drop!

Chapter Forty-Four
Christmas Day 1944

The weather in the Ardennes was awful. It remained freezing, with snow and fog continuing to ground the Allied airpower. We knew so much depended upon the weather, but the forecasters were predicting clear skies on Christmas Day, of all days. This would mean we could finally bring our superior Allied air power to bear. Christmas Day was likely to be an important turning point in the battle.

This was the backdrop to Christmas morning as I led my family into the Manor. I had difficulty concentrating on anything. William was in attendance and took the guests' hats and coats. The new girls, Nancy and Sandra scurried about placing them in the cloakroom, then Mr Jennings appeared in all his splendour walking towards us. Mavis asked if this was His Lordship, and this was even before they put away the coats!

"This is Mr Jennings, our butler; if anybody needs anything, you ask him. If you need to know anything at all, and I'm not there, ask Mr Jennings."

Mildred thought she should shake hands with him, and Gran asked again what his name was. Jennings smiled at me, allowing me once again to draw much needed water from the well. We began our procession towards the Drawing Room. As we entered the Great Hall, the magnificence of Middlebourne

Manor imposed itself upon us. It certainly imposed itself upon the three sisters. Gran was hanging on for dear life to Jim's arm, as Jennings stepped forward.

"If I may, Madam, and with your permission, sir, would you allow me the honour of escorting you to the Drawing Room?"

"That would be very kind of you," Gran said. "What did you say your name was?"

"Jennings, Madam. May I say what a privilege it is to have you grace this occasion. I was but a slip of a young man when I first heard you sing with the choral society. I have never forgotten the sound of your voice. It is a real honour for me to escort you this morning."

Gran appeared to walk six inches taller as she put her arm in his. I wasn't sure if he remembered hearing her sing or perhaps he had done some research but either way, Gran thought Jennings was wonderful.

"As we enter the Drawing Room, the footman will ask who you are," I said. "Then he will announce you, but don't say 'Mildred', just your surname."

"What do you mean, Lily, announce us?" asked Mildred.

"He will say your name so that the family knows who you are."

"But I can say my own name, I'm not that forgetful."

"It's just what they do, Aunty Mildred, tell the man your surname."

Jennings led the way, and we followed. I couldn't help but think we looked like a defeated army leaving the battlefield, not arriving. The three sisters were overwhelmed, and as much as I loved them all, to me they looked as if they were searching for a field dressing station. The exceptions were Jim and my Dad. They looked wonderful in their black bow ties. I placed myself in a prominent position so that I was able to tell them who they were being introduced to. The moment we entered the Drawing Room, Edward sprang to his feet. He could not have made us more welcome and Caroline was especially patient with the sisters.

Dotty and Rob arrived next, Dotty looking fabulous in a red dress. It was rare that she made the effort, which made her impact upon the room all the more eye-catching. The combination of her short almost black hair, red lipstick, and red dress, made quite an impression. Add to that her big alluring eyes, and I just couldn't combine that image with Dotty, the trained assassin. Rob was a little ill at ease at first, but Dotty was just Dotty. She and Edward had become quite pals of late. I suppose that, as with everyone, she didn't give him an option. She just called him Edward and put her arms around him. Everything was going reasonably well until the Strattons arrived.

Once again, I made sure the sisters heard who it was they were being introduced to. There was a bit of, "What did you say, dear," and, "I'm sorry, luv, can you speak up a bit." The real problem for me was Beatrice. I remembered only too well her attitude towards me the first time we met, and it had gradually hardened with each subsequent meeting. Now she found not only a usurper, but her entire family as well. Lord and Lady Stratton were lifelong friends of the family, and if you ignored their terribly superior attitude, they were gracious people. The only contact they had with working-class people would have been tradespeople or servants. Lord Stratton even asked my Dad where he hunted. They simply had no idea!

Elizabeth and Beatrice had been friends from childhood and were very close. I completely understood how it came to be that Edward would almost automatically marry Beatrice. It was bringing together two aristocratic families which they simply took for granted. As much as I wanted to believe that Edward might marry me, I couldn't deny the enormous personal and social pressure he faced. Beatrice had it all, she was a titled lady from a wealthy and powerful family. Not only that, but she was also incredibly beautiful, younger than me, and a really charming woman. I always felt inferior around her, and not without good reason. She didn't like me, but she was far too polite to make it obvious.

Jennings kept watch on us from a discrete distance. Once or twice, he came to the rescue when one of the sisters was causing havoc. They served champagne before lunch and I confess I needed it, and a second. The conversation between the men concerned the first war. Both Lord Stratton and my Dad served in that war. They had much in common, at least as far as a General and a Sergeant could have in common! We quickly found ourselves embroiled in the most unsuitable Christmas Day conversation.

The Great War, Dad said, was supposed to be the war to end all wars, and so why had we failed to learn that lesson? Stratton was of the view that casualties were a necessary and unavoidable part of war. The final straw was when Dotty pointed out that modern warfare had become industrialised, that the word 'casualty' had become the currency of that industry. She had the temerity to suggest that if the Generals had to deal with the enemy face-to-face, a war wouldn't last very long. Stratton was appalled at such a comment, especially coming from a woman like Dotty, wearing a slinky red dress.

"I think you had best leave such discussion to those of us who have the experience, my dear," he said sanctimoniously.

Unusually for Dotty, she thought better about arguing, and I just sat quietly grinding my teeth. Caroline said what should have been said ten minutes earlier.

"This is a most unsuitable conversation for Christmas Day," she said. "It's bad enough those rocket things flying above us, without bringing it here."

"Quite right, Caroline," Stratton said. "When pretty girls see fit to voice opinions on subjects about which they know nothing, then it's time to change the subject."

I looked around the Drawing Room, hoping no-one would say anything. To my profound surprise, it was Edward who broke the silence.

"Actually, Douglas, I feel duty bound to correct you on this issue. Miss Archer has served this country with such distinction that I have put her name forward for the George Cross. Mr Bartlett served alongside Miss Archer; they are both nominated."

"Oh my goodness, I've put my foot in it, please accept my abject apology, Miss Archer. Appearances can be deceptive, and I have allowed myself to be deceived. The George Cross! There is no higher civilian honour. That tells me a lot, Miss Archer. I understand now what your role has been. Ignore my ill-considered comments, Miss Archer, Mr Bartlett; it is an honour to meet you both."

"May I say, Lord Stratton, I've seldom seen a tactical retreat carried out with such dignity and aplomb," I said. "I congratulate you."

"Thank you, Mrs Heywood, regrettably the ignominy of defeat can only be erased by retaking the high ground. In this case, I am outgunned by the highest honour this country can award. I have no option but to regroup!"

Everyone smiled, Dotty included. I have to confess, until that moment, I thought he was a sanctimonious old fool. His wonderful use of language and genuine contrition changed my mind and I warmed to him. However, the contrast between our respective families quickly became apparent when Mavis spoke up.

"What did Dotty say, Lily, that upset that gentleman?"

"She said the wrong thing, Mavis, that's all."

"Must have been serious if he was going to join another group."

"No, he said he would have to regroup."

"Isn't that the same thing? What did Dotty say that has caused all this trouble?"

Beatrice smiled, I couldn't be sure if she was laughing at me or being sympathetic. Suddenly it all became even worse.

"I'm pleased to hear they've awarded Dotty something," Mildred said.

"I didn't realise Dotty had won a prize," said Gran. "Was it in the tombola?"

"I used to play the tombola every week in the village hall," Mavis said. "I didn't win once."

I closed my eyes in despair. It was Caroline who came to the rescue. She started talking to Gran about her singing career, and Lady Stratton overheard. The situation suddenly reversed, and Gran became the centre of attention.

"You must forgive me. I couldn't help overhearing. From what you describe, you must be the wonderful singer we used to call the voice of Middlebourne."

"I don't know who started that silly title," Gran said.

"What a pleasure it is to meet you in person. Lady Caroline invited me to a choral concert here in Middlebourne, in the village hall. It was a part of the centenary celebrations. I shall make a confession now. I was not enthusiastic. I visualised a group of provincial singers screaming like scalded cats. Do you remember, Caroline, I thought they were actually quite good, but then you began to sing, Mrs Taylor. Well, I had heard nothing like it, I was speechless. It was so unexpected, Mrs Taylor, you were simply wonderful."

Gran tried to play down her compliment, and immediately I saw where Mum got it from when we complimented her cooking. Gran dismissed it all, but her beaming face told a very different story.

"It was all a long time ago, but I enjoyed it," she said. "I sing through Lily now, and she's much better than I ever was."

"Do you sing as well, Mrs Heywood?" Lady Stratton asked.

"I used to sing a lot, but the time came when I had to decide between singing as a career or working in my uncle's business."

"It's the only time I have ever disagreed with my granddaughter," Gran said sternly.

"I know, I'm sorry, Gran. It haunts me to this day that I let you down."

"Oh dear," said Lady Stratton. "I didn't mean to say the wrong thing."

"I didn't realise you were a real singer, Lily," said Elizabeth. "When you said you sang the occasional song in the pub, I assumed you meant exactly that."

"It was a decision I took, and I can't go back and undo it. I'll still sing some songs in the pub now and again, but I had to put a stop to any pretensions of being a professional soprano. I would rather do that than go on living a dream."

"That's very sad, Lily. I didn't have the courage to go to that next level, and now you've done the same," said Gran.

"Forgive me, Lily," Edward said, addressing everyone. "When I was in St Hugh's Hospital, Lily sang every day in the wards for the patients. Everyone was so impressed, they asked her to perform for the entire hospital on our last evening there. There was a very good quartet and a pianist. It may have been held in the main hall of a hospital, but it might just as easily have been Covent Garden. Lily, you stole everyone's heart that evening, hardened soldiers had tears in their eyes. I have never heard a voice that could do that before."

"You're very kind, Edward, but I don't think this is the time or place."

"I didn't intend for this to be the time, but you must hear me out now. When you came off the stage at St Hugh's, you told me you would never sing an aria again. You said you had reached as far as your dream could go, that you could never sing better than you did that night."

"That's right, Edward, I needed to let the dream go."

"I'm sorry, Lily, I realise this is not the time nor the place, but I think you made the wrong decision for the wrong reason. Dreams are those aspirations we cling to. We don't abandon them. They have to fade away in their own time. I think you blame yourself for what you perceive as your failure. I think you let your dream go because it is your constant reminder of what might have been. You told me a large part of the reason that you didn't become a professional singer was your own lack of expectation and that you allowed yourself to be influenced by those who said your ambition to become a soprano was not credible.

The only people who would agree with you, Lily, are those with narrow minds, people who are unable to dream the impossible dream. Do you remember, Mother, when you and Father took Elizabeth and me to Covent Garden? It would have been about 1930. I can't remember which opera it was, but I remember hearing Rosa Ponselle singing for the first time."

"I remember, Edward," replied Caroline, "it was an extraordinary experience."

"It was, indeed, Mother, I have never forgotten it. The point I want to make, Lily, is that Rosa Ponselle is considered to be one of the greatest voices of all time. And where do you suppose she started her singing career? She was singing in cafes and motion picture halls and ended up singing with her sister in Vaudeville. Does it sound remotely credible that this woman who had not had any operatic training, could suddenly become a great soprano? Enrico Caruso heard her singing and immediately she was engaged by the Metropolitan Opera in New York. That very same year, 1918, she made her operatic debut singing opposite the great Caruso. Perhaps it is too late for you to become an opera singer, perhaps your performance at St Hugh's was indeed the finest you will ever achieve but please, Lily, do not deny *us* the joy of hearing you sing."

Edward had become quite animated. It would have been even more embarrassing had his comments not been so heartfelt. He was correct in everything he said. When I think back to when Gerry and I would sit in the pub with his docker mates, the prospect of me being an opera singer stretched credibility way beyond its limits. They openly made fun of my ridiculous pretensions, telling me to remember my place. No wonder my expectations were low; I allowed them to determine my path in life rather than thinking for myself.

For everything I achieved in life, I had to work twice as hard, and always because people said my ambitions were not credible. I had to fight that demon every day, I had spent my life fighting against other people's expectations. I could have become an opera singer, I might have become an acclaimed soprano, but what I couldn't do was admit that to myself. I had listened to Rosa Ponselle on gramophone records, she was the singer I once aspired to be. Had I known then that she came from a humble beginning and was literally propelled into stardom, I might not have listened to those naysayers. It was Lady Stratton who broke the embarrassing silence.

"You must forgive me, Mrs Heywood, I seem to have unwittingly raised an inappropriate subject."

"Not at all, Lady Stratton, Edward is correct in everything he says. I have learned, perhaps later than most, that we all have our demons. Why I didn't pursue a singing career is, I'm afraid, something which has always tormented me. The problem is that my decision was made for the wrong reason. I let you down, Gran, and I let myself down, and all because of allowing the naysayers to influence me. There you are, Edward, I've admitted it!"

"Actually, I think Edward has been very clever," smiled Elizabeth. "We all want to listen to you sing now, and it's going to be difficult for you to say no!"

Edward had been clever. He knew full well that they would put me under pressure to sing some arias. I felt a sense of inevitability. Thankfully, I was able to step out of the limelight when Mr Jennings called us to go through to the Dining Room. The change of scenery was very welcome. They placed me between Edward and Elizabeth. They placed Beatrice on the other side of the table, which she was not best pleased about.

Except for the Great Hall, the Dining Room is the most impressive room in Middlebourne Manor. We didn't occupy the entire table, we sat on either side, in the middle. Silver candelabra adorned the table, along with Christmas decorations of holly and pine cones. The silver service caught the light of the flickering candles. Three immense chandeliers hung suspended from the decorative ceiling far above our heads. All around us, a richness of ornate plasterwork flowed from the walls up into the ceiling, and the vast collection of paintings looked down upon us. Every painting reminded us that, whoever you were, you were only ever custodians of that magnificent edifice.

Christmas lunch began with a soup course, accompanied by a white burgundy. It was the most delicious fish soup I had ever tasted. Jennings was on tenterhooks while it was being served. If a disaster ever happens in the Dining Room, it invariably involves soup. It was rich and creamy with the distinct flavour of smoked haddock. No-one else asked what it was, but I'm afraid I didn't know.

"Mr Jennings, what is this delicious soup called?"

"Cullen skink, Mrs Heywood. Traditional Scottish recipe."

"Please pass on my compliments to Cook, will you?"

The following course was smoked salmon terrine. Cook layered the salmon between soft herb cheese before it was pressed and set. They served this with a 1928 Corton Charlemagne, it was another triumph. So far so good, no disasters, and the food was wonderful. The main course was the traditional roast turkey, but with the addition of some pheasants. Jennings and Albert presented it before carving. The red wine was another 1928 vintage, Château La Mission Haut-Brion.

Edward spared nothing for my family. I didn't doubt that it was all a little overwhelming for them, but they must have felt honoured that so much was being lavished upon them. It was all going really well until Jennings came round with the potatoes.

"Would you care for dauphinoise potatoes, madam?"

"That's not a variety I've heard of," replied Mildred. "Have you heard of those, Margaret?"

"No, I only grew King Edwards."

Jennings did his best to explain, but my worst nightmare was coming true. Jim intervened by distracting Mildred, and Caroline, seeing my discomfort, quickly engaged Gran in conversation. For the time being, equilibrium was restored. Elizabeth was very chatty with me, while Beatrice was very quiet. I sensed she had something to say. Dotty was also rather quiet by her standards. Perhaps I was witnessing Dotty on best behaviour.

For all that the three sisters embarrassed me with their deaf ears and malapropisms, I think everyone else overlooked it, mindful of the 266 years that they shared between them. Mum was a little ill at ease, but I noticed Dad giving the impression of getting on well with Lord Stratton. Jim was always relaxed wherever he was and I found him engaged in a lengthy discussion with Edward about the engine design of the V2 rocket! I doubt Edward mentioned our detailed understanding of the V2, but Jim the engineer was asking some probing questions.

"I suppose you're a part of what goes on here at Middlebourne now?" said Beatrice, addressing Elizabeth.

"Yes, I'm sort of a very tiny part of it now," she replied.

"And your friend Dotty over there, I'm thinking she is a part of this as well?"

"She is," replied Elizabeth. "I know it's annoying, Bea, but we don't talk about it."

"It is annoying, it's like your own private club and I can't join."

I don't think Beatrice spoke to me once during the meal, obviously avoiding me. What did surprise me was how well I was getting on with Lady Stratton or, as she insisted, Cynthia. She had volunteered to be a nurse during the last war, serving in France with Queen Alexandra's Imperial Military Nursing service. She must have noticed my surprise when she told me.

"You seem surprised, Lily," she said.

"I confess I am. It sounds as if you were right in the thick of it."

"I was, sometimes it was all we could do to step over the dead bodies trying to tend the wounded. It was truly awful."

"My father served in the last war; he was wounded at Passchendaele. His commanding officer, Major George Miller, was very seriously wounded, and Dad carried him back across no-man's-land."

"Passchendaele was terrible, I was there. I might even have tended to your father."

"George and my Dad both came back from that war convinced it must never happen again, did you feel the same?"

"We all did. Thousands of men dying for the sake of a strip of land which would be recaptured by the enemy the next week. It was collective madness, the mechanised slaughter of the innocent."

Dad was every inch a soldier, I would describe him as being as tough as nails, a man of deeds rather than words. When he tapped on his wineglass and stood up, nobody was more surprised than me.

"With your permission, My Lord, I would like to propose a toast. Forgive me, Lady Stratton, I overheard your conversation with Lily. The 31st of July 1917 saw the first day of the Battle of Passchendaele. The day after, I was lying on a bed inside a field tent. The first thing I saw when I opened my eyes was an angel. That angel was a nurse of Queen Alexandra's Imperial Military Nursing Service. Those nurses saved my life and that of my commanding officer. What greater debt can a man owe but to those who gave him back his life. You were there, Lady Stratton; as you say, you might even have tended me. May I propose a toast to all those brave nurses who worked tirelessly in those appalling conditions, saving the lives of people like me. To you, Lady Stratton."

Cynthia was really taken aback, it deeply moved her, and I was so proud of my Dad. Whatever social divide there might have been around that table, it crumbled in that precise moment. Cynthia was of the same generation and every bit as regal as Caroline. She wore a fabulous evening gown, and she shared with Caroline that wonderful ability to seemingly float in and out of a room. Whatever the situation or conversation, she was above the fray, and yet for all her aristocratic poise, my Dad had just pulled the rug from beneath her feet.

Our last course was traditional Christmas pudding and custard. We were replete. It had been a magnificent Christmas banquet, and all presented in perfect style by Jennings and Albert the young footman. Edward broke with tradition and we all decanted into the Drawing Room together, rather than the women leaving the men to their cigars and port. As we left the Dining Room, Cynthia walked with my Dad, deep in conversation. The sisters wanted to ask Caroline about the rationing because they didn't understand how the house managed to obtain so much food. Dotty and Rob chatted with Lord Stratton who was taking a great interest in them.

Jim was talking to Edward about the progress of the war, and soon that conversation enveloped Dotty, Rob, and Lord Stratton. The Strattons, like everyone else, were unaware what went on at Middlebourne but like everyone else, they assumed the military guard meant we were involved with the war effort. With his General's hat on, Stratton asked Edward to confide in him, being very aware of the German counteroffensive and eager for news. He wasn't the only one because, despite our perfect day, events in France were never far from my mind.

We knew the boys in Hut 3 were working over Christmas and would be following events in France minute by minute. Edward was as desperate for news as I was, and to my surprise he said he would make a phone call. He left the Drawing Room, and I knew he was going to speak to the boys on the internal phone. I felt obliged to join Elizabeth and Beatrice. I had made the rather obvious assumption that Elizabeth would always side with her lifelong friend, rather than with me, so I joined their conversation cautiously.

"Bea is concerned, Lily, that you are taking over the household and turning Edward away from her."

"I didn't say it like that, Elizabeth," Beatrice said, looking embarrassed.

"Maybe not, but that's what you mean, isn't it?" Elizabeth replied.

This was a conversation I definitely didn't want to take part in. I just turned it back towards Elizabeth.

"So what did you say, Elizabeth?"

"I said you're both my best friends and I don't want to fall out with either of you."

"That's very diplomatic of you, Elizabeth," I said, "and I would rather we didn't fall out over this, Beatrice."

"I'm doing my best, Lily, but this is an intolerable situation."

"You're right, it is," said Elizabeth, "but I don't see malice in either of you. Edward is going to choose one of you, and that is not an enviable position for him either."

That conversation had much further to run, and try as we might, I could only see us falling out over it. When Edward came back at the most opportune moment, I seized that opportunity with both hands. The news he returned with was the first piece of welcome news we had received since the whole counteroffensive began. A high-pressure weather pattern had set in over France. The ground was frozen hard, tank tracks could now bite into it and make progress. Best of all, the high atmospheric pressure meant clear skies for the first time during the conflict; the Allied aeroplanes were able to take to the sky. Even for those among us that day who didn't fully understand the situation in the Ardennes, the news that the progress of the war had turned back into our favour was an enormous relief.

The news changed the atmosphere of the day completely. I hadn't realised how much the German counteroffensive had played on everyone's mind. A party spirit filled what was left of Christmas Day. When we came to exchange presents, it really touched me that Edward had organised a small present for each member of my family. I bought Edward another rare first edition because he was so delighted with the one I gave him the previous Christmas. This one was A A Milne, Winnie the Pooh, first British edition, 1926. He gave me a simple but lovely gold bracelet. After the debacle the previous year, he gave Beatrice a very similar bracelet.

The simple act of giving a gift to us both once again highlighted the unseemly position that Beatrice and I found ourselves in. Neither of us set out to be in that position - two women squabbling over a man was not becoming for either of us. If anyone was to blame, it was Edward! If either of us had the courage of our conviction, we would have told him to get on and make up his mind. I knew which way Edward's heart wanted to go and I suspect so did Beatrice. The fact remained that for him, family obligation was sacrosanct. I learned early on that Middlebourne Manor, and the title that goes with it, is held up by various institutional pillars. Each pillar is inviolable in its own right and has stood for centuries. For Edward, knocking down one of those pillars could shake the very foundation of everything that he stood for, but it was a decision only he could make.

The truth of what Elizabeth had said earlier was self-evident, but it was a truth I had assiduously avoided. The realisation suddenly hit me. I was desperate that my future would be as Edward assured me it was, at Middlebourne. The reality was that if Edward decided *not* to knock down one of those pillars, and married Beatrice, I couldn't possibly stay at Middlebourne! If I allowed myself to dwell on that thought, I didn't know where it might end. For the duration of Christmas at least, I would have to put such thoughts to the back of my mind.

Our Christmas Day continued into the evening. In all other respects it was a truly happy day. The three sisters continued with their malapropisms, and their poor hearing led to many more misunderstandings. None of it embarrassed me because they were my family, and that was what they did. Mum was happy, she got on well with Caroline. Dad and Cynthia formed an unlikely alliance, they hardly stopped talking all afternoon. If that was unlikely, Dotty and the General seemed an even more unlikely alliance. He was fascinated by her activities in France and she was fascinated by the workings of the decision-takers in the war. Between them, I suspect they both revealed things they were not supposed to.

Edward got on well with Rob and Jim, talking about all manner of things. That just left us three women, two at loggerheads, and one standing between us. Somehow we remained perfectly civil, we even laughed together. Beatrice was quite something, I had enormous respect for her. Our evening became one of entertainment. Cynthia turned out to be quite an accomplished pianist and accompanied Elizabeth performing some of her cabaret routines for the first time in front of her family. As I knew from that time she sang in the pub, she didn't have the finest voice, but none of that mattered since she overflowed with confidence and personality.

Even with just a pianist, Elizabeth was absolutely fabulous. It must have been an enormous awakening for Edward and Caroline, never having seen her perform. For Edward especially, it was a revelation and he embraced his new experience whole-heartedly. We all clapped and cheered and none more so than him. He was getting to know his sister anew, and he relished every moment. I too have subsequently learnt a great deal from Elizabeth about the art of showmanship, of razzmatazz.

After what had happened that day, and the way that Edward had placed me on a pedestal, I knew they would insist I sing for them. I looked at Edward, as if to say, you have your wish. I tried to explain that singing great arias required so much preparation. I explained that a real soprano would prepare by eating well, all the right kinds of food. They would strictly avoid anything which would dehydrate the throat, such as alcohol or caffeine. And lastly, they would have a practice routine to go through beforehand. I pointed out that I had contravened each and every one of those rules, they would have to accept me as I was.

Cynthia accompanied me beautifully, I started with O Mio Babbino Caro. It was far from my best, but when I finished I could see that they had appreciated me. I built up to Ebben from La Wally, which I found quite challenging. When I came to the last note, a long silence greeted me before the applause. It was an emotional moment. Edward had been so right about me. I had let Gran and myself down, and it was all for the wrong reasons. What he made me realise was that I had to leave my mistake and the naysayers behind, I should lay that demon to rest. I saved what Gran wanted to hear until last, because I knew it would end in tears. I sang Un Bel di Vedremo, and it *did* end in tears!

Chapter Forty-Five
The Diaries

The early hours of 1st of January 1945 started with the usual toast, as we sang Old Lang Syne and drank too much, but apart from that we ushered in the new year with little fanfare. The battle raging in the Ardennes was in everyone's mind; the German counteroffensive had been a salutary lesson for anyone who thought the road to Berlin was ours for the taking. There was a hint of optimism, but it hung in the air as tenuously as the fragrance of a single rose in a summer breeze.

Although the break in the weather was very much in the Allies' favour, it remained a nervous time. The continuance of the Allied advancement depended upon the outcome of the battle, and nobody understood that better than we did. The daily ritual of the morning update in Hut 3 had rarely felt more important. Day after day, Woody gave us his latest assessment, and the days turned into weeks. The Ardennes counteroffensive was to rage on for most of January 1945.

By the end of the month, the German counteroffensive had fatally failed in its objective. The Battle of the Bulge had been a hugely significant conflict, marking the last major German counteroffensive. It was the beginning of the end for the Third Reich and remains the bloodiest battle for U.S. forces in World War Two. When Woody gave us the figures it was one of those sobering moments that was greeted with silence. The Americans suffered casualties of 75,000 which included 8,400 killed, 46,000 wounded, and 21,000 missing. German losses had been even higher. Winston Churchill spoke about the Battle of the Bulge in the House of Commons.

He said, * "*This is undoubtedly the greatest American battle of the war and will, I believe, be regarded as an ever-famous American victory.*"

The month of February 1945 offered us our first taste of genuine hope. The atmosphere in Hut 3 had changed; victory was not yet in sight, but the prospect of defeat had been vanquished. The V1's continued inflicting death and destruction, as did the V2's, but it was only a matter of time now before the Allies overran the production sites. Despite that, hundreds, perhaps thousands of people would still fall victim to those blind assassins. The absurd nature of war demanded that with an end in sight, we had to view the prospect of more casualties stoically, as the ultimate price we would have to pay.

February opened with a very significant meeting of leaders. Churchill, Roosevelt, and Stalin met together in the Crimean city of Yalta. The purpose of the meeting was essentially to carve Germany up into sections where each of the partner countries would retain influence. The agreement resulted in East and West Berlin, sowing the seeds for the 'cold war.' For us, it confirmed that the end was in sight. We continued our work, finding and predicting the V weapon launch sites, and it was never just routine, but I felt I could at last take a day off.

It had been four months since George and Marcia were killed, four months during which I didn't allow myself to grieve for them. It seems absurd in peacetime to consider grieving to be a luxury, but with so many dead and so much responsibility, it had been a luxury I couldn't afford. I'd done nothing about their house, which George had willed to me. It was a big house and no doubt worth a lot of money, but I hadn't even visited it. Dad had been there to check that everything remained secure and to make arrangements about keys. I decided the time had come for me to do something about it and mentioned it to Edward one evening in the Drawing Room.

"I've been thinking about my father today, Edward. I think it's time I went to see the house and make arrangements."

"Would you like me to come with you?"

"Would you mind, Edward? I think I'll need some moral support."

"No, of course I don't mind. I wouldn't want you to go alone."

"Do you have any plans for the house, Lily?" asked Elizabeth.

"I've not allowed myself to think about it, so no, I don't know what I will do."

"When did you have in mind going, Lily? I have nothing pressing tomorrow."

It suited Edward, so we decided to go the following morning. It didn't have to be a rush, but I thought we might as well get on with it. Our train carriage became relatively crowded, which made any private conversation awkward. I shared Edward's newspaper most of the way. I sensed a distinct change of atmosphere when we arrived in London. The collective mood had lifted, and this was despite the continued threat from V weapons. Our Cockney cab driver was typical, he could have been the people's representative.

"Where to, luv?" he asked with an irresistible smile.

I gave him the address near Croydon, which amounted to a sizeable fare so he appeared delighted. We hadn't progressed more than a mile before he started to relate a catalogue of tales, one flowing seamlessly into the next. Obviously well practised, the man was a natural storyteller. Far from being a bore, his recollections were really interesting.

"Which part of town are you from?" I asked.

"If you were a local, luv, you'd know."

"Let me guess, East End, not a stone's throw from Poplar."

"Now, how does a fine lady like you know that?"

"This fine lady comes from Stepney."

"You never do! Well, you could have fooled me."

"They bombed my house in '41, I lost everything."

"Lucky you weren't in it then."

"I was. Well, I went next door, and that was flattened as well."

"And you walked away?"

"Don't ask me how, but yes I did."

"Did you lose anyone?"

"Yes, neighbour and twin boys."

"Do you know, luv, there aren't many Londoners who sit in my cab who haven't lost someone."

"Have you lost people?" I asked.

"My old Mum and Dad bought it, and our son is still at Dunkirk, we don't even have a grave."

"He's in good company, he's with my brother. Do you know what happened to your son?"

"All we know is that two of them were trying to get a wounded soldier onto one of the little boats."

"Were they stretcher-bearers?"

"That's what we were told, yes."

"What day did you lose him?"

"The last day, the 4th of June."

"That's remarkable! Two soldiers carried my brother on a stretcher on the 4th. They were last seen on the mole."

"Good heavens, you don't suppose my boy was one of them, do you?"

"It's a hell of a coincidence, it's the right time and place. I'm going to give you my name and address. If anything else comes to light, you must write to me."

"I'll do the same, luv. Wouldn't that be amazing if they were together?"

"Whoever the two soldiers were who carried my brother, they died trying to save his life. I've always said if they had a grave, I would kiss the ground they lie in."

For the first time, the cabby became silent for a moment. "Do you know, that is a real comfort to me. Whoever my boy was trying to save, I'd like to think there's someone somewhere who honours him for his gallantry."

Of all the cabbies in London, we had chosen to ride with him! We exchanged details, and we kept in touch. I carried out more research after the war, and while we can't be sure, it is perfectly possible that the cabbie's son had been one of Ian's stretcher-bearers. On the anniversary of Dunkirk in 1950, I got in touch with Bill, the cabbie. We travelled over to Dunkirk together and dropped a wreath into the sea in the last known place where we think they had been seen. When grief is shared as an equal burden, it seems to lighten the load.

Bill delivered us safely to Croydon and when we asked what the fare was, he said it had been an honour to drive such a fine lady from Stepney, there would be no charge. I hugged him and Edward tried to insist he take at least some payment, but he remained adamant. This was how it was in the East End. They had little enough to give, but an East Ender would give you the shirt off his back. He made a huge impression on me and I became very emotional.

"What a delightful fellow," Edward said.

"Wasn't he, a real East Ender!"

We turned towards George's house, and the memories came flooding back. It was a very substantial detached house, typical of 1930s design. The moment I touched the garden gate, I re-lived the last time that I closed it behind me. We had just said our goodbyes after dissolving the business. I remembered I'd been fighting back tears as I left, making it as far as the gate before my tears got the better of me. I tried not to think about that and went straight to the hiding place where Dad had hidden the key.

Dad said he had touched nothing, that we would find the house just as George and Marcia left it on that fateful day. It felt like a terrible intrusion into their lives. Cups in the kitchen waiting to be washed, a newspaper open on the table where George had been reading it. A pile of letters covered the hall floor, obviously addressed to them. Opening the personal letters felt particularly horrible, especially the ones from distant friends who probably didn't know what had happened. I would have to write back to them all, and the usual bills would have to be paid.

George had a little boxroom upstairs that he used as an office, he called it his inner sanctum. Everything appeared orderly, George had been meticulous with his affairs. Their bank statements were all filed in date order. He still had everything to do with the business. His original will was there, together with the deeds of the house. Everything was as George liked to say, 'ship shape, and Bristol fashion.'

Edward noticed a row of notebooks in the bookcase. The sheer number of them drew his attention. He counted thirty-two of them, each with the year written on the spine of the notebook. I was busy sorting out the paperwork I needed to take with me when I noticed the look on Edward's face. He sat down with some notebooks open on the desk, whatever they contained seemed to have made quite an impression on him.

"You need to look at this, Lily."

"Why, what is it?"

"Did you know George kept a diary?"

"No, I didn't."

"Put that down and look at this."

He sounded serious, so I immediately took hold of the diary he handed me. It was dated the year I was born. The contents knocked the wind right out of my sails. I had to sit down. They were all diaries, meticulously kept diaries, one for each year. Page one had an underlined heading. *'Pam has given birth to a beautiful baby girl, my baby girl. She is to be called Lily.'* The diary then changed perspective. It continued as a conversation from George to me.

'I held you for the first time today, Lily, and in that instant I hope you know you have stolen my heart. Perhaps that is just as well, because I have no option but to disown you. There are some decisions in life which have far-reaching repercussions, and some which test your courage to the limit. My decision is all those things and much more. You will know Jack as your father, but I will always be there for you every step of the way. In the fullness of time, you will understand everything and perhaps you will be able to forgive me. We will talk every day, Lily, you will never find me wanting.'

The pages which followed detailed the life of a man who had, as he saw it, lost everything. My mum, Pam, remained the love of his life and denying me as well became the final straw that broke him completely. I hadn't realised any of this but it was quickly apparent that in the early years of my life, poor George had fallen into an abyss. His own marriage appeared to be a cry for help which was not forthcoming. He sounded almost suicidal at one point. I was the one thing he had to live for. People can die of a broken heart, and George's diaries make it clear that he nearly did.

I could do nothing else but sit reading them, each page more compelling than the last. Eventually, Edward pointed out that we also had to see the solicitor so we bundled all the papers together with the diaries and put them into bags. The diaries amounted to a heavy load. We left the house and carried them for what felt like an age, trying to find a cabbie. When we did, he proved to be another friendly face like Bill, our previous cabbie. Seeing us struggling with the bags, he asked if we were carrying the Crown Jewels. I replied that was exactly what they were.

I instructed the solicitor on the matters in hand, such as

probate. He was very understanding; he knew George and me well from when we dealt with him throughout the shipping business. It was comforting to have a friendly face dealing with things. It was the culmination of a long and harrowing day as we made our way back to the train station with our bags getting heavier all the while. In the station, enormous numbers of servicemen seemed to be coming and going. Ecstatically happy wives and lovers welcomed their men back, and broken-hearted women said goodbye. Everyone had a story to tell, the station had become a kaleidoscope of human happiness and misery. I had never been so happy to sit down in a first-class carriage.

The journey gave me more time to read the diaries, though it would take me a week or more to read them all. It amounted to thirty-two years of George's life, his hopes and aspirations, his mental turmoil, and above all his absolute devotion to me. The diaries made it clear that George didn't pull himself out of the abyss he'd fallen into until I was approaching my teen years. By then, feelings of rejection had shaped my life. I could see the strained relationship between my parents, with me in the middle, so I well remember feeling a growing dependence on 'Uncle George.' Without me realising it, George became my mentor, and I became his salvation.

During the days that followed, I found it impossible to concentrate on anything else. The diaries had clearly been written for me to read. He vowed not to come between my mum and dad, George's profound sense of obligation towards Dad was a matter of honour. He intended to fulfil that debt of honour by taking his secret to the grave. The diaries were his way of telling me in death what he couldn't say in life. The thirty-two volumes represented a commitment of huge proportions but he obviously knew their benefit to me would justify such dedication. George was right, finding the diaries remains one of the most significant events of my life. They are my most treasured possession, for me they are indeed the Crown Jewels.

Being unsure about your parentage leaves a void in your soul which becomes filled with demons. My father understood that, making it abundantly clear that seeing me struggle with the demon of rejection was as painful for him as it was for me. I so well remember the day when he told me to cast my demons aside, when he told me, 'Walk away from it, Lily, leave it behind and you will fly, you can be whatever you want to be.' He recorded that day in his diary.

'I saw it in you today, Lily, you have an inner strength beyond your years. I think you glimpsed it as well, you are going to make me so proud.'

I was twelve years old when George took me to see my first opera at Covent Garden. His diary comment is enchanting.

'You should have seen your eyes, Lily, I shall never forget your joy. If I did nothing else, I introduced you to the wonder of opera.'

I re-lived so many occasions through those diaries, seeing things from my father's perspective. All those remembered occasions instantly brought me to tears. I would dry my eyes and read on, only for the same thing to happen again moments later. George described the day we wound up the business, and we said goodbye.

'I've had you under my wing all these years, Lily. I have taught you everything I know, and the time has come for you to go out into the world and make your own way. I am fearful for myself, but I have no such fear for you. The day is fast approaching when you will leave the ghosts from the past behind. Come that day, Lily, you will hold your past in the palm of your hand. You are gifted beyond your own expectations, just open your hand, let the past go, and the future is yours.'

The diaries changed my life. George obviously intended they should fill that void in my soul, answering all my questions, and finally laying my demons to rest. They achieved everything he hoped they would, although reading them was a harrowing mix of joy and sorrow. Joy that he shared his inner thoughts with me, and sorrow that he had gone. The act of closing the last diary drew a veil over a very sad part of my life but I left those thoughts behind, along with my demons. George liberated me from my past. I had always been in his debt, now I knew that I owed him everything.

Edward came into the Drawing Room just as I closed the last page. I looked up at him with my eyes streaming. He had become used to seeing me in tears while reading the diaries, so he understood. George's words echoed in my mind, *'open your hands and let the past go.'* I cupped my hands together as if I held a captive bird. As I walked towards Edward, I opened my hands and released that bird into the air above me. He looked at me with some astonishment. I stood looking up at my past as my captive bird flew away.

"Are you all right, Lily? I hate seeing you so upset."

"For the first time in my life, Edward, I'm free. I don't expect anyone else to understand, but my father has given me his final and greatest gift, he's given me freedom from my past, and it feels wonderful."

If my past stood behind me, then my future stood in front of me. I put my arms around Edward and kissed him. As much as he might have wanted to, his aristocratic code of gentlemanly conduct did not include kissing the Chief of Staff in the Drawing Room. Caroline came into the room at that precise moment, and so that became another broken code to add to Edward's list. Initially Caroline had been taken aback to see us in each other's arms, but her reaction quickly changed to a smile.

"I was just comforting Lily, Mother, she is very upset after reading her father's diaries."

"Yes, I am sure Lily was very upset, but your comforting seems to have restored a smile to her face. Perhaps you should comfort her more often, Edward. What do you say, Lily?"

"I agree, Caroline! Edward underestimates how much comforting we women require."

My life changed forever that day, it represented a new

beginning. With my past behind me, the future became my present, and it was all around me. I had a new confidence, born of knowing myself. I had spent my life climbing the sheer face of a mountain, every foothold a vital step towards the summit, I would succeed or fall. My reality was that I could be proud of my East End background. I didn't need to prove myself just because I came from the poor part of town. I could step into the future without looking back. My fellow travellers - failure and success - would always be with me, but now I neither feared the one, nor craved the other.

Chapter Forty-Six
Hope And Despair

February had brought us both hope and despair. Hope that the war was nearing its end and despair that the cost had been so high. The city of Dresden had been known as 'the Florence of the Elba'. Its beautiful architecture and museums had been a defining feature of the city. It was a major transport hub with some industry, but it had never been considered a significant target before. The people of Dresden had lived in relative peace. On February the 13th, British Bomber Command sent 800 bombers to drop 2,700 tons of bombs, and incendiaries on the city. The next day, the US Eighth Air Force dropped another 400 tons of bombs. The following day on the 15th, another 210 US bombers dropped yet more high explosive and incendiaries on what remained of the city.

We had access to the aerial reconnaissance photographs taken shortly after the raids. Maggie handed them to us in Hut 3. We looked at them in silence; Dresden had been razed to the ground. The many timber structures added fuel to the numerous fires started by the incendiaries, the result being one gigantic fire storm. The number of people killed could only ever be an estimation, but something like 25,000 people had been killed, perhaps many more. We immediately asked questions about the necessity of the raids. Dresden's strategic importance didn't appear self-evident to us.

War, by its very nature, could be defined as a dispute resolved by killing each other. It is probably spurious to consider some acts of killing as being more honourable than others, more creditworthy. All those in combat who have 'right' on their side consider they are fighting from a position on the moral high ground. Paradoxically, each side in a conflict prays to its own God and assumes that the moral high ground is theirs. We debated the point in Hut 3. Our conclusion was that we didn't start the war, and the Nazis had shown themselves to be morally bankrupt. Of course, the moral high ground was ours.

"I want to believe that everything we've done during the war, however ghastly, has been done for a morally justifiable reason," I said. "But how can we justify killing 25,000 mostly innocent people?"

"Somebody must believe there's a greater good," said Woody.

"We're fighting an enemy, Lily, one who thinks it's morally acceptable to exterminate millions," said Rolo.

"I know," I replied, "but those Dresden people were not Nazis, that's the difference."

We had no real disagreement; our discussion had been for discussion's sake. It remains very difficult to justify Dresden. There were many subtle ways in which it influenced the outcome of the war. Our opinion was that no gain was worth such a cost, and we valued that cost both in terms of lives lost and the sanctity of the moral high ground. It was only my opinion, but I thought Dresden represented a low point for the Allies.

Throughout that period, we had field agents operating in and around the V launch sites. Our agents, combined with Johnny's reconnaissance, provided us with unprecedented intelligence. The V1 sites were less mobile, and we had considerable success destroying them, but the V2 mobile launchers presented a far more elusive target. They could be launched from well inside Germany, where it was far too dangerous for our agents to operate. On March the 7th, American troops crossed the Rhine, the last substantial physical barrier between the Allies and Berlin. It became only a matter of time before they would overrun the V weapon production sites, and we immediately decided to bring our agents home. We had saved countless lives destroying and harassing V launch sites, it was time to save our own.

The progress of the war moved at pace and the main V weapon production site at Mittelwerk soon became overrun by the Allied advance. Our part in the war was finally over. With hindsight, we might have celebrated, but we didn't mark the event in any way, it felt very anticlimactic. We couldn't officially stand down. We were a fully operational SOE station and we might have been called upon to engage in another mission. The situation became slightly surreal as we found ourselves in this strange hinterland, halfway between war and peace. It became a time of retrospection and relief that we had done our duty and had survived. It affected us all in different ways and laid bare some inner conflicts. I went into the office to find Fiona in tears.

"Oh no, what's happened, Fi, it's not Johnny, is it?"

"It is, we've stood him down."

"Yes, I know, so has anything happened?"

"No, nothing has happened, I'm just so happy, Lily. He's going to survive."

She became absolutely distraught. These weren't tears of happiness - three years of wondering every day if her loved one would come home had taken an enormous toll. The stress was insidious for people like Fiona, working every day while concealing her anguish, deflecting every wave as it crashed against her. Now the need had gone, and those waves combined into a tidal wave which she had been powerless to defend against. It would take her weeks, if not months, to fully recover. We still had Elizabeth helping in the office and so I told Fi to go home.

"Take Johnny to bed and stay there until you feel better," I said.

A measure of how stressed she felt became self-evident when she immediately agreed to go home. Such a decision would normally be viewed as deserting her post. PTSD had not been heard of then, we called it shell shock. It was a far more serious condition than any of us realised. My advice to take Johnny to bed had been well intentioned, but it didn't amount to a treatment plan for the condition which has only just been redefined as 'post-traumatic stress disorder'.

Few RAF pilots flew more hours over enemy occupied territory than Johnny Albright. He would always deliver his film to Maggie with a cheerful smile. When asked if he had encountered any problems, it was always the same, he would say it was a lovely flight, a piece of cake. The reality was that he had been shot down once and managed to parachute to safety. We know there had been at least three other occasions when he came back so badly shot up that the plane barely limped home.

On each occasion, Fiona smiled and said how lucky he'd been. Johnny was the unsung hero of Station M. He stood amongst the bravest of the brave. They awarded him the DFC shortly after the war. The citation emphasised his outstanding courage during the Battle of Britain. His reconnaissance flights for SOE were not mentioned. We were united in the belief that he should have been awarded the VC. It was a magnificent gesture of solidarity when every single member of Station M attended the award ceremony. Mr Jennings and Mrs Morgan attended, even Brenda and the canteen ladies were there. It became a cathartic moment for Fiona, and a very difficult day for her to get through. However, as difficult as it had been, that proud day marked the start of her recovery.

Soviet troops had liberated Auschwitz on the 27th of January. I thought nothing could shock us any further but

I was wrong. April the 15th 1945 became another day to shock the world. British and Canadian troops liberated the Bergen-Belsen concentration camp.10,000 bodies just lay around, unburied. The horror of Bergen-Belsen became something that every person who witnessed it will carry to the grave. The famous British journalist and broadcaster Richard Dimbleby was among the first to enter that hell on earth. Dimbleby had seen it all as a war correspondent, but his words after the event were very poignant. *"This day at Belsen was the most horrible of my life."* To this day, I cannot comprehend how the SS camp personnel could have sunk to such a depth of human depravity.

When Soviet and American troops met each other across the River Elbe on April 25th, it marked an extremely significant stage of the war. Effectively cutting Germany in two, it was only a matter of time now. We followed every twist and turn. Peace seemed to be so close, and yet tantalisingly it remained out of our reach. On the 30th of April, there was an event which, had it been widely known, would have resulted in most of the world cheering. Adolf Hitler killed himself, the Nazi monster had been vanquished.

We found out a day or two later, and our reaction was unbridled joy. The head of the serpent had been cut off, and what was left was in its death throes. Hitler by any definition had been an aberration, a madman. To us, he represented the personification of evil. His ideology of Aryan superiority, and his complete disregard for the sanctity of human life, made him uniquely dangerous. The likes of Goebbels aided and abetted him, together with the rest of his sycophantic followers, but for us Hitler alone had been the embodiment of the devil. What we must never forget is that the German people democratically elected him to power. Those of us who now enjoy peace should be careful what we wish for.

Chapter Forty-Seven
The Savoy Hotel

Throughout the later course of the war, every new month on the calendar offered at least a glimmer of hope for us to cling to. Finally, when I turned over April to reveal May 1945, here was a month offering us the promise of peace. The month of May symbolically represented a new future, simply turning over the calendar filled me with joy.

"I've got to go to London, Lily. Will you come with me?"

"What's the occasion, Edward?"

"I have to attend the House of Lords, well, it's not the House, it's the Robing Chamber for the time being."

"What do you mean, the Robing Chamber?"

"The House of Commons has been very badly damaged and so they meet in the Upper House. The Lords have been relegated to the Robing Chamber."

"I don't suppose there's a public gallery?"

"No, I'm afraid not. But what I thought we might do is stay at the Savoy in the evening."

"I've not been to the Savoy, that sounds wonderful. You're up to something, Edward, what is it?"

Edward appeared slightly evasive. "I would normally stay at my club, but I thought that would be rather stuffy."

"Stuffy! That's not a descriptive term you normally use!"

"Well, perhaps you're rubbing off on me, Lily!"

There was a period of silence and Edward looked towards Elizabeth, but she declined to smile. I was wondering what was going on. I was probably the only person in the room who didn't know what lay behind the silence. We had a lovely evening together as usual, and like everyone else we couldn't suppress the sense of anticipation which filled the air. The prospect of peace being so close was intoxicating. We all felt it, like children given a Christmas present that we were forbidden to open until midnight. People who live in peace take it entirely for granted, but for us it had become the holy grail, the most valuable human condition there is.

Our evening ended uneventfully, and I retired for the night with a sense of anticipation, which continued into the morning. As I made my way down for breakfast, the prospect of the impending peace was all-pervasive, every member of the household staff had a spring in their step. Edward gave nothing away over breakfast, and I didn't ask, but I had the strongest feeling that our trip to London had an ulterior purpose. When it was time for me to pack an overnight case, I tried to visualise a night at the Savoy. I packed a lovely cocktail dress and all of my jewellery - this was when I really missed Florence.

With my case packed, I sat on the edge of my bed wondering what the day held in store for me. In the back of my mind, the ever-present fear about my future loomed large. I had long since come to accept that however much I loved Edward it was no guarantee of a future together, despite him feeling exactly the same. I dealt with that torment by excluding it from my mind. With the end of the war in sight, I knew decisions would have to be made. Station M would be wound up and the Manor returned to its pre-war status. My position as Chief of Staff would fade into memory along with the intelligence section so whatever my future was, it lay in Edward's hands. Suddenly the cold reality of my position sent a chill down my spine, when I realised the timing of our trip to London was not a coincidence.

Albert knocked on my door offering to carry my case to the car and I wondered in what circumstances it would return. He was unable to suppress his high spirits. When I asked him what he was most looking forward to, he simply said he wanted a future which was not shaped by the war. It was a simple enough request, we all just wanted to get on with our own lives. Albert walked ahead of me as I descended the staircase and went into the Great Hall. As I waited there for Edward, both Nancy and Sandra asked me when the wonderful day would be. I could only tell them I thought it would be days rather than weeks. Edward appeared looking wonderfully smart as always, and we went straight out to the car together where William stood by the open rear door dressed in his uniform. I made myself comfortable sitting next to Edward.

"Well, this is unusual, Edward. Do you realise this is the first time since the war started that I've been to London when it wasn't in some way war-related!"

"I think that applies to me as well, I am usually going to the War Office."

William drove us sedately out of the grounds and onto the road beyond. As we left the guard behind at the barrier, I couldn't help but think I might actually miss its presence. I would certainly miss Corporal Harris and our friendly banter. Not having an ever-present concern or worry was a welcome though strange prospect. There would be no more V1's, and a V2 was not about to drop out of the sky. It wasn't until the threat had gone that we realised how much we had become conditioned to live with it, how much of our lives had been placed on hold.

Normally when the clock tower at the station appeared, I associated it with sad memories of the past. It was not so that day, I had finally controlled that demon. My fear was no longer the past, I now feared the future. The sound of the approaching train no longer filled me with dread. When the fire-breathing dragon enveloped us in its breath I ignored its invitation to be fearful. William placed our cases in the first-class carriage and wished us a pleasant journey. I thanked him and waved goodbye. These were the images that now filled me with dread; waving goodbye to William was symbolic of a much greater fear. The train had just started to pull away when a gentleman came running down the platform. Ours was the last first-class carriage, and he just made it in time as the train was beginning to move.

"That was a close shave," he said, "only just made it."

He was a bowler hatted gentleman wearing a pinstripe suit. While he looked a little out of context in Tunbridge Wells, he would become invisible in the city of London. He was the only other passenger, and although he was very personable, I almost wished he'd missed his train. We exchanged small talk for most of the journey, and while he helped the time to go by, he prevented Edward and me from talking. He rushed off at Charing Cross, saying how much he had enjoyed travelling with us. Edward looked at me and we both laughed at the same time.

I had only ever seen the Houses of Parliament from a distance. The taxi delivered us right outside the magnificent building. I knew the Palace of Westminster had been hit during the Blitz, but that didn't prepare me for seeing the heart of Government so badly damaged. Edward took me into what was the Members' Lobby. There was just enough of it left standing to give me an idea of how that magnificent place once looked.

They hit Parliament fourteen times during the Blitz, and the worst occasion was on the night of May 10th 1941, when 505 German bombers followed the Thames up from the estuary. They dropped 500 tons of bombs, and 86,000 incendiaries, hitting the Palace of Westminster at least twelve times. Incendiaries caused the most significant damage. The

Commons Chamber had been completely destroyed, and the Members' Lobby had also been badly damaged. The Lords Chamber didn't escape unscathed, and neither did the famous clock tower.

That same night on May 10th 1,364 people in London were killed, and another 1,616 were badly injured. There was just one crumb of comfort to be retrieved from that awful night. Despite the clock tower being hit and suffering external damage, the clock mechanism epitomised the spirit of the Blitz. It defied the bombs and continued working, as did the famous bell. Big Ben refused to bow to Nazi attempts to silence it. Standing like a colossus, it was a sight and sound that rallied the spirit of the nation, like Saint Paul's Cathedral, defiant to the very end.

Work was being carried out in the Members' Lobby as I stood there. The seat of power might have been damaged, but as long as the will of the British people survived, so would the Palace of Westminster. Edward seemed to be looking out for someone, appearing anxious as he kept looking at his watch. Eventually he said he would meet me back where I was standing and would try not to be too long. His attitude concerned me, clearly he was ill at ease, which added to my own anxiety.

I tried to wait patiently, watching people pass by, some of whom I recognised from photographs in the newspapers. Eventually I found somewhere to sit down, from where I could see along an adjoining hallway. As I sat down feeling more and more agitated I suddenly noticed Edward standing some distance away, having a discussion with someone. It was evident from both men's body language that they were engaged in some kind of disagreement.

It continued for some time until they eventually shook hands and the other man turned to walk away. I recognised him immediately, it was Lord Stratton! The reason for our trip to London and to the Houses of Parliament suddenly became terrifyingly clear. This had everything to do with Lady

Beatrice! I didn't want to be recognised by Lord Stratton so I immediately got up and walked away, my mind racing in all directions. My every thought returned me to my central dread that Edward had been forced to conform to what was expected of him. When Edward found me again he looked agitated, very thoughtful. He obviously thought I looked the same.

"You look distressed, Lily, is everything all right?"

"I'm sorry, I've got a lot on my mind."

"We can leave now, let's make our way to the Savoy. It's not that far, but we need a cab for the luggage."

We left rather hurriedly; I could see that whatever Edward had discussed with Stratton he wanted to get away without seeing him again. There was a cab waiting on the rank and we made our way towards it. The short drive provided the ever-present reminder that London would take time to recover from its wounds. Some buildings were simply missing, those voids in history never failed to make an impression on me. The Savoy itself was not unscathed, and the north-eastern corner suffered a direct hit, killing two people. It was very much the way in London that we just carried on regardless, and so it was at the Savoy Hotel. Regardless of air raids, curfews, and rationing, the Savoy stayed open for business throughout.

The moment the cab stopped at the hotel our cases were spirited away as if by some concealed sleight of hand. We entered through the revolving doors and stepped into another world. It was opulence personified, representing a magnificent image of wartime defiance. Here the spirit of the Blitz had been taken to its furthest extreme. It was a world away from the East End where that spirit started its journey into the nation's consciousness. The black and white tiled floor seemed to disappear away into the distance, punctuated only by its magnificent pillars, hanging chandeliers, and soft furnishings. I had become used to the magnificence of Middlebourne Manor, but the Manor looked tired compared to the Savoy.

Edward spoke with reception and almost immediately we

were escorted up to our rooms. The view across the Thames from my room was magnificent. Edward's room was immediately next door. It was much the same, with the rooms sharing an adjoining door. We had unintentionally timed our arrival to coincide with afternoon tea, and so Edward suggested we drop everything and just go down and relax. I looked at my magnificent room and again at the view, but nothing could dispel the fear which continued to haunt me. The idea of relaxing in the afternoon seemed really decadent and while I welcomed the concept, I was fearful of what might accompany it.

I sat on the bed for a moment trying to control the maelstrom of thoughts racing around in my mind. Edward obviously disagreed with Stratton over something important. It had to be about Lady Beatrice! Would Edward bring me here to be told he was to marry Beatrice? Perhaps it was none of those things. Perhaps it was just to celebrate the end of the war? These were the thoughts tormenting me. There could of course be another reason for being there that I hardly dared to imagine. I knocked on Edward's door and he offered me his hand the moment he appeared. We walked together along the sumptuously carpeted corridor.

Our situation was so far removed from the relentless stress of our hitherto normal daily life, I felt out of touch with reality, as if in a dream. Ours was a love affair with neither a start nor a finish date. We didn't deny it, but neither did we espouse it. It wasn't ours to share but neither was it unrequited. It filled my life with its presence, it was everywhere and in all things, and if ever it ceased to exist, I feared that I too would cease to exist. Edward squeezed my hand several times as we walked together, I tried to draw encouragement from that. His lovely smile was another reassurance, but I was never in doubt that he loved me.

They served afternoon tea in a wonderfully capacious room with a central atrium. We had barely set foot through the door before the maître d' immediately said, "I have a table for you, My Lord." He showed us to a lovely position where we sat down. Moments later, an array of cakes appeared on a three-tier cake stand. As well as the wonderful-looking cakes, there were sandwiches all neatly cut into squares. We both requested Darjeeling tea, which subsequently arrived complete with a silver tea service and bone china cups and saucers. He looked at me with the most disarming expression.

"What are you up to, Edward?"

"To us, and an end to the war."

I repeated his words, and we touched our cups in a toast. The prospect of peace seemed to be an almost alien concept, the war for us had been an all-consuming daily event. We were not prepared for peace, it was going to be like learning to walk again, baby steps into the unknown. The unknown for me was my place in Edward's life. I had all but assumed that our life would be together, and while I understood all the difficulties that I represented for him, I latched onto his words when he said, 'to us.' I found myself looking lovingly into his eyes. He returned that same look as we sat oblivious to the world around us.

He remained preoccupied. Knowing him so well, it was clear to me there was something he wanted to say. A large part of me wanted him to say it, while another part was fearful of what those words might be. I was trying hard to summon the courage to ask him but with every word we spoke I found another reason to delay. I only realised that time had elapsed when I noticed we were the last people sitting there. The wonderful institution of afternoon tea had passed, the people had moved on, thoughts had moved on towards the evening.

"I think we had better go, Edward, do you realise we're the last people here? Was there something you wanted to say before we leave?"

"You're right, Lily, there is something I would like to say, but this is not the occasion. I think it needs to be at the start of our evening, rather than the end of our afternoon."

He sat holding my hands across the table with his eyes telling me he loved me. I knew what I wanted him to say, I had almost convinced myself I could hear those words. It became obvious that my torment was to continue for a while longer, if only it could be anticipation and not anguish. We left arm in arm and wandered about the hotel so I could see all of its magnificent rooms.

It was a different world, as far from the East End as it was possible to get. There was no rationing here, no shortages of any kind as far as I could see. A part of me felt uncomfortable about the inequality of it all. The other part, and I would have to say the greater part, thought I might as well enjoy it. We ambled back towards our rooms with a feeling of relaxed contentment. I remember thinking this must be what peace is like. Edward suggested I should knock on his door when I was ready for the evening. He said he would see me later and kissed me.

As I entered my room, that kiss lingered on my lips. I sat in a full bath of hot water for half an hour, simply enjoying every second, it was wonderful. I wasn't listening for the sound of an approaching V1, had no people to telephone nor decisions to make. I could dream about Edward without interruption. I washed and dried my hair, finishing it just as Florence would have done, except she would have done it better. Wearing my hair up really suited my ruby and pearl choker necklace and earrings. When I finally finished my makeup, I had to admit I was feeling pretty special.

The finishing touch was a new cocktail dress the girls had recently made for me. It was a lovely shade of cream, definitely not yellow, but perhaps a hint. The girls called it 'buttermilk' and it went well with my auburn hair. It had a slightly low-cut crossover front with short sleeves and the waistband gathered the material, which was then draped diagonally from the hip, giving the impression that the crossover top was separate. The knee-length pencil skirt finished it perfectly. It was close fitting and very, very chic. There was nothing more I could do to prepare myself; it was time to knock on our connecting door. I wasn't sure if it was being there at the Savoy, or perhaps it was the prospect of the war ending. Whatever it was, I knew Edward had chosen that evening to tell me something which was going to change the rest of my life. I drew a deep breath and knocked on the door.

"Lily, you look… absolutely beautiful!"

"You're making progress with your compliments, Edward. And may I say you also look beautiful."

"Not sure you're right, Lily, I thought only women were beautiful."

"No, trust me Edward, you are."

He feigned embarrassment, but actually some good-looking men are beautiful, Edward certainly is.

"I haven't seen this dress before, have I? It really is something, isn't it?"

"I'm glad you like it, I had it made with you in mind."

"Then I am deeply honoured, shall we go down to dinner?"

I had always watched enviously as Caroline appeared to float into a room. Even in my high heels, and without a full-length gown, I was beginning to adopt the technique. As we walked arm in arm along the corridor, I became less and less aware of the floor beneath my feet. As we entered the cocktail lounge, I felt Caroline would have been proud of me. I certainly turned a few heads, or perhaps it was Edward as well, but either way it did my confidence no harm at all. He held my seat for me as I sat down. Edward and black bow tie seem to be made for each other. Even accounting for the fact that I was strongly biased, Edward always appeared to be the best dressed man, wherever he was. Sitting looking at him, I was pleased I had told him he was beautiful.

We drank champagne, toasting each other with every glass. He had spent four years trying to keep his distance from me, and suddenly that invisible barrier was gone. The

way he was looking at me told me everything I wanted to
know. My doubts were still there but they were being rapidly
replaced by the most wonderful sense of expectation. I knew
what I wanted that evening to mean to us both and I wanted
to savour every second. I didn't think I was deluding myself,
but I would have to confess to a sudden frisson of fear as the
thought entered my mind.

The maître d' escorted us to our table in the most beautiful
dining room I had ever seen. We each looked at the menu
while peeping over the top at each other. I required no further
assurance that this was to be a very special evening when he
ordered one of the most expensive wines on the list. Edward
said Chateau Latour 1920 was a magnificent vintage, a wonderful example of a wine produced after grafting the vines
onto American rootstock, following the devastating phylloxera
blight. I smiled as if I understood what he was talking about,
but in truth just the sound of his voice made me smile.

When the sommelier presented Edward with the bottle,
there was a considerable fuss made about pouring it in the
glass. Edward looked at it, wafted the aroma under his nose
before tasting it. The sommelier stood waiting in anticipation
of a favourable comment, which was rapidly forthcoming. The
satisfaction on Edward's face was a joy to see. Moments after
the sommelier had poured the wine, we touched glasses again.
Edward was about to say what he had waited so long to say,
when our attention was suddenly diverted as one of the hotel
staff hastily entered the restaurant. He spoke in a loud voice to
attract everyone's attention.

"Ladies and gentlemen! May I have your attention. There
has just been an announcement from the BBC. Tomorrow at
3 o'clock in the afternoon, the Prime Minister, Sir Winston
Churchill, will address the nation. My Lords, Ladies and
gentlemen, tomorrow will be Victory in Europe Day."

People jumped to their feet with a spontaneous cheer
which was followed by clapping and the banging of cutlery

on tables. I doubt the Savoy had ever seen an occasion like it. People rushed about shaking hands with perfect strangers. I was hugged by men in dinner jackets who I had never seen before. For several minutes, it was as un-British as it could possibly be, the most incongruous but wonderful moment. Edward and I left our seats, clapping like everyone else. We hugged and kissed each other, it was all so emotional, we could hardly speak. Being the Savoy, of course, decorum had to be rapidly reinstated, and although everyone sat back at their tables, celebrations continued for the rest of the evening.

"I really thought it would be another couple of days," said Edward. "The Nazis were stalling, trying to get as many of their people away from the Russian side as possible."

"They must have accepted the unconditional surrender terms," I replied. "So tomorrow is the day we've all been longing for, the first day of the rest of our lives."

"Well, that's changed *our* plans, Lily! We thought we would be celebrating at Middlebourne!"

"Yes, I would like to be with them all, but right now I would sooner be here with you."

"I feel the same, so let's enjoy our evening."

That monumental announcement changed the atmosphere of the evening entirely. Everyone continued talking loudly, and the room remained full of excitement and laughter. The meal, the wine, everything was simply perfect. It was an experience like no other, never to be repeated. There was not a person in the restaurant who would ever forget where they were the evening that the announcement was broadcast. Edward now spoke in warm confident tones about the future. We were so close, there were many occasions when I anticipated his every thought. This was one of those occasions.

"You're about to tell me what's on your mind, aren't you, Edward?"

"I confess, Lily, I *have* been planning this evening for some time, although I didn't anticipate that announcement. I hope you agree that I have chosen the best possible occasion to say what I have to say. I have known right from the beginning, but I've struggled to admit it to myself and to you. I love you, Lily. I fell in love with you on that second day in my office. During these past four years, we have become a part of each other, we are two halves of the same person. I love you so much, Lily I can't possibly live without you. Will you do me the greatest honour by becoming my wife?"

I felt as if I had been waiting my entire life to hear Edward say those words. We were holding hands across the table and at that moment, nothing else existed for me. Of course I knew he loved me, and I had long dreamed of hearing those words, but when my dream came true, those words hit me like a bolt of lightning. I wanted to tell him I loved him, I wanted to hold him in my arms, but I could neither think nor speak. He had filled my senses to overflowing. I was overwhelmed.

It didn't matter that we were sitting in the Savoy Hotel restaurant. I was oblivious to my surroundings, only aware of Edward sitting opposite me. I have no memory of getting up from my chair, I just know I must have walked around the table, wherein Edward stood up and we fell into each other's arms. We stood in the middle of the Savoy restaurant, gripped in a passionate embrace. It was the single happiest moment of my life. If every pair of eyes were looking at us disapprovingly, I was blissfully unaware of it. Edward was my North, South, East and West; he was my entire world.

"Does this mean that you will say yes?" he finally managed to say.

"Of course it means yes. My life didn't begin until I met you. Edward, I've *always* loved you."

We stood for a moment just looking at each other, only gradually becoming aware of our surroundings. It embarrassed neither of us in the slightest. We slowly moved back to our seats, our hands parting for a second as we sat down, but our eyes belonged to each other. I reached again across the table but he placed his hand into his pocket and produced a small jewellery box. I knew instantly what it was going to be.

"This engagement ring was my grandmother's, Lily. You would honour me, and my family, if you would wear it."

"Oh, Edward, it's beautiful. I'll wear it with immense pride," I said, wiping tears from my eyes. "I don't know what I would have done if you had told me there was no option for you but to marry Beatrice. I've tried to imagine a life without you, and it just doesn't exist."

"It doesn't exist for me either, Lily. I'm just so sorry I couldn't commit to you sooner. I've been trapped in an awful position."

We were both feeling the same elation, our love that for so long had to deny its name was now free to express itself. I'm not sure that either of us realised the weight of the burden our unspoken love had imposed upon us. I felt as if our cage door had been opened, and like two captive birds we were suddenly released into a world we hadn't experienced before. There were no boundaries to our newly liberated joy, we excitedly flew in all directions.

"Have you any idea what you have put me through, Edward?" I said jokingly.

"Sadly I do but think of what you have put *me* through!"

"What did I do?"

"You have that way of looking at me, Lily! Every time you do that, I want to say I love you."

"I've seen that same look in your eyes. Every evening when I enter the Drawing Room, you stand to greet me with that same expression. Somehow I had to pretend I didn't notice."

"There have been moments when you walk into the Drawing Room, it might have been an occasion, or perhaps you were wearing one of those new dresses of yours, I look at you, and you just take my breath away, you leave me speechless. I've wanted to hold you. I've wanted to tell you I love you. Do you realise the effect you have on me, Lily?"

"I love those moments when you're speechless, it just makes me burst with joy. Those are the moments when I have desperately wanted to tell *you* I love you."

"I know it's my fault but I have been really tormented, Lily."

"I know you have and so have I. Do you remember that day on Westminster Bridge? You said some wonderful things to me, but you didn't say what you really wanted to say, did you?"

"That has been my torment, Lily. I knew you could see right through me."

"We've tormented each other, haven't we?"

"I am to blame, but yes, we have. When I take your hand in mine, you often stroke my palm."

"Do I really, I didn't realise I did that."

"That's not all you do, Lily! There is that thing you do with your toes when you sit in the Drawing Room. I have desperately wanted to take you in my arms when you do that."

"I'll make a confession. It's very sensual stretching your toes into the carpet. When I do it, I sometimes imagine you're holding me in your arms. I suppose I've been shamelessly inviting you to think the same thing."

"I have been thinking the same thing ever since you walked into my office. Did you realise how attractive you were in your WLA uniform?"

"I felt very unattractive in that uniform. Why do you think I spent hours getting ready when you invited me back?"

"When I telephoned George your ex-employer, I found myself praying he would say something to justify me offering you the job."

"You were so rude to me that first time, and then you were such a gentleman. I wanted to be cross with you, but I couldn't. I didn't want to fall in love with you, but I just couldn't help it."

"There hasn't been a day from that first occasion to this

when I haven't longed for you. A gentleman must always behave in the correct manner, but my thoughts alone should disqualify me. Oh, Lily, I've wasted so much time. I don't know how I have managed to resist you."

"If your gentlemanly code of conduct is seeking permission to take me to bed, you don't have to ask Edward. But if you did ask, the answer would be yes, and the sooner the better."

I didn't dream I would ever say such a thing, but I did. The moment I said it the implications of those words made my heart race, every inch of my body felt alive with anticipation. It was no longer Lord Middlebourne sitting opposite me. It was a wonderfully passionate man whose need for me was no less great than my need for him. When those needs combined it was an unstoppable force. They say absence makes the heart grow fonder, well I can tell you; our hearts could not have grown any fonder than they were that night.

There was no discussion, we both stood up from the table. We left the restaurant with our arms wrapped tightly around each other, saying very little. There seemed to be no need for words at that point. The spoken word couldn't possibly describe the longing we felt for each other. We hastened our footsteps the closer we came to our rooms. There was just a moment's hesitation as we decided upon Edward's room. We left four years of wanting each other on the outside of the bedroom door. We stepped across the threshold and into each other's arms. In that glorious moment of indescribable joy, all of creation had nothing more to offer us.

Chapter Forty-Eight
VE-Day May 8th, 1945

I woke in the morning to find myself still wrapped in Edward's arms. In that special time between sleep and wakefulness, I was only aware of the feel of his body next to mine, the smell and taste of him. The second our waking eyes met, we kissed again, and our passion renewed what sleep had denied us. It was every bit as passionate as the night before, but less frenetic, more considered, even more sublime. We agreed, as lovers do, that no two people could be more in love than we were. I thought of all the lovers who have posited that claim, and I knew all the others had failed to take us into account. We spoke in whispered tones about mundane things such as breakfast, but anything which involved separating our bodies seemed impossible to consider.

"Where have you been hiding this side of yourself for all these years, Edward?"

"That person has been locked in chains, dreaming of you, my darling."

"It must have been one heck of a strong lock!"

"Trust me, it has been the struggle of a lifetime."

Eventually when we managed to tear ourselves apart, we agreed perhaps we should go down for breakfast. Glancing at my watch, I saw it was 10 o'clock. We prepared ourselves for what was going to be a tumultuous day, and still clinging to each other, we made our way towards a very late breakfast. There was an air of excitement in the hotel which matched our own. Some people seemed to be rushing about, talking loudly, while others sat in quiet contemplation, some were tearful.

After six years of longing for peace, and enduring all manner of hardship, people's emotions had become stretched to the limit. We all dealt with it in different ways, some contained it within, while some were overpowered by it. I found myself confronting emotions I had tried to contain. My mind was suddenly free to allow my lost loved ones to appear uninvited before me. Ian and Gerry looked down at me, as did Linda and the twins. Then I could see George and Marcia. I had survived the war, all of my dreams had come true, I was going to marry Edward. I had it all, and they had nothing! For many people, VE-Day was a toxic blend of ecstatic happiness, guilt, and profound sorrow.

"Are you all right, Lily? You're thinking of those you have lost?"

"You're right, I am. In amongst all this happiness there is sadness too. So many loved ones are not here to see this day."

"I know, but there will be plenty of time for reflection after today."

"Yes, you're right. I didn't tell you, Edward, I saw you with Lord Stratton when I was waiting in the Members' Lobby."

"I arranged to meet Stratton. Douglas and I had a very difficult conversation. I regret we did not find a mutual under-standing, though I desperately hope we can avoid a permanent rift between our two families. I discussed none of this with you, Lily, because I considered it improper to involve you in the matter. You know that as the Ninth Earl, I have certain family and societal obligations. One of those has always been that I should unite our two families by marrying Beatrice."

"Yes, Beatrice has always made that very clear to me."

"I'm sorry, perhaps that was inevitable. I am afraid Beatrice and her family retain those expectations, regardless of the fact that there has been no encouragement from me. It has been a time-honoured protocol for generations that the Earl of Middlebourne, or the heir presumptive, will make an advantageous marriage. Where that might unite two noble families, that marriage is considered to be a foregone conclusion. My discussion with Douglas left me in no doubt about how he regards the situation with which I presented him. He is of the firm opinion I have reneged on what he considered to be an agreement, and there can be no greater fall from grace than when a gentleman reneges on an agreement."

"Am I going to cause you real problems?"

"Yes, you are! You are the most troublesome woman I have ever met, but I wouldn't want to change a thing. In the end it has been an easy decision to make. Which is the most important to me, my love for you, or my five hundred years of heritage? I would give it all up for you, Lily, without hesitation."

"Oh, Edward, you would do that for me?"

"In an instant, I can't waste another second of my life without you."

"You would give up so much for me, and all I can offer in return is my unconditional love."

"*All you can offer me, Lily*? You offer me a lifetime of happiness, what greater prize is there?"

"What about your mother and Elizabeth, do they agree with your decision?"

"When I discussed it with my mother, she was absolutely delighted. She already regards you as a daughter, Lily, and to my surprise, Elizabeth agrees."

"Oh, that's wonderful, but I'm sorry the Strattons can't accept the situation."

"I am really delighted about Mother and Elizabeth, but frankly, Lily, we are the only two people that matter."

I didn't underestimate the seriousness of the decision that

Edward had struggled with. He was so correct in everything he did, the very personification of a gentleman. Not once had he made what he would have considered being an improper advance towards me. As for Lord Stratton's accusations, the implications were far-reaching. In Edward's world, reneging on an agreement instantly disqualified him as a gentleman. His place in society was potentially in jeopardy. That he was prepared to risk so much for me was quite a responsibility. My heart was ruling my head, but I also understood the dilemma I posed for him and his family.

Much as I wanted to be considered suitable, I knew it wasn't within my gift. They say you can take the girl out of the East End, but you can't take the East End out of the girl. I was to become the Countess of Middlebourne in name, but I worried that in everyone else's eyes I would always remain 'that woman from the East End'. I could change my accent, I could learn everything expected of me, but like a stick of Brighton rock, when I'm broken in half I'll have the words 'East End' running through me. Edward knew that, and we both knew we couldn't live without the other. We would make it work because we had to.

"Look, it's 11.30, Lily, what shall we do? We expected to hear the announcement at Middlebourne with everyone else."

"Yes, I know, but perhaps we should stay here now, we can't possibly miss it."

"I agree, we can celebrate again tomorrow. I'll arrange for another night here."

"Just the one room, Edward!"

The time just seemed to fly by, the mood in the hotel crackled in the air. It was already the most memorable day, I wanted to savour every second and commit it to memory. We hardly needed lunch after our late breakfast, but we went to the restaurant anyway. The usually quiet diners were all chatting excitedly, and we were no exception. The normally genteel atmosphere of the Savoy restaurant sounded more like an army mess hall. The staff were busy making sure there was a wireless set in each of the principal reception rooms, as well as extra seating.

Like everyone else, we went directly from the restaurant to find a comfortable chair close to the wireless. We sat side by side, holding hands, waiting intently. It must have been, and probably will remain, the most eagerly anticipated wireless broadcast of all time. The hubbub in the room gradually diminished as the hour approached. At precisely 3 o'clock, you could have heard a pin drop. Winston Churchill's voice came over, loud and clear.

He told the nation that at 2:41am the previous day, the German high command had signed the Act of Unconditional Surrender. The agreement would be ratified that day in Berlin. Finally the words we had all longed to hear were broadcast to the nation - the German war in Europe was over. The Pacific war against Japan continued, and our resolve must remain strong. Then in typical Winston Churchill style he said we might allow ourselves a brief moment to rejoice. There was a period of silence before the entire room erupted into a cheer. The people went absolutely wild with joy. Otherwise cultured and refined people were jumping up and down with their fists in the air. They were kissing and hugging everyone in sight. It was a spontaneous outburst of pent-up emotion, the extent of which is impossible to describe after the event.

In the euphoria which followed, there was an indescribable need to celebrate with as many people as possible. A lot of the people staying at the Savoy, us included, went outside into the street to mix with the gathering crowd. The Strand was full of revellers, I couldn't imagine where they had all come from. Perfect strangers hugged me, several of them kissed me. Edward seemed to attract every woman for miles around. We walked along the Strand past Charing Cross station, and the atmosphere was the same everywhere. Everyone who could be on the street was there.

Just past Charing Cross, Edward suggested we turn right and walk into Trafalgar Square. It was absolutely packed with cheering revellers. There were men and women dancing without a care in the world, and what I remember most vividly were the well-dressed people standing in the fountain. A young woman stood in the arms of a sailor, soaked to the skin. Everyone had thrown caution to the wind. It didn't matter if you were the Earl of Middlebourne or a barrow boy from Stepney, we were all the same, the war was over. I wanted to be everywhere, I wanted to see everything.

We were at a loss to know where to go next. I would have loved to see the celebrations in Stepney. The magnificent people of the East End knew better than most how to celebrate. Wherever streets had been left standing, there would be street parties in progress. They would bring tables out onto the road, and everyone would give whatever food or drink they had. There would be lines of conga dancers snaking their way from one street to another.

We walked down the Strand towards Buckingham Palace. Our progress was slow as we had to stop every few yards while the crowds surged around us. By the time we entered the Mall, it had become difficult to make any progress at all. There was a moment when I lost Edward, only to find him in the arms of yet another young woman. I grabbed his hand, and we tried to continue on towards the Palace. We guessed that Winston Churchill would make an appearance with the King and Queen, and I so much wanted to be there.

Despite our hesitant progress, we eventually found ourselves outside Buckingham Palace. I have never seen so many people gathered in one place, each one hell-bent on celebrating. They were everywhere, people climbed onto every statue in London, they were clinging onto railings and lamp posts. Union Jack flags waved in the air, and lots of people wore red, white, or blue. There were huge numbers of servicemen in uniform, soldiers, sailors, and airmen, never short of pretty girls to kiss.

When the Royal Family stepped onto the balcony, the roar from the crowd raised our hearts to even greater heights. The noise was deafening, I didn't think it was possible to cheer any louder nor experience any greater euphoria. As much as we loved the Royal Family, this was Winston Churchill's day, and when he appeared on the balcony, I thought my heart would burst. The cheer from the crowd dwarfed everything that had gone before. The ensuing outpouring of patriotic pride was something you had to experience. Men and women alike stood with tears rolling down their faces, we all cheered until we had no voice left to cheer with. No subsequent account could hope to describe it. This was Winston Churchill's moment, and the nation loved him.

It would be nonsense to suggest that Churchill won the war. That honour is shared across the nation, and indeed the world. It belongs to all those who fought and died in the pursuit of freedom, all the people whose contribution, however small, was unwavering. What Winston Churchill did so magnificently was to weaponise the power of the English language. He reached out to the English-speaking people and lifted our spirits and determination to an unassailable level. He said that we, the nation, shall never surrender. We didn't! The outpouring from the masses in front of Buckingham Palace was the nation's homage to its greatest ever wartime leader.

It was the day of days, the greatest celebration the nation has ever seen. All across the country it was the same. There wouldn't have been a single person capable of cheering who didn't join in the celebration. It was much the same around the world. Our great allies in America and the Commonwealth, all those who had fought alongside us, we all celebrated. Edward and I mingled with the crowd all afternoon, swept along on the human tide, with everyone enjoying their hard-earned freedom. All over the country, the celebrations would continue into the night and on into the next day. For Edward and me, it was so much more; not only had we regained our freedom, but we also gained each other. We eventually found our way back to the Savoy. We would end that most momentous day of days safe in each other's arms.

The following morning, I expected to find the nation with a hangover. I couldn't believe that the ecstatic level of joy we had witnessed could possibly last into the following day, but just a glance from our bedroom window confirmed it had. I wondered if some revellers had celebrated right through the night, and when we went down to breakfast, some guests had clearly been up all night. There were many jaded, but happy faces. Edward didn't plan to propose to me on the evening before VE-Day, but I was so glad he did. Our experience at the Savoy was a life-changing event which will stay with us forever, but as sublime as the Savoy was, we wanted to be with our friends and colleagues. Edward and I were really blessed, we had experienced heaven together, but to make the day of days complete, we had to return to Middlebourne.

Chapter Forty-Nine
June 1980

My memories of VE-Day were still fresh in my mind. "If you ask anyone who was there on VE-Day, they'll tell you the same thing, Charlie. Living in peace and freedom is the greatest prize this life has to offer. Sadly, you only come to that understanding when it's too late. The joy we felt that day was intoxicating. It filled our senses, we could see it, feel it, and taste it. Your generation must never forget, Charlie. Guard your peace like you would guard your home and family, because if you lose one, you could lose the other."

"We take it for granted, don't we, Lily?"

"You do, Charlie, and it frightens me. It could so easily happen again."

"*The only thing necessary for the triumph of evil is for good men to do nothing,*" commented Edward, recalling one of his favourite quotations.

"This really worries you, both of you. Do you really see it happening again?"

"Almost certainly, Charlie," I said. "We consistently fail to learn from history. Wars have rarely been started by a democracy, it's always a demented individual with an ideology. And never forget that the German people voted for Hitler in the first instance. Those who would subjugate the democratic system are especially dangerous, they use illegitimate democratic credibility to conceal their true intentions."

"You're right," said Charlie, "but sadly, that's the reason we refer to you as the greatest generation. Only those who have experienced something can truly understand it."

"I have to admit, you're right," replied Edward, "but it doesn't stop us trying."

"When my girls are old enough, I'll tell them what you've told me. My fear is that being another generation removed from the war, well, frankly, I doubt they will believe me. I think perhaps you take yourself for granted, but let me tell you, you were all incredible. Look at my parents, look at what they went through, my daughters have no idea. I didn't even know about it myself. Goodness, you *should know* if your mother and father are war heroes. I've only just learnt about the George Cross nomination. Needless to say, they didn't tell me about that either."

"The only reason that neither of them received the award was because they were a part of Station M, plus our association with Bletchley Park. In the years immediately after the war neither we nor Bletchley existed, we had been erased. You have to remember, after 1945 we went straight into an uneasy alliance with the Russians. Winston thought it perfectly conceivable that parts of his secret army might be called back to duty."

"The fact remains," said Edward, "we should have recognised your parents. There were only 39 female SOE agents operating in France. Just three were awarded the George Cross. Odette Hallowes, Violette Szabo, and Noor Inayat Khan. Dotty stands among those women, the bravest of the brave."

"Do you think she'll ever tell me her story, like you have, Lily?"

"We discussed it, and she knows how I feel. She said she would tell you everything if it was what you wanted. It's going to be quite a story, Charlie."

"You've both been so honest with me. Can I ask you a personal question, Lily?"

"Probably."

"You said you had the words 'East End' running through you like a stick of Brighton rock. You were concerned that people might not accept you as the Countess. I look at you now and you are in every respect the Countess of Middlebourne. What's more, everyone regards you as such. You've achieved so much in your life, Lily. What's been the secret of your success?"

"I think in one word, Charlie, it's expectation. Edward grew up knowing what was expected of him, he wasn't offered any alternative but to strive for those lofty goals. I was born without any expectations attached to me. That's hard, Charlie, it's really difficult to rise above that. What happens is that other people impose their own limitations upon you. I was lucky, George's hopes for me were boundless. For him no ambition was too lofty for his daughter. I grew up as a child with no ambitions, but later when George said I could fly, I believed him. You have to believe, Charlie. If you believe you'll succeed, you will! If you believe you'll fail, you will!"

"You make it sound easy, Lily."

"Life is never easy, Charlie. It takes an inner belief to strive for something seemingly beyond your reach, and your greatest enemy is doubt. When the people around you expect nothing of you, when they say your ambition is not credible, it's because it's beyond the limit of *their* expectation, not yours. Somehow you have to rise above it. Never listen to the naysayers, Charlie, they are the killers of dreams. The seed of doubt only needs a negative thought to grow. Had I known that Rosa Ponselle came from a poor immigrant family and had no operatic training, that would have really motivated me. Within a year of being noticed by the great Caruso she sang opposite him at the Metropolitan Opera. Her fairy-tale story could have been mine, instead I listened to the naysayers who said someone like me doesn't become an opera singer, and I believed them."

"Is it as simple as that, Lily? Never let go of your dream?"

"I think it is Charlie, but it's not easy, we're all influenced by other people. We don't all want to strive for things; some people are content in a world without dreams and ambition. I had dreams, Charlie, and I believed in them. When Winston Churchill said, *we shall never surrender,* the whole nation believed him. Do you know why we believed him, Charlie? We believed because we knew *he* believed it. I believed I could be a Countess, and I haven't let you down, have I, Edward?"

"It wouldn't matter to me if you had, but I don't think you're capable of letting anyone down, my darling."

"I'll make a confession, Charlie. I had a helping hand when we got married because our guest of honour was Winston Churchill. We married in the village church, and initially I had no idea how many of the guest list intended to accept. I'm afraid I let it be known that he was attending. The entire village was there. Every dignitary, whether they were on the guest list or not, was there. Even the Strattons were there! You couldn't see the church for people. I like to think they were all there to see me marry Edward."

"Something else happened that day," said Edward. "Winston was instrumental in preventing your parents from being awarded the George Cross. He described it as a regrettable necessity. After our wedding breakfast, he specifically asked for a private meeting with Dotty and Rob. I have only ever seen your mother completely lost for words on one occasion, and that was it. Rob told us afterwards what the Prime Minister told them. Dotty couldn't say a word but Lily wrote it down.

The PM said, *'It was my honour to speak to the magnificent people of Station M in 1942. I had to tell them the plain truth, that their undertaking was so secret, all references of their existence had to be erased. I also told them they would receive no recognition, there would be no medals pinned to their chests.*

However, come the great day of celebration, I assured them that none would stand taller than those who stood before me that day. I have read the report of your conspicuous gallantry, both before and after D-Day. If the British nation knew of these events, you would rightly be honoured. You would take your place amongst the pantheon of legendary heroes in the hallowed halls of British history. Instead, it falls to me, on behalf of the British nation, to pay homage to your great valour. I am a poor substitute for the recognition you so justly deserve, but I deem it a great honour to shake you both by the hand".

"Churchill said that, to my parents, and they have never thought to mention it?"

"We don't usually talk about any of it, Charlie," I said. "When Dotty and Rob fought their way out of Caen, many people were killed. The German casualties were so high they called for reinforcements, thinking it was the invasion force. Several innocent civilians were killed, and several French resistance people were killed fighting with them. That's something you don't want to live through again, much less talk about."

"I can't comprehend heroism of that magnitude, Lily. Look at Mum, for goodness' sake. She's what she always says she is, Dotty by name, dotty by nature. All the photographs of the time that I have seen show her clowning about, the life and soul of the party."

"Your mother, Charlie, was the loosest cannon on the deck. If anyone was going to do or say the wrong thing, it was her. She's exactly the same now, if you want your party to go with a swing, who do you ask? We never know what we're capable of until we're called. None of us could have dreamed of doing what we did during the war. There's another person inside all of us. When the call came, we had to discover what lay within. In Dotty's case, I think she was as surprised as any of us. Make no mistake, Charlie, your mother was a trained and ruthless assassin. The only way she could live with that was to keep that part of her life completely separate. Never wonder why she hasn't spoken about it."

"I see, now I understand. You don't get to be part of the greatest generation for nothing, do you?"

"We are no greater than any other generation," said Edward, "it's just that we were the ones who were called."

"Perhaps, but there are lessons for my generation to learn. How does Florence fit into all this? She was pouring the champagne at the reunion."

"She is a dear friend. She offered to help with the first reunion, and it has just become the custom that she always does it. Robert Fuller has done really well for himself, their interior design business continues to expand and their son George went into the business as well."

"And what about Greg, did he go back to Scotland?"

"He did. He and Aileen married and had another two children. We still keep in touch. Edward and I saw them two years ago. As you know, Mary surprised everyone, including herself. Well, not everyone, I knew she was capable of taking over from Greg, I just had to convince her of it!"

"Did you manage to restore relations with the Strattons, Edward?"

"Yes, we did, or rather Lily did. It took a little while, but eventually Beatrice married into the Cuthbert family. It seems that honour has been restored."

"We managed to put it all behind us eventually. Beatrice, Elizabeth, and I laugh about it now. Beatrice and I are really close, and I think of Elizabeth as my sister. I was sad in a way when she decided to go back to America. She said it was just for a visit, but I guessed that if she found someone she would end up staying there. Well of course that's exactly what happened, she insists that Larry being one of the wealthiest men in America had nothing to do with it. We see each other at least once or twice a year."

"Those years when I've seen Lady Elizabeth here with you and my mum, I can still see what you mean about them looking alike."

"All this talk about us, Charlie, what about you? When we met at the reunion, you were head over heels about the most beautiful woman you'd ever seen. Joanna, wasn't it?"

"That's right. I remember what you told me that time as well. You said, 'don't lose her, you won't get a second chance.' But I'm afraid I have lost her, I let her go."

"Why are men so hopeless at these things? You really had a thing about her, didn't you? So you're staying with Annie?"

"I felt I had to, but between ourselves, I now realise it's the worst mistake I've ever made."

"I'm sorry, Charlie, you really loved Joanna, didn't you?"

"I did, I still do, I'm an idiot."

"You are, but you're not the first. I know I said you wouldn't get a second chance, but if you want something enough, if you can imagine it happening - well, miracles do happen, Charlie."

"I'm afraid it's a tender point, Lily. Tell me about your singing, did you continue?"

"Would you ring for Reynolds, Edward, I think we need some drinks? Singing remains my only regret in life. I know now I could have become an opera singer, but if I had done that earlier, maybe I wouldn't have met Edward. I suppose even after we married there was still time, perhaps I should have continued. The highlight of my singing life remains that memorable day at St Hugh's Military Hospital, that was my Covent Garden moment."

"What about Christmas 1945, Lily?" asked Edward. "That was an extraordinary experience."

"What happened then?" asked Charlie.

"Edward arranged for a quartet and a pianist to be here on Christmas Eve. He invited all the great and good of the area to attend what he described as a special event. I think I sang well, and it was certainly well received. It was soon after we were married, and I must admit it did wonders for my position in society as Countess."

"Why didn't you carry on, Lily, you were still young," asked Charlie.

"We lost Gran in February 1946, that was a terrible day for me. My uncles had died when I was still quite young. When my family and friends were killed during the war, I didn't appreciate how different that was. My grief came in a parcel wrapped in anger. The Nazis had killed them and I could blame and loathe them.

Gran just slipped away like a butterfly taking to the air. She had her two sisters and daughter sitting with her, as well as her 'three girls'. I was holding her hand, and when she was ready she just flapped her wings, and she was gone. I cried for a week. My grief didn't come wrapped in anger; it was just raw heart-breaking grief. Gran always said she was a part of me and she was right. What she didn't tell me was that I was a part of her; when she died there was a part of me that died with her. I lost my enthusiasm after that. I carried on singing now and again, you know, at Christmas and family gatherings, occasions like that. I guess it's a bit like you and your Joanna, a case of, 'what if'?"

Reynolds came into the Drawing Room. "May we have some drinks, Mr Reynolds? What would you like, Charlie?"

"You know me, a single malt please."

"Edward?"

"Three single malt whiskies, Reynolds, what do we have at the moment?"

"The 25-year-old Lagavulin is opened, My Lord."

"That will do very nicely, thank you, Reynolds."

"May I ask, Lily, about your parents? Did you ever discuss George with them?"

"No, we didn't mention it. I think Mum and I both wanted to protect Dad. It's like you said Charlie, it's a tender point. We go to visit George's grave every year on the anniversary of that terrible day. I stand and talk to him. I know it's silly, I didn't get the chance to talk to him as my father during his life, so I do it in death. Every year, I tell him all the things we've done, what the family has done. When I've told him everything, I still have to ask him if I've made him proud of me, I still need to hear him say that."

"I'm sorry, Lily, I didn't mean to upset you."

"Oh, it's just ghosts from the past. Anyone who went through the war has their ghosts. Give them a reason to come back, and they do. We must always remember, but days like Armistice Day are tough. We lay a wreath every year at the village memorial for those who died when the V1 struck the village. Edward has to say something, it's very hard. There's always a significant date lying in wait for you. The 4th of June, the last day of Dunkirk, is painful because of Ian. The 24th of May was when HMS Hood was sunk, the list just goes on. They call us the greatest generation, but really, we're the generation with the greatest burden of sorrow."

"I suspect that's overlooked."

"Of course it is. Perhaps this is the real generational difference. You, Charlie, look back on history and read about numbers, whereas we look back and we don't see numbers, we see people. Did you know, Charlie, during that awful time, seventy-five million people were killed? Forty million of those were civilians. The Soviet Union alone lost twenty-seven million. The Nazis murdered eleven million people, including six million Jews. The world went mad, Charlie, so many people were killed, but for what?"

"Those numbers are incomprehensible to us today," Charlie said. "It's as if life lost all meaning."

"The Nazis," Edward said, "had a term for it, 'Lebensunwertes Leben' it means, 'unworthy of life.' We faced an enemy led by a cabal of people whose perverted morality had deviated so far from any accepted norm, that it was unrecognisable to civilised humanity. The irony of their unspeakable depravity was that in holding up a mirror against the tide of humanity, what they perceived as 'unworthy of life' was their own reflection. Perhaps what terrifies me the most was the fact that the evil they espoused became accepted by so many. I would remind you of Voltaire. *'Those who can make you believe absurdities, can make you commit atrocities.'*

"That's a terrifying indictment of humankind, Edward."

"It is, and it's why we have to remain vigilant with our politicians and leaders. It all starts with the first untruth. Get the masses to believe that and the following lies sound more credible. The next thing that happens is that 'truth' is portrayed as the enemy of the people."

"All I can say is thank God your generation made that sacrifice! The consequences if you had capitulated to the enemy are horrifying."

"It is impossible to exaggerate those consequences, Charlie," Edward replied. "The world came close to complete disaster. Following Dunkirk in June 1940, most of Europe had been defiled, the lights had gone out, all hope had been lost. In that wasteland of unmarked graves, one lone flower still blossomed. Like a rabid dog, the evil which had laid waste to Europe sat poised with teeth drawn, just twenty miles away across the English Channel. At that most perilous time, Winston Churchill made two of his most remarkable speeches in the House of Commons. Lily said that Winston weaponised the English language, and I believe that was the moment when that most powerful of weapons was used to devastating effect against Hitler's Third Reich. On June 4th Winston Churchill said:

* *'We shall fight in France, we shall fight on the seas and oceans, we shall fight with growing confidence and growing strength in the air, we shall defend our island, whatever the cost may be, we shall fight on the beaches, we shall fight on the landing grounds, we shall fight in the fields and in the streets, we shall fight in the hills; we shall never surrender'."*

"I know you don't like the expression, Edward, but I really feel you and Lily are a part of the greatest generation. What you collectively achieved astounds me."

"If we are the greatest generation, Charlie, then it is only because we were presented with the greatest challenge. The next time this country is called upon, that generation will rise to the challenge, just as we did. We are an island nation, Charlie, we defend our shores. It is what we have always done, and it's what we will always do."

"Edward's right," I said, "it was a terrible tragedy, but one that we had to face."

"Yes, it was a tragedy," Edward continued. "But it was also the greatest threat this nation, or indeed the world, has ever faced. When the call came, our generation were not found wanting, Charlie. In our moment of greatest peril, in our darkest hour, we looked that rabid dog in the eye. We stood fast; we didn't surrender. We turned the tide, which eventually ebbed back towards the aggressor.

The Second World War was the greatest tragedy to befall the modern world. Our only claim to be called the greatest generation is because we averted an even greater disaster. Winston Churchill was one of the few who had the vision to see how that disaster would unfold. He spoke in the House of Commons on June 18th, 1940. He concluded his speech with what proved to be prophetic words. If the greatest generation should ever be granted an epitaph, these are the words, Charlie:

* *'But if we fail, then the whole world, including the United States, including all that we have known and cared for, will sink into the abyss of a new dark age made more sinister, and perhaps more protracted, by the lights of perverted science. Let us therefore brace ourselves to our duties, and so bear ourselves that, if the British Empire and its Commonwealth last for a thousand years, men will still say, 'this was their finest hour'."*

To be continued, Dotty's story must be told.
Charlie's Story has already been told.

Principal Characters

Lily Heywood - Narrator

Edward, Lord Middlebourne - The Ninth Earl of Middlebourne

Caroline, Countess Middlebourne - Edward's mother

Lady Elizabeth - Edward's sister

Jack - Lily's father

Pam - Lily's mother

Ian - Lily's brother

Gerry - Lily's husband

Jim Smedley - Lily's cousin

Gran (Mrs Margaret Taylor) - Lily's maternal grandmother

Spencer Tracy - Gran's dog

Boris - Gran's cat

Mavis - Gran's sister, Lily's aunt

Mildred - Gran's sister, Lily's aunt

Dorothy Archer (Dotty) later Bartlett - Lily's great friend

Fiona Robinson (Fi) later Albright - Lily's great friend

Reg - Farmer

George Miller - Lily's uncle, mentor, employer, father

Marcia - George Miller's secretary/partner

John (Johnny) Albright - Wing Commander Albright (Fiona's husband)

Corporal Harris (Brian) - Corporal of the guard

Private Thomson - Private, soldier of the guard

Greg Norton - Estate manager

Aileen - Greg Norton's wife to be

Fuller - Builder

Robert Fuller - Builders' son

Mrs Morgan (Elsie) - Middlebourne housekeeper

Jennings (Charles) - Middlebourne butler

Florence (later Fuller) - Lady's maid, Lily's great friend

Mary - Housemaid/trainee estate manager/estate manager

Nancy - Housemaid

Sandra - Housemaid

Joyce Evans - Her Ladyship's maid

William Evans - Footman/chauffeur

Albert Reynolds - Footman (later butler)

Caitlin - Scullery maid

Harold (Harry) - Florence's boyfriend

Maggie - Photo reconnaissance analyst

Rolo - Boffin

Corky - Boffin

Woody - Boffin

Patrick - Boffin

Susan - Radio operator

Brenda - Canteen lady

Roberts - Estate lawyer

Roger - Pub landlord

Rob Bartlett (Goldfinch) - SOE agent/Dotty's husband - Charlie's father

Charlie Bartlett - Lily's godson - Dotty's son

Collins - MI5 driver/agent

Freddy - Docker

Thumper - Docker

Lady Stratton (Cynthia) - Friend of the family

Lord Stratton (Douglas) - Friend of the family

Lady Beatrice (Stratton) - Marriage contender

Marion Horworthy (Matron) - Matron, St Thomas' Hospital

Evelyn Riley (Secretary) - Secretary, St Thomas' Hospital

Wiśniewski (Dr) - Doctor, St Thomas' Hospital

General Ashton - Patient in Casualty, St Thomas' Hospital

Patricia (Nurse) - Nurse, St Hugh's Military Hospital

Beverley (Nurse) - Nurse, St Hugh's Military Hospital

Joan (Nurse) - Ambulance nurse

Bill - London taxi driver

Prominent historical figures dramatised to add context to the period portrayed in this book.

* **Winston Churchill.** Sir Winston Leonard Spencer-Churchill, KG, OM, CH, TD, DL, FRS, RA. Prime Minister of the United Kingdom 1940-1945, and 1951- 1955. Popularly accepted as Britain's greatest ever leader, and the most inspirational voice of World War Two.

* This book contains Parliamentary information licensed under the Open Parliament Licence v3.0.

Elizabeth Layton. Elizabeth Shakespeare Nel (nee Layton). Winston Churchill's personal secretary, 1941-1945. The only woman present at the Yalta conference, where Winston Churchill proposed a toast to her.

Joan Bright MBE. Recruited by secret intelligence and fell under the sphere of Lt. Colonel Joe Holland and General Colin Gubbins, later to be in charge of SOE. She later ran the Secret Intelligence Centre, which was in fact a room in the Cabinet War Rooms. From that all-powerful position, she moved to become personal assistant to General Sir Hastings Ismay, who was close to Winston Churchill.

Margaret Jackson MBE. Personal assistant to Colin Gubbins, later Major-General Sir Colin Gubbins, Director General of SOE. Jackson was at the heart of SOE; nothing happened that she did not know about.

Vera Atkins CBE. Recruited by British intelligence in her home country of Romania. A part of the team that evacuated the Polish Enigma codebreakers together with an Enigma machine. Joined SOE in 1941 and quickly became assistant to Colonel Maurice Buckmaster, head of SOE French section. After the war ended, she embarked on a remarkable mission, attempting to account for all the agents who died in her service, succeeding in almost every case.

Field Marshal Bernard Montgomery. 1st Viscount Montgomery of Alamein. KG. GCB. DSO. PC. DL. Nicknamed 'Monty,' famous for the victory of El Alamein. Commander of the British Eighth Army during the campaigns in Sicily and Italy. Commander of all Allied troops during the Normandy landings before handing over to General Eisenhower in September 1944.

Field Marshal Alan Francis Brook, 1st Viscount Alanbrooke. KG, GCB, OM, GCVO, DSO & Bar. As General Alan Brooke, was Chief of the Imperial General Staff during World War Two.

General Dwight D Eisenhower. Promoted to Lieutenant General in July 1942, led the Allied invasion of North Africa ('Operation Torch') November 8th, 1942, and later the invasion of Sicily and Italy. Appointed Supreme Commander of the Allied Expeditionary Force December 24th, 1943. Gave the order to launch the D-Day landings on June 6th, 1944. Became the 34th President of the United States 1953-1961.

General Sir Colin McVean Gubbins. KCMG. DSO. MC. Seconded to SOE November 1940, Gubbins became Head of SOE September 1943 when he replaced Sir Charles Hambro. He helped to transform SOE into a highly effective organisation.

Field Marshal Erwin Rommel. German Field Marshal, popularly known as the Desert Fox.

Claus von Stauffenberg. German army officer, best known for his attempted assassination of Adolf Hitler.

Adolf Hitler. Austrian-born German politician. Dictator of Germany 1933-1945.

Joseph Goebbels. Chief propagandist for the German Nazi party 1933-1945.

Juan Pujol Garcia. MBE. Spanish spy who acted as a double agent for British intelligence, under the code name of 'Garbo'. Recruited by MI5 during Operation Double Cross, played a prominent role in the German misinformation campaign.

General Omar Bradley. US Army officer who commanded the Twelfth Army Group, which helped ensure the Allied victory over Germany during World War II; later he served as first Chairman of the U.S. Joint Chiefs of Staff (1949–53).

General Hastings Lionel "Pug" Ismay. 1st Baron Ismay. KG. GCB. CH. DSO. PC. DL. Winston Churchill's chief military assistant during the Second World War and later served as the first Secretary General of NATO.

Sir Hugh Cairns. KGB, FRCS. An Australian who spent most of his life in England. Set up the Nuffield Department of Surgery in Oxford, became the first Nuffield Professor of Surgery. A key figure in the development of neurosurgery as a speciality, the formation of the Oxford University Medical School, and the treatment of head injuries during the Second World War. Instrumental in the creation of the hospital for head injuries at St Hugh's College Oxford.

Sir David Petrie. KCMG, CIE, CVO, CBE, KPM. Director General of MI5 from 1941-1946.

Major General Sir Stewart Graham Menzies. KCMG, DSO, MC, Chief of MI6, 1939-1952.

Robert Anthony Eden. First Earl of Avon. KG, MC, PC. British Foreign Secretary on three occasions, then Prime Minister 1955-1957.

Herbert Stanley Morrison. CH, PC. Home Secretary 1940-1945.

John Anderson. 1st Viscount Waverley. GCB, OM, GCSI, GCIE, PC(Ire), FRS. Chancellor of the Exchequer 1943-1945.

Osbert Peak. 1st Viscount Ingleby. PC. First Secretary to the Treasury 1944-1945.

Sir Arthur Harris. 1st Baronet. GCB. OBE. AFC. Marshal of The British Air Force. Commander-in-Chief of RAF Bomber Command 1942-1945. Popularly known as "Bomber" Harris.

General S Patton. General in the United States Army. Commanded the Third Army during the Battle of the Bulge.

Eric Sykes. Englishman, best known for his work with William Fairburn. Expert in close quarter unarmed combat, recruited by SOE to train its agents. Developed the infamous Fairburn-Sykes fighting knife with Fairburn.

William Fairburn. British Royal Marine and policeman. Taught martial arts to the Shanghai police force. Later trained SOE agents in unarmed combat and pistol shooting techniques.

Rosa Ponselle. American soprano. Little known singer who was singing with her sister in vaudeville until she was noticed by Enrico Caruso in 1918. At Caruso's instigation, Ponselle joined the Metropolitan Opera in New York, where that same year she sang opposite Caruso. Widely considered to be one of the finest sopranos of the 20th Century.

Enrico Caruso. Italian operatic tenor.

Jack 'Spot' Comer. Son of Polish immigrants, born in Whitechapel. Notorious East End gangster.

Printed in Great Britain
by Amazon